Blood Fire

Books by Sharon Page

BLOOD FIRE

BLOOD SECRET

"Wicked for Christmas" in
SILENT NIGHT, SINFUL NIGHT

BLOOD WICKED

BLOOD DEEP

BLOOD RED

BLOOD ROSE

BLACK SILK

HOT SILK

SIN

"Midnight Man" in *WILD NIGHTS*

Blood Fire

SHARON PAGE

APHRODISIA

KENSINGTON PUBLISHING CORP.

www.kensingtonbooks.com

APHRODISIA BOOKS are published by

Kensington Publishing Corp.
119 West 40th Street
New York, NY 10018

All Kensington titles, imprints, and distributed lines are available at special quantity discounts for bulk purchases for sales promotion, premiums, fund-raising, and educational or institutional use.

Special book excerpts or customized printings can also be created to fit specific needs. For details, write or phone the office of the Kensington Special Sales Manager: Kensington Publishing Corp., 119 West 40th Street, New York, NY 10018. Attn. Special Sales Department. Phone: 1-800-221-2647.

Aphrodisia and the A logo Reg. U.S. Pat. & TM Off.

ISBN-13: 978-0-7582-7829-6
ISBN-10: 0-7582-7829-2

First Kensington Trade Paperback Printing: November 2012

10 9 8 7 6 5 4 3 2 1

Printed in the United States of America

Acknowledgments

With many thanks to my wonderful editor, Audrey LaFehr, for sharing my enthusiasm. It is so terrific to work with you. Also with thanks to Martin Biro for all the many things he does.

As always, I am indebted to my agent, the amazing Jessica Faust, for her encouragement and savvy.

As always, to my family for your belief in me, your support, and your smiles.

I

A Lady's Erotic Quest

London, March 1821

"I want the delicious, delectable, and thoroughly handsome Lord Sutcliffe," Lady Octavia Grenville said in a whisper. "And I want him exactly as he is shown in my book: without a stitch of clothing."

Leaving her best friend, Eliza, staring at her in shock, Octavia slipped out of her bed and crouched on the floor. She held her finger to her lips as Eliza began to protest. Eliza frowned, but rolled onto her stomach on the bed.

Octavia took one last glance at her closed bedroom door. The door was safely locked, key in the keyhole. No one could interrupt or come in. Taking a deep breath, for it was hard for her to move so quickly, she drew out a large, leather-bound book from beneath the bed. A piece of satin ribbon stuck out from the top.

She hauled the heavy book onto her comforter; then she sat on the edge of her bed. Her legs shook from just that little bit of exertion, and her arms were weak and tired. Her heart struggled to beat, but she was not going to give in and rest.

She wasn't going to just close her eyes and let herself die. She had too many things to do first.

She flipped open the book to the place she had marked. On the page, there was a colored print of a young man. A young, *naked* man. The picture depicted him lying on his side on a disordered bed. Sprawled on a counterpane of dark blue, he grinned toward the viewer. The artist had rendered rugged, sensual lines that bracketed his beautiful mouth. And dimples—beautifully depicted dimples that made her heart ache each time she looked at his smile. Dark chocolate-brown hair fell rakishly over his brow. As for his magnificent body . . .

Octavia let her gaze move down his body, and her heartbeats sped up. Her pulse was strong and thundering, not unsteady. Her skin went warm, instead of being chilled and covered in goose bumps. She felt weak and achy, but in a good way.

Lord Sutcliffe's body was like nothing Octavia had ever seen. Of course, as a delicately reared young miss, she had never seen a real, live, in-the-flesh, undressed man.

Her upbringing had been rather unusual. She drew the illustrations for Father's books and stories on his travels, which sometimes required her to depict the male body in very little clothing. But the gentleman in this erotic picture made every painting, statute, and real male pale in comparison.

He had the most spectacular muscles. Enough to make her drool. He had slender hips and long legs. The artist had drawn *all* of him. Even his male part—the privy part—and it stuck up straight along his abdomen, pointing at his navel.

She glanced to Eliza. Her friend's cheeks were bright scarlet. Octavia waved airily at the picture. "That is what I want," she said matter-of-factly. "Before I die, that is what I want."

Eliza's blush vanished in an instant, and she went pale. "Stop speaking of dying. You are not going to die, Tavie. You are going to get better."

Octavia sighed. She had been afraid for a long time—afraid

of dying, of losing the rest of her life, of never having love or a husband, children, and household of her own.

But fear eventually wore you out. You couldn't feel it anymore. You were simply too drained.

Now that she couldn't feel anymore, Octavia had decided that if she was going to die, she was going to experience a few things first. For a start, she was not going to die a virgin.

"I *am* going to die, Eliza," she said. "I am certain of it. The physician is, too."

She had come to terms with dying. But the people she loved had not. "I know Father believes I am going to die. He has tried every cure they can think of." Octavia shuddered as she remembered the bloodletting and the noxious concoctions she had drunk. Father had even brought in men who were not doctors, who sold quackery. Of course nothing had worked. "Father is fighting it, but deep down in his heart, he believes it is going to happen. I can see despair in his eyes, no matter how much he tries to hide it. I know that if my father has given up hope, I am done for."

"But why on earth would you want to do . . . things"—Eliza glanced nervously to the closed bedroom door—"with Lord Sutcliffe?"

"I don't think I have enough time to find a husband before I go." She gave Eliza a buoying smile. "So it will have to be a love affair. Perhaps one that will only last one night. In that night, I intend to experience everything."

"Tavie, you can't ruin yourself with Sutcliffe. Your father despises him."

Octavia felt her cheeks heat. "I'm not going to ask Father's permission, for heaven's sake. I don't want him to ever know about it."

"You think Sutcliffe would keep it a secret?"

"Sutcliffe will not know who I am."

"How are you going to do that? How could he not know

who you are when you are"—Eliza gave a strangled sound—"naked with him."

Imagining that brought a pleasant rush of warmth through Octavia's body. An ache followed it—one that throbbed between her legs. It agitated her as much as an unreachable itch. "I have a plan, but since I am not supposed to go outdoors, you are going to have to help me."

"Help you plot your own ruin? How can I call myself your friend if I do that?"

"I can't ask anyone else. Anyway, when I am dead and gone, how will you feel if you deny me this last wish?"

"Stop that!" Eliza cried. She nibbled her fingernails. Octavia heard the crisp sound of them snapping beneath her teeth.

"I don't know when I'm going to die, Eliza. Please help me with this." She met her friend's troubled gaze with a pleading one. "You will feel terrible when I've gone and you know you didn't help me."

Eliza chewed through another nail. "What do you want me to do?"

"Help me put together a costume, of course. And hire a hackney for me—so I can sneak outside and go to the masquerade two nights from tonight."

"What masquerade?"

"The one held by the Duke of Glencairn—"

"You are not going there! It's not a respectable event!" Eliza cried. "Everyone knows the duke holds that for his shockingly scandalous friends, and the only females there are demireps and courtesans."

"I can hardly interview gentlemen for the position of bed partner during the afternoon stroll in Hyde Park."

Blushing fiercely, Eliza pursed her lips. She looked up to the heavens, her raven curls bouncing, and as though she'd been given divine help, she asked, "How do you know the Earl of Sutcliffe will be there?"

"I invited him," Octavia said, and it was hard not to be smug at her cleverness.

"*What?*"

"I forged an invitation—Father has some correspondence from Glencairn, so I used my artistic skills to fake one."

For years she had drawn and painted pictures to go with Father's books of his travels. Her years of painstaking work had come in handy for forging. "So will you help me, Lizzie? I could go without a disguise. I could even walk across London to get there."

The Duke of Glencairn did not have his scandalous parties at his home, a massive ducal residence on Park Lane. He had acquired a house on the fringes of Mayfair for his bacchanalias.

Glencairn had been a patron for some of her father's travels. But despite His Grace's generosity, Octavia had always disliked the duke, since he was so heartless toward his wife. The duchess was young and pretty, but the duke's infidelities had seemed to sap away all her vitality and strength. The duchess was always pale and unhappy.

Octavia wondered what it was like to live with heartbreak every single day. She knew what pain was: She'd felt it dearly when her mother had died. But eventually that hadn't hurt so much. Marriage to an unfaithful man must be a living hell.

But she was willing to use the duke to get the one thing she wanted so desperately: Lord Sutcliffe.

"Everything is set up perfectly, Eliza. There's nothing to worry about. Nothing can go wrong."

Eliza bit off a bit of her thumbnail. "All right, I will help you. But I don't know what you are going to do afterward when you become healthy, but you are ruined. You will get better, you know. So you will have to marry Sutcliffe."

Octavia didn't argue, but she *wouldn't* get better. There was no reason to fear a forced marriage with a man known as the worst rake in London. It was reputed the Earl of Sutcliffe had indulged in the wickedest things on his travels: bacchanalias, opium dens, brothels where the pleasures involved punishment and pain. It was said Sutcliffe had learned how to make a woman reach pleasure by just speaking to her.

Octavia had never known pleasure. But she'd heard about it, and she wanted to know what it was like.

Her father had adventured around the world; so had the Earl of Sutcliffe. She had never gone anywhere, or done anything exciting. And now that she was dying, she wanted to live as much as she could.

In two nights, she was going to have an adventure of her own. She knew she was never going to get well. She knew the doctor believed she was so weak that she could die any day now.

She had one night—one night in which to fit a lifetime of pleasure.

Someone had forged him an invitation to Glencairn's orgy.

Matthew Winthrop, the Earl of Sutcliffe, studied the crowd packed into the duke's ballroom. Sexual acts were being performed around him with enthusiastic abandon, but he felt nothing. He was dead inside.

His younger brother's death had killed him.

It was strange. Six months had passed since Gregory's death. It had been half a year since his brother had been transformed into a vampire, and he been forced to hunt down his brother, forced to stop Gregory from attacking innocent maidens for their blood.

Damn.

Matthew shook his head as if throwing off the memories. But he couldn't escape them. He held an empty glass. He'd long since drained the liquor in it. He wanted to be deadened to the pain and grief, but he didn't deserve any escape, did he?

To his right, a young viscount had pressed a giggling courtesan against the wall, pushed up her skirts, and was now thrusting into her. The young lad's hips pounded with the speed of a panicked rabbit. The girl was drinking port above the lord's bowed head and flashed her eyes at other, more rugged and experienced men.

He used to love an event like this. It felt empty, cold, and soulless now.

Just like he had condemned Gregory to be.

In the Carpathian Mountains, Matthew had accidentally unleashed a powerful and ancient female vampire, known as Esmeralda. Beautiful and alluring, Esmeralda had hunted his brother, seduced Gregory, and turned him into a vampire.

When he had found Gregory, he had done what was necessary. A stake to the heart at first, then he had carried out all the other acts that were supposed to prevent a vampire from rising: He had sawed off his brother's head and stuffed the mouth with garlic. He had tried to tell himself he was just doing it to a corpse and that his brother was gone, but he felt Gregory's eyes staring at him as he did the work. The local villagers had insisted his brother would walk the earth as an undead demon unless he did exactly as they asked.

After traveling the world, he'd grown used to discovering strange and brutal customs. Still, he hadn't been prepared to discover vampires were real, and to learn what he had to do to destroy his brother.

He wanted to go back and retrieve his brother's body. He wanted to bury Gregory on English soil. His brother deserved to be home.

He also had to return to hunt and destroy Emeralda. He had gone to the Royal Society for the Investigation of Mysterious Phenomena looking for help. With vampire slayers, he was going to mount an expedition and find the female vampire—

"You look glum, milord." Giggling, a woman sashayed up to him. She pressed her chest against him and wriggled her breasts. "Let us find a spot where we can fuck."

He gently pushed her back. "No, thank you," he said, coolly polite.

She laughed at that—a drunken laugh close to a screech. But then the young Duke of Sandhurst cupped her bosom from behind, and she spun and fell into the duke's arms. "I'll take you up on your offer, my bountiful wench."

Laughing, they left Matthew; he was part of the crowd, yet completely isolated and alone.

He looked over the large, drunken, half-naked group. For a fleeting moment he wished he could forget grief. He wanted to laugh and enjoy pleasure. But he would never forgive himself— he should have taken better care of his younger brother, and hell, in the end he had been the one to destroy Gregory.

He couldn't feel joy or pleasure anymore. He was empty and cold. And no woman, no matter how tempting, would change that.

In fact, he would not have come here if it had not been for that fake invitation.

Who had sent it and why?

A threesome sank to the floor in front of him. The buxom woman in the middle did not even lose her grip on the two men's cocks as she lowered. She was in a costume that consisted of a short tulle skirt that barely covered her arse. She wore nothing underneath, and it allowed the men easy access as they sandwiched her from either side. Soon she was writhing in pleasure, and the men were both staring at her and taking care not to look at each other.

Matthew gave a short laugh and moved through the crowd. Sex was everywhere. The smell of it hung in the air like a miasma.

He had brought the two invitations with him. The real one

he had surrendered to a servant at the door. He drew the fake one out of a pocket in his costume.

Without the authentic one at its side, it was hard to tell this one was the fake. Gilt rimmed the edges of them both. The wording was quite similar on the two. But on the first one he had received, a week before the second, Glencairn had scrawled a personal note.

Glencairn wouldn't bother to send him a second invitation. And, while the ducal crest on the second card was almost a perfect copy, there were some small flaws. It was a forgery.

Who was desperate to get him to attend an orgy?

She was in trouble.

Octavia surveyed the glittering crowd that filled the small ballroom of the duke's house. Where was Sutcliffe? That was one flaw with her scheme. This was a masquerade, though it seemed the idea was to wear as little as possible, at least for the female guests. All the gentlemen were masked.

Even a small strip of a black mask around a man's eyes changed his appearance to an astonishing degree.

Octavia stared at dozens of men, trying to distinguish features disguised by the various masks, but she was certain she had not seen the Earl of Sutcliffe.

He was a notorious libertine. Surely he would have taken the bait of the invitation. Most of the women here were almost *naked*. Some wore only their corsets and stockings, along with heeled slippers. Their private parts, bottoms, nipples were entirely on display. Other women wore gauzy, fanciful costumes.

Octavia sipped champagne from a flute given to her by a footman—a footman who had been bare-chested and wore only breeches and boots. Nervously, she looked around.

She saw two fairies with jewel-rimmed gossamer wings. Brightly colored satin skirts barely covered their derrieres.

In polite society, it was shocking to show one's ankles. Here, it seemed shocking not to reveal one's legs or breasts. One woman wore only veils in the style of Salome. Another was also dressed as a harem girl, wearing a sparkling jeweled top over which her full breasts jiggled. Her stomach was bare, and a large ruby flashed in her navel.

To think Eliza had been shocked by her costume. It made Octavia smile to remember the way her friend's jaw had dropped when she'd emerged from behind the screen in her bedchamber. She wore a draped Grecian style dress with no underpinnings beneath. Her breasts moved freely beneath the clinging, silky fabric, and the skirt fit tightly to her hips and legs, outlining their shape. She had needed an easy costume, and one she could readily hide with a cape. Her arms and shoulders were bare, and the flowing skirt was slit, revealing her legs.

She felt deliciously shocking.

She had braided her blond hair in an elegant Grecian style, and her gold mask covered her face from her hair to the top of her lip. The excitement of wearing the costume and then sneaking out of her house had made her feel stronger. She'd felt the way she had before she became sick—happy and excited.

It had been all the more thrilling when she'd thought of what was going to happen. When she'd imagined what she would say and how bold she would be with Sutcliffe.

Yet now, she couldn't find her quarry, and she stood on tip-toe to take another look around the crowd—

"You are unique, my dear. Unlike every other woman in this room, you are mostly covered up."

The deep, masculine voice rippled over her shoulder at the exact same moment fingertips brushed down the length of her spine. The silk of her dress was so thin it felt as if the man touched her bare skin. Octavia jerked around, gasping.

Blue eyes gazed down at her. The man's lids were sultry and heavy, rimmed with dark lashes, but his sapphire irises appeared empty and cold. His dark brown hair fell in waves to his shoulders and drifted over his mask.

It was Sutcliffe.

He was dressed as a wizard, with a flowing robe of black silk belted at his waist. Stars and moons were embroidered on it with silver thread. He wore a tall, pointed black hat, one that was crooked at the end. His robe was slightly open at the top, revealing his bare skin.

Was he naked underneath?

All the witty and provocative things Octavia had intended to say left her head. She stared at him, her lips slack. This was the man whose naked body she'd stared at for hours. She'd touched herself while looking at his picture. She'd put her fingers between her thighs and imagined it was his hands caressing her there. She had cupped her breasts in front of his painted eyes.

And now . . . what did she say to him to get him into bed?

It was so much easier with pictures. She could make up anything she liked.

Think, Octavia.

"Cat got your tongue, love?" he asked gently. His gaze moved slowly over her, filled with . . . not sexual interest but suspicion. "You are a pretty thing. I don't think I've seen you here before."

"N—no," she managed to stutter. "I've never been here before."

"Sweetly awkward, too. Just off the stage from the country, are you?"

He smiled, but it was a wry and jaded one. It appeared he didn't suspect she had lured him here—he was suspicious because he believed she didn't belong. She was about to reply when his large hand settled on her bottom. Just that touch made her legs quiver.

"This is too intense a place for a country innocent." He gave her a little push. "You should go, sweetheart, before you find yourself in trouble. Come back when you've gained some experience."

"I have experience," she said desperately.

His brow lifted. Even with his mask, she could read the doubt in his expression.

"I do," she insisted. "I came here for more."

Good heavens, she'd imagined trading clever repartee with the earl, not blurting out these idiotic things.

Maybe she should touch him and keep her mouth shut. Taking a deep breath, she boldly pressed her hands to his chest. Her fingertips touched bare skin at the top of his robe.

And that made her knees tremble. Especially when she stroked his chest and remembered all the things she had imagined doing next. "You are very handsome, my lord," she purred. She ran her tongue around her lips in the most sensual way she could.

He let his head fall back, and he laughed.

It was as if a wildfire had started on her cheeks. How could he laugh at her? She wanted to fall through the floor. She was accustomed to dealing with irritating, arrogant, condescending men: The Royal Geographical Society was filled with them. But she'd wanted her fantasy gentleman to be different. She'd wanted desire and passion. Now, she just wanted to kick him—

He shook his head, still laughing lightly. "Don't, my dear. Don't try to play games. I liked you awkward and honest. Now, why don't you tell me your name?"

Awkward and honest. But his gaze was tender, and that eased some of her embarrassment. "You want to know my name?" Octavia hadn't even thought of that. She hadn't thought she needed one. There was gossip that he seduced women and never even bothered to ask for names. "Why?"

"I've traveled the world. It's my habit to name intriguing

creatures—unless the fascinating specimen in question has a name."

He cupped her cheek. The contact made an amazing sound drop off her lips—it was a strangled moan.

She'd landed in a quandary. Did she reveal that she knew him? Would it reveal who she was? While Sutcliffe and her father were rivals, their meetings and arguments had always taken place at Royal Geographical Society lectures or at their gentlemen's club. Perhaps Sutcliffe knew her father, the Earl of Morton, had a daughter, but she doubted he would ever realize who she was.

She needed a courtesan-sounding name. But she was at a loss. She'd heard stories about mistresses, but about women with ordinary names like Harriette. "My name is . . ." Then she saw how hopeless this was. Talking would get her nowhere. She remembered she could be dead in a week, or a month, or even in days. She gathered all her courage and gazed at him evenly through the eyeholes in her mask.

"Take me to bed, my lord. No names. No questions. Just— just bedding." She had meant to say "just sex," but the word wouldn't come out.

"Here? Now?" he asked.

She spotted the amused glint in his eye. Then he began to undo his wizard's attire at his waist, and she realized what he was doing. He really did mean here. *Right* now.

"No," she said desperately. "In a bedchamber."

"Frightened you, did I? You should go home."

"No, please. My lord, I came here to find you."

"Indeed." His fingers closed on her chin. As he held her face firmly in place, his blue eyes searched hers. He must be looking for a hint of her identity. "Who are you?" he demanded.

"Perhaps I might tell you . . . once we are in a bedchamber."

The holes of his mask revealed narrowed eyes, filled with suspicion. "Why were you looking for me?"

"I have watched you lecture, my lord. You are famous throughout England for your exploits. I have admired you for years."

"And you want me to make love to you?"

"Y-yes."

"All right. Let us find a bedchamber." He offered his arm. Relieved but trembling, she laid her hand in the crook of his elbow, her fingers curled around the sleeve of the silk wizard's robe. Without another word, he led her through the crowd.

Her heart galloped with nerves, but he had said *all right*. That meant it was going to happen. It had worked. She was going to begin on an adventure. Within minutes she would know what it was like to touch the most perfect male body in the world. She would know what pleasure was.

Nothing could go wrong.

2

Yours to Command

Octavia quickly discovered there was an enormous problem with pretending she had experience.

In the wild fantasies she had as she'd lain in her sickbed, she'd dreamed of Sutcliffe sweeping her into a bedchamber. He would be kissing her silly as he did it. He would push her up to the wall, trap her there by bracing his hands on either side of her head. Then he would do all sorts of hot, lovely, naughty things with his mouth. She'd dreamed of how lovingly and daringly he would kiss her. With his mouth open, his lips firm and hot, his tongue dallying with hers.

He would be wild and mad with desire for her.

Instead, Sutcliffe calmly walked her to a bedroom, shut the door behind them, and removed his robe and his hat in an instant.

Octavia gaped at him, struck mute by the cool, almost disinterested way he took off his wizard's robe and laid it over the arm of a chair. Beneath it, he wore an open white shirt, black trousers, and shoes.

He was not acting as though he were excited at all.

She had seen young men sent to fetch punch for debutantes

display more trembling excitement. The earl was behaving as though this was of no consequence. As if it was not even mildly *interesting*.

In the time she had stood, slack-jawed, stunned by the way he was stripping without even speaking to her, he had removed his mask, then pulled the hem of his shirt from his trousers. He paused.

"I thought you would be removing your dress," he remarked. The rest came out a bit muffled as he pulled his shirt up over his head. ". . . you could manage on your own."

She could see his abdomen. The real thing, not just a painted image. In the naughty picture, his stomach had been so muscular it looked like it had been made of rows of cobblestones.

A picture couldn't do it justice. The light skimmed along the flat plane of his belly, highlighting the striations of muscle. His navel was a small, tight little indent of dark shadow. His trousers sat low on lean hips—heavens, his hip muscles jutted beneath his bronzed skin. She felt the most intense longing to touch them, to know what they really felt like. And, heavens yet again, his pants rode so low she could see how the line of tawny hair that ran down his tummy began to thicken at his . . . private parts.

He pulled off his shirt completely and tossed it to a chair. "Do you want help?"

I want romance. I want passion. I want your eyes glazed with desire for me, your breath coming in desperate pants, your head filled only with the need to make love to me.

But she wasn't courageous enough to shout her demands at him. Should she go? She didn't feel hot and quivery now. There was a painful tug in the pit of her stomach, and it was not a pleasant one. But maybe it would get better. Maybe, once they began, it would improve.

"With your gown," he repeated, as if she were simple. "Do you want help?"

"No, I can manage."

He was beautiful. Even if he wasn't going to be passionate, she was going to have his gorgeous body for her own. She would be able to touch him. She would know what it was like to have a man's body stretched over hers, to have his . . . parts inside her.

Perhaps this night could still be spectacular. Even if he had the personality and seductive skills of a marble statue, she could touch and feel and explore him. Perhaps that would be enough.

It would have to be. Fingers trembling, she undid the fastening at her shoulder. Silk tore a bit.

Hadn't that been one of her fantasies? Tearing silk? She'd imagined *him* tearing her clothing, desperate to take it from her.

"Here, let me help you. You don't want to rip your costume to shreds." He prowled toward her. His scent enveloped her. She smelled the tart freshness of witch hazel astringent from his shaving, the sultry aroma of sandalwood, along with earthy hints of leather. She took a deep breath and drank in more.

His long-fingered hands moved over her dress with confidence and speed. He opened the fastenings at the sides first. Then he undid the shoulders. Sometimes his hands brushed her skin. She found she waited for his touch, almost unable to breathe. She wasn't afraid, though. She was hungry for this. Octavia began to think he was deliberately letting his fingers brush her breasts and his palms bounce them.

It melted her. Made her feel sensuous. Made her so hot between her thighs she thought she was going to catch fire. It was actually *painful*, she wanted him so much.

Then reality stormed in. She was going to do something magnificent, something she'd dreamed of day and night, something that had kept her alive with hope and yearning. Literally, her fantasies had kept her alive.

It would happen with a gentleman who was almost a stranger.

She knew Sutcliffe. At least she'd thought she did. She had watched him lecture in the Royal Geographical Society about his journey across the cold ice of Siberia. She'd heard him tell of how he had narrowly escaped catching the malaria that had killed his traveling companions on the coast of Africa. His words there had been full of passion. He had made her feel the horror of watching a man fling himself off a cliff into the sea because he was mad with fever. He had made her know what a tiger smelled like, and how the fur looked in dappled sunlight.

But she didn't really know him.

She felt a spurt of panic. Then he pulled her dress up.

She moved to stop him, to grasp the silk of her gown and keep it in place. Then she fought to quell her hands. She *couldn't* turn back. After all, she didn't know when she would die. How many nights she had left, she couldn't guess. This might be the only one.

"You can't take off my mask, though," she said softly. "I want to leave it on."

His brow rose. "All right. Who are you that you are so concerned about your identity?"

"I cannot tell you." She looked at his eyes. He still wore his mask too. It made him look . . . dangerous and sensual. "We will both leave our masks on."

"Fair enough. But the dress comes off you," he said.

Taking a deep breath for courage, Octavia lifted her arms. She let him draw up her costume, take it off her, drop it to the bed.

He let out a soft whistle. "Nothing beneath. You are a fascinating creature."

An experienced woman would be confident, wouldn't she? Let him look his fill. Octavia pressed her back against one of the tall bed columns. The position thrust her naked bosom forward. But she couldn't look down at her own body. She could let him look, but she wasn't courageous enough to review what he was looking at.

Was he even pleased with her nakedness? With her sickness, she could barely eat, so she wasn't generously proportioned anymore. Her breasts and her waist were small, her hips more lean than round. She could count her ribs. No doubt Sutcliffe could, too, even with just his gaze.

His gaze moved over her with the same slow, intense curiosity that she gave to the stuffed creatures her father brought home, when she was preparing to sketch them.

"You've been ill, haven't you?" he asked.

"Yes." Then, "I'm sorry. That's why I am so thin."

"Sweetheart, I am the one who is sorry. Are you recovered now?"

She shook her head before she even decided how much she should reveal. She might as well give the truth. "I am dying. I don't know when it will happen, but doctors believe it will. It is just a matter of time."

His face revealed nothing. His lips were set softly, his eyes devoid of feeling. "It is always a matter of time, my dear. I hope you mean you still have years left."

Her throat closed and grew sore and aching, making it hard to speak. "Days. I think I just have days. That's why I wanted you—"

"Did you send me an invitation to this party?"

She started. How had he known? She had thought her forgery was marvelous—

"I received two invitations. One was obviously a fake."

Heavens, she hadn't been thinking clearly at all. She had been certain this was the sort of event he would attend—which logically meant he would be sent a real invitation.

"So you have wanted to seduce me for weeks, and you created a fake card from a duke to lure me to an orgy."

"I admit it sounds a bit mad—" It sounded utterly insane, as though she were pursuing and stalking him the way Caro Lamb had chased Lord Byron. "I suppose the fear of dying addled my wits. But you must understand how much I want to experience pleasure before . . ." Her lips wobbled helplessly. She fought it. ". . . I die."

His brows were high with disbelief. "My dear girl, you sound like an obvious novice to me. I am sympathetic to your situation and flattered by your interest, but I don't ruin women."

"You won't be ruining me! I am experienced. But my lovers have been . . ." She waved her hand airily, praying she wasn't blushing again, and she tried to appear jaded. Then she remembered she was not wearing anything but her stockings and shoes, and she put down her hand. Thank heaven she still had her mask on.

"Ordinary," she managed to say. She searched for something that made sense—that would make her seem awkward but not virginal. "My lovers were . . . pedestrian. I've heard there are all kinds of things that can be done in bed that I have never tried."

"I wouldn't want to hurt you."

"You won't." She didn't care, even if he did. But was he going to send her away?

"I'm a lady's dying wish?"

Tears leapt into the corners of her eyes. "I guess you are." She tried to blink away the itchy tears, but two rolled beneath her mask to her cheeks, then dripped from her skin.

"No tears, love," he said softly. He moved close to her, his trouser placket open and hanging to the side to reveal his underclothes. "If it's a sexual education you want, I'll provide it. My cock is yours to command, love."

Matthew knew he'd changed.

Once he would have pleasured this woman without a second thought. Even with the mask obscuring much of her face, he could tell from her delicate chin and full lips that she was pretty. It wasn't a complete surprise that his mysterious invitation had come from an obsessed young woman. He was a wealthy earl. And his travels, books, and lectures had given him fame.

She blushed scarlet when he told her she had command over his cock.

Innocent. She had to be an innocent.

Though, in truth, some widows were essentially virgins. They'd been exposed to the physical act of sex, but none of the fun that went with it. His mystery lover had made no mention of a husband, and she had spoken of lovers—more than one.

She fascinated him. For a few moments, she had made him forget . . . forget his brother's death, forget all the damned mistakes he had made, all the guilt he insisted he must carry.

He had never been a woman's dying wish. Perhaps, for a while, he would humor her desires.

She was blushing deeply now, beneath her mask. In fact, she was blushing in many places. Her chest was rosy, as were her thighs and her shoulders.

He grinned at her, and his gaze dropped to her small, sweet breasts. The nipples were puckered and were a delicate pink. "Do you have a command for me?" Matthew asked.

"I—I don't know." Octavia knew she was flushing from her hairline to her toes. She knew, because she looked down and saw her skin turn as pink as her nipples. And her nipples had hardened to erect tips.

Sutcliffe's tongue traced his lips as if she were a particularly tasty dish.

He lifted his arms and put his hands against the column above her head, an action that made the large muscles bulge in his bare arms. He bent forward. In a heartbeat, her right nipple was in his mouth. The speed left her breathless. She'd expected a . . . warning. That he would say, "I'm going to suck your nipples now."

But he would think she knew all about this. Since she was supposed to be experienced, she would know that once he was close to her breasts he'd dive in for taste.

His mouth tightened around her nipple, his tongue flicked over the tip, and Octavia had to close her eyes. He sucked, drawing her nipple in, tugging at her entire breast. Then his tongue circled her nipple and her legs turned to fluid beneath her.

"Oh goodness," she gasped. She grasped his shoulders, clutching them for support.

Even with his mouth filled with her breast—an astonishing sight—he chuckled, and she heard the raw, lusty tones of it. At once his laughter died away, and he worked at her breast, sucking so hard she could not bear it. Her hands pushed at his shoulders; she sought freedom. His teeth grazed her nipple and panic jolted her.

"No. It hurts. Stop."

He moved back. "Don't like that, love?" His voice was gruff. "You didn't tell me what you wanted."

"I—I don't know," she admitted. "I don't know exactly what I want."

"Then relax and enjoy," he murmured. He turned his attention to her left breast. His arms, the closeness of his body kept her trapped. But this time, he was gentle. His lips lightly kissed and teased her nipple until it was plump as a thimble. He nibbled her breast, but only with his lips, so it felt like silk skimming over her skin. The most delicious sensations rocketed through her.

She sagged against his mouth. Her arms slid around his neck. He had a strong neck and straight shoulders. She let her fingers coast along his upper back. His skin was velvet-smooth. Slightly damp from heat and sweat. His muscles were powerful and hard. She focused on his partial nakedness, rather than the fact that *she* was completely undressed.

Then his hand slid up her inner thigh, and she squeaked in shock.

He sucked her nipple with more force, making her moan. Her legs melted even more, but she didn't fall. She couldn't, because he was cupping her private parts and holding her up.

The pressure of his hand there was amazing. He pushed up with the heel of his hand, rubbing deeply against her. The hoarsest groan she'd ever heard fell from her lips. Followed by sobs. She throbbed between her thighs, yet she wanted him to rub *harder.*

Needing it, desperate for it, she arched against his hand. Oh God, yes. It felt so good to move rhythmically against him. He accommodated her by increasing the pressure.

Her head lolled against his shoulder, and she sucked in harsh breaths. Never had she even dreamed it could feel like this. Under her bedcovers, she'd given herself pleasure with tentative touches. Sutcliffe's hands behaved quite differently. He cupped her right breast now, while rhythmically sucking her left nipple. His fingers stroked the wet lips between her thighs. He touched her lightly, but she was close to screaming with delight.

Pictures were lovely to fantasize over. The real earl was proving to be spectacular.

He stopped licking her nipple, and she almost cried out with shock. *Don't stop. Please don't.* But she didn't have the courage to voice the demand.

"Can I make you come, my dear, with just my fingers?"

"Come where?" she whispered dazedly.

His fingers moved, parting her nether lips. She gasped as a flood of warmth seemed to wash from her.

"You're soaking wet," he muttered hoarsely. His voice was terse, but she did not think it was a bad thing. The sound of it sent shivers of pleasure down her spine.

She gazed up at his eyes—blue eyes, but they were so bright with lust, she could barely see the color.

His fingers moved, sliding up between her damp curls until he found the sensitive place. Softly, he brushed his fingers there, and she was shaking like a leaf. Then he pressed harder, as he'd done with the heel of his hand.

"Oh—oh no," she began. "No, stop."

"In this, trust me, love." He whispered it with hot breath by her ear.

She tried. She did. Making fists, Octavia waited and let him stroke that place that brought so much sensation. She knew how to touch herself; she did it gently, with teasing brushes that led to explosions.

He was much more forceful. Probably because he was male. They were rougher in everything. She was aching and close, but tension kept the pleasure away. Tantalizingly close, but not quite there.

Then, his touch lightened, and he murmured, "I'll stay still. You move my hand as you wish."

She throbbed with yearning. Inside she was all coiled up and ready to burst. But weren't they supposed to wait? "Not yet though?" she whispered tentatively. "Shouldn't I wait until we're together in the bed?"

"One now." He laughed gently. "It will make my thrusts all the more delightful."

One *now*? She hadn't known there could be more. He seemed to think so. She hadn't even given him her name, but she felt so close to him. The intimacy was breathtaking.

Her fists flailed, bumping his neck, but he didn't appear to mind. Wonderful feelings grew inside. There was agony, too, but in a good way. How that made sense, she didn't know. She knew real pain from her illness. This was an ache, but a glorious one.

"Yes," Sutcliffe encouraged her, but the word came rough, bitten-off. Then, softly, "Pleasure yourself."

Octavia had to close her eyes. This was what she did beneath the covers in her own bed. Not in front of a man she'd watched lecture in front of a crowded room. She moved against him, thinking he would stay still. But he didn't. Once she had rocked back and forth, panting and feeling pleasure build, he began rubbing her. Matching her rhythm.

She couldn't reach the peak standing up, could she?

It didn't matter what she wanted, what she thought she could do. Her body ached for more. Her legs rocked of their own volition. She went faster and faster.

Sutcliffe helped her, spreading his fingers, rubbing them along the sides of the mysterious nub that felt so good.

She was going to melt. Or go up in flames.

She was clinging to him and sobbing and moaning. Her hips rocked like wild. She was going to dissolve in front of him, or die. He was watching her breasts jiggle and bob. He could see her at her most intimate moment. . . .

She didn't care. It was too good.

Then . . . oh God . . . pleasure exploded inside her. Her body rocked with it, and she would have lost her balance, but her fists were pressed to his chest. He caught her mouth in a kiss, his tongue playing with hers. She couldn't kiss him back. All she could do was moan and cry out against his mouth.

The peak buffeted her, and she rode it with her eyes shut. She was riding on his hand, and it was the most scandalous, delicious thing.

He gave a soft groan, a gentle laugh at her squeals and cries and sobs.

Shared pleasure was wonderful. Much better than being alone and making up fantasies.

Then he set her on her feet. "Get into bed, love."

It was both soft suggestion and harsh command. On shaky legs, she obeyed. The house belonged to a duke, and even though it was a second home meant for his parties and orgies, the bedroom was a beautiful room. An enormous bed stood in the middle of it, topped with a soaring bed canopy of tasseled silk. Pillows were mounded upon a soft, embroidered coverlet.

Octavia glanced back at Sutcliffe as she approached the bed. He hooked his thumbs in the waist of his trousers and pushed them down. She had dreamed of seeing him naked. She had just thrashed around in ecstasy against his chest. But she felt far too shy to stare at his completely nude body.

She tugged at the counterpane. Tugged and tugged until she pulled it free. Then she slid underneath. Her skin was on fire— but with blushes. Her legs still tingled, and she felt achy between her legs. She had never brought herself to that intense, climactic moment more than once.

She didn't feel tired, though. She wanted more.

Sutcliffe had stepped out of his trousers. He threw them over a chair. Long, relaxed strides brought him to the bed. Octavia peeked at him from beneath the covers. She'd drawn them up, over her nose.

This was the body she had drooled over for weeks. It was glorious to watch him move, to watch his lean legs casually swallow up the distance between them. Each step made the muscles of his thighs bunch, then relax. His stomach was flat, beautiful defined with bands of strong muscle. He had lean hips. His arms were undeniably strong, with taut, hard forearms, and bulges that brushed his chest when his arms were relaxed at his sides.

And the rest ... the privy part ... the part depicted in the naughty drawing ...

It was remarkable. It swayed as he walked, the firm head of it bobbing. Thick curls of dark brown hair surrounded it and almost obscured the sight of full, heavy ballocks dangling below. The rest of his body was so hard and firm, nothing jiggled. But his . . . his penis danced merrily as he came toward her.

He drew down the sheets. Gently, he reached down and pushed her legs apart.

It was truly going to happen. Her very first time. Sudden realization made her body tense and made her legs resist him.

"Touch me," he commanded softly. His eyes were hot with lust, but not overly confident. His word had been both a hungry, vulnerable request and the demand of a lusty man. "Please, sweet nymph, stroke my cock."

She hadn't thought of touching that part of him. Shoulders, chest, back, even his buttocks—those places Octavia had imagined running her fingers over. But not down there.

She lay on the bed, completely naked to him. Yet she was afraid to reach out and . . . Well, what did she do? Rub it? Grasp it? Pull it? What would he like?

His lips curved, his white teeth flashed, but she was astonished to see his smile looked uncertain. "Touch me like this?" he asked.

Before her stunned eyes, he wrapped his large hand around the shaft of his penis. What had terrified her, he did with ease. It was obvious he had touched himself before.

He gave one long stroke of his hand along the shaft, groaning. When his palm reached the head, he squeezed. Clear fluid bubbled out.

While she stared, amazed at the things the picture hadn't depicted—the fluid, the agonized look in his face, the shiny tautness of the head—he clasped her hand and put her palm to the hot shaft.

It pulsed gently against her skin. She tried to stroke as he had done. But her hand stuck to his skin and tugged hard. He grimaced, and she gave a stumbling apology.

She loosened her grip and slipped her hand up to the head. She squeezed but with barely any pressure. He urged her to do it harder, and Octavia obeyed, then he gave a pained squeak.

Instantly she released him. She had no idea how to deal with this appendage of his.

He fondled his ballocks, letting them spill over his fingers. Octavia stared—it was one of the most erotic things she'd ever seen, watching the soft pouch, intriguingly wrinkly, fall over his fingers. She knew it was a sensitive place, yet he was surprisingly rough. No wonder he had nipped her nipple.

She tried to fondle the soft sack and his firm testicles as he had, until he delicately moved her hand away, and she realized she'd hurt him. Wearing a wry look, he stroked her face. "You aren't experienced, are you, love?"

"I am." But she knew she wasn't convincing—she'd practically injured him while fondling his private parts.

He frowned. Then he got off the bed and stood beside her.

What had happened? She'd revealed that she had lied about her experience. But did that really mean he was going to stop?

She hadn't been any good, and obviously he didn't want her

To her horror, a sniffle broke the sudden, awful quiet. Sutcliffe jerked his head down—he'd been staring up at the bed canopy—and he looked at her.

"You're crying."

Even with her mask, he knew. She was embarrassed to show her emotions so blatantly. "I wanted . . . passion. And you gave me some when you—you kissed my breasts." Octavia winced as her cheeks caught flame again.

But this was her one night, and she wanted it to be as close to her dreams as possible. Sutcliffe was listening, so she had to explain. "You were passionate before; now you seem so cold. What have I done wrong?"

* * *

Matthew couldn't deny her accusation. The icy guilt he had been trying to fight had swamped him as soon as he'd realized she was definitely lying.

His nameless lover might be innocent, but she was sharp and perceptive. For those last two qualities alone, he should lead her back to the ballroom and take his leave of her.

"You've done nothing wrong." He couldn't explain what had happened, why he'd drawn back. She had been gazing at him with such trust, guilt had roared up in his heart. He was responsible for his brother's death. She was a starry-eyed innocent who probably saw him as an adventurous hero. He was no hero.

"Apparently, I have more conscience than I thought," he said tersely. "I can't bring myself to ruin you."

Clutching the sheet to her, she sat up. Her chin stuck out stubbornly. "I'm dying," she whispered. Her lip wobbled, but determination glowed in her blue eyes. "I want one wicked night with you before that happens."

"Why me? Come, sweetheart, if you want me to do this, tell me why you've chosen me. I can't offer you anything after this night. There would be no question of marriage. But I suspect you were hoping for more than just a night of passion."

"How could I?" she asked bitterly. "I won't have a future."

Was she really dying? He couldn't deny that she was obviously ill. She was thin, with collarbones that jutted beneath her skin, and bony knees and elbows. If he left her, would she find another man to ruin herself with? Any other man here would accommodate her without guilt or remorse. Most of them wouldn't take care with her. Most of the gentlemen who attended the duke's orgies were interested only in their own pleasure, not their partner's.

Never had he expected to feel damnably guilty for not ruining a woman.

He sighed. "All right."

He was certain he heard her softly whisper, "Thank heavens."

He got back onto the bed, positioned himself between her spread thighs. She was a slender sylph beneath him. Her hair was falling from her pins. Suddenly, he realized her hair was vaguely familiar. Somewhere recently he had seen a woman who possessed thick, golden hair like this. He dimly remembered how he'd looked at a woman and had noticed her pins could barely restrain her hair's unruly waviness. Where had he made that observation?

"You will be gentle," she whispered, "won't you?"

Apparently she must have been watching him for a while before she had decided to lure him to a seduction. "Yes, very gentle," he promised.

He'd pushed his cock into her snug heat only inches before the taut head gently nosed against her barrier. She drove her fingernails into his back.

Suddenly, he knew he had a choice to make. He could stop, though his body was urging him to thrust his hips forward. His cock throbbed with pain, yearned to be squeezed tight inside her. But he could force himself to pull back. He could break her heart and send her away. It would be the gentlemanly thing to do. Protect her, whether she liked it or not.

Or he could ruin her like a blackguard, knowing she might want this now but she would be in tears in the morning.

He had unleashed a demon because of his arrogance. He hadn't saved his own brother's life. He was already condemned to Hell, wasn't he?

He might as well have his pleasure . . . and ruin her.

London teemed with mortal life.

Esmeralda prowled through the shadows of a street notorious for its gaming hells. Gentlemen were everywhere around her, and the very smell of them made her slowly lick her lips. She had never seen so many delectable men. They were unlike those of her home. These were not grizzled men accustomed to the hard work of peasants. These men smelled of soap and cleanliness. They wore elegant clothes. She admired their wide shoulders, their narrow hips, the trousers that clung to their legs.

Beautiful. They were so beautiful.

She was so thankful to that handsome man who had set her free. He had dark, lush hair and eyes as blue as a clear spring sky. He had been a foolish man. He had not listened to the warnings of the villagers. How she delighted in arrogant English peers. If it had not been for his belief in his superiority, the poor, handsome fool, she would still be trapped in her prison.

She had wanted him, but he had managed to escape her. His brother had not. His brother had been young and very handsome. He had been a wonderful playmate in her bed, and his blood had been so plentiful and so sweet.

Eventually she would find the gorgeous male who had freed her. She wanted him. But for now . . .

She would find a man now. She would lure him into a night of carnal pleasure. Then, when she was well satisfied, she would take the ultimate prize.

She would drink his blood.

Slowly, she watched the gentlemen walk by. Many were drunk on spirits. Some looked bleak with despair. She had learned that men gambled their money here, and some lost fortunes in these places.

Then she saw him. The perfect prey. A lovely young man with curly, blond hair. He could not be more than one-and-twenty years of age. His jaw was smooth, and he looked like an angel.

Esmeralda stepped out of the shadows. She wore a gown of

dark red, one that clung to her voluptuous figure. Her pale breasts almost spilled over the neckline. She smiled and spoke to the young man through her thoughts.

Come to me, my beautiful lover. Come to me, and I will show you heaven.

It did not matter what she said. No mortal man could resist a demoness like she.

The young man turned and obediently trotted after her. She was slick with arousal, her heart pounding with desire and hunger.

Here was the perfect place—a shadowy alley. The moment the young man appeared at the entrance, searching for her, she dragged him into the darkness and shoved him against the brick wall. Her fingers tore the placket of his trousers, releasing the earthy scent of his cock.

How young and sweet he was. She bent on one knee, drinking in the rich, erotic smells. He moaned as she took his lovely staff into her mouth and sucked. He was enthralled, caught under her spell, and he rocked his hips to thrust into her mouth.

She sucked him until he was thick and rigid, his cock engorged with blood. She felt it pulse against her tongue. She dragged her fangs along the ridged length of him, making him shudder. She was creamy now, her nipples erect with hunger and need. The pump of blood along the tip of her fangs was so thrilling and erotic, it made her want to howl with delight.

She could bite now and feel his blood spurt out.

But no, she wanted to be pleasured first.

She released him and turned him, so she was pressed against the wall, and he was positioned between her thighs. His long, youthful, rock-hard penis was wedged between her skirts.

"Push them up," she whispered, panting with lust. "Fuck me."

He did so eagerly, and she savored his first long, hard thrusts. He was an eager young man.

But then, as her orgasm built, she wanted the ultimate pleasure.

As the climax roared through her, Esmeralda sank her fangs into the young man's neck. Together, they both sank to the ground.

And she gave her last spasm of an orgasm, as he slumped, lifeless, from her arms.

3

The First Time, Finally

Octavia braced herself for the twinges of pain that she'd heard newly married ladies whisper about.

But Sutcliffe withdrew slightly, making her mewl in frustration. She could feel the swollen head of his penis resting just inside her.

She wanted him inside. Though she feared the pain, she yearned to be filled by him. The need was so strong, she almost wanted to scream.

Braced on his arms over her, Sutcliffe arched a brow, looking very lordly.

"How can you stop?" she asked in a raspy voice. She ached and throbbed inside. She felt as if she would burst if she didn't do this. Why wasn't *he* so desperate and lust-driven that he couldn't stop?

"I don't want to stop. At any moment my hips might surge forward whether I like it or not, and the deed will be done." The earl panted, and it lent a sharp rhythm to his words. "But every time I try to just take your innocence, my conscience stops me."

"Don't listen to your dratted conscience," she whispered. In a heartbeat, she wrapped her legs around the backs of his thighs, trapping him so he couldn't get away. Who was this wild woman who held a man captive? It was she, and she had never been so driven and obsessed in her life. Her roaring heartbeat filled her ears. Her throat was dry and tight with anguish. He couldn't stop now. He just *couldn't*. She wanted this—needed this. Something in her heart, or in her womb, or deep in her soul refused to allow him escape.

"I've seen tentacles with less ability to cling," he muttered. Then he let out a harsh breath. "You really want me to ruin you?"

"Yes." She thrust her hips up, taking his shaft deeper inside, and she gasped in shock at the sudden, lancing pain.

He arched his hips forward, then he kissed her lips, her cheeks, her forehead. He stroked her cheek softly with one hand, rubbed his thumb against her nipple with the other. With so much sensation, she could barely think of the pain. And it eased. Now she felt fullness, as his shaft invaded a bit, pushing between the soft, wet walls. It seemed amazing to think his large penis could fit, even though they were intended for this.

Her private place still tingled from the orgasm she'd just had, and she felt *soooo* sensitive. She whimpered as Sutcliffe stroked his shaft slowly in and out. It was a sensation that swamped her mind, that made her fingers and toes curl, made her sob and moan.

He lowered his head, groaning. "You believe you don't have a future," he said hoarsely.

"I don't. Please."

But his penis slid back. With a quick jerk of his hips, he withdrew from her. He moved down her body and bent to nibble her nipples on the way. Octavia squeaked, but loved the way he tenderly took each pink tip between his lips. His fingers stroked her aching nub. But it wasn't enough. She wanted to be filled by him.

But he moved down her body, down to the crisp curls between her thighs. As a scholar of the world, her father had collected sketches and paintings of mating rituals. She had looked through them without Father's knowledge. She thought she knew what Sutcliffe was about to do.

Still, it was one thing to look at pictures, and another to watch a beautiful, naked man settle between her thighs, part her legs, and lower his mouth to her quim.

He licked her there. With his tongue. She almost leapt off the bed. Of course, she couldn't, for he was between her thighs, with his arms wrapped around her bare legs. She gasped as his tongue stroked her nether lips, then slid up, to touch the sensitive nub at the apex of her lips.

His tongue was so hot and wet, and just a little rough.

Pleasure exploded inside her. She shut her eyes and gasped as rainbow colors shot across the darkness. She cried with the pleasure. It rushed through her, a wave of sheer delight. "Oh, Sutcliffe! Oh heavens!"

He laughed huskily. Then he moved over her.

"*Now*. Please now," she commanded. "Do it now."

She cried out as he slid inside her. The ache eased at first, then he thrust and the twinge of agony came back, stronger and more intense. It was an ache that needed his long shaft stroking inside her. She clung to his back, holding him as tightly as she could.

He drove his shaft deeply into her. His hips collided with hers, and when he thrust to the hilt inside her, he lifted her off the bed.

She loved this. This was perfect. Heaven. All she'd dreamed. Sutcliffe's eyes were a brilliant blue with desire. His mouth was tense. The harder he thrust, the more he sweat. It beaded on his head. It made his chest and back dewy.

She loved this. She'd never dreamed sex would be so sweaty.

That she would be panting as though she'd run miles. That it would smell so lush and exotic.

He bent and captured her mouth, thrusting his tongue into her mouth at the same pace as he buried his shaft inside her. Each deep plunge made her moan and shiver, made her grip his shoulders and scratch his back, and pleasure shot through her. She felt pleasure in every nerve.

He kissed her hard, his mouth open, and he thrust so deep, she felt his groin bang hard against her—

"Oooooooh!"

Octavia arched up to him, driving her nails into his skin, wrapping her legs around him. She bit his neck. She sobbed against his warm, dewy throat. Screamed and cried and came apart in a million pieces and rushed back together—

Then everything went black.

"My dear, are you all right?"

Octavia blinked. "Where—?" A strange canopy loomed over her, one painted with naked nymphs. She jerked up in a panic. Where was she?

"Sweetheart?" asked a gentle voice.

Lord Sutcliffe was in the bed beside her. Suddenly, everything rushed back. The sex, the pleasure—the amazing, intense pleasure that had left her so dizzy she'd passed out.

"I'm all right." She shyly looked toward Sutcliffe. She lay back down on the bed.

"Did you actually lose consciousness?" He lay beside her, on his back, and he pillowed his arms beneath his head.

"Yes. Is—is that unusual?"

"Very, my dear." His beautiful grin widened. "You are re-markable. That was better than anything I've had for—" He broke off. He rolled onto his side and gathered her to him. "It's amazing that your mask is still in place."

He peered intently into her eyes, and she feared that he could guess who she was. She felt for the mask ties behind her head. They had loosened. Octavia was thankful the fire was almost out, and they were shrouded in darkness.

Gently, Sutcliffe traced the lace edge of her mask. His fingers reached the place on the right side where the tie connected to the leather.

"No," she said quickly, heart thudding. She pressed the mask to her face and scuttled away. "You mustn't."

"You know, you are the first nameless, mystery woman with whom I have shared a bed. Normally, I know who my lovers are."

"Well, you can't. Not with me. It's so much better if you don't know my identity."

"That only intrigues me more."

Oh heavens. "You are supposed to be a rake. I thought it wouldn't matter to you." She scurried to the edge of the bed. Really, he had the reputation of bedding a different woman almost every night. Why was he so interested in knowing who she was? Given his notorious behavior, he should be happy she'd only wanted one night.

She hadn't thought of what would happen after lovemaking. Never would she have dreamed it involved Sutcliffe's deciding he needed to know who she was.

Sutcliffe slid across the sheets to her, and she hung onto her mask, about to protest, when he kissed her. And what a kiss. It left her as liquid as fresh honey. She wished she could stay all night like this, underneath him, hot and languorous and so well pleasured, while he did wonderful things to her mouth.

A sharp rap sounded on the door. "Are you done in there?" shouted a deep, masculine, autocratic voice. "We need a room."

"Find another. We are busy," Sutcliffe yelled.

A muttered curse sounded through the closed door, along

with a female giggle. Another hard thump came—a fist pounded in frustration—but Sutcliffe shouted again, sounding both autocratic and irritated. "Bugger off and find another room."

Would this come to a fight? Octavia froze with worry. Then she heard heavy footsteps heading down the hall, and a trail of giggling that grew fainter.

"Sorry, my luscious mystery lover," Sutcliffe murmured. "We can't stay here." He sat up, then slid out of the bed. He had his trousers on in seconds.

As he fastened them, he faced her. "You need to go home. If you stay, another man will expect to bed you. I will escort you home, lovely creature."

Octavia panicked. Not because she wanted to stay at the orgy, but she couldn't allow him to take her home. "No, it isn't necessary. I found my way here; I can certainly return home. I hardly want my family to see me with a strange gentleman."

"What family would that be?"

"That is neither here nor there. They are a family, and therefore will disapprove of . . . of scandalous behavior." They wouldn't disapprove, that was the worst of it. Instead, her father would be devastated and heartbroken. She felt she could live with his rage. But knowing she had caused him pain would destroy her.

"All right. But I will see you to your carriage." He pulled on his shirt, then asked, "Did you bring your own carriage?"

She shook her head. "No." She did not want to tell him she had come here in a hackney, and that she had snuck out alone from her home before she'd summoned the vehicle. She had brought a dagger from Father's collection of artifacts. As she'd walked, she'd had the knife hidden in a pocket of her cloak but kept her hand wrapped around the hilt. If anyone had attacked, she would have used it.

"Then I will see you on board a hackney. I could ride with you—"

"*No.*" Sutcliffe had been to her house. He would guess who she was at once. Though, did it matter? It wasn't as if she was an innocent ninny who had been seduced. Sutcliffe had told her she was not to expect a proposal of marriage. He would hardly change his mind if he knew she was the daughter of his rival.

It did matter. What if he told her father what she had done?

"All right," he said finally. "Let me help you dress."

It was strange to get dressed with him and not speak. Neither of them said a word. But what could she say? She could hardly ask him if he was going to enjoy the rest of the orgy while she was gone. It shouldn't matter, there was no future for her, but she didn't want to think of him going to other women.

With his help, she had her Grecian gown in place and fastened in minutes. He summoned a servant to fetch her cloak. Then they waited, again in awkward silence.

Finally he cleared his throat. "My dear, I don't want to believe you are actually dying."

She didn't want to talk of this. She did not feel weak. Her body still felt tingly and almost light as a feather from pleasure. But she met his gaze and said, "Thank you. But I have accepted it."

"What is it that ails you?"

"I don't know. No doctor has been able to understand it."

"Perhaps you have not seen the right doctor."

"I've seen many, many of them." She sighed. Father had employed one physician after another; each one had visited the house and examined her—well, had spoken to her and asked her questions. Only one doctor had placed a thing called a stethoscope to her chest and had listened to her lungs.

Father had held onto hope, but finally he had begun to give up after she had been visited by at least half of all the doctors in London. He was convinced he had brought some virulent and mysterious illness back with him from one of his travels, and she had caught it. She had argued that Father was obviously healthy, but he pointed out there were those who never got sick, yet who managed to spread disease while they remained untouched.

If it was a disease from somewhere else in the world, it was unheard of in London. For no one had been able to give it a name or cure it.

Sutcliffe was watching her, regret and tenderness in his eyes. "It is strange."

"It is," she said briskly. The pain in his face was hard to look at. Anyway, she couldn't give him any further explanation about her illness. How could she reveal that it might come from some other place, like Russia, or Turkey, or Africa, without revealing her father's identity?

Sutcliffe and her father were rivals—could Sutcliffe be the kind of man who would use what she'd done to hurt her father?

She felt his gaze on her and lifted her head. He studied her, eyes frankly curious. "What kind of symptoms do you have?"

"Many things. Weakness, generally. My legs become so tired and shaky, they won't hold me up. My heart beats without a regular rhythm, and my pulse becomes faint. It's hard for me to breathe. My body aches everywhere. But some things ease it." She'd spoken the last before she thought.

"What things?" he asked, which was quite natural.

She couldn't tell him. She was too embarrassed to say that touching herself had always made her feel better and stronger.

"Come, my mysterious lady. Tell me. Perhaps I can help."

"You did. I feel better now."

A grin. "Thank you. I'm pleased to know I helped." He had pulled on his wizard's robe. Now he put his pointed hat back on his head.

The servant returned her cloak. Sutcliffe put it around her.

"There." He nodded. "An exotic bird should hide its plumes when it walks amongst hunters. Now, mysterious beauty, I'll take you downstairs, acquire a hackney for you, and send you safely away."

Octavia nodded, but her throat had gone tight. Her one night was over. It had been glorious, thrilling, sensual, and exciting. But it was done.

She had thought she would cling to the memory of pleasure and it would help her. But she found she wanted to look ahead. She didn't want to just remember pleasure; she wanted to experience more and more of it. She yearned for another night like this. *Many* nights like this.

But there wouldn't be any. She had to accept it.

A half-hour later, Matthew stood in shadow on a street in Mayfair, fighting a surge of guilt. He had followed his nameless young lady. He had assumed she was someone's gently bred daughter. He had never dreamed she would be Lord Morton's bluestocking daughter, Octavia.

He lit a cheroot. Now he knew why that mass of golden hair had been familiar to him. He'd seen it when he had attended her father's lectures at the Royal Society. He had seen it when he'd been a guest in her father's home.

He supposed he deserved this for having sex, for thinking of pleasure, when his brother was dead and would never know any pleasures again. This had to be his punishment. He had ruined a respectable woman. Yes, he could argue that she had begged for it.

But he couldn't say that and believe it. It didn't relieve him of responsibility.

Hell, he hadn't known Morton's daughter was dying. No wonder the old man had been arguing with him so much of late. Normally, they sparred—they both wrote books and lectured about their exotic travels; they were rivals. But her father had been unusually irate lately.

Matthew threw away the cheroot. Now he understood. The poor man thought his daughter was going to die. Morton was suffering all the grief of loss, but before it even happened.

Matthew shook his head. His recognition of Morton's pain hit him like a blow to his heart. Having lost Gregory—and his father and mother long ago when he was a child—he knew exactly how excruciating grief was.

But to have to watch someone you loved fade away before death, and to watch it happen to a child? Hell, that was more than any man should have to endure. And Morton was a good man.

So what did he do now? Decency demanded that he walk up to the house and ask for Lady Octavia's hand in marriage. Good sense told him that Morton would probably rather shoot him than have him for a son-in-law.

Lady Octavia had insisted this was only to be for one night. Why couldn't he quell his conscience and just accept what the lady wanted? She'd wanted a man to show her what a fuck was like. He'd done his duty.

She didn't want anything more from him. The last thing he needed was a bride, certainly not one who did not like him. Anyway, he had no time to engage in a wedding. He had to return to the Carpathians. Right now, he had an appointment with Mr. Sebastien De Wynter, a member of a different Royal Society from the Geographical one—the Royal Society for the Investigation of Mysterious Phenomena. De Wynter had insisted on meeting at this unusual time—in the middle of the night.

Matthew intended to return with De Wynter to the Carpathians and hunt vampires. It was the only way he could get any kind of vengeance for his brother's death.

He had been the one to unleash a demon. That made it his duty to destroy her.

Octavia stared through her open window at the tree that grew beside it and the thick ivy that shrouded the wall like a shawl. She could not believe she had managed to climb the tree and the ivy to reach her bedroom. Her hands still stung from the tree bark, and her bare palms were stained green.

In truth, she should have been too weak to do such a thing. And, after so much exertion, she should be ready to collapse where she stood.

For weeks, she had been barely able to draw a deep breath. Today, she had done all sorts of energetic, mad, dangerous things; she felt powerful and alive. She felt like twirling on the spot until she fell down dizzy.

She didn't feel ruined. Or wrong. Or mortified and ashamed.

Instead, her heart danced happily when she thought of what she had done. . . .

There was so much to remember, and it was all so wonderful. How could she ever forget the soft-as-silk feel of the beautiful skin of Sutcliffe's back? The way his smile had widened when she had grasped his shoulders in her pleasure. The hitch of his breath as she wrapped her legs tightly around his hips.

He had liked it. Octavia felt thrilled to have given him something he liked.

She felt full of laughter and joy. She felt . . . strong.

She wanted more. Another night. If she felt this strong, perhaps it meant she wasn't going to die right away. Maybe she did have more time. Time for more nights with Sutcliffe . . .

Could she do that? Savor as many nights with him as she could before she finally got too weak to do anything?

Or, by tomorrow, would she feel sick once more?

She didn't know. She didn't know what the morning would bring. Right now, she must brush her hair and braid it for bed. She would pretend to have slept in her bed all night. There were still a few hours until dawn. If she still felt this wonderful when she awoke, she would get out of bed and dress. She was tired of being sick and spending all her time in bed.

Her brush lay on her vanity. Foolishly, Octavia stretched

her hand toward it, though it was across the room. She would have to go and fetch it—

The silver brush rattled on the vanity.

It must have been her imagination. There had been nothing that had made such a vibration.

She took a step toward the vanity, but the brush suddenly spun around so the handle faced her.

That . . . that was impossible. Brushes could not move by themselves. Was this something new from her illness? Was she now hallucinating?

"Well, if I am, what if I envision the brush flying across the room to me?"

She held out her hand. Was she going out of her mind? Perhaps she had an awful fever—she had hallucinated terribly once before when she'd had a high temperature.

The brush spun madly as though it was trying to fly but was bound to the marble top of the vanity.

Then it broke free. It rose up in the air and swooped toward her. It came so fast, Octavia ducked. A loud crack and a clatter told her the brush had gone over her head and tumbled across the floor.

Of course it hadn't. She was seeing things that couldn't really happen.

She blinked and looked at the vanity. The brush would be there, just as it should be—

It wasn't.

Octavia whirled, not ready to believe the impossible. Yet there was the brush. It had skidded across the varnished floor and had come to a rest against the fireplace.

She pressed her hand to her forehead. It wasn't hot, and if she had a fever that could make her see flying brushes, she should be burning up.

She didn't care about her hair anymore. Wearing only her

shift, not bothering to change into her nightgown, she leapt into her bed and pulled up the covers. The strength she'd thought she had must be an illusion.

She shut her eyes, but she knew she wouldn't sleep. What she didn't know was if she would live through the night.

Men were such weak creatures, utterly enslaved to their cocks, Esmeralda decided.

She lifted her riding crop and brought it down hard on the bare buttocks of the young man tied up in front of her. The smack of leather upon his bottom sang through the room. Writhing against the metal chains that held him, he moaned in agony and submissive pleasure.

She had been spanking him, carefully, for almost half an hour. She did not want to break the tender skin of his firm arse yet and make blood flow.

She stopped whipping. The young man half turned. "Have I displeased you, mistress?"

How beautiful he was. Five-and-twenty, with lean muscles, narrow hips, and the most delectable bottom. "No, you have pleased me well. As a reward, I will give you some pleasure. But you must not come until I give you permission."

She grasped an ivory wand intended to go deeply inside her young slave's arse. She did not apply the oils she used on such a device for herself. No, she wanted him to feel some pain along with his pleasure.

He was ready, arching back so she could shove the wand inside.

Then a searing pain filled her head. The wand fell to the floor. She almost collapsed. She, who was one of the strongest vampires in the world, had to clutch a table for support.

A silvery haze covered her eyes. And she had a vision—of a young woman with blond hair. The girl was carefully making her way up a tree. Even in the vision, Esmeralda knew the young woman had recently had sex.

Power emanated from the woman. Power and strength.

This woman had just taken a piece of a man's soul, and she glowed with it.

Finally, after hundreds of years, it had happened again. One of the most powerful succubi had been awakened by finally having sex.

It meant they were all ready. She, the vampire, was finally free of her prison. Now the succubus had been awakened from her dormant state. All she needed to do was find this girl. Then she would bring all six of them together: the female wolf, dragon, and hawk-shifters; the most powerful witch; the young succubus; and herself.

Together they would destroy most of the male preternatural beings and enslave the rest. They would subjugate humankind.

Together, they would rule the world.

"Please, mistress?"

The young man's begging broke into her thoughts. Esmeralda straightened and stared at the tight, naked rump of her slave. "Not yet," she said impatiently. "You will have to wait for your pleasure, and you will do so obediently."

4

Sexual Healing

Vauxhall Pleasure Gardens, London
One week later...

Attending an orgy to hunt Lord Sutcliffe had been daring. Going alone to Vauxhall Gardens was madness.

Gathering her courage, Octavia stepped down from her hackney, paid the driver, and joined the large, boisterous crowd outside the pleasure garden's gates. She held her hood forward to shadow her face. There were no masquerades at Vauxhall anymore, so she had not worn a mask. Instead, she'd secretly bought face paint. She'd darkened her brows, rimmed her eyes with kohl, and reddened her lips. She looked like a different woman.

Octavia paid her admittance fee and followed the laughing groups down the main walk. Lights sparkled in the tree branches. They wavered and bobbed in soft breezes, twinkling like a sea of diamonds. Stars glittered above, and moonlight splashed down.

Musicians played in a central building, like a rotunda, and the strains of a European waltz danced through the air.

She was alive when she had expected to die. And being alive made her appreciate *everything*. It was as if she had never truly seen lights and greenery, heard music, or smelled the scents of flame and food before this night.

Ahead, she saw the area of supper booths. Curtains were tied open, and the diners sat at raised tables. Octavia recognized many of the people in the booths—all nobility, peers of her father's. She strolled along the row, furtively glancing at the people inside.

Father had mentioned that he had seen Sutcliffe with men who belonged to the Royal Society for the Investigation of Mysterious Phenomena. Most people did not even know the society existed. Father had said they investigated things such as vampires, werewolves, and witches.

Father had told her such things existed. He had written notes about all sorts of strange and remarkable creatures he had found on his travels. About the unexplained things he had witnessed.

Father never made any of those notes and findings public. He kept those under lock and key. She had recopied his rough sketches into fine ink renderings of the monsters. If Father accepted them as real and true, she had no reason to doubt him. Father was a scientist and a scholar, and she took him at his word. Ever since her health had improved, Father had been much happier and stronger. And she had been well ever since her forbidden night with Sutcliffe.

The day after, she had felt so strong she'd gotten out of bed. She went outdoors and did sketching for Father's latest book. She had even gone shopping on Bond Street. Instead of being pale, she had color in her cheeks. She could draw deep breaths without pain. She could make a fist without her arm's becoming instantly weak. She even had an appetite.

She'd thought that one night with the Earl of Sutcliffe might have been her last. But since she'd made love to him, she'd felt so alive and healthy.

It was like . . . magic.

But she had an enormous problem. Since she was not going to die, she was now ruined.

She'd tried not to care. She wasn't going to marry anyway, since she didn't know if she would get sick again. So it didn't matter that she could no longer marry because she was no longer a virgin.

If she was not going to become a wife, there was nothing stopping her from having another night of passion with Sutcliffe.

First she had to find him.

Two women in low-cut gowns passed her, large bosoms wobbling well ahead of them. Garish feathers danced on their turbans. They wore as much facepaint as she did, but she didn't think theirs was for disguise. They hoped to look attractive. They sipped punch from large cups. One pointed ahead. "Look, it is the Earl of Sutcliffe."

"Ooh, 'e's a 'andsome one! Let's see if 'e wants to 'walk' on the Dark Walk with us."

Octavia's heart sank. Was she going to be too late? She followed the two light-skirts. They scurried ahead, giggling madly, and she moved through the crowd as best as she could.

Then Octavia saw the courtesans's destination. It was one of the supper booths. It had walls adorned with elaborate paintings and an ornate railing ran across the open front. Behind it, inside the booth, a long table gleamed with silver, crystal, and bright white china. Sutcliffe sat at the end, with a beautiful dark-haired lady seated across from him.

Jealousy panged, but then a blond gentleman who sat beside the lady leaned forward and conversed with Sutcliffe. It was hard to see the party in the booth, for the courtesans stood on tiptoe to gaze at Sutcliffe, but Octavia recognized the blond man. He had come to several of Father's lectures. He was Mr. Sebastien De Wynter, brother to the Earl of Brookshire. The dark-haired lady was Lady Brookshire.

One of the light-skirts sashayed up to the booth. She curtsied to the party, then spoke quietly to Sutcliffe. Then the courtesan retreated, linked arms with her friend, and they both crooked their fingers at him.

Mr. De Wynter laughed, and his brow rose. Octavia moved close enough to overhear.

"If you would like to leave to take a stroll on the Dark Walk, feel free," De Wynter said to Sutcliffe. Then he winked.

Lady Brookshire giggled softly. "My husband has promised to take me for a walk on the famed Dark Walk."

"Indeed," Mr. Sebastien De Wynter said. "I feel like stretching my legs myself."

Octavia was startled as both the earl and his brother gave seductive smiles to Lady Brookshire. The beautiful countess blushed, but rose quickly. "Then let us go."

Unfortunately, Sutcliffe left too. He helped Lady Brookshire down the steps, then her husband and brother-in-law joined her, the two men walking on each side of her. The flashy courtesans quickly claimed Sutcliffe, and he strolled through the crowd with a bosomy woman hanging off each arm. One woman gave his buttocks a pinch.

Octavia wanted to scream in frustration. She should go home, but she had worked so hard to get here. It would break her heart to simply give in, trudge back to the gate, and hire a hackney to take her home.

But she would be an utter twit to believe she could tempt Sutcliffe away from the large-breasted courtesans.

She trailed after them. She could hear how curtly he answered them, how distracted he appeared to be. Was he really going to make love to the two of them?

She wasn't naïve—there had been illustrations in that erotic book of all the various ways human beings had sexual relations. From it, she'd discovered people liked to copulate in groups. One picture had been unforgettable—an entire dinner party had been depicted having an orgy on the dining table. Plates had been flying everywhere, crystal goblets strewn on snowy tablecloth and floor. Some gentlemen were feasting while making love, and women were swallowing wine straight from the bottles. They had all been having sex.

Now, watching Sutcliffe walk with two women, Octavia felt the air fairly crackled with their intent.

The Dark Walk certainly lived up to its name. There were no fairy lights here, and masses of bushes and trees blocked moonlight, creating vast seas of black shadow. Rustling sounds came from thick bushes. Soft moans and heavy panting could be heard everywhere.

Three more lovers would be going in the bushes, too. If her heart sank any lower, she would tread on it.

She should *leave*. Admit defeat. She had said she was only going to have one night with Sutcliffe. But for some mad reason, she was obsessed with the idea of doing it again.

She was so obsessed that she stepped forward. "Lord Sutcliffe?"

He stopped and turned. The two women weren't just clinging to his arms now; they were sagging against him. Apparently they'd indulged in a few cups of punch. They glared at her, and Octavia could tell they were furious at the interruption.

Even with her hooded cloak and her facepaint, he recognized her as his one-night lover. The way his eyes widened in shock and he stepped back proved it. As he jerked back, the drunken courtesans swayed, and one almost fell over.

He righted them both. "I'm afraid our stroll is over, ladies. Go now, and find a gentleman who will be better company."

"There's two of us," one protested, fluffing her henna curls. "Only one of her. You can't mean, my lord, that you prefer *her.*"

"The lady is a friend, and it is my duty to offer company." He bowed to the courtesans. "I bid you good night, and thank you for sharing a pleasant stroll."

Octavia squared her shoulders as one of the harlots flashed a glare so filled with hot anger, it should have set fire to the trees around her. The courtesans stalked off with chins in the air.

Octavia could not quite believe Sutcliffe had sent away two courtesans for her. She took a step toward him, ready to do something mad—like wrap her arms around his neck and kiss him.

But icy cold exuded from him, and she stopped in her tracks. "What are you doing here?" he growled.

It wasn't the greeting she had hoped for. She had come here for him, but suddenly that was the last thing she wanted to reveal. But what else made sense? "I—I wanted to see you again."

A breeze rustled leaves, sounding like ghostly whispers. The night was warm, but shivers tumbled down her back. She wanted to move closer to him. Seeing him, his strong body, and his broad chest made her yearn to press against him. She wanted to feel his warmth. She wanted his arms around her.

Shadows clung to his face, making it look stark and hard. "I thought we were supposed to have one night together," he said icily. "I thought you were dying. You played on my sympathies, my dear, and had me behaving like a scoundrel."

His accusatory tone startled her. "Well, I am sorry, but I thought I was. But I got better."

He looked frustrated.

The irritation he displayed hurt. She lashed out with words. "I apologize for having caused you such grief with my fear."

"You didn't need to bother with the hood and the facepaint. I know who you are, Lady Octavia."

"H—How did you know?"

"I followed your hackney to your home, the house of the Earl of Morton." Displeasure glared from his eyes. "You lied to me, Lady O. You tried to hide the fact you are—were—an innocent maiden. Worse, you are the daughter of a good friend."

"Friend? You and my father argue and fight all the time."

"We debate, and I would never intentionally do him harm. Taking his daughter's virginity is the biggest and most painful insult I could have inflicted on him."

"He doesn't know."

"So I assumed. Otherwise I expect I would have had to meet him over pistols at Chalk Farm."

Branches clattered together, the sound eerie and forlorn. Her cloak blew around her legs. Fear gripped her heart. "You wouldn't have dueled with my father."

"What do you think your father would do, if he finds out?" He raked his hand through his hair. "I ruined you—and I can't understand why a proper, unmarried young lady was so determined to throw away her virginity."

"I was dying, and preserving my maidenhead hardly seemed to matter. It would rot in a grave along with the rest of me."

"What do you want from me, Lady Octavia? I can offer you nothing. Certainly not marriage."

She recoiled. What she had wanted was another night. Even after this argument, her body still ached and throbbed with desire for him. Even when his talk of a duel had frightened her, she still yearned for him. Her desire was worse now that she was so close to him. His scent seemed to lure her, drugging her, making her giddier than if she'd drunk wine.

How could she still desire him when she wanted to smack him across the head, then storm away?

"I wanted pleasure, but at this moment, I would rather die than touch you," she spat. Then she whirled around, ready to stalk away. But she actually paused, hoping . . .

"Go then," he snapped behind her. "Leave me the hell alone. I don't need you pestering me. I don't need you on my conscience."

The next night . . .

Matthew groaned and rubbed his temple. Since his confrontation with Lady Octavia last night, he'd had a pounding headache. Now he had to look through books about vampires.

It was almost dawn and his host, Yannick De Wynter, the Earl of Brookshire and a vampire slayer, set a lamp down on the long table in the center of his library.

After Lady Octavia had walked away from him, Matthew had returned to Brookshire's supper booth. There he'd waited, drinking Vauxhall's watered-down punch, until the earl, his brother, and his wife had returned from their stroll.

He had been so happy to see Lady Octavia was alive, so happy he had forgotten the voluptuous women clinging to his arms. With relief, he'd noted how much healthier she looked since their night together. Her eyes had sparkled; her cheeks were pink. Even her breasts had looked fuller.

The instant he'd noticed that, lust had slammed into him like a runaway carriage.

Guilt had followed quickly, trampling over lust.

"I do not think you are listening to me, Sutcliffe," Lord Brookshire said.

"Sorry." He had been thinking about Lady O—she was the

daughter of an earl, and he had no right to touch her again. "What did you say?"

"The library is yours to explore, Sutcliffe." Brookshire pointed to towering shelves that framed the large fireplace. "Those are the volumes on vampires. The lower three shelves deal with vampires of the Carpathian Mountains."

Matthew groaned. "Now I understand why your brother laughed when I insisted I could gain sufficient information on vampires in a few days."

The earl smiled. "You need to know your quarry to hunt it, as you are well aware. Now, if you will excuse me, it's almost dawn. I've been up all night, and it's time for me to retire to bed."

His host bowed; Matthew returned the gesture, then Brookshire left.

Matthew studied the shelves. Brookshire and his brother, Sebastien De Wynter, were organizing the trip to hunt the demon he had unleashed. They had two weeks before they would be ready to sail, and he was to learn everything he could in that time. With so many books to read, he should get started.

But Matthew leaned against the fireplace mantel and ran his fingers through his hair. The curt, cruel things he had said to Lady Octavia rang in his head.

The moment he'd seen her on the Dark Walk, he'd wanted her, like he had never hungered for any woman before. His heart had thundered, and his blood had raced so quickly to his cock that he had almost fallen over with dizziness.

He'd never had that kind of intense reaction. Certainly not for a woman he should not lust after. What had happened between them at the orgy had been a mistake. He knew she hadn't lied to him about her illness. Discreet questions of his servants had revealed the truth. Servants gossiped, and Lady Octavia's mysterious and devastating illness had been much discussed by maids.

So she hadn't lied, and somehow she had made a miraculous recovery.

He knew what that meant.

He owed her marriage. That's what had made him so damned hard and cold with her. Even so, it was not her fault. He had walked into the parson's legshackles himself. He didn't have to fuck her. He could have backed out. He'd had no right to be so damnably rude to a girl who had been deathly ill and frightened.

And what if she was with child?

Her surprising and unexpected recovery changed everything. He couldn't just walk away from this.

So what should he do? In two weeks, he was going to travel to Europe to hunt vampires. He could marry her and give her his name—it would be the gentlemanly thing to do. But he remembered how she had stalked away from him. She might be stubborn enough to reject him.

She had asked for one night. He had been honest about what he was offering. He'd told her he wouldn't give her marriage. Why was he supposed to insist on marriage now so that he could act the gentleman?

After all, he'd let his brother die. . . .

That was the reason he could not just walk away from Lady Octavia now. But he didn't want to marry a woman who hated him.

First he had to ease away her anger. If he was going to take a bride he didn't want, he at least wanted her not to be spitting venom at him.

That meant courting her.

Hothouse orchids. These were exquisite, with silk-soft petals and lush green stems. There were twelve of them, gathered in a crystal vase. The footman presented them to her and handed her a small card of smooth linen.

Octavia flicked open the card. The signature drew her eye first. In sprawling letters, the name *Sutcliffe* filled one half of the card. On the other half it said, *Apologies for my rudeness. I was happy to see you well.*

Father glanced up from his breakfast, surprised but pleased. "A suitor, then, Tavie? A besotted one by the looks of it. Who is it?"

Sutcliffe's apology was nice, but she wished he hadn't been so flamboyant. How did she explain this? Father was leaning toward her, waiting to find out who had sent such an expensive token.

She couldn't tell him it was Sutcliffe. But if she lied, she might end up accidentally exposing herself. She struggled to think of a harmless reason the earl would send flowers. The instant one sprang to mind, she admitted, "It is from Lord Sutcliffe."

"Sutcliffe?" Papa's fork bounced off his plate and flew to the floor. A footman came forward to retrieve it; another brought a clean one.

"We had an argument recently. He is apologizing for behaving in such an ungentlemanly manner."

"An argument?"

Father and Sutcliffe had almost come to blows in the Royal Society's lecture theater yesterday. For a moment, she'd feared her father had found out what she and Sutcliffe had done together. But it hadn't been that at all. Father had admitted it was about something Sutcliffe had called "natural selection." Sutcliffe was proposing that animals changed—that they adapted to their environments, and transformed over many, many generations. Sutcliffe insisted there had been species of animals on earth for thousands of years, and they had evolved over that time. He said the earth was much older than was believed.

Father, she knew, had been proposing these ideas himself, but in secret. He had insisted the Royal Geographical Society was not ready to hear such ideas. Since they shared essentially the same opinion, she'd feared the fight must be about her. But it could not have been.

She would have known. Father would have been heartbroken and shocked by what she'd done, and she doubted he could hide such emotions.

"We argued about your latest book," she lied, though she hated telling fibs to her father, "on your explorations along the coast of Africa."

"Ah." He nodded with satisfaction. "I can see why the irritating earl would drive you to sharp words. I'm relieved to hear it was not a lovers' quarrel. There is no risk I might be addressing him as my son-in-law."

She had blanched, startled at the word *lovers,* and she was sure a telltale blush had swept over her face. "No, no risk at all, I assure you. I despise the man."

"Good, good." Father nodded his approval. He had absent-mindedly stroked his ear, and now a blob of jam resided there. "He infuriates me to no end, so if you have not developed a tendresse for him, it means all is well with the world. Today"— Father gave a happy smile—"would you accompany me to the museum?"

"Yes, of course." But when she stood, her legs felt as if they were draining away beneath her. She almost fell, but slapped her hands to the table to catch herself. Father swiftly rose to his feet, and one of the footmen lurched away from the wall to help, but she waved them away. "I am fine. I must have just stood too quickly."

"We will not go to the museum today, Tavie. You must rest. I will stay here and work in my study. There were items I had wanted you to sketch for me, but it can wait."

She tried to urge Father to go alone. She didn't want to go back to bed. After spending weeks in it, she wanted to be free.

Father insisted, and she ended up in her room. But instead of putting on her nightgown and getting into bed, Octavia dismissed her maid and paced the floor. A few days ago, at Vauxhall, she had been filled with strength. Now, her limbs felt weak and shaky.

She must be growing ill again. But why? And why had she gotten better so miraculously after no medicine, or bleeding, or prayers had worked?

She had felt healthier almost immediately after she had made love with Sutcliffe.

She'd overheard maids, in their furtive, naughty discussions, refer to things like kisses and touches as "magical." Were Sutcliffe's kisses magical enough to cure illness?

Octavia paused by her bed. No. That would be madness. It couldn't be possible.

But she couldn't explain her feelings toward him. After his cold, cutting words on the Dark Walk, she should have pushed him from her mind. But she couldn't. No matter how hard she tried, she simply couldn't stop thinking about him. She even dreamed about him, wild, erotic dreams that plagued her all night long. She would wake up so aroused and needy that she had to pleasure herself. So aroused that she only had to lightly stroke between her legs and she exploded in an orgasm.

After her orgasms, she also felt stronger. But it was only a temporary effect and would ebb away.

Did lovemaking have healing properties? She couldn't ask Father, obviously, even though he was a great scholar of human nature and existence.

So was Sutcliffe.

Perhaps the Earl of Sutcliffe knew why pleasure—and thoughts of him—made her feel better. Perhaps he could explain it to her.

If she knew the secret, then she wouldn't need Sutcliffe.

* * *

Octavia sat in the very back row of the lecture hall of the Royal Society, while Sutcliffe spoke in front of the packed room of ardent young scholars and middle-aged men.

She had no idea exactly how to ask the questions she must ask of him.

Can you actually make magic when you make love?

I feel better after I have erotic dreams about you. Do you know why?

She certainly couldn't do it in front of a crowded room. She had to get him alone.

From beneath the veil attached to her bonnet, Octavia watched Sutcliffe describe astonishing sights he had seen on his last voyage to Africa. His words painted pictures in her head. He really was . . . magnetic when he spoke.

She was not the only woman in the hall—there were six, and all the rest looked very much like bluestockings. She was the only one wearing a thick lace veil to hide her face. She had wondered if Sutcliffe would notice her and stare at her. But he let his gaze flit over the crowd as he spoke of the remarkable species he had found in Africa, and how most of the creatures had developed methods to blend into their environment, thus helping with their survival.

She didn't blend in here. In her disguise, she stuck out. But he had not looked at her even once. He appeared to be carefully avoiding her. Whenever he faced her side of the room, he kept his gaze on the first rows. Then he would abruptly turn on his heel and pace the other way.

Sutcliffe came to a stop behind his lectern, rested his hands on it, and gave the crowd a handsome smile. "Are there more questions?"

Octavia's heart pumped hard. He would be finished soon, and she intended to approach him. And . . . well, she also had to proposition him.

She had to get better again. She had to see if sex with him could make her well again.

But a dozen hands went up, and she almost wept. It would be a long time before he was finished and she could get him alone.

Would he even acknowledge her if she did? He had apologized, which did not mean he wanted to see her again, but the lovely flowers were more of a gift than he had needed to send.

Now he was ignoring her.

There were hundreds of reasons. It was a public place. He was giving a lecture and certainly couldn't suddenly jump over the chairs to reach her and sweep her into a kiss. Not without causing a scandal—

In front of the crowd, he bowed. "I thank you all for coming today, and I hope you enjoyed my talk on 'Survival of Certain Species of the African Plains and Jungles.' "

All the young men stood and applauded.

Octavia waited at the back of the crowd. People streamed past her, and when the last one had left, she looked toward the lecture area.

It was empty.

Sutcliffe had left through a different door. Avoiding her.

"Miss, there's not supposed to be anyone in here."

She turned to see a youthful footman in the doorway. "I wished to speak to Lord Sutcliffe," she said, as imperiously as she could.

The servant's brows shot up. She was a woman alone, after all, and that usually meant scandalous and sordid things. In truth, she had to do shocking things with Sutcliffe. To see if they made her well.

"You will have to leave now, miss."

"Of course. But where has Lord Sutcliffe gone?" She asked the question without a quiver, as though it was her right to know.

"He left the building, miss. Mentioned he had a party to go to. One of his footmen was talking about it."

"And the host would be . . . ?" she prompted.

"Don't know. Wasn't the sort of party ladies attend. Didn't know they did things like that in the daytime, I didn't." The lad was trying to appear to be a stoic servant, but he blushed so red, his freckles seemed to leap off his face.

It had to be an orgy.

She had to find out where it was.

5

Erotic Fire

"I will now prove that a woman can pleasure eight men at once."

The Duke of Glencairn held up his hands as he made the statement to the gentlemen of the *ton* who packed his drawing room. Matthew heard laughter and mutterings of doubt wash over the crowd. He lifted his brandy snifter and took a long swallow.

"But first, gentlemen, there will be wagering."

"Who's the tart who is going to pleasure all these men?" yelled the Earl of Durbrooke.

Glencairn gave a wicked grin. "The courtesan with the most remarkable rack of tits in England. Harriet Bird."

The gentlemen in the crowd hooted with delight. Matthew drained his drink.

Most men enjoyed the sight of the extremely bosomy Harriet without her clothes. Normally he did, even if he was only studying her so as to speculate on how such large breasts defied gravity.

All he could think of right now was Lady Octavia Grenville.

Embarrassed, he knew why he was here at Glencairn's event. This party was intended for the truly depraved—the gentlemen who wanted to spend several days at an orgy. This particular one had been going on for three days straight, or so he'd been told.

He'd run here as an escape. He had needed time before he approached Lady Octavia. He had sent the flowers and intended to work up to making a proposal of marriage. Then she was there, in the lecture theater, and it had surprised him. He hadn't expected her to pursue him again.

He knew he had to make that offer of marriage. And once he'd seen her, knowing he was on the brink of making a duty marriage, he'd panicked. A long time ago, he'd planned to wed for love. He'd wanted children. After his father's suicide over an intense, unrequited love for a woman who was not his wife, Matthew hadn't trusted in love anymore.

After Gregory's death, he hadn't been able to face the idea that he would someday have a family while his brother was lying in a coffin with a stake in his heart and his severed head stuffed with garlic.

"Good God, those things would smother you," breathed a young man at his side.

Matthew jerked his gaze upward. Harriet Bird had emerged from behind a translucent screen. Her large breasts bounced and swayed as she moved seductively toward Glencairn.

Vaguely Matthew wondered what Harriet would do with eight men. In his loud baritone, His Grace asked for volunteers. Seven men were easily found. Then Glencairn looked to him.

"Sutcliffe, care to be the eighth? You are soon to leave for foreign shores. Perhaps you would care for a taste of an English tart before you leave?"

Then, across the crowded drawing room, Matthew caught a glimpse of a black lace veil. Lady Octavia? She'd hunted him here? Bloody hell. She'd told him she wanted nothing more to do with him. Yet here she was. Apparently his flowers had worked, and she forgave him.

He just hadn't expected her to follow him.

He remembered Sebastien de Wynter's smug grin when Matthew had sent the flowers. De Wynter thought he was trying to win Lady Octavia's heart.

Nothing could be further from the truth.

He was just trying to ease her dislike. He certainly didn't want any woman's heart. Love had killed his father. He had loved his brother, and after Gregory's death, he never wanted to know the pain of love again.

Would stubborn Octavia be satisfied with a duty marriage in which the husband and wife lived separate and distant lives? She would have to be. Whether she wanted love or not, she was not going to get it—he couldn't give it. As soon as they were wed, he was leaving to hunt vampires. Their marriage might prove to be a very short one.

One woman was going to pleasure eight men? All at once?

Octavia could not believe what she'd heard. She stared at the group in the center of the room. Even the courtesan herself wore a look of uncertainty as the men approached the small daybed on which she sat. Each gentleman was taking off a different amount of clothing. Two were stripping entirely—they were shirtless, bootless, and working on the fastenings of their breeches.

Another had opened his trousers and appeared to be unwilling to remove any clothing at all. Two more had removed coats, waistcoats, and cravats.

Octavia looked at the woman, who was very bosomy and had long, red hair that fell to her bottom. The woman arranged herself provocatively on the divan. Her fingers stroked her nipples as one of the completely naked men stooped onto one knee before her. Heavens, her breasts were so big that one gentleman was supporting the right one with two hands while he was kissing the erect, doe-brown nipple—

"What are you doing here?"

The terse, masculine question startled Octavia. She turned and met Sutcliffe's furious blue eyes.

Behind him, she saw the eight gentlemen climbing on the daybed—and on the courtesan. It was odd to see the hairy legs and bare bottoms of men she actually knew. It made her giggle. Giggles that threatened to take control and never stop.

Sutcliffe grasped her elbow and he stalked across the room, away from the spectacle on the daybed. He carted her with him. Once he had her close to one of the corners of the room, where they were on the edge of the crowd watching the spectacle, he growled, "Lady O, I thought after Vauxhall you had decided you never wanted to see me again. I hoped you would change your mind, but I never expected you to come here."

"I had to." She tried to stop walking, but he was pushing her so quickly her slippers were tripping across the floor. "I needed to see you again." She felt a hot blush hit her cheeks under her veil. "I have to . . . um . . . go to bed with you again."

He shook his head. "That's what you want from me? Sex? Christ, why did you have to pursue me?" he muttered. "Why in blazes didn't you just find a nice gentleman and marry him? Why are you tempting me again?"

"Because sex with you makes me well."

That stopped him in his tracks. Men had turned to look at them, so he pressed her quickly against a nearby column and braced his arms on either side of her head. His back shielded her. To anyone in the room, it would look as if he were preparing to ravish her.

But to her, he frowned. "What are you talking about? You mean you enjoy—"

"No, I mean I got better after our night. I was healthy again by the very next day. And I stayed that way for days. It's only now that I've started to get sick again."

He bent very close to her, as though he were going to kiss her. Instead, he murmured, "Lady O, this is impossible."

Heavens, he had a nickname for her?

"Sweeting," he continued, "perhaps you just felt better because you had fun."

"No. I was *truly* better. Before you, I could barely get out of bed. I was weak, and I couldn't keep food down. But after we made love, I was like normal. There is no other explanation. Making love to you made me well. I want to know why it would be so."

He gave a gruff laugh. He was so close the soft shudder of his chest brushed his coat across her bosom. And that soft caress made her shiver. "Well, I can't tell you, my dear, because I can't see how such a thing is possible."

He moved one hand from the column and scratched his jaw. His chin was framed with dark stubble. "There is one phenomenon that would explain it. I've seen men recover from fevers that should have killed them. They were given potions that were innocuous, nothing more than flavored water, yet the men believed the concoctions were medicine. Even after drinking nothing but these false cures, they did battle the illness and survive. Believing that they had potent medicine was enough to cure them."

She pushed up her veil. He was shielding her so no one could see her. "But I did not *believe* making love with you would heal me. I didn't expect it would, so I wouldn't have convinced myself it did. It just happened."

"There's one thing to do." He bent to her throat. His fingers stroked there, and his lips came so close to her ear she moaned softly. Yet he didn't kiss her. Instead, he said hoarsely, "We'll have to try it again."

* * *

Why had he said that? As a gentleman, he was supposed to marry her, not seduce her. But Lady O was pressed against the column, with her veil tossed back and her breasts lifting with her quick breaths. With her soft, shimmery lips, sparkling eyes, dewy skin, she looked like an iced cake presented on a silver dish.

It was as if he had never discovered until now, until he'd looked at Lady O, how beautiful a woman could be.

Matthew bent to her neck and nibbled her skin. She smelled of roses and soap. He wanted to seduce her here, against the column. He wanted to kiss and suckle her beautiful, pert breasts. Lift her skirts and find heaven between her legs.

She had the most beautiful mouth. Her lips were wide, but not full, yet they were incredibly expressive. When he watched her mouth, he couldn't look away.

Even with Harriet moaning and shrieking, even with a wild carnal display taking place behind him, he was more entranced with Lady O's mouth than with busty Harriet's orgasm.

Never before had he met a woman he would call irresistible. At least, not before Lady O.

Matthew grasped her arm more roughly than he intended. "Octavia, I want to fuck you," he murmured. "I would love to do it. Hell, I need to do it. But first—hell, for what I need to do, we cannot be here."

They had to pass through the room to get to the door. Fortunately everyone was watching Harriet. She was bouncing on top of one man who lay on the chaise. Another gent was on top of her, obviously buried in her arse. Balanced on her elbows, she held two men's shafts in her hands, played with another two cocks with her toes, and suckled the seventh man's cock. The eight was straddling her back, pointing his cock toward her generous rump, and obviously intending to slide his prick beside that of the man already in her.

Once upon a time, Matthew would have been intrigued to

watch. Humans invented a staggering number of sexual pleasures—learning what they would do was like finding a new species of animal. But right now, he had no interest at all.

He hustled Octavia around the back of the crowd, hoping she would not see what was happening on the daybed. He feared she could, especially when she gave a huge gasp.

He steered her to the front foyer. A sharp summons had her cloak brought to her. By the time he had her at the sidewalk, his carriage was rattling to a halt in the street.

"Where are we going?" she asked.

"I should take you home. I have no right to touch you, not now that I know who you are." *Not until I propose marriage and you accept.*

"But I—I want to feel well again. Please—I learned you are leaving England, so I won't have many chances. But before you go, couldn't we do it a few times? I want to feel strong again. *Please.*"

God, she was lovely. Unspeakably beautiful, with her lush, voluptuous mouth and hopeful blue eyes.

"We could begin in the carriage," she said matter-of-factly. "Should we undress?"

"Not yet," he said tersely. He was certain he could already smell the rich, erotic scent from between her legs, but given the layers of skirts how was it possible? She was unbelievably tempting. It was as if she had cast a magic spell over him.

"I'll do it," he said, "if you agree to marry me."

"If I do *what?*"

Octavia stared at Sutcliffe as he stretched his long, lean form along the carriage seat. He rolled onto his back. "Sit on my face, Lady O."

She gasped at his blunt words, yet understood what he wanted. She stood, crossed to him, but the carriage lurched in a rut.

Laughing he caught her. Releasing her hands, he lifted her skirts. As she swung her leg awkwardly across his chest, he let go of her skirts and pulled her quim onto his mouth.

She gaped down at him. "What are you doing? You asked me to marry you."

"This is to convince you."

Muslin and petticoats flopped over him, hiding him. But she felt everything he did. Gently, he tugged her nether curls with his lips. Just that light tug and the heat of his breath sent shivers everywhere.

Her palm flattened against the velvet seat, and she let her nether lips lower onto him. She was right on his mouth, her legs wide. He was devouring her with his mouth. His tongue played, but it was the suckling on her nub that made her want to go mad.

She thrust against his mouth in her excitement. She mustn't do that—it must hurt him. How could he breathe?

But when she tried to pull back, Sutcliffe gripped her rear firmly. His hands were big and strong. If he wanted to smother himself with her cunny, how could she argue?

It made her feel naughty but so good. . . .

Embarrassed but lovely . . .

She thrust madly on him, praying she wasn't hurting him, and then he suckled her clit, harder then softer, in the same wild rhythm. Perfect . . . it was so perfect. . . .

The carriage lurched, and her hands slipped. She was balanced on his mouth, and he was . . . merciless. He nuzzled her, his stubble tickling. Then he suckled really hard, really intensely.

She screamed loudly enough to deafen them both when the orgasm exploded in her.

God . . . God . . . God.

Exhausted, sobbing with delight, shaking, she slumped on him.

Then realized she was on top of his face.

Octavia tried to scramble off him, aware he would want to breathe again. With his long body sprawled along the velvet seat, her foot caught, and she stumbled.

He launched up and caught her again, wrapping his strong arms around her.

Suddenly, she was on his lap, and he was embracing her. The carriage swayed, but he ensured she didn't fall off his firm, slightly spread thighs. He gave her the most beautiful smile. Her breath caught. She had never seen a man smile like this—his eyes literally glowed at her.

He captured her mouth with his. She tasted an earthy, salty taste—the flavor of her cunny.

As amazing and impossible as it should be, already she felt stronger. Octavia glowed with strength and delight, and she wanted to share. "I want to do this to you."

Matthew blinked. He thought Lady O had just told him she wanted to pleasure him with her mouth. He gently laid her onto the soft velvet of the carriage seat. He began, gruffly, "I don't expect you to—"

"I want to," she said quickly. "But—but shouldn't I be on top?"

She was so sweet in her innocence. And innocent, gently bred ladies did not suck men's cocks. He should not let her—

She grasped his trousers and efficiently unfastened the top two buttons. Her graceful hands went to the next fastening, and his cock strained against his underclothes. He'd been thinking of something. Something he had to do. What was it?

Oh yes, he'd intended to stop her. But he couldn't . . . hell, he couldn't . . .

Her knuckles brushed his linens, and the muscles of his gut tightened reflexively. She wriggled on the velvet. "What do I do?" she asked ingenuously. "I have no idea. I've seen pictures—"

"You've seen pictures?"

"One of Father's books. He collects erotic books in his studies of human civilization. I suppose they do show a lot about society."

She was adorable. "They depict what people—mainly men—fantasize about," he said. "Not necessarily what they do."

"Well, it showed women holding the man's privy part in their mouths. But you lick and suck at me, so obviously it cannot be as easy as just holding you between my lips."

Dear God. "Sweeting," Matthew managed to rasp, "I would not mind just being held."

"But you made me have a peak of pleasure. An orgasm." She frowned. "I want to do the same for you, but you must tell me how."

She was going to kill him. "Lady O, you do whatever you want. Whatever you feel comfortable with."

She undid the last button of his trousers, though she was breathing hard. She squirmed on the seat.

He'd forgotten—she was wearing a gown and a corset. She couldn't be comfortable. He was going to marry her, so he asked, "Can you spend the night with me?"

"What?"

Holding her arms, he lifted her to a seated position. "Stay with me, and I can remove your clothing." With fumbling fingers, he undid her cloak, then dealt with the fastenings of her dress. Once the bodice was falling off her, he drew the sides off her shoulders, and undid the bow at the base of her stays, and loosened them.

Freed from her dress, Octavia lay down again, on top of her cloak and the seat. She felt strength coursing through her whole body. She would spend a night with Sutcliffe if she had to move heaven and earth to do it. "Yes."

But he had asked her to marry him.

Could she? Was he in love with her? Had he fallen in love with her while making love to her?

"Good, because I want to be naked with you." As the carriage rumbled along, he grasped his trousers and pushed them down. Even with the vehicle swaying, he managed to get his trousers down around his ankles, and get his coat, his waistcoat, and his shirt off.

He was certainly determined to get undressed.

She certainly loved seeing him naked.

Once he was nude, she suddenly discovered how erotic it was to lie on her back while he straddled her. Above her, his ballocks dangled, wrinkly and intriguing. They swayed with the carriage motion. She put up her flat palm and bumped them gently. She wanted to stroke, but knew they were sensitive, so she just cradled them. Even that slight touch made him take a sharp, hard breath.

His erection pointed straight up. Now she could see all its fascinating details. The thick shaft was not smooth, but seemed to be made of three long, tall stalks, and veins encircled it. His curls were a dark brown, and his shaft rose out of the thicket of them, so amazingly straight.

Octavia tentatively wrapped her hands around him. She couldn't touch her fingers together near the bottom of his shaft.

It was utterly straight, stiff as iron. The head looked glossy, and a droplet of moisture rolled off the full, smooth crown.

What would it taste like? It looked clear, like champagne. She wanted to know. She opened her mouth and touched her tongue to the head. . . .

Salty. Ripe tasting. Intriguing. She clumsily ran her tongue over the tip of his member. It bobbed away from her, so she clasped it with two hands—it was like holding a sword. She tried to tug it down, but it didn't want to come to her mouth, and she didn't want to hurt him.

He put his hand on the shaft, near the hilt. Ruthlessly he

pushed it down. He was breathing fast, faster than he'd done even when making love to her.

She arched up, opened her mouth wide, and gobbled him inside.

It was so astonishing. The head of his cock was soft, but obviously full. Against her tongue it felt as smooth as silk. She hadn't thought it would be so hot. The taste was . . . not at all like her, but it tasted intimate.

"You—you can suck it if you like."

He sounded hesitant. For all his arrogance, he didn't make demands now. It was rather . . . mmm . . . sweet of him.

How did she do this? He had thrust this shaft in and out of her quim. That had stimulated him, so she must try to do the same with her mouth. Holding her lips tight around the shaft, she took him deep inside. As deep as she could, before she realized how big he was, how much he filled her mouth.

Goodness. Her cheeks were hollowed so much, she must be hurting him with suction. She couldn't quite breathe. She let his member slide out a bit.

She'd wanted to be good at this, but it was complicated. How did the women in the pictures do it?

Sutcliffe, however, was smiling. He looked utterly delighted. Then he frowned with concern. "Are you all right? You look like you're choking. You don't have to—"

"Did I do it right?" She waved away his concern, blushing. She hated showing her innocence so plainly. Though what did it matter? He knew what she was now. He'd even asked her to marry him, after they'd been to bed once. She could not be that bad. But to make sure, she asked, "You liked it?"

"Yes." His voice was so soft, she barely heard it over the creak of the rolling wheels. "Watching you do that is the most miraculous thing I've seen."

She felt her brows shoot up. "You've stood almost at the rim of Mount Vesuvius. You've seen the sunrise from Mount Kilimanjaro. You have seen exotic jungles and the beauty of the East. This can't be—"

"It is," he murmured.

Boldly, she grasped his bare legs and lifted, so she could graze his ballocks with her lips. He closed his eyes and moaned. She felt the most remarkable surge of power. And she felt strong.

This was scandalous, shocking, wonderful—to be underneath him, taking his erect cock in hand and guiding it back to her lips. His legs were amazing. His thighs were rock hard, his calves beautifully shaped. His hips were lean, his stomach a plane of defined muscle.

He was a gentleman, but also an adventurer. He had climbed mountains, paddled wild rivers, had ridden everything from a camel to an ox to an Arabian mare. All that adventuring gave him the body of a Greek god and made him heartbreakingly beautiful.

He wanted to marry her. The thought of it made her dizzy with delight.

When she was ill, she couldn't even think of marriage. If she married Sutcliffe, she would be healthy again. All the time. She could bed him all the time.

She suckled hard. Suckled and suckled . . . until her jaws ached . . . and though his hips rocked and he breathed hard, he didn't seem to be reaching any peak. He had made her melt in mere minutes. Why couldn't she give him the pleasure he gave her?

He reached down and gently eased her hands away—she was gripping the hilt of his thick cock, trying to stroke and pleasure where her mouth could not reach. Then he eased out of her mouth, and she was struck with a sense of failure.

This was her wildest adventure. And she hadn't been good at it.

"I—" Did she apologize? Should she? The thought of it was so embarrassing. She had wanted to do well on her adventure.

"I can't let you make me come," he said softly. "It would take me too long to recover. After all, my duty here is to give you as much pleasure as I possibly can, to ensure you become healthy." He gazed at her with the studious seriousness he'd displayed in his lecture. "If climaxes heal you, I have to last as long as I can to ensure you have many orgasms."

"How many?" she whispered.

A slow grin brought out deep, sensual lines to bracket his beautiful lips. "We'll find out how many you can enjoy."

She'd never dreamed—even in her maddest fantasies—she would end up in Lord Sutcliffe's bed. Yet here she was.

Octavia drew the covers up. Sutcliffe's sheets were a dark blue satin; his thick counterpane was embroidered with silver. A mountain of pillows propped her up.

He had helped her hastily dress in the carriage, had placed her veil and her cloak back on her. She prayed she had been sufficiently disguised. He might have offered marriage, but she didn't want Father to hear any gossip about this. He had dismissed his footman at the door, after giving the man instruction to have the other servants leave them alone.

She clasped a brandy balloon. Lifted it to her lips, and took a small sip, a little bit for courage, as he stripped off his clothing—he had fastened it only enough to leave the carriage and get up his stairs without his trousers falling down.

He climbed on the bed, naked, and took the glass from her fingers. He set it on the bedside table. His breathing was harsh, and he whispered, between pants, "I've been hard for you for almost an hour. You have no idea how much it hurts...no, perhaps you do. I've no call to complain. I just want you to know how much I ache for you."

She loved him like this: when he smiled at her and she felt so close to him.

This was what their married life would be like. She had dreamed of adventure for her entire life. Marrying Sutcliffe, leaving her home, having a family—this would be her dazzling, wonderful adventure.

His fingers stroked her sensitive clit, and she cried out in pleasure. How could just the brush of his fingers make her feel as if she were flying?

When he lifted his fingers from her and gently held them to her lips, so she could taste her own juices, she blushed fiercely with shyness.

He licked his fingers, making her moan and squirm.

She was ready. So very ready for this—

He faced her with a serious expression. "First we must get on with the matter at hand. I've ruined you. You told me you were dying; otherwise I would never have deflowered an innocent maiden. I want you to understand that about me. I'm known as a rake, but I'm not a rogue, or a scoundrel. I'm not the sort of man who ruins women's lives. So, because you are well, I owe you marriage."

"You asked me to marry you because . . . because you *have* to? You don't really want to?"

"It's a gentleman's duty."

"What about love?"

He shook his head. "I'm sorry, Octavia, but I am not in love. I doubt very much I will ever be. I don't believe I am capable of falling in love with you."

"I—I don't understand." This was awful. Humiliating and embarrassing and dreadful. He was telling her he would never love her. Telling her he was not capable of falling in love meant he was not even willing to try, didn't it?

"As you know, I am leaving England on a voyage. My ship sails in a few days, and I cannot take you with me—it's too dangerous for you, where I am going. There will be enough time for me to acquire a special license and for us to be wed. I have to warn you though . . . I might not come back."

"I am driving you away from England?"

"No, no, not that. I am going to the Carpathian Mountains on a hunt, and the beast I am hunting might kill me before I can destroy it. You may be a widow very soon. If so, you will have my name, and if you turn out to be with child, the baby will be legitimate. Every detail will have been satisfactorily taken care of. No loose ends."

Her jaw dropped. She actually felt the muscles ache because she was gaping at him with a wide open mouth. If she didn't agree to this, she would die. But what would happen to her if he didn't come back? She would grow ill again anyway. He didn't seem to even be concerned about that. Perhaps, since he was insisting he wouldn't love her, he didn't even care.

"I won't do this," she spat, in humiliation. "Go and leave England and forget about me. I would never marry you—you are utterly heartless."

She gathered up her clothes.

Tears burned her eyes. Her heart felt as if it were on fire. It seemed to be burning in her chest. Was this heartbreak—that feeling that her heart would be reduced to ashes?

A loud roar sounded behind her. It was a huge sound, sort of like an explosion. She felt a burst of sudden heat at her back.

Clutching her clothes to her, Octavia swiftly turned around.

Giant flames leapt in the fireplace. The small fire had exploded into an enormous blaze. Sutcliffe wasn't even looking at her. He had grabbed the fireplace poker and was trying to approach the blazing fire.

She didn't know what had happened, and she didn't care. Sutcliffe was busy jabbing into the heart of the fire, tugging at the logs, trying to gain control of the flames. It gave her time—she couldn't go out into the corridor naked. She stopped long enough to fling on her dress and stuff her feet into her shoes. She didn't bother to fasten the gown. Instead, she pulled her cloak over it, held the bodice to her chest, and ran from the room.

Maybe she would die if she never saw Sutcliffe again. But her heart hurt so much she no longer cared.

6

Sex on a Desk

It was one of the most tempting sights Matthew had ever beheld. Dressed in sprigged muslin, with a bonnet perched on her golden curls and a parasol held in her gloved hands, Lady O looked the picture of maidenly innocence. While she studied the voluptuous form of a naked Greek statue.

At the sight of her, his cock bucked up like an unbroken horse, wild and refusing to obey commands. He had to duck behind a glass case while he studied ancient Egyptian pottery—something that should quell his ardor in an instant. Lady O was not alone—her friend Miss Eliza Compton was with her. That meant he could not whisk Lady O into a quiet corner and seduce her into marriage.

Or just seduce her.

For two days, since she had run out of his house, he had been plagued with desire for her. Raw, irritating, unstoppable sexual yearning.

He had no idea what was wrong with him. He had made her an offer of marriage. She had refused it. Hadn't he done his duty?

But he felt he hadn't. He wanted to behave like a gentleman, which meant he had to marry the lady he had ruined, even if he had to tie her hand and foot and carry her to the altar over his shoulder.

His brother, Gregory, would have never ruined a woman. Gregory had been the perfect gentleman, noble and good. So bloody good he had trusted his wild, arrogant, selfish, thoughtless older brother, and it had cost him his life.

Matthew had never acted like a gentleman—and when he had sealed the crypt on his brother's mutilated body, he'd sworn he would change.

Gregory had always urged him to act like a gentleman and do what was right.

Marrying annoying Lady Octavia was what was right. So Matthew adjusted his trousers, stepped out from behind the glass case, and strolled over to her.

Her friend spotted him first.

Miss Compton plucked Octavia's sleeve. She whispered something, and he caught a bit of it as he approached. It sounded like, "It's him" and "erotic picture."

Lady O turned, pursed her mouth, and then stalked to him. She met him in front of a large stone sarcophagus. "What are you doing here, Sutcliffe?"

He'd come to take her to a private place, ravish her, make her come until she agreed to marry him between her cries of pleasure. But she glared at him, and for some reason it brought out the devil in him, the ungentlemanly part of him. "I brought some of the items that adorn this exhibit," he said coolly. "I came to see how they were doing."

"I expect, since the pieces you brought back with you were several thousand years old, they haven't changed much."

Damn, he did not want to stand here in public, sparring with her. She walked past him, but he caught her wrist, stopping her. Giving quick glances to the other visitors, he murmured by her ear. "I came in pursuit of you. You are to be my bride. And since you left me unsatisfied in my bedchamber, I came searching for you to finish what we started."

"*No,*" she whispered, her voice low but fierce. "I won't marry you out of duty. I will not."

"Do you still believe sex with me keeps you well?"

She caught her breath. Her expression changed. All the anger seemed to drain out of her. "What difference does it make? You do not care. You plan to marry me and leave, whether I am sick or well. You were very clear. You want to marry me so you can ease your conscience, but you said you would never love me—you would never even *try* to have love between us."

"You drive me mad," he growled in a low voice. He saw Miss Compton watching them intently, as she pretended to study a display. "I don't know what's wrong with me. I can't love you, it's true, but I lust for you like an addict needs opium. I'm half-insane with desire for you."

"Well, I'm sure you'll recover, once you have left England."

"Damnation," he swore, which was not something he was supposed to do in front of a lady. Even one he'd fucked. "I have to go."

"Are your voyages so very important to you? I've wanted to travel my whole life, and I've never been allowed to. I am supposed to accept all the limitations a woman has and be happy. You men refuse to give even an inch for anyone else, even someone you love."

Matthew had to be insane. He was throbbing with desire for her, hard as a brick. His heart thundered like native drums. "Would you believe me if I said I had to go back because it was my arrogance and stupidity that unleashed a powerful vampire? I have to go back to the Carpathians to kill her."

"I—A *vampire?*"

"What?" Miss Compton breathed. She had crept up behind them.

Holding Octavia's wrist, he dragged her against his body. He had to marry her. Had to. And, God, this close to him, her scent was drugging him like opium. He had to have her.

In the middle of the Egyptian exhibit, in front of numerous members of Society, he yanked her into his arms and hungrily French kissed her.

It was the scandal of the Season. Drat Lord Sutcliffe.

But that shocking and scandalous kiss in the middle of the British Museum was not the only reason Octavia had not left the house for a week.

Sutcliffe was determined. He had delayed his voyage to the Carpathians. He had sent her a long letter that detailed everything that had happened to him on his last journey there: his trip to a forbidden cave, his foolish exploration that had unlocked the prison of a vampire, the attack on his brother, the fact he had been forced to kill his own brother.

He had explained that his heart had broken with his brother's death and that he believed he could never love anyone again.

She knew how painful grief could be. She had never lost the grief she'd felt after her mother had died. Sutcliffe felt responsible for his brother's death, which must make the pain a hundred times worse.

She understood how he felt, but that did not mean she was willing to enter into a loveless marriage.

Unless he could be healed . . .

No. It was ridiculous. He'd told her he refused to even try to open his heart to her. Anyway, she suspected he would be so determined to avenge his brother he would probably get himself killed in the Carpathians.

In his letter, he'd written that he feared she would think he was crazy for saying that vampires really did exist.

She believed him because Father had told her such things existed . . . and because she had discovered there was something wrong with her. Slowly, Octavia faced her fireplace. The fire was laid, but not burning. But she knew what would happen if she looked long enough—

With a *whoosh*, flames burst from the logs. Heat flooded into the room from the fire. The blaze consumed the logs, turning them to ash at an impossible rate.

She stepped back, shaking. She was certain she had started the fire. These things kept happening. When she grew angry . . . glass shattered, or wood splintered, or liquid suddenly frothed out of pitchers. Or fires suddenly started.

She was so scared Father or a servant would notice. She'd avoided the dining room, the parlors. Again she was hiding in her bedchamber, just as she'd done when she was sick. Hiding the fact she appeared to be a witch. And brushes flew.

She had read everything in her father's journals about witchlike women. The words he had written were now burned into her mind, as if they had been imprinted on her with a searing brand.

The things she could do were definitely like witchcraft. His sketches had belied the truth of her vision of witches as wizened women surrounding a cauldron, chanting spells. In his pictures, many witches were young and beautiful. And they did not need spells to change the weather, make crops die, or cause people to grow sick and weak.

She didn't consciously do things like starting fires. But the only logical explanation was that she was a witch.

How could she marry Lord Sutcliffe? She knew he had told Father he intended to offer for her hand. Her father had been stunned. But Sutcliffe had told Father he loved her. And that had convinced her father to agree and let the wretch court her.

The liar.

And she had one more damning secret. Every morning for the last few days, she had been sick. She had missed her menstrual courses.

That had nothing to do with magical powers or with her illness.

She was pregnant.

Octavia stared at her reflection in the mirror. Her heart felt as though an efficient maid was wringing it dry. "Since you are carrying his *child*," she whispered, "you have to say yes."

With a sharp *crack*, the glass of the mirror split in half.

Swans paddled on the water, and one honked and hissed as she and Eliza hurried through St. James Park. In the nighttime, the park was notorious for liaisons between gentlemen—something ladies were not supposed to know about. But this was a sunny afternoon and, Octavia reflected, the park was quiet.

"You are going to hunt Lord Sutcliffe down in the park?" Eliza asked.

"Not in the park, ninny. Across the street, on Birdcage Walk. The Royal Society has its offices there."

"It does?" Eliza puffed behind her as Octavia strode swiftly to the elegant building. She had no idea why she was almost running. She was about to accept an offer of marriage from a man and lie to him while doing it. Yet she wanted to get it over with, while she had the courage.

Eliza stared up at the soaring marble columns. A servant stood by the double doors, which were glossy black and festooned with brass. A plaque that read THE ROYAL SOCIETY FOR THE INVESTIGATION OF MYSTERIOUS PHENOMENA was fastened to the wall beside the doors.

It took only minutes before a servant returned and brought her and Eliza into an office. Sutcliffe was there, and the servant announced them, to him and Mr. Sebastien De Wynter. Before the men had finished their bows, Octavia blurted, "I came to say 'yes.' "

"Excellent." Sutcliffe jerked his head toward the door, then looked pointedly at De Wynter.

"Ah," murmured handsome, blond Mr. De Wynter. His brows rose, then a spine-melting smile curved his lips. He turned that smile on Eliza. Her friend gaped, dumbstruck. "Miss Compton, would you care to join me in one of the parlors? Lady and Lord Brookshire are here today, and always take their tea now. I thought you might enjoy a refreshment."

He offered his elbow. Dazzled, Eliza slipped her hand in the crook.

The moment she was alone with Sutcliffe, he let out a sharp breath. "Thank God," he muttered. "Those last few moments were agony. Ever since you breezed into the room, smelling of gardens and sunshine, I've wanted Lady O."

His voice was raw, like that of a man truly in severe pain. She blinked, and in that heartbeat, he came to her, took hold of her around the waist, and hoisted her on the desk. In an instant, he bunched muslin and petticoats at her waist. She wasn't wearing drawers, which were considered fast.

He was fighting to undo his trousers. "I have never wanted a woman like I want you. It is like you have a magical power over me—"

"Surely not," she said quickly, but his attention was on the falls of his dark trousers. He pushed them down, shoved his linens down his hips. She gasped at the sight of his erection—it was thick and more rigid than she'd ever seen it, rising along his flat, hard stomach. It seemed so scandalous to see his bare bottom and his naked erection in an office of the Royal Society. He cupped her bottom and dragged her to him. Her legs were open, and she moaned as her bare quim nestled against his shaft.

Oh yes.

She had ached for this, too. But first, she must tell him she was going to have his child. And she could not let him guess she was a witch. "I have decided to marry you—"

"Don't talk. Wrap your arms around my neck. Make love to me."

She hooked her arms around his strong neck, resting them on his broad shoulders. Bending his head, he kissed her. Then he pushed his erection inside her.

He filled her; the stroke of his shaft touched sensitive places inside that made her sob and tremble. So many intense sensation rushed through her, she had to bite her lip to keep from screaming in delight as he thrust slowly in and out.

She pressed her lips to his stubbly jaw, kissing and licking as he moved his hips gracefully and fluidly, teasing her deep inside.

It was so good. So *very* good.

She had to stay quiet. If she cried out or moaned, someone could hear. What a scandal that would be.

But the risk . . . the danger . . . made this hot and thrilling.

"I can't last, Lady O," he whispered throatily by her ear. His hips moved faster, arching forward, pressing his groin to her to drive deep inside. His shaft rubbed along her tingling, aching clit. Each stroke made her whimper against his skin.

It was magic. Pure magic. She clutched his shoulders, moving with him. It was like chasing something. Pleasure was there . . . so close . . . and if she just thrust madly against him as he buried himself into her, she would find it.

With a soft roar, the fire burned brighter. Papers flew off the desk. As they fluttered wildly around the room, the climax took her. Her fingers drove into his shirt. He gave an intense moan at the exact same instant, and he shoved his hips forward, burying his erection to the hilt. He rocked slowly, groaning, coming into her.

Then he stopped, bowed his head. Gently, his lips moved over her, touching her forehead, her lashes, the tip of her nose, then her lips. "Mine," he whispered. "My wife."

His lying wife. Reality hit her with more power than the orgasm. Papers had landed everywhere. How did she explain that?

He was kissing her, long and slow, and she couldn't even enjoy it. She was staring over his shoulder at the pieces of paper she could see. The fire was now a huge blaze. Wouldn't he begin to wonder why fires went mad when she was near them?

Sutcliffe eased back.

She stayed perched on the edge of the desk. He quickly pulled his linens up, tucking his softening shaft into them. It felt so intimate to watch him casually arrange himself inside. Then he did up his trousers.

Sutcliffe walked around the room, collecting up the papers. The office of the Royal Society looked like a normal gentleman's study, except there were strange weapons arranged on the walls between bookshelves. "There must have been a breeze," he muttered. "The rush of air must have made the fire flare up. Just as it did in my room."

Octavia couldn't say anything. She didn't trust her voice to stay steady.

He plunked the pile of papers on the desk and smiled at her. She still sat on the edge, her skirts bunched at her waist. Taking her hand, he guided her back on her feet. Her skirts fell, but they were crumpled and wrinkled.

He smoothed them, and then he drew a folded piece of paper from his pocket and held it up. "Special license. We can be wed instantly if we want."

She *must* do so for the baby, but she panicked. How could she keep this secret from him? After spending time with her, wouldn't he realize she caused these things to happen? Then what would he do? Kill her? Burn her at a stake? "I—"

"Or do you want something large, ostentatious, with a grand breakfast and royalty in attendance?"

"Heavens, no. This is a duty, isn't it? We . . . we are not in love, and I don't want to pretend we are . . . if we are not." Now she was glad he wouldn't love her, because if he did, she would hate lying to him. This way she could argue he wouldn't care.

"I'm sorry," he said softly. "If you are hoping for love, I am afraid you will be disappointed."

"I know. Because of your brother. It is all right. I don't care that you don't love me."

"Lady O, do you love me?"

"I—no. And I won't, as I'm sure you would not want that."

He stared at her, curiously. "Then why did you agree to marry me?"

"I am going to have a baby," she said bluntly. "Our baby. That's the only reason I said yes."

When a husband broke his wife's heart before the wedding, did he get a wedding night or not?

Matthew tore off his cravat, then tried to yank off his form-fitting coat as he paced his dressing room. Helms, his slender, finicky valet, rushed forward. "My lord, allow me. You will tear the seams."

"I don't bloody care. I want the thing off."

What did it matter if he destroyed clothing when he had just married an unhappy woman and tomorrow he would be leaving to hunt the powerful vampiress who had killed his brother?

Helms turned stark white. "But my lord, the cloth . . . the tailoring . . . You must not treat such a work of art with such disdain. This is the morning coat of your wedding—"

"Don't remind me," he growled.

Fussing, Helms stood on a step stool to reach his shoulders

and eased the coat off. It was driving Matthew mad to have his clothes taken off with care.

When Helms paused to brush his coat before dealing with his shirt, Matthew snapped. "That's enough. Go away."

Pouting, Helms left him alone. Why was he in such a hurry? He had no idea if Octavia would welcome him into her bed. True, she was his wife, and he could demand she do her duty, but he refused to make love to an angry woman.

This morning, he had stood beside her at the altar. Then he had been at her side at their wedding breakfast.

He had spent the morning beside her, and he had never felt more distant from anyone in his life. Even his mother, who had been distant and ice-cold after his father's suicide, had been warmer to him than Octavia had been on the morning of their wedding. After the ceremony, she had not smiled once. At breakfast, she had barely touched a bite of food. She had accepted congratulations from the few friends in attendance, but when no one was looking at them, he saw such pain in her eyes, it had twisted his heart.

What in Hades was he supposed to do?

The ceremony had reminded him at every moment that Gregory wasn't there. It had reminded him of how empty and hollow his parents' marriage had been. His father had been in love with another peer's wife, a woman who refused to become his mistress. Matthew had never learned who the woman was, but his father had committed suicide over her. Father's devotion to the mystery lady had broken Mother's heart and had destroyed her.

As Octavia had sipped wine and refused to meet his gaze, he had regretted what he'd said to her. He should have lied. Should have told her he was in love. He could have faked it; she would have been happy, and if he died in the Carpathians, she never would have learned the truth.

He hauled his shirt over his head. Nerves gave him enough

strength to drag off his own tight-fitting boots. Then he took his trousers off and put his robe on.

It was easy to stride into the parlor that separated his bed-chamber from Octavia's, but almost impossible to dredge up the courage to rap on the door. It was insane, but he preferred to stand there, with his elbow resting against the door, than knock and find out she didn't want him.

Hades, how was he going to hunt vampires if he couldn't face a confrontation with his wife?

He rapped on the door.

7

After the Wedding

There was no answer. Matthew felt he should walk away, leave her alone, but this was to be their wedding night. Even if she threw something at him in her anger, he had to face her. He grasped the doorknob, turned it, and began to open the door.

Then he heard it. A soft, helpless sob.

A bride should not be crying on her wedding day. Even he knew that. His mother and father had reputedly been filled with joy at their wedding—and it had gone sour. What hope for happiness was there when the bride began her new life in tears?

He pushed the door open the full way. "Don't cry, Octavia," he said gently.

Octavia was seated on the edge of her bed, wearing her gown. She looked up; her eyes were red and puffy, and tears had streaked down her cheeks, leaving glistening traces.

Damn.

What words were there? Just the lies he could give her. Maybe, if he told her he loved her, if he pretended he was capable of it, he would stop her tears.

Or maybe he needed to distract her.

"There are some advantages in being a bride," he said softly, awkwardly.

She stared at him as if he had lost his mind. "If you mean pleasure, that's what got us into this mess. And what will I do, when you've gone away for months? I'll grow ill again."

He crossed his arms over his chest. He didn't know how to answer that. "Have you felt sick? It's been a few days since we last made love."

"I feel sick with the baby, but not the kind of sickness I felt before."

"Then you are probably well." He had to believe that, because it was his duty to hunt vampires and destroy what he had stupidly unleashed.

"Thank you. Now that you've said I am," she said in a prickly manner, "I suppose I must be."

He felt like his father, saddled with a wife who was angry, sharp-tongued, and determined to jab at him. And like his father, he was responsible for his own disaster. He couldn't believe that sex with him was keeping Octavia well. It made no sense. But seduction was the only method he knew to ease her anger. And if she believed it made her feel better, he had to provide her special form of healing.

Could he be good enough in bed to make his wife retract her claws and purr?

Oh, she was *furious* with him.

And furious at herself for seducing him in the first place—without thinking to ask him to take precautions against making her pregnant. If she hadn't been so impetuous and impatient, convinced she was dying, she would have avoided a loveless marriage.

But mostly, Octavia was scared.

Before Sutcliffe had come in, she had lost her temper, and all her perfume bottles had exploded on the vanity. At least she'd only had three. She had quickly opened the window to air out the room, then had swept the shards of glass into her wash basin.

Now she was shaking with horror and fear. And Sutcliffe could see that.

"Shh," he murmured. He lifted her to her feet, embraced her. Softly, his lips brushed the top of her head, and his large hand stroked down her back. Her husband was gentling her in the way a man did with a frightened horse.

Her simple ivory dress was loose, but she had sent her maids away when she had realized her perfume bottles were rattling on the marble vanity top.

Sutcliffe drew her gown down from her shoulders. He ran his lips gently over the nape of her neck. The bodice, tugged down over her arms, kept them trapped. She closed her eyes and let him kiss her.

What should she do? She was angry with him because he insisted he would never even try to love her.

Should she fight not to feel anything? Or should she let herself enjoy sex with him, because it was the only tenderness she could hope to have in this marriage?

She didn't know. Why did she have to even make this choice? Why did he have to be so stubborn and wrong?

He undid a few more buttons on the back of her dress and gave her bodice a tug. The sleeves went down to her elbows, and the bodice slid to sit below her breasts.

He gently kissed the swells of her breasts. Of course it tickled and tingled and felt wonderful.

Even if she tried, she couldn't stop showing her pleasure. His mouth suckling her nipples made her moan.

Then he scooped her in his arms. Carrying her, he bent to her bosom, and he sucked her nipples once more.

She was trying to be annoyed, but it was *sooooo* good.

Next minute she was on her stomach on the bed. She gasped as he threw her skirts up and her bottom was bared.

She had bathed last night. She'd wanted to be clean and fresh to start her new life, even if it wasn't a happy start. And bathing had given her something to think about other than watching the hours tick away to her wedding to the man who didn't love her.

"You smell beautiful," he murmured. "Like roses."

To her astonishment, he kissed her bottom. She twisted to see. His mouth dropped dozens of kisses on the curves of her derriere.

"I bathed." She blushed fiercely. She had had no idea men kissed *bottoms*.

"Now that you are my bride, I can do everything to you I've ever fantasized about."

But men did not do that with wives. That was what she'd learned from gossip. Gentlemen were supposed to be gentle with their wives in the bedroom, and take their . . . wilder interests to mistresses.

The Earl of Sutcliffe, her husband, clasped the naked cheeks of her bottom with both hands. He parted them gently, scandalously exposing the valley between. Then he kissed—*kissed*—the opening there.

It was shocking. Stunning.

If he was doing this and he wasn't going to love her . . . what desires would he take elsewhere?

It was hard to think as he stroked her in that forbidden place with his tongue. Hard to remember he didn't want to love her. Hard to be afraid of losing him to a mistress and of being unhappy . . .

What he was doing was so very good.

He lifted her bottom in the air. Then something stiff and

hard brushed against her nether lips from behind. It was his shaft, and the stroking made her slippery and wet.

He slid his member inside. His hands reached around, and he clasped her breasts.

She had seen how animals mated from behind. Never had she expected to do the same thing. Though, now that she thought of it, there had been a scene like this in the erotic book.

It was as if he knew all the scenes in the book and was showing her every one . . .

In this position, his hips collided hard with hers. Each thrust, each time his groin hit her bottom, her cheeks jiggled. It was so very erotic.

His hands cupped her breasts, then he began pinching and tugging on her nipples with each thrust.

She couldn't see him, but she could feel everything he was doing. She didn't know what he was going to do. He released her right breast, then slid his fingers down to her nether place and stroked her clit, and she came.

Instantly. With screams. And gasps. She rocked madly beneath him. Her arms shook, then gave out, and she fell on the bed.

He fell with her, still thrusting. He went deep inside her. The taut head of his erection stroked in new, fascinating, thrilling places.

She'd barely finished gasping from her first climax when the second one hit her, making her shout. And scream.

Heaven, heaven, heaven.

Her marriage might be a disaster, but her husband was giving her a glimpse of heaven.

Then he withdrew, and she sobbed. Gently, he eased her over. Her wedding dress was a wrinkled mess. But when she saw the hungry gleam of lust in his eyes, she didn't care.

"More," she whispered.

"At your command, my lovely wife," he whispered. He

thrust deep inside her and made her come again and again and again. . . .

Her husband collapsed beside her. Sweat gleamed on his handsome face. The hair on his chest was damp with perspiration, and his back was slick with it.

"That was amazing," he growled. "You made me come so intensely. Watching you reach so many climaxes was unbelievably exciting."

Octavia couldn't speak. Her throat was too tight. She'd had six orgasms. So many that she did not believe she could have another one without exploding into a thousand pieces. She was so sensitive that even the brush of his breath on her skin made her feel close to a climax.

But nothing had changed. They still had a duty marriage, an empty one. She was going to share a future with a man who was determined never to love her.

"I'm exhausted," he muttered. "Let's sleep now. I have to sail tomorrow."

She let him put his arm around her and cradle her to him, but she could not relax. He was going to leave in the morning. Nothing had changed. Being married had not chipped away any of the ice around his heart.

He was still going to leave her, even though she was expecting their baby. Even though she didn't know if she would become sick again.

The only good thing was that if he was far away, he would never find out she was a witch. But she still had to hide the truth from her family, her friends, the servants.

She might be married, but she felt completely alone.

Late April, 1821

Flakes of snow swirled around him as Matthew emerged from the tiny, warm inn in the small village of Bistritz, at the foot of the Carpathians. It was the last village before the Borgo Pass that led through the mountains into Bukovina. This was where he had stayed with Gregory months before. This had been their "base camp," from which they had left to hunt for the supposed tomb of a demoness and had found the vampire Esmeralda.

The memories of the last few days he had spent here with Gregory hit him hard and fast. The memories had forced him out of doors. He had been inside, struggling to interpret as Sebastien De Wynter questioned locals. Matthew could speak some Russian and some Czech, but De Wynter had been talking to men in dialects he did not know. He had taken it upon himself to buy the drinks.

He had recognized two of the words: *vrolok* and *vlksolak*. Both meant the same thing—vampire or werewolf. One was Slovak, the other Servian.

When one old man looked at them with pity, then crossed himself, Matthew knew what it meant. Now, outside, he stamped his feet, for his toes felt ice-cold in seconds. De Wynter came out, coat open and scarf flying in the blustery wind. The man never seemed to get cold.

"What did you learn?" Matthew asked.

De Wynter shook his head to brush off a dusting of snow, then plopped his hat on. "The men I spoke to said they had seen a woman demon near the village. She was hunting for children and young men. They think she has gone. They believe she bought a coffin, filled it with earth, and paid gypsies to take her to the Danube, where she traveled by ship. She has not been seen since."

He groaned. "So we return?"

"We should make sure first," De Wynter said. "We should go to the cave in which she was entombed."

The snow had begun falling more heavily. It soaked up all sound and brightened the night sky. In England, it was spring.

Here, blizzards still raged and snow covered the earth in ten foot-deep drifts.

He and De Wynter returned to their carriage, but the driver refused to travel through the pass. "Too much snow," he said in his native language. "Threat of avalanche. Not at night. Never travel the pass at night."

"Could we ride?" Matthew asked De Wynter.

"We won't go on horseback," De Wynter said. "Not through the pass in the middle of the night. Wolves would tear us apart before we made it a quarter of the way."

Matthew was impatient to go, but he recognized the sense of his friend's argument. They took rooms at the small inn. An excellent chicken with paprika was served, and many bottles of red wine, but he had no appetite.

He had gone to his room when De Wynter knocked, then walked in. His friend casually handed him a cheroot and strolled over to the window. "What's troubling you, Sutcliffe?"

Matthew lit the cigar and drew a lungful of smoke. "Hunting vampires isn't the obvious reason?"

"No. You're a hunter by nature. You would enjoy that. And I don't believe it is guilt over your brother's death. It's something else, I suspect."

"I've left my new bride to go on a quest that will probably kill me," he growled.

"Indeed. You know, you didn't need to come. I could have assembled a group of slayers and hunted the demon Esmeralda by myself. This is too dangerous for a newly married man." De Wynter puffed on his cheroot. "You're going to be distracted during the hunt, Sutcliffe."

"It's my fault the demon got out of her prison. I couldn't leave the job of killing her to someone else. It's my responsibility."

So instead of reneging on that responsibility, he had acted like a blackguard with Octavia, leaving her alone while she was with child and was worried that she might grow ill again. She had seemed so strong and so well, he was certain she was going to be all right.

And now it looked like he had come all this way only to turn back and return to the town of Buda on the Danube. Where in Hades had the vampire gone from there?

Even if he gave up on his mission to destroy Esmeralda, it would take him weeks to return to England by sea.

"For a man who has convinced himself he is doing the right thing, you don't look happy," De Wynter observed. The vampire slayer sighed and turned from the window. "Talk to me," De Wynter urged. "My—my brother's wife is with child again, and I find I worry about being so far away when she is close to her time. Hearing your problems would be a distraction for me."

"It's a wild tale. Hard to believe."

"You would be surprised by the wild things I've seen. Try me."

With the sweet scent of the smoke filling the room, and his blazing fire finally warding off the damp cold, Matthew related the entire story to De Wynter, beginning with Octavia's mysterious illness and her even more astonishing recovery. This wasn't about confessing his sins; it was about airing his fears. What if she did grow ill again? Why had sex apparently made her well?

"It's impossible, isn't it? Pleasure couldn't—"

"No, it's not impossible. It's actually very believable and very easily explained."

"What are you talking about?"

De Wynter shrugged. "It makes perfect sense if your wife is a succubus."

8

Escape

The village of Marlybowe
August 1821

It was the letter that had made her run.

Octavia plucked the kettle of boiling water off her simple stove. Heat filled the small cottage kitchen, and the summer sun spilled through the tiny paned windows. Beyond were meadows and the fields of the farms around the village of Marlybowe, forty miles west of London.

Octavia poured tea into a small, cracked cup. Cradling the cup in both hands, she sipped and walked back into the tiny parlor. No servants lived in to tidy the house or cook her meals. For the first time in her life, she had to look after herself. It was lonely. She missed Father terribly. And Eliza. But she'd had to run away—because of both Sutcliffe's letter and the fact that she couldn't hide the truth from her father anymore.

Not the truth about the pregnancy. Father knew about that—she'd admitted it to him, but only a fortnight after the wedding. What she had fought to hide was the fact that she was a witch.

She was utterly certain about it now. Sometimes she could control her power and cause anything she wished to happen just by desiring it. Other times, her magical powers went mad, and terrible things happened...which meant she'd had to leave London before people began to suspect.

The uncontrollable nature of her magical powers terrified her.

Sometimes she feared she might accidentally will the baby away.

She didn't want to lose her baby. She wanted to be a mother, to put the baby to her breast, watch its smiles, its first steps. She could not give up her child.

But she didn't know how she was going to look after her baby alone and in hiding.

Her powers had allowed her to acquire money. She had wished for it, and that time her magic had worked, and by remarkable good fortune money had actually appeared—a great stack of pound notes and sovereigns. Now she had a good nest egg.

One she needed to keep away from her husband.

Somehow, Sutcliffe had discovered what she was. He had figured out that she was a witch. He had spoken of her powers in his letter, though he didn't directly call her a "witch." But he had to believe she was bad and dangerous—why else would he intend to make her a prisoner?

She had received his letter one month ago—it had taken a month to reach her. He had told her he would return to London as quickly as he could, once he had exhumed his brother's body and he had traced the route of escape of a vampiress named Esmeralda. When he arrived, he planned to take Octavia immediately to one of his most northern properties—an old and crumbling castle—and keep her hidden there.

Forever.

So she had run away—first out of London to the small village of Wharton-Upon-Loo, where she had taken a small cottage. She had told people she was a widow, though she noticed village women pointing at her and whispering. At first, they thought she was a scandalous ruined woman. It was almost laughable, considering she was a *witch*.

When she was agitated or nervous or angry, she could not control her powers at all.

In the milliner's shop in Wharton-Upon-Loo, she had caused all the hats to fly off their stands. Quickly she'd commanded the door to blow open, and she'd pretended there had been a strong breeze. Anytime she went near a fire, it suddenly exploded and began to rage out of control. Glass would shatter for no reason. Horses grew frightened when she went near them.

Then the word *witch* was spread. She lived in Wharton-Upon-Loo for three weeks before she'd had to leave. The next village she abandoned in a week. Here, in the third village in which she'd lived, she barely left her cottage, terrified she would do something to give herself away.

Father would be worried about her, but she had written a letter of explanation—she had told him she had gone to visit relatives of Sutcliffe's. This way, she could be absent and Father would not come in pursuit of her. She didn't want her powers to get her father into trouble.

Had Sutcliffe returned to England yet? Octavia had no idea what he would do once he reached London and found her gone. Would he pursue her? Or would he not bother to try; would he be happy to be rid of her?

But she was carrying his child.

For that one reason, she didn't think the Earl of Sutcliffe would let her simply disappear. No, he would come after her, and if he found her, he'd want to lock her away.

Octavia set down her half-finished tea.

Today she must purchase more food, which meant a trip into the village. She could not avoid the excursion any longer out of fear of what she might do.

She put on her pelisse, clamped her bonnet on her curls, and hooked her basket over her arm. If she was careful and she didn't get upset, perhaps nothing would explode or burst into flame. Perhaps this time, nothing would go wrong.

Octavia strode briskly up the rutted track. It was a shortcut from the village back to her cottage, and passed through a grazing field of a farm. She had spent the day in the village, purchasing food that now weighed heavy in her basket. The sun had set;, the sky was the soft purple of twilight, and she was hurrying home before dark.

Here, in the field, she was safely on her own. So when she reached the stile at the edge of the next field, she willed her body to soar over it.

It was much easier than clambering over it in a skirt and stays, with a rounded belly. There was no one to see. No one but sheep, and while they bleated mournfully, they couldn't speak of the magic they'd seen.

"Where are you going, my pretty one?"

The male voice stopped her. Deep, seductive, it sent shivers through her. It sounded like . . . it sounded like Sutcliffe, and she froze in her tracks. She had nothing to fear—he knew what she was, she had nothing to hide anymore, so she could use magic to escape him. He was not going to make her a prisoner.

Slowly, she turned around.

Screamed.

It wasn't Sutcliffe. The creature that faced her, that stood on the path behind her, his arms folded over his chest, was not even human.

He had horns. Curving horns that erupted from his forehead, and fangs, and skin so pale it was almost marble white. He had goat's legs like the mythical satyr. With a soft clopping sound, he approached.

Shock held her in place, her stupid legs too frozen to move.

This *couldn't* be real . . . yet she could smell the dank odor of his fur. She could hear the snorting sound of his breathing. He cast a shadow on her as he moved closer, and she could hear the squishing of his hooves in the mud.

The beast smiled at her. "What a beauty you are. Once I learned a new creature had been unleashed, I had to see for myself. It will be a shame to destroy you, but first, I intend to take my fill of pleasure with you."

A new creature? *Destroy* her? This *had* to be a mad dream. Octavia grasped her forearm and pinched as hard as possible through her sleeve. There was a stab of pain, and the horrid realization she was wide awake.

Had she conjured up this monster? Had her magic done this?

"I've never made love to a being like you before," the satyr-like monster casually said. He stroked his hand down his furry stomach. As though mesmerized, she felt her gaze follow the movement of his hand. Then she saw it—the evidence of his arousal. It was an awful parody of that beautiful part of Sutcliffe's anatomy. The satyr had a thick and heavy penis. It was a brownish color and looked like a club. Thick, unattractive veins roped around it.

She backed away. She must say something, but her mouth was dry and she couldn't force words from her lips. Finally she screamed again. "Leave me alone!" she managed to shout. "Go away and leave me. Or—"

"Or what?" The beast had features that looked almost human, and he smirked at her. "What can you do to me?"

She had her basket. She could hit him—

She had her *magic*. She'd never used it to defend herself. Shaking, she stared him and willed him to fly backward.

It worked. The goat-like monster flew heels over head and landed with a hard thud on the ground. But he jumped up swiftly and roared like a lion. "I'll kill you first, you witch," he shouted. He lowered his horns and rushed toward her.

She tried to use magic to push him back again, but it didn't work. Fire always went out of control when she was angry or afraid . . . but if she started a fire in the field, she would probably burn to death also. It might consume the whole field, then take the farm and the village with it.

She had to stop the satyr—

An arrow streaked through the air. It struck the monster in the back, and the force of the strike sent the monster sprawling on the ground. The thing howled and writhed. With its powerful arms, it tried to pull the arrow from its back. Blood poured from the wound, and Octavia's stomach roiled.

She was afraid to run in the direction where the arrows were coming from, which was back toward her cottage. She whirled around. She would run toward the village, toward people. For the first time in months, she longed to be with people—

Stumbling on the uneven ground she raced like a mad woman. Her skirts tangled around her legs, and she tried to pull them free. Her foot landed in a deep rut, her ankle twisted, and she fell, like a useless heroine in a gothic novel.

She rolled over and sat up as fast as she could.

The satyr was on its feet. Two arrows were in its back, two stuck out of its arms, and three were in its strong, hairy legs. The beast began to retreat toward the woods that bordered the field. It waved a fist. "Blast," it roared. "You have her now, but you have not won."

Then it turned and ran toward the strip of forest. It crossed the field with impossible speed on its hind legs. To her, it looked like a blur of gray. Another arrow sliced through the air, but landed well short; it stuck into the ground. The satyr vanished into a grove of trees.

She couldn't see her rescuers. There was no sign of anyone who had shot arrows.

Her heart thundered. How could it be? The arrows had come from behind the satyr creature, and there was only open field there. Suddenly, grass swayed and rippled in the breeze. Sheep bleated. But there were no other sounds and no sign of archers.

How could it be?

Then the air in front of her seemed to . . . to flutter. It looked like a pond when a stone was thrown in. Circular ripples flowed through the air, and then two dark forms took shape.

She tried to scramble back, but caught her heel on her skirts. Using magic, she willed herself up on her feet.

Two men in breeches and tailcoats emerged from the eerie whirlpool in the air. They held strange-looking bows, had quivers of arrows on their backs.

One turned and spoke back into the vortex in the air. "Should we pursue?"

"No." The voice was female. "He has gone now. You will never catch him."

A woman stepped out from the wavering air. She held up her hand, and the air magically smoothed out. The woman stood unusually tall and wore a gown of severe black, but a pelisse of rich amethyst velvet. A velvet bonnet was perched on pale gold curls. Her face was pale, her eyes dark with such thick lashes it was hard to see the color of her irises. Large, pale pink lips smiled gently. "Do not be afraid."

The woman's voice was soft, melodic. It reminded Octavia of her mother's voice, which she'd last heard when she was very young.

"Thank heaven we found you when we did, Lady Sutcliffe,"

the woman said. "If we had been a bit later, he would have attacked you. I fear he would have raped you first, and then he would have killed you."

"How do you know my name?" Who was this woman? Had Sutcliffe hired her to find his runaway bride? But what sort of woman could emerge out of thin air? What sort of woman was quite calm about confronting—shooting at—a mythical beast? "W-who are you? What was that *thing?*"

"That was a satyr. My name is Mrs. Darkwell. I have been pursuing you for three months now. I recognize that you have moved from cottage to cottage, and you rarely venture outside. You are afraid that people will discover your powers and become afraid of you."

"How do you know all this? How could you?" Even her father did not know about her powers. "Did Lord Sutcliffe send you?" she demanded, though she felt guilty about being so sharp with someone who had saved her life. Yet she was afraid. The whole situation struck her as eerie and unsettling, highly suspicious, and she was still shaking at being confronted by the beast with the horns and goat legs.

It was one thing to become a witch and another to see an impossible mythical being, and one that obviously meant her harm.

Mrs. Darkwell elegantly shook her head. "Lord Sutcliffe does not know about me. I do know you are carrying his child. I also know that he has no idea how to properly take care of you."

"What do you mean—properly take care of me? Why are you not afraid of that monster? Why does it want to kill me?"

"I have a great deal to explain to you, Lady Sutcliffe. Please let me help you. I run a house in London that is a sanctuary for young women like you—"

"I have heard of sanctuaries that are really brothels."

"I am not like that. As you have seen, I am aware of the fantastical elements of our world. I protect girls who are witches, vampires, werewolves. Young women who have no means to protect themselves. It is my duty to teach you how to survive with your powers. I know you are special, my dear. All the young ladies in my house are special. They all have powers and, because they did not understand their magic, they were frightened by them. They were confused and afraid, and fought to hide what they are. You have tried to do the same thing, but you couldn't, could you?"

"No, I couldn't," Octavia admitted. "But why do you do this? How much money do you want?"

"I do not want money. I am paid to do what I do by a benevolent patron. I can help you, but you must trust me."

"I need to know more. I can't just trust you."

"Of course I understand your hesitation, Lady Sutcliffe. My patron is a duke, one with a fascination with the occult, and with preternatural beings. Unfortunately, by the terms of his patronage, I cannot reveal his name. I can tell you that he was a leader of the Royal Society—a group of vampire slayers. But after a decade in command of the group, he realized that people with special powers should be helped, not hunted. He purchased houses in London that would be sanctuaries for preternatural beings. I run his house for young ladies."

She didn't know what to do. Mrs. Darkwell had saved her.

"Lady Sutcliffe, I believe the satyr was commanded to assassinate you."

Hysterical laughter hovered, and she swallowed hard. "*Assassinate* me?"

"Yes, due to your great power. You are unusually strong, and because of your destiny, you will be a target for all the powerful male preternatural beings. The satyrs will try to destroy you. As will the dragon-shifters and the werewolves. The vampires—"

"I don't understand."

"I will protect you and ensure no harm comes to you. And I will explain everything. But I cannot do it here, where you are at risk. You must come with me to London."

On blind faith, did she go with this woman who had saved her life? Octavia's hand strayed to her stomach. It wasn't just her life at risk, in any decision she made. She had to think about the baby. What if the satyr returned? How could she fight him alone?

"You are afraid for your child," the woman observed. "You will have a safe house during your confinement and the best of London's physicians for the birth. We must keep your baby safe, too. If these monsters want to kill you, they will also kill your child."

Octavia knew she must accept the truth. She couldn't live alone and unprotected anymore. "All right, I will come with you."

Octavia had been at the mysterious London house for two days—two days of delicious meals, clean, silk sheets, the constant chattering of other, apparently contented young women—when she was summoned to Mrs. Darkwell's private rooms.

"Are you going to tell me what is happening—" she began impatiently, but Mrs. Darkwell stood up from behind her desk and put her finger to her lips.

"Not yet, Lady Sutcliffe. We have to ensure you and your baby are both well." She nodded toward the wall.

A white-haired gentleman came forward. He carried a bag with instruments. He set it down and bowed to her.

Mrs. Darkwell glided out from behind the desk and across the room, hands clasped in front of her. "This is Dr. Hogkins, Lady Sutcliffe. He will examine you and ensure all is well."

Octavia sank down onto a settee. She glanced around the room, for this was the first time she had seen it. The rest of the house was elegantly decorated in the latest styles. There was a

Grecian room, filled with graceful chaises, Grecian vases, and statues. There was a vivid scarlet Oriental room. There was a room used only in the mornings that was filled daily with vases of fresh flowers. In short, this house was very much like her old home and Sutcliffe's mansion.

But Mrs. Darkwell's room was very different. It was dark—the walls were paneled in dark wood. It looked like a gentleman's study. Pictures of horses adorned the walls.

"How do you feel, Lady Sutcliffe?" Dr. Hogkins asked jovially.

How did she feel? Frightened. Nervous. Frustrated because she had come here hoping for answers and had none yet. Worried, for she was living in a house only a few blocks away from her husband. She knew Sutcliffe was back in London—he had arrived a fortnight after his letter. Could she really hide just a few yards away from him? But the doctor was talking about the baby. "I don't feel nausea anymore. Yesterday, I felt the baby kick."

Dr. Hogkins felt her belly for only seconds, asked her more questions about her health and her eating habits, then he glanced to Mrs. Darkwell and nodded. "Lady Sutcliffe is quite well and progressing as should be expected. I shall make another examination in a fortnight."

She thanked the doctor, who bowed and departed.

Mrs. Darkwell settled on the chair across from her and smiled. "There, now that is done, there are other aspects of your health to be discussed."

"I want to speak about the satyr and what you told me—that creatures will be trying to kill me!"

"I wished to speak of something of more importance first. Your carnal desires."

"My *what?*"

"It is quite common for a woman with your powers. You

have a heightened degree of sexual desire. You desire pleasure often. That is why your relations with Lord Sutcliffe made you feel better."

"How could you know that? I never told you—"

"I could guess, my dear. Now, while you are expecting the child, you will be protected from your desires. It is a good thing if you pleasure yourself, as well. It is quite harmless for the child, and enjoyable for you. I suggest that you dream of a man you desire."

Octavia launched out of the chair. "I don't want to talk about this. I want to find out why a satyr wants me dead."

Mrs. Darkwell held out her hand. Octavia eyed the woman with suspicion, but she stopped. This mysterious woman had given her safety and a place to stay, and here she was learning how to control her magic powers. But despite all this help, Mrs. Darkwell refused to give her any real information. Yet, even knowing the woman would not tell her what she needed to know, Octavia found she was lowering carefully back into her chair.

"You have very strong magical powers," the woman said softly. "Whenever someone comes into strong power, as you did when you first made love with Lord Sutcliffe, members of the metaphysical world can sense it. They know things. They have spies everywhere, as well. So they learned about you. Women with such power are threats to the males—to male vampires, werewolves, dragon-shifters, satyrs. If the most powerful women were to join their powers, they could enslave all the men. There are six special magical females who can combine their powers—they can literally bind together—and who could control the world. So the men fear them. Over centuries, men have hunted and destroyed the most powerful women, to ensure that there never have been all six in existence together at once."

Her wits were whirling. "Six women? Which six women?"

"A vampire. A female wolf-shifter, as well as a dragon-shifter. A hawk-shifter. A witch. And a—a demoness."

"But how can I be one of these women? I knew nothing of having powers. I don't want to have these powers, and I certainly don't want to use them to hurt anyone."

"I know that, Lady Sutcliffe, but these creatures do not. Unfortunately, it is because you are new to your powers that you are the perfect target for them." Mrs. Darkwell clasped Octavia's hands and squeezed gently. "But that will not happen now. Not with me to protect you. Now, go to bed, my dear. In your room, you will find a variety of implements to gratify yourself. After the baby's birth, then you will be free to pursue gentlemen. As many as you wish."

Octavia's head reeled. "As many as I wish? But I am married."

"You can no longer live with Lord Sutcliffe. Your decision to leave him was quite right. You must live independently, my dear. There is no other way. Otherwise he will try to quell your powers. If he tries to do that, he could very well kill you." Mrs. Darkwell patted her knee. "There is no reason an independent woman cannot satisfy her needs."

Octavia bundled all of Mrs. Darkwell's strange "implements," which included long wands, beads, and balls on a chain into her arms, and she pushed them in a drawer without using them.

She dropped into her bed, pulled up the sheets, and closed her eyes, hoping for sleep. But one never slept with whirling wits. She was one of the most powerful of the preternatural creatures. How could that be possible? A few months ago, she had been a normal, but ill, young woman, and she had never made a fire start or a mirror crack. Surely, if she were a powerful witch, she would have had some sign of it before going to bed with Sutcliffe.

As for dreaming about gentlemen . . .

She only wanted one man. Just one. Sutcliffe.

She couldn't have him. She couldn't live with a man who refused to love her and believed she should be locked away.

In his letter, he had outlined his entire plan. First they would go together to his most remote estate on the Scottish border. He would have to return to London, but she would not. She would have to live in his old castle, to ensure that no one learned of her strange "abilities," as Sutcliffe put it. A small group of loyal servants—well paid for discretion—would be her companions.

She would be cut off from the world. A prisoner.

Well, she had cut herself off willingly, but on her own terms. She could imprison herself; she wouldn't let Sutcliffe do it for her.

Not once in his letter did he say that he would live with her, or even visit her. Perhaps he intended to store her away, and he didn't care if she rotted.

But he would care about a child, wouldn't he? If he had married her for the sake of the child, he would not abandon it; she was certain of that. A boy would be his heir.

What frightened her was the fear he would take the baby away from her. She would be left in the middle of nowhere, and Sutcliffe would live away from her, with their child.

She couldn't bear that.

Mrs. Darkwell had promised she would learn to control her powers, and there was no way her magic could ever hurt her child.

Octavia closed her eyes. The strangest sensation fell over her—it was as if she had dropped through a black hole and was hurtling down. Was she literally *falling* asleep? Dreaming? She opened her eyes and jerked up in the bed.

She wasn't *in* bed.

It was impossible, but she was in a garden, one she had never been in before. She *must* be dreaming.

In the garden, it was daylight. Warm sunlight slanted into the beautiful place like ribbons of gold. She had to close her eyes for the rays were blindingly bright. When she took a deep breath, she smelled roses—masses of them, and their rich perfume was enough to tickle her nose and make her sneeze.

Octavia snapped open her eyes, sure the tempting garden would have vanished.

No, it was still there. A breeze made petals flutter. Hummingbirds darted, and somewhere a fountain made a splashing sound.

When was a dream ever so vivid that she could smell things? Octavia saw flagstones below her feet. The roses were high, growing in ordered rows. They made it impossible to see where she actually was.

She followed the path, winding up and down rows of flowers. She took one last turn and a tall man stood before her, his back to her. A coat of dark blue stretched over his shoulders and brought out the richness of his brown hair. His legs were slightly splayed, outlined by formfitting trousers that disappeared into tall, gleaming black boots.

It was Sutcliffe, the man she had intended to avoid. She had run away from home to escape him, yet here he was, standing right in front of her. But instead of retreating, running and hiding again, she approached. Sutcliffe turned. She expected him to look annoyed. Instead, the softest smile curved his lips. For once, he actually looked delighted to see her. His blue eyes sparkled. "I've worried about you."

"I—" She steeled for the argument. She had to protest against all his plans.

But he pressed his finger to her lips. Surprised, she quieted. He had stripped off his gloves. "For months, I've longed to be with you. To make love to you."

She looked down at her rounded belly.

"It won't hurt the baby," he whispered. "I want something sweet with you."

He bent and kissed the swell of her breasts with soft lips. She should run away from him, but she couldn't. Her cunny ached with need. How she loved the way his full, firm lower lip traced the lacy edge of her scooped neckline. Sensation sparkled there, making her skin tingle.

It felt so real, but it couldn't be. Octavia sighed with delight in the warm sun, under his warm kisses. "Oh yes," she whispered. "More."

"You are so sweet, Octavia. I want to taste you. Nipples first. Then more." He cupped her breasts through her dress. "Much fuller now that you have the babe inside. They're spilling over my hands." His boyish grin of pleasure made her legs tremble.

She found the fastenings of her simple day dress, undid them to let her bodice sag. Wrapping his hands around the globes of her breasts, he tilted them up. Her nipples basked in the sunlight, hardened in anticipation.

Opening his mouth wide, he took the right nipple in his warm mouth.

Oh yes. Greedily, he sucked it, taking quite a bit of her breast along with her pointed, sensitive nipple. Then he slid back, and he sucked so hard on the firm tip, she almost leapt out of her slippers.

Never had she felt anything so intensely. Explosions of pleasure, pain, shock, delight went off in her head at once. She felt him laugh against her breast. Dizzy with erotic excitement, she realized they were friends only when pleasuring each other.

Then he suckled her other nipple. After that he moved his head swiftly back and forth, lavishing his attentions on one and then the other. Both nipples turned cherry red and became thimble-sized. Tingling sensations washed through her everywhere, like wine swirled in a glass.

This was so lovely. Octavia arched her back, pushing her breasts right into his face. A gruff laugh was his response, before he attended to his sucking again. Her hips squirmed and rocked, her cunny aching to be touched.

Tightness grew. The tension of mysterious muscles, the throbbing ache—she knew what it meant. Her fists were tight balls. But he was just sucking her nipples. Surely, he couldn't make her come just by doing that—

Oh God. One hard suckle at her breast ignited the burst of pleasure. Her cunny pulsed, her womb contracted, and the force of it rippled through her, making her sob, making her fists wave, then land on his coat-covered back.

He kept his mouth latched on her nipple through her entire storm of ecstasy. But he released her to strip off his coat, pull off his cravat. Then he stood straight, and she set at once to yanking the tails of his shirt out of his trousers.

Golden sun blazed over his golden skin. She placed both her hands on his chest. His heart thumped beneath one. Hair tickled the palms of both.

How had she thought to stay away from him?

In reality, she had to. In dreams, she could come with him.

He sat down on a stone bench. She touched the smooth stone seat. Her hand felt the warmth radiating because the stone had absorbed the sun's rays. Two petals fluttered, and one landed on her eye. She dashed it away, opened her eyes again. His trousers were open, his erect cock sticking upward. It was dewy on top of the head, ready and eager. Daintily, she lifted her skirts and straddled him.

But she didn't sit down. Not just yet—

* * *

Matthew groaned and rolled over, faintly aware of darkness, of a soft mattress beneath him. Then he slipped back into his delicious, enticing dream.

His hand skimmed up Octavia's calf to her garter. Silk stroked his hand, along with the soft lace of her stocking, then his palm touched the warm, satiny skin of her thigh.

She carried his child and she glowed with it, smiling down at him. How many times had she smiled for him before he'd left for the Carpathians? Very few and only when they made love. It was a treasure to see one now.

Cupping her bottom, he lifted her, and brought her down on his cock. Months had passed since he'd known the heaven of sliding inside her.

She was scalding hot, wet, and tight. Pleasure shot through him as he buried himself deep inside her. He fought for control, but he gave one thrust, and exploded with pleasure—

Matthew jerked up, sheets falling away from his sweaty back. Moonlight spilled into his room in the small, village inn. There was no garden, no sunshine, no delectable hot and sweaty Octavia stroking his back.

For two weeks, he'd been chasing her across the English countryside. He had tracked her here, to a tiny cottage, but he'd found it deserted. This was the closest he had been to her since his wedding night and it had just been a dream. Hell. It had been the sweetest session of lovemaking he'd ever had, and it had been entirely a figment of his imagination. An uncomfortable, wet stickiness was on his sheets. He'd climaxed in his sleep. Groaning, Matthew fell onto his back, away from the wet spot, and covered his eyes with his hands. "Just a dream. How bloody tormenting . . ."

"Actually, it wasn't a dream," a voice said.

Matthew got up so quickly, he fell off the edge of the narrow bed. He landed on the worn, knotted rug and launched to his feet, naked, as Sebastien De Wynter strolled out of the shadow. The vampire slayer was fully dressed and moved casually, as though spying in another man's room was an everyday occurrence for him.

"What in hell are you doing in my room?" Matthew barked.

"Observing. I had to see if she would come to you."

"Come to me? You mean she was here?" He shook his head. What was he thinking? "Impossible. It was a dream." He was protesting, with his now limp cock swinging between his thighs. He yanked a sheet off the bed and wrapped it around his hips.

Strangely, he'd been to orgies, where he'd been oblivious to male nakedness as there had been so much female nudity about. But in his room in the village inn, with an unexpected guest, he preferred to be covered.

"She's a succubus. This is what she will now do," De Wynter said, as though explaining addition to a particularly dimwitted child. "She has to visit men in her sleep."

"Men. Not just me?"

"You have to understand it's not just a dream, Sutcliffe. I've explained what a succubus does. Each night, she is really coming to you and making love to you. Each time she does, you lose some of your soul. Eventually she will drain all of your soul away."

"What does that mean?"

De Wynter's eyes reflected the moonlight. "It means she will kill you. When you lose all your soul to her, you're dead."

"You're joking. What is this—vampire slayer humor?"

His friend grimly shook his head. "I wish. It's not a joke, Sutcliffe."

Hell. This couldn't be possible. How could sex with his wife kill him? He had read about succubi, but he still couldn't believe Octavia was coming to him in a dream.

"To save yourself," De Wynter continued, "you could stop her coming to you—"

"No, I don't want her to stop coming to me. If I do she'll go to another man, won't she?"

"It's her nature as a succubus. She has to go to men in their sleep and attack their souls through sexual pleasure. We can ensure she only comes to you, but it might kill you."

"I don't care. And I don't want to make love to her in dreams. I want it to be real."

De Wynter nodded. "Then we'll help you find her. The trail may have gone cold at the cottage, but she had to go somewhere. However, there is a small problem. I noted evidence in that cottage of another presence. A recent one. Someone else looking for her, I believe."

"I didn't notice anything."

"You wouldn't, as you weren't trained to hunt vampires."

"There was a *vampire* in her cottage?"

"Worse," De Wynter said. "A satyr."

9

The Perfect Prey

Esmeralda knew she would find the perfect prey amongst the drunken, boisterous young men in the country tavern.

She only had to look at the young man she wanted for a few moments. He stopped laughing and slowly turned to meet her alluring gaze. One smile was all it took to make him stumble to his feet and approach her.

Still, though she anticipated spicy sex and delicious blood, frustration burned in her.

She had tracked the succubus here, to a tiny cottage on the outskirts of this tiny, horrid little village. How she hated such backward hamlets—and villagers with their closed-minded ignorance. She had lived for thousands of years and had endured war, famine, persecution. She was superior.

A satyr had tried to attack the succubus—Esmeralda had been able to discern that by the scents left around the cottage. The succubus had escaped, she knew, for the villagers had spoken of a blond lady in an ebony carriage who had taken their mysterious new resident away.

Whoever this woman was, she was able to cloak the succubus's scent. Esmeralda should have been able to track the girl by her primal, sexual smell. But she could find no trace of it.

Which meant someone with knowledge of their world was protecting the succubus.

And now, her dinner had come to her.

The young lord raised her hand and bowed over it. She leaned forward, allowing him to look down at her brimming décolletage. "Let us go to bed," she said softly. She looked toward the table at which his friends were drinking and laughing. They were all, including this one, in their early twenties. Young, strong, delectable.

"Perhaps some of your friends would care to join us?" she asked.

He nodded obediently, thoroughly captivated. Grinning boyishly, he hurried back to his companions. What a lovely young man he was. Wheat blond hair was arranged in tousled curls over his handsome head. His skin had the dewy smoothness of youth. A darling shadow of stubble graced his jaw.

As for his body . . .

He was young and slender, with a lovely combination of a stripling's lean hips and coltish long legs, but a man's broad shoulders and muscular arms and chest.

His friends were equally delicious. One had dark hair, and looked proud and arrogant. How she loved to make such young men quiver with fear as she sampled their blood. The third young lover she would have possessed auburn waves.

She smiled at them, taking care not to reveal her fangs. She did not even need to give the number of her room to the eager young men. Her powers of allurement would draw them to her.

In her room, she extinguished all the light except for the reddish glow from banked coals in the grate. She stripped naked, then lay on her bed. In her view, this was a meager room. She was accustomed to a bed on which a dozen men could lie with her.

She despised this place; she despised the English country-side. But as soon as she found the powerful succubus, she would rule the whole world.

There was the legend that six powerful female demons could join together and rule the world. But there was another way for the world to be ruled: During their blending, one woman could take the power of the other five and turn herself into an all-powerful demon.

Esmeralda planned to command the world alone. If there was one thing that centuries of existence had taught her, she did not like to share.

After spending four centuries in imprisonment, she was determined to have ultimate power.

Her door slowly swung open, and her gentlemen callers stepped in. "Come in, please, my darlings," she purred. "Come in of your own free will, for the most wonderful sexual pleasure awaits you all."

They giggled together like young maidens—young men were most adorable. Then they all stepped willingly inside.

She moved with lightning speed. She rushed around each young man, tearing his clothes off. The scent of their skin was like a drug for her.

When she was finished, when she had them all nude, they stared in shock at her. And looked nervously at each other, then at their piles of clothes on the floor. She had truly ripped their clothing off.

But of course, when she had finished with them, they would have no more use for clothing.

The dark-haired one scowled. "What in Hades—?"

"Do not worry about such trivial things as clothes," she murmured. She cupped her hand beneath her large left breast and lifted it, offering it to him.

She had so much power the young man forgot everything. His cock hardened as he came to her, until it was thick and perfectly straight. He bent to her breast eagerly and began to suck hard at her nipple.

She had not had a group of young lovers for centuries, so she was too eager to waste time indulging just one at one time. Playfully, she pushed the young one at her breast away. "No, go to the bed. I wish to be filled with all of you."

They were all unique, her bevy of lads. The dark-haired one possessed the biggest and straightest cock. The blond had a long penis, and it curved upward. It had the most darling head on it. The young man with auburn hair had a shorter erection, but it was very thick.

She kissed each one, then lay on the bed. "Two of you inside my rear," she commanded. "And one to fill my cunny."

She used her vampiric power to control them, and the blond obediently lay on his back on the bed. The muscular, auburn-haired youth got on top of him, spreading his legs to allow the blond's penis to rise from between his thighs.

Esmeralda lowered slowly, willing her anus to open, to take the two cocks deeply inside. As a demoness, she needed to be filled intensely, to be taken to exquisite limits of pain and pleasure. Being filled completely satisfied her needs.

She breathed hard as she took both men inside her tight rump. Moaned as she pushed her bottom down to take both rigid cocks deep inside. She never allowed her lovers to move—she willed and controlled their movements to ensure she received the greatest pleasure.

Men had no trouble pleasuring themselves. It was hard for them to always successfully pleasure a woman.

She loved the thought of the two iron-hard shafts rubbing against each other, the heads squished together and held tight by her hot arse.

Using thought, she brought the dark-haired man on top of her. He fought her a little—he grunted, "I've never shared a woman with men before. Usually I have a group of women."

Oh, do you, you arrogant boy? She laughed, then moaned as his long shaft slid into her wet cunny. Very soon the over-confident youth would learn his lesson.

But for now, there was pleasure to be had. She closed her eyes and enjoyed Dark Hair's thrusts while she worked her rump on the other men. After years of imprisonment, she climaxed at once. Stars burst before her eyes. Orgasms were heavenly for the undead.

She forced them to keep thrusting vigorously, until she came four more times.

Then she allowed them their orgasms. Their last orgasms.

They collapsed in their exhaustion. Dark Hair laid his head on her large breasts, gasping for breath. She pushed him off and extricated herself from the pile. The three young men did look surprisingly innocent as they lay, sated and vulnerable.

She chose the blond. She did not want to begin on Dark Hair. It would be much more fun if he bore witness to his fate, if he had sufficient time to become afraid.

Pulling the blond man close to her, Esmeralda licked his neck. Her tongue touched the all-important vessel of blood, and she felt it pulse. The sweet young lordling gave a moan of pleasure. He reached for her breasts but she batted his hands away.

Shuddering with pleasure at the smell of his blood, Esmeralda plunged her fangs into his neck.

10

Seduced to Death

Octavia.

Just thinking of her name made Matthew hard and made him ache with desire. He and De Wynter were riding down a dark and quiet stretch of road, and Matthew fought to stay awake. But despite the fact that he had to remain alert, his wayward thoughts went to their wedding night. And to the very first time they had made love, when she had seduced him while masked.

He shifted in the saddle, but it was impossible to find a comfortable position. Riding with an erection was proving to be torture. He spurred his mount, trying to cover more ground faster, but his horse was also tired.

"You are right," he called to De Wynter, who was riding a few feet ahead of him. "I have to stop for the night. Neither my poor horse nor I can go forever without rest. I saw a signpost for a village. We should be able to reach it within the hour."

"A good plan," De Wynter answered. "You need sleep."

But if he slept, Octavia would come to him.

Every night he had vivid dreams about her, the most erotic dreams he'd ever had. Dreams of sweet sensual pleasures, filled with laughter. Every night had been a different enticing act, and each one came as a delicious surprise. Even when he had spent his day developing a specific fantasy, his dreams took him somewhere else.

And they felt so real.

One night, in the dream, he had lain on a blanket in a sun-drenched field, and Octavia had planted her bare pussy on his face while she deeply sucked his cock. He'd loved the sensation of lying in the hot sun with her hot, creamy quim against his mouth. Roses had dangled around her, the perfect backdrop to her sensual beauty.

The next night, they had been at a house party. Every detail had been astoundingly realistic. Octavia had been there, a gleaming angel in an ivory silk gown. First they'd danced. . . . Then they had escaped to the library and made love on the carpet in front of the fire. It had been sweet, laughing with her, kissing her as he plunged deeply inside her. The risk of discovery had obviously lent spice to the lovemaking for her.

De Wynter had told him the dreams felt real because in essence they were. But Matthew couldn't understand it. How could she come to him, yet not actually be there? How could something that felt so good be killing him?

After reaching London from the Continent, and seeing to Gregory's burial in his family's crypt, he had left town and chased for more than two weeks across the countryside to find his wife, only to learn she had gone back to London. At the last inn, he and De Wynter had learned that a woman who matched his description of Octavia had been traveling to London with a beautiful dark-haired woman, who had used the name Mrs. Smith . . .

"Wake up, Sutcliffe. You almost fell off your horse."

Matthew opened his eyes and found his horse had stopped and that De Wynter had caught him by the shoulder and stopped him falling to the ground. Ahead, lights twinkled.

"There's the village. Can you stay awake for a few more minutes, or"—De Wynter gave a cocky grin—"or do you want to ride on my horse in front of me, and I'll lead yours by the reins."

"I can stay awake. And I want you to tell me who that dark-haired woman is. I saw the expression on your face when we got her description at the last inn. You recognized her."

De Wynter shook his head. "I thought I did—I made an assumption and I was wrong. I thought she was one of the vampire queens. They like to meddle in the affairs of preternatural creatures. I thought one of them might have decided to help Lady Sutcliffe. But I should be able to sense the presence of a queen, and I don't. This dark-haired woman does have some kind of power, but I don't know what it is."

"Wonderful," Matthew growled. "My wife has been captured by some woman with unknown powers. She will be hidden from me in town. Finding her in teeming London will be next to impossible."

"I don't think she is being held captive." De Wynter eased his horse into a rhythm at Matthew's side. "I suspect this woman is protecting Lady Sutcliffe from the satyr."

"Why is a blasted satyr pursuing her?" he barked. Matthew couldn't let himself imagine the satyr's capturing Octavia—otherwise he would go mad. He had to believe she was safe. If this mysterious woman was providing safety, he had to admit he was relieved—but he was furious Octavia was hiding from him.

"One of two reasons," De Wynter answered. "The satyr could be attracted to her—succubi are extremely alluring, and satyrs are known for their lusty tendencies—"

He glowered at De Wynter.

"Or the satyr has been sent to destroy her."

"Christ, why didn't you tell me that before?"

"It was sufficient for me to know about the danger. I've

sensed the presence of the satyr along the road, but he obviously did not attack your wife. I assume this means her companion knows how to keep a satyr at bay."

They had reached the edge of the village's green. Even though it was the middle of the night, light spilled from the local public house. Matthew urged his horse to trot toward it. Exhaustion made his head swim.

"Damnation," he muttered. "I don't understand why she ran away. Who is this mysterious woman she has accepted help from? Where in blazes is she going in London? Her father is sick with worry about her, and I'm going mad. She's in danger, and I could have kept her safe. Why did she run when I vowed to protect her? She vanished the night she received my letter."

"One might assume the letter influenced her decision," De Wynter remarked. Despite having been awake for several nights, he looked bright and alert. "What did your letter say?"

The obvious question. De Wynter was right—obviously his letter had driven her to run. "I promised to look after her. I insisted I would."

De Wynter nodded as though it was an expected answer. "Of course. The very thing that makes a woman run."

"Are you being sarcastic?" He was itching to work off anger and would be happy to stop his horse in the middle of the village and fight De Wynter.

"How did you intend to look after her?"

"I can't let her go to men at night in her dreams," he said hoarsely. "I can't let her be accused of witchcraft because she has magical powers. I told her I would take her to my most remote estate. That way she could stay away from people. I would keep on just a few loyal servants to look after her—"

"So you proposed that your married life would be an imprisonment for her? No wonder she ran."

"She must know I'm trying to keep her safe."

"I would guess she read possessiveness in your words, not protection."

"There's no difference. She is my wife."

"There is a world of difference, Sutcliffe. Come, let's turn into the inn and get some rest."

"You never look like you need any. You're usually fresh as a daisy at night."

De Wynter slid him a glance. "Noted these things, have you?"

"I've noticed you behave like a vampire. But since you are a vampire slayer, I assume that hunting vampires has taught you to work at night and sleep in the day."

"It's rare that I hunt vampires now—only the truly dangerous ones like Esmeralda."

He must be groggy from tiredness. "There are harmless vampires?"

"There are those who try to live in peace with mortals and who do not treat the living like dinner. I mostly do research now, trying to learn about them. In that, I am like you. You travel, observe, learn."

He suspected De Wynter was reminding him to have an open mind. Matthew moved with the gentle trot of his horse, his thighs flexing. But his leg muscles throbbed, his neck ached, his arms felt like lead. "If vampires can live without attacking mortals, does that mean Octavia doesn't have to have sex and take souls? Doesn't it mean her demonic nature can be overcome?"

"I don't know," De Wynter said. "But you can't imprison her out of fear. You have to believe in her. You have to love her no matter what, and accept her for what she is."

"What kind of advice is that?" Matthew growled. "You told me that sleeping with her would eventually kill me."

"No relationship is perfect."

After that, Matthew was too tired for more conversation. He managed to stay awake long enough to give their horses to grooms, buy two rooms, and stumble upstairs to his bed. He fell on it, fully dressed. He shut his eyes. With an exhausted body and worried, ravaged soul, he felt himself slide into sleep quickly. He was groggy, but still slightly aware.

Suddenly, he was aware of something sliding around his wrist, and his hands were jerked together. Scratchy softness tightened around his wrists, locking them together. His lids flew open.

He was naked in bed, and Octavia was straddling his chest. Her blond hair tumbled loose down her back. Her full breasts swayed, and her tummy was a taut, lush curve, rounded with his baby.

Humming softly, she was tying his arms to his headboard.

Octavia could not believe what she was doing, but in her dream she felt naughty and confident. And wanton. Very wanton.

She wrapped a silky cord around her husband's wrists, and her cunny ached as she did. She should not be doing such a thing. Yet she was soaking wet between her thighs and throbbing with desire. Why did the sight of a cord around his wrists excite her like this?

But it did. He had elegant, masculine hands, with strong wrists and big, hard forearms. Veins showed on his forearms, and the fact that she had this strong, powerful man under her control was thrilling.

She was astonished he was not angry. But in the dream, he was smiling at her. That special smile he gave when he desired her.

Feeling utterly devilish, she looped the rope through the carved curlicues on his headboard, so he was trapped. He gave a tug on the rope, but she felt it was more to prove he was captured, than to escape.

Why was he not enraged? Instead, he winked at her. "Now that I'm your prisoner," he asked huskily, "what do you plan to do to me?"

"I—uh."

"What do you want to do to me?"

Heavens, all kinds of naughty things.

"Since you are in command," Sutcliffe said, "you should climb on top of me and fuck my brains right out of my head."

She gasped in astonishment. But he lifted his hips hopefully, and she gathered her courage. Swinging her leg over, she straddled his hips. She had never even ridden a horse astride, never mind a husband.

"You'll have to hold my cock up," he suggested.

Awkwardly, she did. She grasped it and held it upright. She touched the head to her nether lips. Then she sank down on him.

What did she do now? She tried rocking up and down.

"Perfect." He grinned. "You are perfect. And your bouncing breasts are beautiful."

She looked down and saw her rounded bosom lurching up and down as she bounced on him. It felt pleasurable. She bounced harder. She loved letting her quim come down hard, loved the feeling of her bottom striking his legs.

"Touch yourself," he rasped.

She slid her fingers down and with each bounce, she stroked her aching clit. Oh heavens, yes, it was perfect. This was why he liked to thrust hard and fast—it felt so good.

She rubbed hard . . . harder . . . then fireworks burst in her head, and pleasure took her, and she rocked madly on him.

She shut her eyes, feeling her muscles pulse and twitch, sobbing with delight as each wave of pleasure took her. He was close to coming too, his face contorted with the agony of sheer pleasure. Harsh lines ringed his mouth as he gave restrained moans. He jerked his hands, wildly rattling the headboard as he lifted his hips hard and fast to drive his cock into her climaxing quim.

It was stunning to watch him fiercely working toward orgasm. Beautiful to behold. Why did he have to be so cruel, wanting to imprison her?

Octavia wanted to take him to ecstasy. She ached for this to be real. Yearned for it. She wanted to be with him—

"Why are you here? What is your special magical power?"

Somewhere a woman was speaking to her . . . but Octavia did not know where. She was half asleep and dreaming of something naughty . . . of tying Sutcliffe's hands together.

Octavia jerked groggily back to reality and saw white bed curtains tied with lavender ribbons and her now familiar vanity table and painted white wardrobe. She wasn't with her husband; she was in her bedroom in Mrs. Darkwell's house. Banked coals glowed in the grate across the room, and they threw a soft, reddish-gold light on the pale face of the ghost who stood in her room—the apparition who had spoken to her.

She sat up, and her sheets tumbled away. She was ready to fight, to run, when the figure stepped back swiftly and squeaked with pain when she bumped the door.

Octavia held up her hand. "Don't go. I'm sorry. You startled me."

It wasn't a ghost. One of the other girls had sneaked into her room. The young woman had pale blond hair and wore a white nightgown. Her face was terribly white; her eyes were a dark blue and ringed with thick black lashes.

The girl stepped forward. "I'm Ophelia. Yes, named for that Ophelia, the mad one. I have been here the longest, for it's impossible for me to marry. You're the newest, the one who is *enceinte*."

Mrs. Darkwell had made it clear the girls were not to visit each other's rooms after bedtime. In fact, whenever the residents of the house were together, either Mrs. Darkwell or her housekeeper, a thin woman named Pratt, was always there.

Since they were all hiding, or had nowhere else to go, they obeyed the rules.

Ophelia must know the rules. But Octavia saw such a look of sadness in the girl's dark eyes, she knew why Ophelia had come. She must want a friend. She must want to talk.

"Come here, and we can talk." Octavia scuttled over to the side and held open the covers. Ophelia had bare feet and must be cold. But to her surprise, the girl sank down to the floor and burst into tears.

Confused, Octavia leapt out of bed, feet hitting floorboards she knew would be chilly. Her rounded, taut stomach made it hard to move decorously, but she rushed to Ophelia's side. She began to put her arm around the girl's shoulder.

As though seared with fire, the girl moved away before Octavia could touch her. "You mustn't touch me. Go back to your bed. I can't be nearer to you than three feet. That way, if I forget to be vigilant, I won't hurt you."

Octavia frowned. "That can't be so."

"It's my power—my *curse*," Ophelia hissed. She wrapped her thin arms around her chest. "If I touch anyone, I make them very, very sick, or I cause them to die."

Once she never would have believed such a thing. But she was a witch, and sex made her healthy, so she could believe anything now. "You truly cannot touch anyone ever?"

Ophelia bowed her head as if this were her fault. It was obvious she feared her power—and with such a terrible one, how could she not? This power must have left her alone and isolated. "So I cannot hug you?"

"No." Ophelia kicked the air with her bare foot. "You go back to your bed. I will sit at the end of it. That way there is no chance I will hurt you."

Octavia hesitated. She wanted to comfort the young woman but there was nothing she could do. She went to her bed, but she stripped the counterpane off and left it in a pile at the bottom of the mattress. Then she sat on her bed and waved toward the foot of it. Slowly, Ophelia went there and perched on the very end. But she did wrap herself in the comforter.

"How did you find out this is your power?" Octavia asked.

"How do you think? I killed my parents and almost destroyed my brother and sisters. I almost killed a young man who wanted to marry me simply when he kissed me. I began to see that someone died after I touched him or her, but I didn't want to believe it was really true. It seemed *insane*. Then Mrs. Darkwell found me and told me it was true."

"She brought you here to protect you?"

"She brought me here to protect everyone else *from* me. I overheard her speaking, and she said you are very powerful, but you don't hurt people."

"No, but I am afraid sometimes that I could."

"I know I can," Ophelia said glumly.

Octavia's heart ached for the girl. "Could Mrs. Darkwell teach you how to control it?"

"No. I shouldn't even have come to you. I'm forbidden from going near anyone else. It's why I cannot marry, so of course there is no hope that I will ever leave here."

"What do you mean? Why can't you leave if you cannot marry?"

"I can't marry, so it doesn't matter. Mrs. Darkwell would never let me. She would be protecting me, too, as well as any poor man I married. If I hurt someone else—one more person—I couldn't stand it. I couldn't live with myself. I would kill myself."

"But, my dear, what does being married have to do with whether you leave? This can't be a home for unmarried girls—I have a husband."

"You do? I heard Mrs. Darkwell call you Lady Octavia, as though you were not married."

"Well, I am. My husband is Lord Sutcliffe—" She spoke his name without thinking. Should she have revealed so much?

"Mrs. Darkwell is like a matchmaker," Ophelia explained. "Normal young ladies have matchmakers to engineer marriages with the most eligible gentlemen of Society. Mrs. Darkwell is a matchmaker for girls like us—girls who are not normal, who are vampires or werewolves, or witches, or who are like me. But my powers are so deadly she does not believe she can find someone for me."

"She never told me she was a matchmaker." Why did this bit of information make her feel so nervous? It did not matter to her; she was already married. But she wished Ophelia were not trapped. After all, she had run away to escape imprisonment.

But what did this mean for her? Octavia had believed she could leave any time she wished. But with satyrs, vampires, and other monsters chasing her, she was too afraid to go.

Ophelia sighed. "I wish . . . I wish I could be normal. I wish I could go to dances. If only I *could* marry, I'd be willing to live in the middle of nowhere, even in some crumbling old castle, but at least I wouldn't feel like a prisoner."

Octavia winced. The very thing she had escaped was Ophelia's idea of perfection. To change the subject, she asked, "Does Mrs. Darkwell ever care if her charges fall in love, or are these just arranged marriages?"

"They are arranged, but Mrs. Darkwell believes that she finds our soul mates. The men we should love. She says that even if the marriages don't start with love, it always blossoms. No girl can resist her true soul mate, she says."

What was Sutcliffe to her? Hardly a soul mate, as he didn't seem to care what was in her soul. Since she was a witch, did she even have a soul? "How would she know who our soul mates are?"

Ophelia's eyes opened wide. "That, she claims, is her special power."

"I can't be awake. Not *awake*."

Matthew let his head fall back against the pillow as he let out a howl of frustration. His cock arched like an over-tightened bow. Hard, heavy with blood, it curved up from his crotch, bowed toward his navel, and dribbled fluid. It had been so close to release, it hurt.

His hands were free, though he could still feel the tickling sensation around his wrists, from his dream about ropes. Something had stopped his erotic dream in its tracks, leaving him rock hard and aroused to the point where he was panting like hissing steam.

He didn't want to have to take care of his erection himself.

He wanted to finish the dream.

Footsteps sounded softly in his dark room. "Wake up, Sutcliffe."

Recognizing De Wynter's soft drawl, Matthew growled, "I am awake, damn it, though I'm trying to recapture one of the most sensual dreams I've ever had."

Why had Octavia stopped in mid-dream? Did it mean she had gone to another man instead of him? Or something worse—she had been attacked?

He scrambled out of bed and grabbed his small clothes. They didn't fit well, given how erect and swollen his cock was, but he pulled them up over his hips, wincing.

"What are you doing?" De Wynter asked. "It's only four o'clock in the morning."

"I was having a visit from my wife and was interrupted. Since she's come to me every night, I fear it means she's in danger. I intend to start riding now and keep riding until we reach London."

"It's close to dawn," De Wynter said slowly. "I was hoping to sleep today and ride when it grew dark again."

"I have to get there. You're free to stay and rest and catch up to me later."

The vampire slayer shook his head. "You're my friend and on a search to find your missing wife. I would be remiss not to be at your side. If she is in danger, it may be a beast that you are unable to fight, Sutcliffe."

God, he'd thought of that but had pushed the thought away. His heart clenched hard. Pain shot from it, through his gut. His blood felt like ice.

"It might not be that. Perhaps she was awoken by something else. Althea—my brother's wife—has a hard time sleeping when she is pregnant."

"I pray it is only that," Matthew muttered. He was going to ask why De Wynter had come to his room, but he could guess the answer. His friend was afraid that Octavia was going to drain his soul and kill him. The truth was—he didn't care. He was willing to risk death to have Octavia.

Deep inside, a voice whispered, *If you feel that way, it means you've fallen in love with her.*

The thought brought guilt—for his brother, who would never have love. And even if Matthew did love her, he had driven her away.

When he found her, he had to make her understand he intended to protect her. Whether she liked it or not.

London
Three months later, November

He couldn't find her.

He had searched London for three unbearable, terrifying months. Matthew was losing his mind. In Brookshire's office, in the headquarters of the Royal Society, he paced, dragging his hands through his hair. "My wife must be near the time to give birth and I cannot find her or Mrs. Smith anywhere in London."

It was as if the woman could use magic to keep hidden.

At least he believed Octavia was still alive. Each night she came to him in erotic dreams. When he woke up, he couldn't remember any clues as to where she was. And when he slept, he couldn't bring enough conscious will with him to ask where she was or ask for any clues.

But the fact she visited him for nocturnal carnal play meant she must be alive.

"I still do not know why she was being hunted by the satyr." He stopped in front of Brookshire's desk and faced the earl. "If you know why, will you not tell me? Damnation, I have a feeling every vampire slayer in this damned building knows the truth, but none of you will tell me."

The blond earl looked haunted. He ground the lit end of his cheroot onto a porcelain dish. "Hades, Sutcliffe, we are doing everything we can. As is the Royal Society. What point in worrying—"

"I want the truth, Brookshire. For three months, I've asked for it. Each time, you've reassured me that we are going to find my wife. I have to admit, I let you keep the truth from me because I needed your help. But I refuse to be kept in the dark any longer. Why is my wife being hunted?"

"Your wife, as a succubus, also possesses magical power. The power to start fires, for example."

Start fires? He remembered the way the fire had exploded in the fireplace in his bedchamber. Hell, that had been Octavia's power.

"A woman with strong power is a threat to men," Brookshire continued. "For that reason, the male vampires, werewolves and satyrs are hunting her—"

"I think we owe him the truth, brother."

Matthew turned. Bastien de Wynter lounged in the doorway. "We know the truth and we have to tell him. She is his wife, after all."

Slamming his fists on the desk, Matthew growled at Brookshire. "Damn it, tell me. What is the blasted truth?"

"There are six extremely powerful women amongst the preternatural creatures," the earl said softly. "Six who are capable of combining their powers. They can actually change into one, all-powerful female and in that form could rule the world, enslaving all men."

"And you are going to tell me my wife is one of those women."

"Yes."

"Then why has this never happened before?"

"Because men have destroyed these women before it could happen. The vampiress Esmeralda is one of them. With her escape, for the first time in the history of humankind, all six women could actually join together at once."

"My wife—I could not envision her doing this."

Brookshire sighed heavily. "She may not have a choice. Esmeralda will be determined to do this and she will try to force it on your wife. That is why the male beings are determined to stop it."

It was night, and while many of the *ton* had left London to spend Christmas at country estates, some remained in London. When Matthew went to bed, Octavia would come to him as soon as his head touched his pillow. All he had to do was go to sleep, and he was with her. But that was a luxury he could not have tonight.

Instead of going to sleep and having a night of unbelievable pleasure with Octavia, he was attending a hot, crowded ball.

He hated balls.

He was determined to question Octavia's friends. Like a hunter pursuing prey, he'd singled out the young women who had been her companions and had peppered them with questions. The only one who appeared to know anything was her bosom bow, Miss Eliza Compton. He believed Miss Compton was hiding something from him.

He stood amongst the crowd entering the foyer of the Duke of Glencairn's Park Lane home. This was the first social event of the duke's he had attended in a long time that wasn't an orgy, that wasn't being held in the duke's rented townhouse.

Several matrons eyed him, no doubt wondering why he was here and his wife was not.

Scanning the crowd, he searched for Miss Compton. The instant he spotted her, he stalked over.

She turned white and stammered as he bowed to her. But after fifteen minutes talking to her, he had to admit defeat.

Miss Compton didn't know where Octavia was. Damn it—it was his last hope. The crowd was a loud roar around him. Heat built up under his shirt and coat, making his back sweat. It was as if the room was filled with steam and he was being boiled alive. The endless chatter and artificial laughter grated on his nerves.

He had to escape.

He felt like he had on the night he'd lost his brother—when he had realized Gregory had left their rooms and had walked into the forest alone, bewitched by the vampire Esmeralda's call.

Raw panic seeped through his veins. *Get out. Get out. Get the hell out.*

Turning on his heel, he stalked away. He couldn't run—he'd look like a lunatic—but it was a fight not to break out into a mad dash.

What in hell was happening to him? He had the sense of a presence. Of something following him. But when he jerked around to look, there was nothing there. Just the crowd—all watching him with eager eyes, intrigued by his actions, sniffing a scandal.

Storming into the corridor, he wound through the large house, passing suits of armor, elegant Italian paintings, gilt-trimmed details, until he reached the library. Dark and empty, it was a sanctuary.

Entering the library, Matthew closed the door behind him. The fire was still blazing. The air felt soaked with heat, making him yawn.

A settee of embroidered dark blue silk sat invitingly near the fire. Matthew stretched out on it, boots hanging off the edge.

Could Octavia come to him here? Was having her in his dreams the only way he could have her?

He closed his eyes.

In the next instant, soft, slender hands ran over his body. Many hands caressed his chest and shoulder, his jaw, his arms, and his legs.

Matthew jerked up from the couch. Candles burned every-where, and pretty young ladies in dresses squirmed around him, trying to touch him.

Where was Octavia? Why would this be what they were going to dream?

Musicians struck up a dance. Several girls grasped his arms, trying to lead him out to dance. Now he could see that his sofa had been placed near the doors to the ballroom. He was dragged inside. The room was crowded. All of them were talking about his wife.

Then the crowd parted, and he could see Octavia standing there, in the sudden opening. It was as if she had parted the sea. The crowd silenced at once. The room instantly became bright, as though all the candles had just been lit.

"I am here," she said softly. "I wish to dance with my husband."

She was beautiful. Her gown clung to her figure—she looked as she had when he had left for the Carpathians. The swells of her breasts rose from the scooped neckline of her gown. Her skin looked like silk and shone like pearl. Her hair was pinned up in a style that looked uncontrolled and tousled, yet so sexually appealing it made his knees weak. Her lips curved in a catlike smile that made him want to howl up to the heavens.

The young women who had been clamoring for him faded away. He stepped forward, hand outstretched to claim his wife.

He wanted her, and as he pulled her into his arms to waltz with her, he had to fight not to fuck her in the middle of the dance floor.

She rested her gloved hand on his shoulder, fingers curled into his neck.

As he twirled her, Matthew saw the women were still there, watching them together, some looking breathlessly enthralled, others disappointed. They hadn't disappeared; he had just been unable to see them. All he had been able to see was Octavia.

Under the chandeliers, she gleamed like a jewel, and she moved like a dream. Her eyes were luminous and blue, her lips glossy and soft as she smiled.

"Love, let us go somewhere private," he began.

"No, I want to dance with you."

But he was finding it hard to dance with a fierce erection. He wanted their dream to move onward, to the pleasure. She only shook her head, and wore a mischievous smile.

"It's Lady Sutcliffe." The drawl belonged to Viscount Brant. "It is said she is looking for a lover, to keep her pleasured while Sutcliffe travels. They were barely married a few days before he went to the Carpathians."

"Indeed." The group of gentlemen with Brant said the word together. Each one was blatantly appraising his wife's charms.

Damn. He twirled her away, watching her cheeks turn pink. She knew men were looking at her. She did not meet any of their eyes, but she must know the power she possessed. Her figure was lush and curvaceous, and her skin tempted a man to touch. She looked like sex in a gown, and he would wager no man could resist her.

He would prove to them all that Octavia was not going to stray from him. She was not going to take other lovers because he would keep her so well pleasured she would barely be able to walk.

He would prove it.

In front of the *haute ton,* he stopped dancing and drew his wife into his arms. He coaxed her low bodice to drop a few inches lower, and her breasts popped up and fell out of her bodice. The soft, pale globes rested on the lace neckline like it was a shelf. Her pink nipples went hard; her cheeks flushed from a pale peach to deep scarlet.

Then he hiked up her skirts.

She wrapped one leg around him. It made it hard to get his trousers open, but he managed to do it. Rigid as a doorknocker, his cock jolted forward as soon as he got the placket open. The head grazed the soft, sweet, wet place between her thighs.

He held her thigh and lifted her. His cock was so hard and she was so wet, it slid readily inside her. The entire crowd was transfixed. He heard the sharp breaths exhaled by other gentlemen as his long prick disappeared entirely inside her. She kept her arms around his neck, her leg around his hip. She wrapped her other leg around him, so her thighs gripped him tight. He held her lush bottom to support her.

Then he thrust hard into her. The orchestra continued to play, and he and Octavia fucked to the music. His legs shook with the exertion, but the pleasure of being inside her, of having his shaft stroked and squeezed in her heat was so good, he couldn't stop.

Women gasped. Gloved hands clapped to mouths. Matthew took Octavia so fiercely her hair fell out of its pins and poured down her back.

"Yes," she moaned to him. "Yes, yes. Please don't *ever* stop."

Sweat ran down his back, under his shirt. He fought to hang on, but then she came. In the middle of the ballroom. In front of hundreds of awestruck guests.

She screamed with the power of her orgasm. Her nails scratched his back through his coat and shirt. Her wails filled the room. Even the orchestra stopped, their bows skipping sharply over violin strings, and watched her in her lovely climax.

He lost control. His legs shook hard enough to fall apart as he came. He felt the powerful surge of his seed shooting up inside her and almost collapsed.

"Mine," he growled aloud. "Always mine. No one else but me is going to have you, Lady Sutcliffe. Ever." His cock was softening and slid out of her. She let her legs slide down, and as soon as her pretty slippers reached the floor, she pushed away from him. Her skirts tumbled back down.

"You've proved I love you," Octavia said softly. "You've shown how much I desire you. But I refuse to be yours if you intend to make me a prisoner."

She lifted her hems, stuck her chin in the air, and swept out of the ballroom.

He tried to run after her. But he lost his vision—suddenly Matthew couldn't see anything around him but darkness.

Sound faded away. He felt softness beneath him. Groping with his fingers, he realized he was on the couch in the library.

She'd run away from him in the dream. Did it mean she wouldn't come to him again? He had to get up. Once again, he had no clue as to where she was. He had nothing.

He tried to push off the sofa, but his arm wouldn't obey his command. . . .

God, he couldn't lift his arms or legs. He couldn't draw breath. De Wynter had warned him she would drain his soul. Apparently, she had done it.

He was dying.

11

Birth

Something cracked him hard across his cheek, knocking his teeth together.

"Wake up, Sutcliffe," growled a masculine voice. "Wake up."

The voice belonged to De Wynter. Matthew had opened his mouth to protest the blow to his cheek when cold water splashed in his face.

"Christ Jesus!" Matthew opened his eyes. Icy water dripped off his lashes. Levering up on his arms, he glared at Sebastien de Wynter. "What in hell was that for?"

"You were unconscious, with very little pulse. But before I assumed you were dying, I thought I would try to rouse you."

Matthew wiped the back of his hand along his brow, aware of rivulets of sweat. "What were you planning to do if you couldn't rouse me?"

"I don't know. You might have been rewarded with eternal life."

Moving his shoulders beneath his damp shirt, Matthew jerked his cravat open and glared at the vampire slayer. "What in Hades are you talking about?" It was hard to speak—his voice was raspy and it was as if he couldn't bring in enough air to talk. His chest ached as if his heart had been torn out of it.

De Wynter grinned. "I'm a vampire."

That stunned him. "You're a vampire *slayer*—"

Resting his boot on the arm of the chair, De Wynter cocked his head. Firelight touched his bright gold hair, making him look angelic. But his smile was anything but sweet. "It's true that I've hunted vampires—evil ones who refused to try to live with mortals without hurting them. But I was a vampire first."

Matthew shook his head. He had to be dreaming still. Or going mad.

"If you were close to death, I could have rescued you by turning you—"

"You can't be a vampire."

"Why can't I?" De Wynter asked. "You know the creatures exist. Give me one reason why it's impossible."

He struggled to find one. It would explain De Wynter's penchant for sleeping in the day and being awake at night. He had seen De Wynter go outside during the day, but admittedly the slayer did wear a heavy greatcoat and keep his hat low to shade his face. But—"I've never seen you drink blood."

"I'm careful about how I do it. I never attack an unwilling victim."

Matthew stared in disbelief. "There are willing victims?"

"There are always those who will service you for money. There are many women—and men—willing to bare their throats for money, if they are guaranteed to live at the end of it. But most of the time I take my blood from a glass."

"What of the Royal Society? Do they know?"

"They do. It would be impossible to hide."

"And they let you hunt vampires?"

De Wynter shrugged. "What is the first thing you do when you explore, Sutcliffe? You find a native guide."

It was true, and thinking about it that way, it was logical. If the Royal Society wanted to hunt vampires and demons, shouldn't it take advice from one of the brethren?

Matthew glanced to the door, straining to hear sounds of laughter and music. There was quiet, but not the tomb-like silence of a house where everyone had gone to bed. "Is the party still going on?"

"Yes, otherwise you might have been found by some poor, hapless servant."

It meant they had to be careful in their conversation. Matthew tried to stand. He could will his limbs to move, but they were weak. De Wynter grasped his forearm and hauled him to his feet. Once upright, Matthew found he was feeling stronger, but he leveled a glare at De Wynter. "You would really have changed me into a vampire?"

"Yes."

He scowled. "I wouldn't have wanted that."

A wry smile quirked the vampire's lips. "You're a friend. It would be hard to just stand by and watch you die."

"De Wynter, that would be what I would want. I would never want to be transformed into . . ." He lowered his voice to a mere grunt. "The undead."

Broad shoulders shrugged, then De Wynter perched his hip against the arm of the sofa. "I can personally attest that it is better than death, but I now know your wishes, and I respect them. So tell me what happened to you. Since you were asleep, I assume it was another visit from Lady Sutcliffe, one that came close to killing you?"

Ruefully, Matthew nodded.

"I can teach you how to keep your soul closed to her. She would not be able to get to you—she couldn't reach you through dreams."

"No. Hell, even if our dream sex kills me, I don't want that—I couldn't drive her away."

"So you're willing to die for love?"

"I'm not in love. That's impossible for a blackguard like me."

"You are an idiot, Sutcliffe," De Wynter said cheerfully. "So was I when I fell in love. But now, we've got to find out where your wife is. Was there any clue in the dream?"

"Nothing. It took place . . . here. She came to me here, and we made love in the middle of the ballroom."

De Wynter gave a grim smile. "Then you're going to have to go home, go back to sleep, and hope that her succubus nature drives her to you again. And this time, get some answers before it kills you."

Matthew flopped back onto his bed, naked on top of the covers, and closed his eyes. He stretched his arms above his head. In their last dream, she had flounced away from him—this was him crawling back to her.

"Let me come to you, Octavia," he muttered softly aloud. "Wherever you are, let me come to you. Let me make love to you in your bed. Let me know that you are safe."

Nothing.

The one thing Octavia had done on his terms was marry him. Now it appeared he was out of luck. Anger rose—she was carrying his child, she was his wife, and he was tired of this game. He fought the anger. De Wynter had told him she wouldn't come to him for a confrontation; she was coming for passion.

All right. He would take her terms. He would take *any* terms.

"Would you truly? Why don't I believe you?"

He opened his eyes and she was there. She stood at the foot of his bed, completely naked. Her hair was loose and spilled over her shoulders. Her arm was wrapped around the bedpost, the curve of her full, lusciously naked breast pressing against it. She looked like Eve personified: natural, beautiful, tempting.

Her belly was large, tight, and well rounded. Matthew swallowed hard. He'd traveled all over the world, studying every type of wild animal, but he knew almost nothing about the childbearing of humans. She was much larger than he'd expected. Her breasts were heavy and sat almost upon her rounded tummy. Her navel jutted outward.

Mentally he counted months, and he swallowed again. She was very close to giving birth.

He slid out of the bed and held out his hand to her. "All I wanted to do, Octavia, was keep you safe. You have powers—powers that have put you in grave danger. What is wrong with a man wanting to protect his wife?" He approached her, because she did not move. She had a pained look on her face, and she was breathing hard. Then she met his gaze, and there was a confused look in her cornflower blue eyes.

Finally they were going to talk. He never usually bothered with words—words were for his books and his lectures. They were for expressing discoveries, describing journeys, documenting scientific principles; words could change the world, he'd discovered. But with women, he usually only used a few words before using his mouth in different ways to convince them to get into bed. With his brother, he had rarely talked. There was no talking to his father. And his mother had always been too upset and hysterical over his father's betrayal, then his suicide, to speak to her son.

"Why did you run before I returned, before I even had a chance to explain what I was trying to do?"

"I—Oh, it's so hard to explain. I didn't want to be a prisoner, but I've learned that I am one anyway. I ran away from you, and now there are monsters who want to kill me. So I let a woman give me sanctuary. It gave me safety, but I am still a prisoner. I can't leave there. I'll never be able to leave. I was furious with you, but now I've realized I don't want us to be apart."

"Then tell me where you are, and I'll come for you."

"I—" She doubled over and clutched her belly. "It's hard. My tummy has gone so hard." Then she jumped, and the carpet suddenly was wet. "Oh heavens, my water . . . broke. Goodness, it's time—"

Matthew ran to her, but as he reached the end of the bed, she disappeared. So did the water on the rug.

No. No, damnation, no.

He spun in a circle, fists clenched. But of course his room was empty now, except for him. "Octavia, where are you?" he shouted. "Tell me. Let me come to you. I want to be with you."

"I can't. I'm not allowed to tell you. It's too much of a risk—"

"I want to be with you for the birth of my child. I want to protect you." What did she mean it was too much of a risk? She had to tell him where she was. He needed to be with her. What if something went wrong? And what happened after the baby was born, if she would not tell him how to find her? "Damn, Octavia, do not take my child from me—"

But there was nothing but silence. She was gone, and she was not going to come back.

He had to find her.

Matthew ignored the carefully expressionless look on De Wynter's face. If De Wynter told him that this mad dash was proof of love one more time, he'd stake the vampire—

Hell, he wouldn't. Yes, he cared about Octavia, but he could not love her. Every time he thought about love, he remembered Gregory, who had been cheated of love, happiness, and life. He thought about his father, who had wasted away over an impossible love and had finally taken his own life.

Even if he did love Octavia, he still had to do what she didn't want. He had to keep her safe against her will.

"Where are we going? I thought your wife gave you no clues."

"She refused to tell me. She said it would be too great a risk to tell me. What did she mean? Is she afraid of me?"

"I think it must be that she feared some other being might sense what she told you. It might mean that she was warned that some of the beings searching for her could read her thoughts if she tried to project them to you."

"What about when we've made love in dreams? Would some of these creatures read our thoughts then?"

"Of course," the vampire said. "And demons and satyrs are the worst voyeurs."

"Why didn't you tell me?" Matthew snapped. His heart burned with anger. He hated to think of demons watching his wife make love.

"What else were you going to do? She needed you. So where are we going now?'

"I'm going to break into Miss Compton's bedchamber. If Octavia wrote her letters, she'll have them there, and hopefully they will give me a clue to where Octavia is."

"I thought you said Miss Compton was no help."

"She's a vapid young woman. There might be clues she completely overlooked. I'm not certain if the girl would even have the wit to look at the postmark of the letter."

He had to do something. De Wynter had told him that laboring could take a long time. He was wild with the need to find Octavia. What if something went wrong? What if she were in pain or in danger? He needed to be there.

When they reached the street on which Miss Compton lived, he got out of the carriage and slipped down the mews. The November air was cold, the ground hard with frost. Silently, De Wynter followed. The vampire helped him climb over the back stone wall, then De Wynter easily jumped over it.

Stunned, Matthew followed him to the house. A barebranched tree grew beside the house. He climbed it and jumped over to a terrace, then broke in. It didn't take long to find Miss Compton's room, conveniently empty as the family was out at social events. Nor did it take more than a few moments to find a bundle of letters stashed in her writing desk.

His heart lurched at the sight of his wife's signature. There were no postmarks on the letters, but he read them quickly. When Octavia spoke of watching nurses pushing perambulators in the park, and when she mentioned a certain fountain in the square outside the house, he knew where she was.

"Come on, De Wynter." He retied the bundle of letters and pushed them back in the desk. "We've got to hurry."

He wasn't going to give up. This was his child. If Octavia truly thought he would walk away and abandon her, and ignore his child, she was mistaken.

If she had told Sutcliffe where she was, she could be screaming at him right now.

With each contraction, Octavia found she was shouting and groaning at everyone else. Maids rushed in with heated water and towels, but she had no idea what they were to be used for.

Guided by the physician, Mrs. Darkwell was admonishing her again. "You must not push now, Lady Octavia." Mrs. Darkwell held her hand and had told her to squeeze as hard as she needed.

"I. Cannot. Help. It." Octavia tugged her hand free. It was Sutcliffe's hand she wanted to squeeze, but Mrs. Darkwell had warned her she mustn't send him any clue where she was.

How could she not push? For twelve hours, she'd had contractions. When they had come just five minutes apart, she'd thought her baby would come soon. She had been wrong.

But all the while, Mrs. Darkwell had assured her this was actually an easy birth. The physician was quite pleased with the progress. But it hurt. It hurt almost more than she could bear. She was struggling to stay calm.

How did women go through this? How did they survive? She feared the baby would never come.

"You may push now, my lady," the physician urged. The man was blushing. But she was only relieved. She panted and pushed. The physician lifted the sheet draped over her legs. Perhaps she should be embarrassed to be seen in such a way, but she was far too weak to care.

She pushed. And breathed. And sobbed. And cried, and did any number of embarrassing things, then Mrs. Darkwell declared with triumph, "The head. Lady Sutcliffe, the baby's head is crowning. We are so very close."

She sobbed with hope. Someone grasped her hand, and held tight, and encouraged her to keep breathing. It was so intense. So very intense. She feared it would go wrong, that her baby could not be born. Mrs. Darkwell said firmly, "You must push once more, to birth the shoulder."

The *shoulder*? What about the head? But Octavia pushed and felt a swift, slippery sensation, and the pain vanished. Relief rushed through her, and she laughed and cried in delight as she heard the soft cry of her baby.

It was the sweetest sound—most indignant—and her heart ached for the poor little one. How frightening it must be to go from warmth and darkness into a strange world.

The cord must have been cut, and she was exhausted, but Mrs. Darkwell wrapped her child in swaddling clothes, and brought the small baby back.

Octavia cradled her little infant to her breast. But with the cloth on—

"A little girl," Mrs. Darkwell whispered. "You have a baby girl."

A daughter. She held her baby girl closely. The little eyes

were closed, the pink lips pursed. She gently kissed her satin-smooth cheek. The baby flinched, wriggled a bit within her swaddling blanket. Relaxing against the pillow, Octavia let out a deep breath. Her lashes flickered shut as exhaustion stole over her. Her hand spanned the belly of her little girl. She smiled softly.

Then hands came down and wrapped around her child. Fighting exhaustion, Octavia opened her eyes and rolled to look. It was one of the maids, and she lifted the baby to her gray gown-covered bosom.

Octavia held out her hand. "Where are you taking her? Can't she stay with me?"

"My lady, I must put her in the bassinet. You could roll atop her, and you might not hear her cry. You could smother her."

Surely she couldn't. But the baby was so small, her tiny cries so sweet and quiet. What if it could happen? It would be horrible.

"I will bring her to you when she needs to be fed, my lady."

Through a narrow slit between her heavy lids, Octavia watched the maid turn and carry her baby out of the room, after warning that she would return in about three hours for the baby to feed.

The physician was not yet finished—he began to massage her belly, then something else slipped out of her. After a while, he announced that he believed the bleeding was stopping. She heard Mrs. Darkwell sigh in relief.

"It is all done, my lady, and you did admirably." Mrs. Darkwell smiled down at her. "A healthy baby girl, and all has gone well for you. Now you must rest. We will take you to your bed."

Octavia was lifted by a strong servant and carried. She wanted to walk, but Mrs. Darkwell insisted she should not. She was laid in a large bed in a new room, one with clean sheets.

She was so tired; she had to sleep. She closed her eyes.

Her baby was her family, and Octavia would take care of her little one forever. . . .

The next thing she knew, she felt warmth on her face. Slowly, she opened her eyes, dazed, confused. . . . Light was pouring in through the curtains. She wanted to burrow deeper under her covers. Then she realized—

It was morning. She had slept through the night. No one had woken her to feed her baby.

If her water had broken so many hours before, Octavia must have had the baby.

Matthew drained his brandy. He tossed the glass toward the large table that sat in the center of his library. The empty brandy balloon slid across polished wood, smashed to the floor on the other side.

He'd thought he had found her, only to discover he had been outsmarted. He had found the house where the letters supposedly had been sent from, but it was empty.

Why hadn't she let him come to her?

Thud. Thud. Thud.

His terrace doors were rattling. Half-drunk, he lurched off his chair and stumbled to the door. A young lad stood outside, getting pelted with cold rain as he pounded on the glass.

What in Hades? Matthew wrenched the door open. The urchin clutched a wet cap and had streaks of mud on his cheeks. Rain dripped off his small, upturned nose. Matthew looked the boy over from head to toe. "Exactly what are you doing in my yard, young man?"

The boy wiped the droplets from his cheeks. He gave a look of complete honesty—it appeared to be a look well practiced to con gentlemen. "I heard ye're looking for Lady Sutcliffe, milord. Me brother told me you were asking questions around Birdwell Lane."

That was the street he had been to today. "How can you help me?" he asked sharply.

"I know where she is, milord," the boy said, wide-eyed.

Hope flared. A mad hope that made him hunger to go at once. Instead, he held the door open. "Come in, dry off, and warm yourself." Grasping the boy by the shoulder, he led the lad to the fireplace. "How would you know where Lady Sutcliffe is?"

The boy held small, pale hands out toward licking flames. He gave a sigh of pure pleasure. "Mrs. Darkwell, the lady that runs the school, pays me to take messages for 'er."

Mrs. Darkwell? Was that the real name of Mrs. Smith? Was the boy's tale the truth? He couldn't trust the beguilingly innocent look on the boy's face. On the other hand, why would the lad lie? "What school is this?"

"It's one for orphaned ladies, milord. Mrs. Darkwell has a house east of Mayfair, and she gives a 'ome to girls that don't 'ave families. Wellborn ladies, like the one ye're looking for."

"All right, lad. You take me there, and I find you're telling me the truth, you'll receive a generous reward. What is your name?"

"John, milord. How much reward? Me brother said it were to be two gold sovereigns."

"John, if you take me to Lady Octavia, I will give you five pounds."

The boy's eyes lit up and he spun away from the fire, rubbing his hands together. "I'll take ye now, milord."

Matthew walked up steps to the deserted-looking house on the eastern boundary of Mayfair. The stone steps were chipped, the windows shrouded on the inside with faded drapes, and paint hung in strips on the door.

"Here?" He turned, but the street was empty except for his carriage. The boy had run.

That didn't surprise him. It did surprise him the lad had fled *before* he got his money.

The rain had turned to thick, wet snow. The streets gleamed with wetness. It was possible the mysterious Mrs. Darkwell was keeping Octavia a prisoner inside and the boy had run in fear.

Why would a woman who ran a house for homeless girls take in Octavia? Who was this woman? A healthy instinct about danger had protected him in the past—the only time he had blatantly ignored it was when he had found Esmeralda's tomb in the Carpathians. His instincts were on alert now.

He was sure Octavia was not safe with the woman—she was in danger.

Matthew tried the door, found it locked. He retreated, then charged, and slammed his shoulder into the wood. It was half-rotted and gave way easily, sending him stumbling inside. Given he'd already made enough noise to wake the dead, he shouted, "Octavia? Are you here? Mrs. Darkwell, I am the Earl of Sutcliffe. I demand to see my wife at once."

The house was gloomy, and he stood in a foyer that contained no light, no servants, nothing but the smell of damp. It wasn't dusty, he noted, and a faint line of light gleamed at the base of a door opposite him. The house had been elegant once. Eight marble columns soared around the circular foyer, with delicate fanned designs at the top, supporting a domed skylight. Rain streaked on the glass panes.

"Octavia?" He shouted it again. Unease settled heavily on his shoulders. With nothing but silence answering him, he made for the door.

Pushing it open, he breathed in a sweet, heavy, perfumed smell.

The scent was drugging. One breath and his head felt dazed. It made his skin grow hot, his heart pound. Arousal hit him—

Matthew was instantly sexually aroused, but for no reason. Where in hell was the smell coming from?

His feet were moving down the corridor. There was another door at the end, and the light he had seen came from under that door.

Was he in a dream again? Would he open the door and find Octavia there, naked and ready for him? Was any of this real?

He must be losing his mind. Of course it was real. He had not gone to sleep. Anyway, Octavia had left him when her water had broken—she had run away because the baby was coming. Would she be coming back to him for sex right after the baby was born?

Given she was a succubus, he didn't know, but he didn't think so. So what in hell was this place? He kept walking forward, though logic warned him of danger. He couldn't stop his legs moving. By their own compulsion, they took him to the door, one painted a glossy black. Unlike the others, it looked used.

He didn't touch the door, but the knob turned and it began to swing open. A bevy of feminine giggles drifted out to him. A woman cried happily, "At last he has come. I have been so *hungry!*"

Matthew hesitated. He had a pistol, but De Wynter had taught him in the Carpathians that his gun would not be a protection against the undead, and the instant he saw the women, he knew they were vampires. It was obvious by the long, pure white fangs that lapped over their full, crimson lips.

They were all nude, lying in a tangle of arms and legs on an enormous oval daybed. He could see their full, bare breasts, their rounded rumps, their long seductive limbs. There were six women in all, all of different shapes, all endowed in different ways. Two were sleek, with small breasts—though one had large, dark nipples, and the other possessed tiny pink ones. Two were of more 'average' endowment, though one had round plump breasts that sat high on her chest, the other had longer, tubular breasts, with thick, chocolate brown nipples. The remaining two vampires had the largest breasts he'd ever seen. The two sets of huge bosoms were being petted, licked, and kissed by the other four girls, while all six women watched him.

Now he could see exactly what they were doing. Their legs were spread, flung over each other, and each woman was sliding a large dildo in another woman's quim. They licked their lips and thrust the toys more vigorously. The room was filled with the carnal noise of thrusting and with the ripe smell of aroused women.

"Watch us," whispered one of the women with the biggest breasts. "Enjoy the sight of our climaxes, and let your cock grow ready for pleasure."

He intended to back away.

Instead, his feet moved him forward, to a large chair that sat facing the daybed and the writhing women. He was flung into it as though pushed by an invisible hand.

In front of him, the women squirmed over each other. They began suckling each other's pussies, working their tongues around the thick, flesh-colored dildos inside them.

Once this would have aroused him; now he was just aware of the wasting of time, and the unsettling feeling of being a prisoner. "I'm here for Octavia," he said coldly. "I'm not interested in watching.

"Octavia? There is no Octavia here. No, you were brought to us for another reason entirely."

He had indeed been an idiot. "What reason? Who the devil are you—all of you? Or who employed you to bring me here?" Who would organize an orgy with vampires and drug him, forcing him to come in here? Somehow, that smell had affected him like opium, stealing his wits.

"We can help you find your beloved Octavia."

Shoving hard on the arms of the chair, he tried to rise to his feet. He could not move. "Do you know where she is? Tell me. Every moment counts."

"You fear she has had her child, do you not? You wish to have your child. To hold the sweet babe, and kiss its tiny, fragile head—"

"A babe. How delicious," breathed one of the smaller-breasted women, who had long, blond hair. She licked her sharp fangs.

He recoiled, revolted. In the Carpathians, he had rescued children from demons like this. Unfortunately, he'd been too stupid to save himself this time. The women rose to their haunches, like wolves, smiling seductively at him. "Come to us. Take us all. You may do anything you wish. Imagine the pleasure of having all of us at once—"

"No. I will never touch you." Ever since he'd been with Octavia, he hadn't touched another woman, even before they had married. He didn't want these women now, but his cock was hardening against his will. They seemed to have a magical control over him.

His hands went to his trousers. "No," he roared. "I will not do this."

He had to get to Octavia, and no team of naked vampiresses was going to stop him. She deserved his protection. And he . . . he needed her. He couldn't face life without her. He was not going to be damned, not when he had to save her. With a roar of fury, he wrenched his hands from the buttons of his trousers. Stoking his anger, his impatience, he shoved off the chair.

There, the bloody spell was broken.

At his side was a delicate, polished wood table. He picked it up and smashed it to the floor. Hissing, the female demons moved back, hugging together. He kicked the legs off the table, stomping them with his boots. They broke with sharp, splintered ends. Grabbing two of them—one in each hand—he held them out, like stakes. "Do you know where my wife is? Or should I stake you in pairs?"

The vampire women leapt to their feet, their toys falling out to the daybed. They suddenly spun in circles, dissolved into twinkling stars that hung like dust in the air. They streaked across the room toward a door opposite where he stood.

He was going to lose them, lose his chance to find Octavia. Matthew ran . . . but the door suddenly flew wide, slamming against the plaster. Real dust flew up. The sparkling demonesses disappeared through the door, and a woman floated into the room.

A different woman. One swathed in white furs with pure black hair that hung in curls to the middle of her back. Her gown was made entirely of silver thread. Her fur robe trailed behind her in a train of several feet. The hem of it hovered a few inches off the floor, moving smoothly over the carpet. Then he saw her feet were levitated as well.

I am afraid you cannot leave, Lord Sutcliffe.

It was madness. She was not speaking, but he could hear her voice in his head. It was deep and echoing.

You destroyed the young man who was to be my soul mate, my young lover for all eternity. Your dear brother, Gregory. You staked him in his heart and cut off his head. You stole children from me that I needed to feed upon. You hid the succubus from me. But you are going to pay for all the trouble you have caused me. Now, you are mine. You are going to help get me what I want.

He lifted his stake. But it turned searing hot in his hand. He rushed forward, fighting the pain, sickened by the smell of his own burning flesh, but determined to drive a stake into the vampire's heart. The broken wood pieces suddenly exploded into dust in his hands. Hollering with the pain, Matthew clasped his burnt hands together. Before his eyes, the beautiful vampire's face changed—it turned into a skull of jet-black, mouth opening wide to reveal long, razor-like teeth.

A screaming sound filled his head, like the shriek of a hundred dying souls. Then Esmeralda launched forward and flew through the air toward his neck.

12

Turned

Esmeralda's fangs slashed against his neck as he tried to shove her away. Matthew howled in pain as the sharp tips cut his flesh and drew blood.

If there was one time in his life he needed De Wynter, this was it. Madness: He needed a vampire to fight a vampire.

He yanked his pistol out of his trouser waistband and fired at the vampire. The shot slammed into her stomach. It wouldn't kill her, but it drove her back. Esmeralda howled in fury and jerked off him. He turned and ran, leapt over a sofa. He was near the fire grate, but the windows were still about fifteen feet away. Blood soaked into Esmeralda's white furs. Her face had changed back to a human-like one, but she hissed at him, baring her fangs. His blood dripped off the tips of her teeth.

He had been a fool. He had followed the boy alone, and now he was going to be killed by a vampire—

Not if he could help it. There was a full complement of fireplace pokers, but he knew none of the iron bars would help him. He needed another wooden stake. According to the slayers, he had to stake her through the heart—or shoot a crossbow bolt through it—then cut off her head. But since she had turned a stake to ash in his hand, he didn't know how he was going to do this.

What would he do if he were out in the wild?

Most explorers would send some unfortunate native to try first. He had never been that sort of man. He never considered anyone expendable.

This time, however, he was going to be the expendable one, losing his life to be a vampire's dinner, unless he could get the hell out.

He backed toward the windows. For some reason, Esmeralda hadn't attacked. She hovered above the ground and smiled at him. A sickening, triumphant grin that flashed her fangs.

"This would be more fun if I were not encumbered," she whispered.

Suddenly there was a blur of motion. He tried to watch her but he couldn't; he was forced to blink. When he opened his eyes, a mere instant later, she was gone, and an enormous bat swooped over his head. He dove to the ground, desperately searching for a weapon. He pulled his knife out of his boot, knowing it would do him no good. The bat gracefully beat its wings, wheeled in the air, then charged at him again.

He scrambled to his feet and ran for the window. He was going to leap through it—he had jumped off the ground when talons caught him by the shoulder. The bat dragged him back, claws piercing into his skin through his clothes.

She pulled him to the ground, slamming him down. Blood leaked from the wound in his throat, soaked into his shirt and coat from his shoulders.

In an instant—so fast he couldn't see how it was done—the bat was gone, and Esmeralda was sitting on top of his chest. Nude. Her large, heavy breasts swayed over him.

True, with her black hair, ivory skin, red lips, and lush body she was unusually beautiful. But to him, she looked like a beast. He moved to shove her off him, but she caught his wrists. He tried to buck her off, but she was too strong.

"I have a choice, Lord Sutcliffe. I could simply drain your blood and kill you. Or I could give you immortal life."

"Get the hell off me, you whore," he growled.

Her eyes were black, but reflective, shining like an animal's eyes did at night. They flashed with fury. "So this is how it is to be. I offer a gift, and you insult me. Just like a man. You think your paltry insults will bring me to my knees. That I will sob and cry before your moralistic judgment." She laughed, and it was the high-pitched laugh of a madwoman.

Then she arched forward. He tried to jerk away, but she grabbed his hair. She yanked his head so hard that if he'd tried to resist, he suspected she could have torn his head off his neck.

Esmeralda twisted his head, arching his neck. The pain was excruciating. He kicked; he jerked his body underneath her; he tried to fight.

"Come now," she said coldly. "Surely you can push a mere woman off you. Surely, just as a woman should be able to fight off a rapist if she really wanted to, you could fight me off. I can only do this to you because you really want it—"

She broke off. He was trying to absorb her words—and the spitting fury behind them—when she suddenly roared. He swung with his arm—

She grasped his wrist and snapped it. As pain shot through him, she plunged her teeth into his neck.

He could feel his blood rushing out of his body to her mouth. But he could feel something else . . .

Christ, it couldn't be. His cock went bolt upright, hard as a brick. His body felt like it did when Octavia's lush, hot body was against him. His heart was pounding with desire; he was panting with lust.

He didn't feel anything but revulsion for this woman. Yet

for some insane reason, having his blood drunk was making him aroused.

Damn it, this was a nightmare. He should be fighting. But the intense sexual heat roaring through him made it impossible to fight. It made him want more.

He was going to die, damn it, because of lust.

I will spare you if you help me.

He could hear Esmeralda's low, throaty, accented voice in his head. He was writhing underneath her, trying to fight the intense sensations of sexual pleasure. Her teeth were fastened into his neck. He couldn't get free.

Help her, Lord Sutcliffe. Help your wife, the succubus. You cannot protect her. If you keep her a prisoner, she will die. If you let her fuck you, she will kill you. A succubus does not belong with a mortal man. Tell me where she is, and I will take her. I will train her. I will teach her how to survive. Give her freedom. Save your pitiful life.

There was no way in Hades he would give Octavia to this monster.

You stupid fool. Do you think going from one man's bed to another will be good for her? Do you think she will be happy to kill you? I can free her.

"How?" he croaked. He was weak from blood loss.

You men will destroy her. I will not. With me, she will have the power to rule the world. Once we unleash that power, she will no longer be a servant of Lucifer, forced to harvest souls through sexual pleasure.

"A servant of Lucifer? Hell, not Octavia. She's not a demon."

She is. It is what she was born to be. She must do her duty and take male souls, or she will be destroyed. She can never live like a docile mortal wife, which is what you want her to be. Let her be what she is supposed to be—powerful, sexual, seductive.

"No!" he roared. "She is my wife. I will not permit that."

Do you not understand that you have no power, you stupid

man? You men always believe you are in charge, that you have all the control. This time you do not.

She sucked harder at his neck. His legs felt weak and numb, as did his arms. But he still had a raging erection.

Damn it, he was going to come. He refused to. He refused to let this give him pleasure. Octavia gave him pleasure—she was beautiful and sensual and good. She was the only woman he desired. Not this monster who was draining his blood.

If he let Esmeralda kill him, he would not be able to protect Octavia. He had to find out the truth about what Octavia was. He did not believe Esmeralda: He didn't think this monster was going to protect his beautiful, gentle wife.

"I'll help you," he rasped. "I'll do it. But I don't know where she is. I've been trying to find her for months. Let me live, and I'll search for her and find her for you."

I could just release you now, but you would die anyway. I've taken too much blood. I'm going to make you one of us. But I have to do something special with you. Your wife will reject you—she will sense you no longer have a soul. So I have to make you into something different. A vampire with a soul.

"What? I'm not going to be one of you," he managed to mutter, but he was losing consciousness. He fought to keep his eyes open, yet his lids were too heavy. He couldn't move his arms or legs. He was sure he could feel his heartbeat slowing.

Then something wet and slippery pressed to his lips. It was the vampire's wrist. She pressed it to his mouth. Slowly, he realized it was her blood flowing into his mouth.

He fought to pull back and spit it out, but he couldn't will his body to move.

Whether he liked it or not, his body wanted to drink.

In the hallway outside Mrs. Darkwell's private room, Octavia stopped. Through the closed door, she heard sobbing. Inside the study, a woman was crying as if her heart was breaking.

It could not be Mrs. Darkwell. It must be one of the other girls in the house, and Mrs. Darkwell was breaking this poor child's heart, just as she was trying to destroy Octavia's.

To think all her life she had yearned for a dangerous adventure, like the kinds Father went on, the type of exotic and glorious adventures Sutcliffe had experienced in foreign lands.

Now all she yearned for was peace and a normal life. Octavia wished she had stayed at Sutcliffe's London house—that she hadn't run away and that she hadn't learned that beasts wanted to kill her.

For it would have meant that this morning, she would have held her daughter.

Squaring her shoulders, she pushed open the door and stormed into Mrs. Darkwell's private room. To her surprise, Mrs. Darkwell was alone. Her golden hair was immaculately styled. Her clothes were perfect, and her face did not look as if she'd been crying. For a moment, Octavia was mystified.

Then she realized she didn't care what was going on. She stalked forward and slammed her hands on the desk. She winced, trying to absorb the soreness of her legs and her private place. Apparently it took a while to recover from giving birth. She snapped, "Where is my daughter? Why did you not bring her to me? Why do your servants refuse to fetch her for me?"

Mrs. Darkwell merely set her quill back in the pot of ink, a placid expression on her face. She settled her hands on her silk skirts. A small strand of pearls glowed at her throat. A turban decorated with pure white feathers sat atop her head.

Octavia was so furious: While stealing a *child,* the woman had been well able to select fashionable clothes.

"What is it, my dear?" Mrs. Darkwell asked gently.

Octavia ripped the quill from the ink and flung it across the room. How dare this woman smile so patiently at her?

"Where is my baby?" She glared at the ledger in which Mrs. Darkwell had been writing. It rose and flew off the desk. Sheets of paper suddenly tore from it. They tumbled to the fire grate, where they landed on the coals and began to smoke.

"Is my daughter in this house?" she demanded.

But Mrs. Darkwell ignored her, shoved back her chair, and stood. She stalked to the fire and salvaged her ledger pages. Then she glared in annoyance. "Stop this, Octavia. Setting the house on fire will not help."

Octavia rushed to the desk and jerked open the drawer. She pulled out letters, searching for something that would tell her where her daughter had gone.

Mrs. Darkwell snatched the letters from her hands. "There will hardly be the clues you seek in my correspondence. Perhaps you might have found something in the ledger you just destroyed. Did you think of that?"

The woman moved to her and Octavia flinched, expecting an attack. But Mrs. Darkwell embraced her.

Oh no. She pushed the woman's elegant hands away. She did not want to be soothed, or stroked, or lied to. She needed the truth. "I must know where my daughter is. You had no right to give her away. I am a married woman—a countess, and I am able to raise my daughter by myself."

"My dear, you are in danger from satyrs, vampires, werewolves. To keep your daughter would have been to put her in grave danger. You still do not have complete control of your powers. What if you hurt her unintentionally?"

"I wouldn't—"

"You might. Do you not want her to be safe? If she is away from you, with a good family, you know she will be. To explain why she is not with you, you will say your daughter was stillborn. In truth, she will be alive and well, and she can be raised by people who will teach her how to live with her magic powers."

"My daughter has powers?" Octavia whispered. It seemed madness, but she had not even thought of that. That magical powers must be inherited. She must have been given hers by her mother.

"Yes, of course. Just as you do. Not as strong as yours, for her father was a mortal with no special magic. Powers such as yours lessen with each generation that contains more mortal blood. She will learn how to live with them, how to use and control them. Obviously your father tried to deny that you possessed magic. Yet that did not help you. His attempt at protection simply left you unprepared to cope when you unlocked your magic."

"But she is my child. Why can I not be with her?" She had married for the sake of the baby. That was why she had agreed to a loveless union. She would not relinquish her baby now!

Mrs. Darkwell grasped her shoulders and gave her a gentle shake. "If we make the world believe she died, she will be safe. Otherwise, she could be kidnapped or hurt as a way of getting to you. The beasts that hunt you would happily use the child to lure you into a trap. Then they would kill you both. And there is Sutcliffe. . . . He will not let you disappear with his *child*. Unless you want to live as his prisoner—"

"No! I—" She didn't know what to do anymore. "Won't he still hunt for me?"

"Will he? Or has he been pursuing you because he believed you might be carrying his heir?"

That made her freeze with surprise. She had never thought that without the baby involved, he might just let her go. He had told her bluntly he would never love her. If he'd intended to lock her away in a castle and leave her there, wouldn't he stop hunting for her? . . .

"But my daughter deserves to have love, not just to be schooled in magic powers—"

"The family who will raise her will treat her like their own child. They have desperately wanted their own baby, but could never have one. They will shower her with love, even as they teach her to live with her powers. She has gone to a good home."

Octavia shivered. She knew what Mrs. Darkwell was saying: Because of her magical powers, she must face spending the rest of her life alone. But she—she couldn't. "My daughter should be with me," she cried. "I don't want to give her away as though she is an inconvenience. She is my child. I want to care for her, I want to love her, and I want no one to do it but me. She is my *family*."

"You are doing this for your protection and hers. You are free to leave Sutcliffe, to completely disappear. I could find a man who is destined to be your true soul mate. He could become your lover and protect you. Sutcliffe would not look for you. You could even make Sutcliffe believe you are dead, and then you would be completely free, as you wanted to be. But, Lady Sutcliffe, you cannot survive alone. You require love and pleasure to live. It is part of your magic powers."

Octavia shook her head. "I could disappear with my daughter! Either way, my husband will have to think his child is dead." She didn't think he would care about losing her, but it would break his heart to think his daughter was gone.

But if her daughter had magic powers, too, Sutcliffe's solution would be to keep her a prisoner, too. She could not let that happen.

"I am a mother now, and I *choose* to be one." This time she yanked the pages from Mrs. Darkwell's hands. On the desk she smoothed the singed pages of the ledger. There had to be some clue here . . . a payment made to a name . . . to the family who wanted to take her child—

Mrs. Darkwell walked up behind her. "Octavia, your daughter will grow up in a happy family," she said softly. "You must understand this is the only way she can be safe."

"It's not her fault that creatures want to murder me."

"But she will pay the price for your choices. You must think of her, Octavia. To want to keep the babe is selfishness. You have powers you do not understand and which you cannot control. You need to be taught, and you are not ready to be the mother of a child. Your daughter will be raised as the child of this couple. She will have a dowry at her disposal when she is older—I have taken care of all of this. She will have a bright future. Do not steal that from her."

Steal it from her. Was she being selfish? How she longed to see her baby. She had been so exhausted after the birth she could now barely remember what her daughter looked like.

But would she be hurting her baby? Would the monsters who wanted to kill her be able to get to her and the baby?

Mrs. Darkwell guided her to a chair and pressed her to sit in it. Her legs ached, and she hurt when she sat, but she slumped onto the seat. She wrapped her arms around her chest. This would be for the best. In her heart, she knew it. In her soul, she wanted to deny it.

The best thing for her daughter would be if she stayed out of the poor child's life and never saw her again.

She wanted to cry, but she hurt too much even for tears. Her stomach contracted on a sharp, vicious pain, as if she'd been punched. Her arms ached to cradle her baby.

It would never happen. It could never happen.

Hands smoothed her hair back and cradled her cheeks, and she looked up into Mrs. Darkwell's strange black eyes. "You are doing the wisest thing," the woman said.

"Wh-who is she going to live with? What are their names? Where do they live?"

"You must not concern yourself with that. They will bestow much love on the baby."

"But what kind of people are they, that they can teach my daughter magic? Are they witches or demons?"

"They are not demons—they do have the power of witchcraft. For that reason, they have made English society believe they are members of the country gentry. They appear to be only thirty years of age, though they have been on earth for a very long time."

"Will my daughter ever know of me?"

"I believe it is best if she does not. Now that you are no longer pregnant, it is time for you to find the gentleman intended to be your soul mate. We will teach you to control your powers. You will find the appropriate man—and then you will have a future filled with love."

She shook her head. "I don't want another man. I simply . . . don't."

"Do you love Lord Sutcliffe? I am afraid, my dear, he will never come to love you. He will never be able to accept what you are. I suspect, like his father, he will die very young. There is tragedy in his family—his father took his own life. You would be alone. If you leave him now, if you make him believe you are dead, he has a chance to survive."

"I don't understand—"

"My dear, your powers hurt mortal men. If Lord Sutcliffe is your lover, each time you make love together, your powers take a little of his . . . strength away. You will drain the life out of him. You need an immortal man as your lover. You deserve happiness. I can find you a gentleman who you will love, and who will love you in return. This is what I do—I help young ladies like you, ladies with special powers. I help them find love."

She pulled away from Mrs. Darkwell. "How can I kill Sutcliffe? I think that's a lie! How can it be possible?"

"My dear, how can you start fires with your thoughts and move objects with your mind? Aren't those things impossible?"

It was the truth. Was it possible she had to escape Sutcliffe to protect him, not just her own freedom? "Why are you doing this? Why do you care whether I have a lover? Why do you care about making matches for women with powers?"

"It is how I survive in this world," Mrs. Darkwell said dryly. "Pleasing the duke who is my patron keeps me alive. Otherwise I would be poor, I would be cast out, and I would die. It makes me happy to see women find love. You would be in danger out in the world. If I had not brought you here, you would have been murdered by now. Now I must find your soul mate—a man who loves you—to look after you."

"No!" Octavia shouted. She didn't want anyone to "protect" her: to control her, imprison her, keep her from finding her child. Suddenly the fire exploded in the fireplace. The windows burst, and glass shattered into the room.

Mrs. Darkwell ran behind her desk. She swiftly pressed hard on the wallpapered wall, and a panel sprung open. Octavia could not see what she was doing, but when the woman turned back to the windows, she held up a crossbow.

But there was no foe. Octavia's heart pounded, her chest was heaving with fast breaths, and she was shaking with despair and anger. She was doing this.

Fire leapt out of the fireplace and caught on the rug. A line of flame rushed across the patterned carpet toward the wall, propelled by the wind coming through the windows.

This wasn't an attack by monsters. She was doing this, and she couldn't stop it.

"Get out," she screamed to Mrs. Darkwell. "Get out before I hurt you."

Or would the woman just shoot her with the weapon? Octavia kept her gaze fastened on it, until she coughed on smoke. Mrs. Darkwell stared over Octavia's shoulder, horrified, and Octavia turned.

The whole wall was on fire, and the wood door was a panel of blazing flame.

"The other girls," Octavia cried.

She had spent her nights locked in her room, reading books on spells, trying to learn how to control her magic. She had to try now. Holding up her hands she shouted, "Quench the fire. Make the flames disappear."

The drapes exploded into flame, and the fire leapt from one to another. The chair cushions were burning. Thick smoke was filling the room, and there was no more wind coming in the window.

Octavia snatched up the ledger pages and ran to the flaming door. She folded the pages and stuffed them in the bodice of her dress.

Let me through the door without injury, she commanded by thought, though without much hope after her lack of success with the last demand.

But the door crumpled before her, falling like ash. The fire leapt out into the hallway beyond. Octavia covered her head, and she ran. Servants ran toward her: panicked-looking footmen, maids who were screaming and clutching their skirts, even the burly cook was running.

"The girls." Octavia pointed to the stairs. "We must get the girls to safety."

Fire was already licking at the banister. It caught on draperies on the landing and set those ablaze. She could hear female voices shouting.

She closed her eyes and sent a spell over the other girls. *There is a fire, but you must be calm. You must get out of the house. Get out your windows. Go to the back stairs and get out.*

The servants were rushing up the stairs. She looked back: A door in the corridor opened, and Mrs. Darkwell stumbled out. There had been a secret door. Now, her face pale with shock, the woman was rushing toward the stairs.

Octavia lifted her hems and charged up the stairs. This was her fault. She had to ensure everyone was safe.

Even if she died in the attempt.

* * *

He hungered for blood, and he had been chained to a bed for a week.

Matthew roared in frustration, as he did most nights, jerking in fury at the shackles around his wrists. If he could get his hands free, he would grab a stake and end his owned damned existence.

Scratching sounded at the thick, oak door. The six demonesses lurked on the other side. Their seductive laughter rippled around the peeling wood, but the sound was muffled because the door fit tightly. They sang to him, songs that would have tempted him to them, but the magical cuffs around his wrists and ankles kept him bound to the bed.

The women wanted to take his blood, even though he was a vampire now.

Esmeralda had left him here. Apparently she didn't trust him, didn't believe he was really willing to help her.

Or maybe she was trying to force him to grow accustomed to what he was.

On the first night after she had turned him, she had brought him a young boy of about ten. It was sickening: He was expected to drink from the child. He had fought with her to save the boy. The child had escaped; he had almost ended up destroyed. Esmeralda had kept him chained but had forced him to stand out on the balcony in sunlight. He had howled in pain as his flesh burned on his body, but he had relished death. He was willing to die.

She wasn't going to let him. She had dragged him back, chained him up. Slowly, his body had healed.

Then the craving for blood had begun.

Each night she had brought him an innocent victim. Each time he had saved the victim and had been punished for it. But as his hunger grew and he got weaker, it was harder to resist the scent of blood. Right now, he could smell the demonesses' blood, and it made him aroused, erect. It was making him writhe on the bed in agony and need.

"Let us in," the demonesses chanted. "We will feed you. You can drink from us. And then you can fuck us in any way you wish. All of us. All together . . ."

It was as if he could hear their voices in his head. Some magic kept them on the other side of the door. There was some kind of spell infused in the door that meant they couldn't open it. To let them into the room, he had to open the door and invite them in.

Matthew lay back on the bed.

That would never happen. He would never give in to them—but he would also never drink from an innocent victim. He had to escape. Esmeralda wanted to break him. She'd said she wanted to turn him into her lover, then use him to find Octavia. If he refused, she would destroy him.

But he had fought against the chains for a week and hadn't found a way out. He didn't know why it was taking Esmeralda so long to give up on him and destroy him.

Octavia must have had their baby. He didn't know if she was still safe. He had to find her, yet how could he go to her as a vampire?

Damnation Sutcliffe, are you in there?

Where had the voice come from? He jerked around, but he saw no one in the room. It sounded like—

It is Bastien De Wynter, man. Let me know if you are in there. If I have to confront six naked demonesses, I want to know I'm doing it for good reason.

"De Wynter," he shouted, though his throat was raw from thirst—for blood—and his voice was a weak croak. "I'm in here and chained to a damned bed. Get me out of here. Please."

Had he ever said "please" before in his life? Likely not. There was nothing like being held captive to make a man humble.

The cooing and giggling on the other side of the door grew louder. It sounded like thousands of bees.

"Back, back!" De Wynter barked. "Let go of that. I'm a happily married man."

One of the women gave a burst of screeching laughter. "Don't try to put that in your mouth, you foul harpy," De Wynter yelled.

What was happening out there? Matthew strained to sit up. He had no idea what De Wynter was talking about—the man was not married.

Though that was the most insignificant thing to worry about.

Even if De Wynter got through the door, how could he help with the locked shackles? Esmeralda kept the key around her neck, and as Matthew had proven, they were too strong for even a vampire to break.

The door flew inward and slammed onto the floor. Matthew dropped his head back in shock, frustration, and fury. Damn, damn, damn. "De Wynter," he shouted. "We're supposed to keep those foul women away from us."

He jerked his head up as footsteps sounded. Sebastien de Wynter stood in the doorway with three naked women hanging off him. One was wrapped around him like a boa constrictor, her large breasts pressed to his side, her legs tight around his thighs. Another had her arms around his neck, and she clung from behind. The third was gripping his leg. De Wynter looked down at her. "Let go. I'm dragging you across the floor."

"You are mine," the woman cried. Her fangs were elongated, her mouth distorted so that her lips were wide open. She looked like a snake ready to plunge in her teeth. Those teeth were aiming for the man's thigh.

"De Wynter—"

Before Matthew could finish the warning, De Wynter reached down, grasped her shoulder, and flung her off him.

"I'm sorry, my angels of hell," De Wynter said, "but I have to use this potion on you." He pulled a vial out of his pocket, poured some into his hand. It smelled like . . . like something that had gone bad. He sprinkled some on his shoulders and around him.

Hissing, the women backed away.

Matthew wasn't surprised—the stuff was noxious. Laughing—amazingly the man looked like he was thoroughly enjoying himself—De Wynter approached. He dumped some of the clear, pungent fluid into his hand and sprinkled it on Matthew's bare legs.

Matthew moved to hold up his hand in protest, but the shackles stopped him. "Gah, what is that stuff?"

"Something to make you less tasty."

"I appreciate your coming to get me, but I'm chained to the bed and the harridan Esmeralda has the key."

"No, problem. Guidon suspected as much." De Wynter pulled out a small key ring. A half-dozen silver keys jingled. "He knew the type of shackle she would use—it is a thousand years old."

"Guidon? Who in blazes is he?"

"The historian of all vampires," De Wynter said.

Four quick turns of the key, and Matthew was free. The demonesses were cautiously approaching, fangs bared.

"Are you sure this stinky stuff is working?"

"We are about to find out."

"I can't believe we got out of there alive."

Matthew pulled the carriage door closed as De Wynter, who had climbed in ahead of him, sank back on his velvet carriage seat. Stretching out his arms, De Wynter cocked his brow. "We aren't alive, Sutcliffe. We are both undead."

Wonderful. He'd been saved from certain destruction, so that he could embrace destruction. Matthew had forgotten that he was now a monster. He slumped down onto the edge of the seat opposite De Wynter. Worse, the scent of blood surrounded him—he was highly attuned to the aroma of blood exuded by people around him. By mortals.

"Close your legs, Sutcliffe. Remember, you are wearing nothing but my coat."

Esmeralda had stripped him naked to keep him prisoner. She'd left his clothes with the demonesses. Apparently the fanged harridans had been so aroused by his scent they had ripped his clothes to pieces in their lustful frenzy, and had had sex together on the tattered remains of his shirt and trousers.

So he had borrowed De Wynter's tailcoat. He clamped his knees together and arranged the coat to cover more of his bare legs, and definitely his bare crotch. Surprisingly, he didn't feel the cold of the November night, but that must be because he was now a vampire.

De Wynter suddenly frowned and pulled open his cravat. Two small puncture wounds stood out on his pale throat. "Dratted succubi," he muttered. "That one clinging to me managed to bite my neck."

"They were succubi?" Matthew asked hollowly. "Like Octavia?"

"Not like your wife. I apologize for what I said. They are vampires, and are not succubi at all. I used the term facetiously, and I had no right." Then he gave a smile that was obviously forced. "Now what? I thought of White's, but of course, you need clothing."

"White's? Are you insane? How can you relax and ask 'now what?' I'm a vampire. The first thing I should do is destroy myself for the sake of humanity."

De Wynter retied his cravat in an elegant knot. "Interesting. If that's the first thing, what do you plan on doing second?"

"Obviously there would be no second thing, which is why I can't drive a stake through my own heart just yet. I have to find Octavia. Esmeralda told me that making love to a man without a soul would kill Octavia. She said she would turn me into a vampire, yet leave me with a soul. Is that possible?"

De Wynter shook his head. "I do not know."

"Esmeralda wants Octavia. She destroyed my brother and now she wants my wife. Damn, will I destroy Octavia if I make love to her? I can't even destroy myself, leaving her a respectable widow, since I have to protect her. But I do not dare bed her, in case Esmeralda's claim that I have a soul is a lie. Damn and blast."

"There may be another solution. . . ."

"Tell me, then. Don't sit there stroking your jaw. Enlighten me."

De Wynter reached out. With the tip of his index finger, he flicked the side of the tail coat aside.

Matthew grasped it to close it. "Do you mind?"

"There's a mark on your chest, just below your heart. I didn't notice it before. Did Esmeralda make it?"

"No, I don't believe so. It wasn't there earlier today. I don't know how it got there." He'd been trapped for a week with nothing to do but fight his chains and look down at his naked body. And now there was a foreign black mark on his chest. Not a stain, it was a definite shape, with crisp edges. It looked as if someone had drawn on his skin with ink. It looked like a heart, but one shot through by a lightning bolt. "I don't know what it is."

"I do," De Wynter supplied. "It's a brand."

"Like what is done with horses or sheep?"

"This is different. Vampire queens can do it. It usually carries a curse. If you are wearing it, it means you are cursed."

"Of course, I'm cursed. I'm a vampire."

"This is something completely different, Sutcliffe. We have

to get to your home. You need to dress. Then we have to pay court to the vampire queens."

"I have to find my wife—"

"Damn it, Sutcliffe. You cannot go near her until you know what kind of curse you've been damned with."

13

Apologies

It was a brothel on Curzon Street, a private one, known only to select men, for it was one that catered to gentlemen who sought male lovers. The bedrooms were filled with the grunts, sighs, and panting of men.

"God, yes," grunted a male voice from behind a closed door. "Deeper. Plunge deeper into me."

A hoarse male laugh answered the request.

Matthew's enhanced vampire senses let him hear what was happening in the various bedchambers. De Wynter grinned, but Matthew felt his neck turn red. Surprising, given the number of orgies he'd attended. Becoming a married man had changed him.

That fact alone should unnerve him. But surprisingly, it didn't.

Becoming a vampire had definitely changed him. He had been forced to wait a day before coming here with De Wynter. It had been close to dawn when they had escaped last night. They had visited the vampire librarian Guidon, then the need for day sleep had hit Matthew hard. De Wynter had first taken him to a different brothel from this one—a place where women willingly allowed vampires to take some blood.

De Wynter had watched over him, had stopped him before he took too much. But even with the woman's consent, the experience had horrified him. Appalled him. After that, he had fallen into sleep, learning that as a brand-new vampire, he had almost no ability to fight the need for day sleep. It would take days or weeks before he gained more control.

De Wynter had also taught him how to shift shape into vampire form. Another hellish experience.

"The vampire queens are here?" Matthew lifted a doubtful brow.

"Where else would they be, with so many handsome, virile, blood-filled males on display?" De Wynter asked.

He had no idea. The vampire queens sounded like Esmeralda, who had been enraged with him for stealing his brother from her—she'd intended to make Gregory her sex slave for eternity. "The vampire queen I wish to talk to will be in there," De Wynter said.

Matthew pushed open the bedroom door and saw the woman referred to as a vampire queen.

A woman with coal black skin was watching two blond men—one was on his hands and knees, the other slamming into him from behind. She wore a loose-fitting, open robe of black lace and nothing beneath. Firelight glanced along the muscular form of her body, turning her ebony skin to a remarkable sculpture of black, silver, and blue. She had large brown eyes and the fullest dark crimson lips he had ever seen.

She was breathtaking, certainly, but not as beautiful as Octavia.

Both of the young men had stripped off their shirts and pushed their trousers down to their ankles. A fire burned in the fireplace, and both men glistened with sweat.

He had never desired sex with another man, but he had to admit the scene was arousing him: the harsh thrusts, the moans and groans. This time he didn't blush. Instead, his cock ached at the thought of being gripped in tight heat. The way the hard haunches of the man on the bottom rippled when the upper man slammed his prick deep. The scene aroused him.

But since becoming a vampire, he found everything aroused him.

"She is the queen I want," De Wynter murmured. Matthew caught his friend's broad grin in his peripheral vision. "Do you want to just walk over or shift shape and fly, Sutcliffe?"

Fly? Matthew felt the usual sense of horror at what he now was. "I—hell," he bristled. "I'd prefer to walk instead of shifting shape and enjoying the pleasure of stretching my body like it is on a rack." That was what changing into bat form had felt like. "Nor do I want to shift shape and lose my clothing in this place."

De Wynter shrugged, then stepped into the room.

Matthew knew De Wynter had been trying to make a joke, to make light of what he now was. He knew De Wynter wanted him to accept it. But he couldn't. He didn't want to shift shape and turn into a giant bat, even though he could do it now.

After his first experience with drinking blood, he now refused to do anything a vampire was supposed to do. What he would do when his hunger got strong, he did not know, but he could not face plunging his fangs into a human's neck.

He followed De Wynter. He used to crave the exploration of unknown worlds. He had traveled the planet in search of the new, the adventurous. Now he lived in the most novel world of all, but the vampire world was one he wished he could leave behind.

The queen was not just watching now. She was feeding.

She was drinking from the neck of a young, muscular, dark-haired man. At the sight of De Wynter, she released her victim, patted the six-foot-tall man on the rump, and murmured, "That will have to be all for tonight, my dear. Come tomorrow."

The vampire queen smiled as De Wynter gave her a flourishing bow. Matthew hesitated, then bowed, but without the theatrical sweep of his hand and hat.

White fangs flashed as she smiled coyly and seductively at him. "You fear I hurt my young, handsome friend?" Her voice was rich and throaty.

Do not offend, De Wynter said in his thoughts. *Treat her like a queen.*

This was the first time he had seen De Wynter look nervous. So he knew he had to play along. "I don't, Your Majesty."

She laughed. "You did. But do not worry—I would never kill him. The poor, young, sweet boy is dying of a disease, so when I finally bestow immortal life, he will be spared a painful death. It is not all torment and agony, Lord Sutcliffe."

His brow rose.

"Yes, I know who you are. The queens were aware that Esmeralda had turned you. So why are you here? Is it to be set free? I cannot do that for you."

"But could I be?" Hell, he'd never even thought of it. "Set free?"

Dark shoulders moved with fluid elegance in a shrug. "Sometimes it is possible. It depends on a great many things."

"Queen Nivar, Sutcliffe was cursed when he was changed," De Wynter said. "He bears a mark on his chest, just below his heart."

"Does he?" She licked her lips. "Let me see."

The lip-licking made Matthew apprehensive, but De Wynter jerked his head as if to say: Go on. Matthew opened his coat, then waistcoat. The two men were rutting passionately, which meant no one was paying them any attention.

He jerked up the hem of his shirt, revealing his abdomen, then his chest and the strange brand. Standing motionless, he waited as she moved close and bent to study the mark.

The vampire librarian Guidon had not been able to help them. At first Matthew had been surprised by the librarian's troll-like appearance and his enthusiasm to learn everything he could about a newly made vampire. The small librarian had hopped up and down with excitement. Matthew had told Guidon what Esmeralda had said before she took his blood. The words were burned into his brain, and he had repeated them:

But I have to do something special with you, Esmeralda had said. *Your wife will reject you—she will sense you no longer have a soul. So I have to make you into something different. A vampire with a soul.*

Guidon had not thought the curse mark had anything to do with the words. But he could not be sure.

"Very interesting," Queen Nivar said. She stroked the muscles of his chest, then laid her fingertips on the mark. "But this was not given to you by Esmeralda. Yes, she left you with your soul, but this has nothing to do with her. This is a curse. You must come with me, so I can discover what it means."

"This is the largest I have ever seen."

Matthew let out a low whistle as he surveyed Queen Nivar's dark library. She moved through the moonlit room as if floating over the ground, just as Esmeralda had done. Her black lace gown swayed over her slender, tight bottom as she moved. A scarf of black velvet, decorated with enormous jewels, held her hair.

She waved her hand. "Of course. That little gnome-like librarian Guidon believes he has all the knowledge about vampires, and he refuses to share it with us, the queens. We have to pay him to be told things. So we have built our own library. Now . . . let me see . . ."

She drew out a book—a thick book that her hand could barely grasp. It smelled of dust, and the leather binding was split and old. "Here. I thought as much. That mark comes from the touch of a god. A god or goddess must have visited you in your day sleep and has put a curse on you. Let us find out who . . . and what the curse says. It is fortunate for you that I am one of the queens who is versed in ancient magic."

"Taught to you by Guidon," De Wynter remarked casually.

Baring fangs, Nivar hissed at him. "It is a good thing you are married to a very special lady, or I should kill you with pleasure for your insubordination."

"Married?" Matthew looked to Sebastien. "You aren't married."

"I am." A shrug. "It's . . . complicated."

Nivar closed the book with a snap. "I must touch your curse. I can make it speak to me."

Matthew again opened his waistcoat and jerked up his shirt. Again, the queen touched the scar. This time, she closed her eyes, parted her lips, and made soft moaning sounds.

Finally she moved back. Her shiny brown eyes glittered. "You have been given a way to escape. It is because you still have your soul. Esmeralda may have turned you into a vampire, but the goddess of love—Aphrodite—has given you a way to free yourself."

"*Aphrodite?* You must be joking?"

"Sutcliffe, you are a vampire. Of course I am not joking. You can become human again. Mortal. It is a way out, but only if you prove you deserve it. It is the ultimate gamble. You will die in a fortnight—you will be destroyed, cease to exist—unless you break the curse."

"What do you mean 'die in a fortnight'? You mean if I try to change back?"

"No, I mean you are destined to die. In two weeks. That is your curse."

He reeled back on his heels. To think he'd worried about being a vampire for eternity. He had two weeks.

He had never been a man to gamble at dice or cards. He gambled by taking dangerous voyages. His games of chance were played on storm-tossed ships, in disease-ridden jungles, in wilds where there were creatures that would eat him for dinner.

"What do I have to do to break it?"

She stroked her full lower lip with a fingernail that was like a talon. "It is really quite simple, my lord. All you must do is capture a woman's heart. If you can make a woman truly fall in love with you, knowing that you are a vampire, you win. You will be free. Mortal and human once more."

What woman would love a vampire? How in blazes could he woo a woman in two weeks? He couldn't even find Octavia, and she was his wife. Octavia was the only woman he wanted. It would be easy enough to seduce her and make her happy in bed, but to make her truly fall in love . . . when he was a vampire? That was insane. She already despised him, apparently. Now she would be afraid of him.

"Her love for you must be more than infatuation," Nivar said. "It must be deep and strong. There is one other caveat. Aphrodite has chosen the woman in question. She knows that you have married a woman without love, and you have driven that woman away."

"I did not drive her away," Matthew said through gritted teeth. "She ran away."

"You offered her imprisonment, in return for protecting her name. That hardly nourishes a woman's soul," the queen responded, sounding annoyingly like De Wynter. "Offer this woman real love and make her love you in return, and then you will live. You will live with a soul."

"But after that, making love with Octavia will kill me."

"Perhaps. But otherwise you are guaranteed to die in two weeks."

So to save his life, all he had to do was make Octavia fall in love with him.

"Hell," muttered De Wynter. "You have a fortnight to find your wife, apologize, make her forgive you, and win her heart. After you drove her away."

"I did not drive her—"

"Yes, you did," De Wynter and the vampire queen broke in, together.

"All right," Matthew growled. "Let's say I did. If Aphrodite, the goddess of love, wants me to make amends to my wife in two weeks, how does she expect me to do that when I can't find her?"

Nivar shrugged gracefully. "I imagine she has thought of that. Goddesses tend to be very clever—almost as brilliant as vampire queens. I expect you will have help on your quest. Your quest to seduce and court your wife." Her deep, throaty laugh filled the room. "How delightful—a husband given a do-or-die quest to court his own wife. That is very clever. I must remember it, and next time I want to bestow a curse, I know what it shall be."

"Finally, we've found the woman who has kept my backside on a saddle for almost an entire week." De Wynter grinned as he reined in his horse in the shade of an elm tree, in front of a country manor house. It was sunset; the sky was red. De Wynter wore a hat pulled low, a greatcoat and gloves, and kept his skin out of the sun.

As did Matthew. De Wynter had shown him how to rouse himself from the day sleep, so they could travel in the afternoon, as long as they were protected. As a vampire, Matthew didn't feel the cold of the November evening, but he had to protect himself from sunlight.

He frowned, studying the simple, square brick house and the snow-crusted garden out front. The vampire queens had agreed to give him one advantage in his hunt—they had given him the ability to sense Octavia. He could almost smell where she was, even when miles away—and that had aroused him beyond belief.

Using his new, magical awareness of her, he had followed her here, to the small village of Layton in Hertfordshire, but he had no idea why she had come here.

His heart pounded; his palms were damp with nervousness. In minutes he would see her again.

He missed her. Had she had their baby? Had the birth gone safely?

Once he'd felt anger when he thought of how he had been cheated out of holding his newborn. Now all he wanted to know was that both Octavia and the baby were safe and well. He was a vampire—how in Hades could he be a father now? The only way he could be a father to a child was to get free of this curse.

That meant winning his wife's heart.

He tied the reins of his horse, Demon, to a gatepost, then walked up to one of the front windows, taking care as he paced through the slumbering garden. His hands shook with nerves. Through the panes of glass, he saw several people, seated and talking. He crouched by the window and looked in. Here he was: a vampire, one shrouded in a cloak so he wouldn't burn to a crisp in the late afternoon sun, and he was taking great care not to put his boot on any of the dormant plants.

Through the window, he saw his runaway wife.

He had expected . . . He hadn't known what to expect. Not Octavia's fashionable gown of bronze silk, with its neckline that hinted at the swell of voluptuous breasts, or the elegant turban with tall feathers. Poised elegantly on a chair, she exuded wealth and power. As far as he knew, she had run away from her home with nothing. Where had she gotten the money for clothing? Had it been from Mrs. Darkwell?

Given that she was a succubus and needed to seduce men to survive, had she become a man's mistress?

Something gave a loud *crack,* and he felt it jab his hand. He'd snapped his riding crop in two.

Suddenly, Octavia jumped up from the seat. Despite her straight spine, her hands shook. The country lady also swiftly stood, but Octavia waved her hand as though waving concern away. Using his vampire senses, he could hear what his wife said through the window.

"I was wrong," she whispered hoarsely. "I apologize for my accusations, but I have been desperate to find my child."

Find their child? Shock speared Matthew, and he straightened with a jerk.

"But my lady," said the country lady, "if you are in danger, is it not better the baby is with a family and will be safe?"

She had given their child away? He was stunned into immobility. Then Octavia scrubbed her glove across her cheek. Was she brushing tears?

The woman squeezed Octavia's shoulders. "My lady, I think it would be wise for you to give up the search. The family who has taken your daughter will love her and take good care of her. Mrs. Darkwell chose only families who would welcome and love a child. We desperately wanted children but could not have our own. We have raised many of her charges—babies of the young ladies she trains and cares for. Your child will have grown to think of that family as hers. Is it not better your child is with a family and will be respect—?"

"I am not like Mrs. Darkwell's other women," Octavia interrupted. "I am married."

The woman looked startled. "You are? Oh, I beg your pardon, my lady; I did not realize."

"I know. Most of the women who are with Mrs. Darkwell are not married."

"But why is your husband not looking after both you and your child?"

Why indeed, Matthew thought darkly.

"My husband cannot accept what I am. And I don't believe my daughter is better off or safer with strangers." Tears broke free and fell to his wife's cheeks. "It has only been days. Surely my baby will not forget me so quickly."

He seethed with frustration. Why did she not see that he did accept what she was, that he was willing to live with it, as long as he could keep her safe and his alone? He left the window, and he'd reached the small stone path when the front door flew open. Octavia rushed out, her hands in fists. She might be crying, but she looked more determined than he'd ever seen her. She wore a fur-trimmed cloak.

"Octavia."

She stopped, whirled. As she saw him her eyes widened, then narrowed. She looked as if she'd like to drive a spear through his heart.

How had he ever thought she'd obediently marry him and obey him? Every moment of his life—or his undead existence—was going to be like this. A battle. With her glaring at him.

Madness to want it.

Anyway, how was he going to win this angry woman's heart?

"What are you doing here?" She crossed her arms over her chest.

Her chest was considerably more ample than it had been. Her breasts were lushly round and generous, swelling delectably over her scooped bodice.

"I would appreciate it if you met my gaze," she snapped.

He obeyed, jerking his gaze up, until he was speared by her glare. "I came here for you, Octavia. I offered you protection; I intended to take care of you, and you ran away. I've been worried about you."

She stopped glaring. And rolled her eyes. "You offered me a future of loneliness, locked away in your most remote estate." She gave a quick glance at the paned windows, where he'd just been eavesdropping. But the woman of the house had not pursued Octavia. His wife's lower lip wobbled. "All because I am a witch," she whispered. "It is not my fault. Your idea proved itself idiotic—I've learned how to control my . . . well, what it is that I can do."

"A witch? Octavia, you're a—"

"Good afternoon, Lady Sutcliffe. It is a delight to see you again."

Damn De Wynter. Why had he chosen this moment to interrupt them?

He swept a flourishing bow to Octavia. "Sutcliffe, why not escort your lovely wife to her carriage? Perhaps we could all dine together at the inn in the village? It would be a more conducive setting for a discussion than someone's garden."

"I am staying at the inn," Octavia said. "But I do not know if we have anything to speak of."

"Yes," Matthew began, "We do—"

"Yes, your husband has to begin apologizing for his high-handed behavior," De Wynter broke in.

Matthew was going to sputter out a retort in his defense, when he saw a small smile curve Octavia's lips. Since he was supposed to work to win her heart, he assumed he was better off keeping his mouth shut.

"All right. Meet me at the inn, Octavia. Dine with me, and I promise I'll start groveling."

She looked startled, but she nodded. The sun had dipped

below the trees that lined the horizon, so he no longer had to worry about direct sunlight. "I will escort you to your carriage."

"No. No, don't. I need some time to think before I speak with you. We will talk at the inn."

Hades, she was his wife. He had been hunting for her; she was in danger. She did not just tell him to heel when he needed to be with her. He needed to know what had happened to their child. Their *daughter*. He had a baby girl, and how did she expect him to damn well wait?

Let her go, Sutcliffe. We need to speak alone first. De Wynter spoke in his thoughts. *It's important.*

Nothing is more important than knowing she is safe and knowing where the baby is.

This is, Sutcliffe. Trust me.

Tightening his fists by his hips, he watched Octavia walk away. Seconds later, he heard her speak to the coachman, heard the creak of the door, of the steps, then the clop of hooves and the rattle of wheels on the frosty ground.

"I looked inside her thoughts, Sutcliffe," De Wynter said. "Let's ride to the inn and talk about it."

But Matthew grasped the vampire by the shoulder. "You saw inside her thoughts?"

"Vampires can do that. See thoughts and push our will onto people. But not with people we love. Their thoughts are blocked to us. So if you can't see into your wife's thoughts, it means the two of you are in love. I assume there is more happiness in a marriage when a husband and wife don't know each other's thoughts. It's easy enough to say something one regrets, and a lot easier to think it."

"I don't want you looking into her thoughts," he barked. Then he paused. "What was she thinking about? What did you see in her thoughts about our child?"

"Apparently, Mrs. Darkwell took the child for its protection, but she does not agree with the idea."

"This woman took an earl's child?" Matthew sputtered.

"Your wife is being hunted, and the woman believed it was for the child's safety."

"Damnation."

"Calm yourself. You have to charm your wife, remember. Also, Lady Sutcliffe thinks she is a witch. I believe she has no idea she's a succubus."

"I should tell—"

"Don't tell her, Sutcliffe. She is a gently bred woman. The fact that she is supposed to steal men's souls through sex is not something she needs to know. It will be shocking and painful."

"We—we have to face it sometime."

"Win her heart and her trust first," De Wynter said. "Remember, she needs to have sex to survive. You have to keep her satisfied. In addition it may help her fall in love with you. If you do a good job in bed."

Matthew scowled. "I always do a good job in bed."

He saw her in the yard of the inn, stepping down from the carriage. Matthew dismounted and handed the reins to a young groom, watching his wife stride across the hard ground toward the entrance of the inn. This was madness. She was his wife, but he had no idea how to approach her.

Finally he shook off the sense of awkwardness, and he stalked after her. He caught hold of her wrist as she reached the door. "I will reserve the parlor for dinner," he said softly. "Come down and join me there. I want to find out what has happened to our daughter. How in heaven's name could you have let her be taken away?"

Octavia paled. She tried to pull her wrist free, but he wouldn't loosen his grip. "I had no choice. I was fooled, and then she was taken from me. She is safe, and this was done to ensure she is safe, but I—I want to find her."

"So you don't know where she is."

"I know she is safe," Octavia hissed, her blue eyes wide with pain. "I know she is with a family. I don't want to speak of this here, now, Sutcliffe. Let me go."

"I want to help you search for our child," he murmured. He moved close to her, so his lips were close enough to kiss. He drank in her warm, fresh lavender scent, and his cock bucked with yearning. His mouth ached to kiss her.

This had to be the vampire in him. Finding his child was the most important thing. He was still angry—how could she not have protected their daughter? He had been denied the chance to do it.

She pulled her arm free. "And when we find her, what will you do? Do you want to imprison us both?"

"Stop glaring at me as though I'm an enemy. I'm not. I want to help you."

"You don't want to help, you want to dictate to me. And blame me."

"This is not about blame—"

"You want to order me about, Sutcliffe. I refuse to be treated like chattel. I know what I am, and if you cannot accept it, I refuse to let you be my jailer."

She stalked away from him, through the doorway, to the desk of the inn, and she rapped sharply on the bell.

Matthew stayed where he was as the burly innkeeper came out.

Octavia was going to drive him out of his mind. To seduce her, he knew he had to be conciliatory. He couldn't coax her into bed while they were snapping at each other.

He had to stop feeling anger because his daughter was gone, and work to find the child. He was willing to do that. But Octavia would not let up for an instant. All she wanted to do was fight with him.

He could win her heart much faster if he could be making love to her. Not in dreams, but in reality. Since she was certain their daughter was safe, he believed he could manage to make love; then they would go on their search.

The first times they'd made love, Octavia had propositioned him. Now he had to find out how his wife wanted to be seduced.

She was breathing hard, and she felt weak and shaky, but Octavia had enough strength to open the door to the inn's maid, and eye the bouquet the girl carried with suspicion. It was a collection of evergreens and silvery twigs and ivy leaves. They had obviously been cut from the rambling shrubs that grew around the inn. The greenery smell was lovely.

"From Lord Sutcliffe, my lady." The young maid, Alice, curtsied. "He has ordered a special private dinner for you, too." The girl gave a shy smile. "An intimate dinner, he said." Her voice dropped to a soft, girlish whisper, then she giggled. "The parlor's been set aside. You are to come down as soon as you are ready, my lady."

"Yes, he told me he planned to do that. Lord Sutcliffe is my husband."

"Oh!" That news startled Alice.

"At the moment, we are estranged."

Alice's eyes enlarged to the size of dinner plates. "I beg yer pardon, my lady—"

"We are fighting." It was on the tip of Octavia's tongue to send a refusal by maid. She didn't know if she had the strength for a battle with Sutcliffe.

But the girl set a vase, one that was chipped and somewhat dirty but filled with water, on her vanity table, and Alice plunked the greenery in there. "His Lordship cut them himself. Mr. Jones—the innkeeper—wished to send one of the servants, but Lord Sutcliffe insisted he would do it. He scratched himself something fierce on the shrubs."

He wanted to hide her away in a gloomy northern castle, yet he cut a bouquet for her himself. The man made no sense.

Alice fiddled with the bouquet of green until she had arranged them in a way that made her smile. "He was ever so fussy about what he selected."

Octavia faced the girl with playful suspicion. "How would you know that, Alice?"

The maid went red. "I admit I did watch him, my lady. I had to dust the parlor, and the leaded windows look out over the garden. He blushed when he requested the dinner. I think—"

"What do you think, Alice?"

"He is sweet on you, my lady, and I would think he don't want to fight anymore."

"I am sure he doesn't," Octavia muttered, so softly the girl would not hear. "As long as he gets his own way."

"I think," Alice breathed, starry-eyed, "Lord Sutcliffe is like a knight in shining armor."

Octavia twisted her lips in a wry grimace. A husband who wanted to lock his wife away was hardly a besotted and noble knight. . . .

Of course, he insisted he was doing it to protect her. He had searched England to find her. But was that out of love, or out of annoyance, possessiveness, and the male need to be always right? She knew that from dealing with gentlemen of the Royal Geographical Society.

Perhaps he was not bad, just dense, as men could tend to be.

Bother, she mustn't weaken toward him. She was not going to be a prisoner—it was as simple as that.

She would have to meet him in the parlor and confront him.

Either he had to bend to her wishes, or she had to leave him. And he had to stop pursuing her.

She stood, determined to do this, when she suddenly felt dizzy. It was as if all her blood had drained from her body. Her arms and legs shook, and she felt boneless. Spots of gray burst in front of her eyes.

She hadn't felt like this for months. It had suddenly happened now, after seeing Sutcliffe again.

Octavia reached for the bedpost, but her fingers felt numb. She was holding it, but she couldn't feel it. It wasn't giving her any support. The room lurched about her, and she let her hand slide down the post. She sank to the edge of the bed and let out a small sob.

She hadn't felt this sick even when expecting her baby.

What was wrong with her?

If she was getting sick again, would sex with Sutcliffe make her feel well?

"Are you all right, my lady?" Wide-eyed, Alice leaned over her. "Should I fetch smelling salts? Cold water on the wrists? . . . That always helped me mum when she felt faint—"

"I am all right, Alice. It was just a dizzy spell, and it will go away. But I will need your help. I must get ready for my dinner with Lord Sutcliffe."

If she had to go to bed with Sutcliffe again to be well, she would. This time, she would not make the mistake she'd made months ago. His arrogance had made any love she'd had for him wither and die. This time, she was wiser, much wiser. She would not fall in love with him again.

She would just sleep with him.

Octavia's decision had given her a small burst of strength— enough to propel her down the stairs and across to the private parlor. The inn appeared to have been built during the reign of the Tudors and had low ceilings of heavy beams, and a fireplace large enough to fit a boar inside.

She avoided the fireplace.

But she caught a glimpse of her hair, her face, her dress in an oval mirror above the mantelpiece.

She felt like an actress on the Drury Lane stage. She wore an elegant, low cut gown of sapphire silk. Her bosom almost spilled over the neckline, but her breasts weren't full or sore anymore.

She knew it meant her breasts had given up hope of finding her baby, that *they* no longer expected to have an infant to feed. The first few days after her milk had come in had been excruciating with no baby. She hadn't even been able to stand the pressure of her shift on her breasts. Any touch against her nipples had prompted her milk to flow.

But she was not giving up hope. She was going to find her baby. Then her breasts, she prayed, would make milk once more.

If they didn't, she had no idea what to do—

There he was. Her husband. He lounged at a table set for two, but he rose from his chair as she reached the doorway. At least she had the strength to walk, to do so without looking weak. Even if she had clung to the banister to get downstairs, she looked strong now.

She refused to let him know she was ill again. She didn't want him—her enemy—to know she had any weakness.

"Octavia."

He came forward and she knew, in one heady glance, it was going to be very easy to sleep with him. She was furious with him, but her foolish body *wanted* him.

He looked even more handsome than he had before he'd left for the Carpathians.

In fact, Sutcliffe looked more handsome than he had an hour

ago, when she had seen him in the inn's yard. How was that possible?

His eyes were a stunning silvery blue, and they reflected firelight so intently, it looked like flames flickered in his eyes. His skin was paler, but his features seemed even more perfect. His lips were full but sensually masculine.

Looking at his lips made her heart beat faster. It made her ache between her thighs—an ache so strong she wasn't sure if she could walk. She was so wet between her thighs.

He seemed to tip his head, as though he was scenting her.

Then he smiled. "I wanted to apologize to you."

"Did you really? Or is this a trick?" At first Octavia's question raised Matthew's ire. Then he saw the way she hugged herself and the sad, downward curve of her mouth. She really didn't believe him.

It wasn't a trick. In this moment, he felt damnably sorry. "I shouldn't have made it sound like I was going to imprison you."

"Do you still intended to lock me away?"

"Of course not." But he had intended to do exactly that to keep her safe and to keep her for himself. She thought he was selfish, arrogant, and possessive. Perhaps he was, but he knew he was right. With his brother, he'd made the mistake of being arrogant and selfish, and he had not been protective or possessive enough.

This time he intended to be very possessive with his wife . . . and with their child.

So she was correct—he was not really sorry about what he had done. He was sorry he hadn't made her understand it was for the best. She turned toward him, frowning. The position sent warm firelight cascading over the swells of her breasts. "I don't believe you."

He was aroused and hard enough to bend iron with his

cock. Right now, he wanted to lock her away. He wanted to keep her his prisoner in bed. He crossed the room, moving toward her.

De Wynter had warned him not to tell Octavia she was a succubus. And he had to begin to capture her heart. As he'd realized before, he had better stop talking and put his tongue to better use.

When he reached her, he put his finger to her lips. "Don't speak. I want to seduce you. I want to make love to you for real tonight, not just in dreams. Give me the chance to try."

14

Hunger

Sutcliffe walked around her and blew a soft, warm breath gently across her neck. Octavia shut her eyes and let her head fall back. That brush of heat and air made her bones melt. It made her tingle everywhere.

"You are sure our baby is safe?" he asked softly. He cradled her breasts as he spoke. It had been so long since she'd felt his hands on them—not in a dream, but in reality. It felt so good, she moaned.

Then she whispered, for she was too weak with desire to speak normally. "Yes. I know at least she is safe."

"Then tomorrow we will find her." He tongued her neck, from the base of her hairline to the top of her dress. Shivers rushed down her spine; heat raced through her blood.

"It's better if we hunt during the day," he said softly. "The monsters come out at night."

She nodded. She had vowed she would not return to him. But the thought of having him with her, protecting her and their child, was tempting. So very, very tempting.

She had to remember the price for his protection.

"What did you call her?" he asked softly.

He kissed along the neckline of her dress in the back. Kisses that made her melt. But at the same time, she admired him for the controlled way he was asking questions.

He must be furious, but she couldn't hear anger in his voice. Or even sorrow. She heard only . . . gentleness.

"I—I didn't have a chance to give her a name. She—she was taken away from me." Octavia tried to speak calmly. But her voice wobbled. It felt as if the words were scratching their way out of her throat. Then something hot and wet spattered to her cheeks.

Sutcliffe turned her, and he kissed her tears away. His lips brushed them from her face. He looked at her tenderly, when he should be furious.

Never had she dreamed she would have his sympathy. That he would understand. Then she was telling him everything: about the satyr that had attacked her, about Mrs. Darkwell and the house, about soul mates and escape, and losing their baby. "But I have the names of families she would use to keep a child. I am going to find our baby."

"We are going to find her."

"All right," she breathed. "We will do this together."

What was she doing? She wanted sex with him tonight to regain her strength. She didn't want more than that.

He kissed her throat, making his way down to the hollow where her pulse pounded. It was good. She didn't want words. Talking was making her tense.

He licked in that hollow. Her tension snapped. "Just seduce me," she begged. "Just get on with it and seduce me."

The first time she'd seduced him, she had needed the same thing she needed now: sex to make her well. She hadn't *known* it, but a mysterious instinct must have guided her to get exactly what she'd needed. But she'd felt like a girl then. It had been romantic and daring and wonderful to seduce the man she'd dreamed of.

But it was different now. She felt lonely even with Sutcliffe. She felt empty.

Perhaps because she wasn't a normal, starry-eyed girl anymore. She now knew the truth: She'd never been like other girls. She was a *witch*, one who didn't belong anywhere, and one who might end up dead.

Sutcliffe didn't love her. How could he, when she was a witch? How could any man love a witch? Even if he did, which she couldn't believe, how could they have a normal family, a normal marriage, or happiness? She was a danger to their family.

Mrs. Darkwell had been right—

Her husband undid the fastenings of her dress. It snapped her out of her fears. In seconds, he lowered her gown and held her hand so she could step out of it.

Her arrogant husband gently laid her dress over a chair, then undid her corset. He didn't say a word, as she'd asked, but he was breathing hard. Attentively, he undressed her. He got to one knee to do her slippers and stockings, a gesture that made her blush and feel awkward.

She was panting, and the room was becoming hot. Sultry, steamy, and hot from the fire, from their panting, from the heat of their skin.

"You. Naked." It was all she could manage to say without using too many words.

He complied. She could see how aroused he was before he was naked. He had to struggle to open his trousers as his erection strained them so much. Watching him fight, she smiled. Until he undid the buttons and his cock sprang forward.

It was bigger than she'd remembered. Much bigger. How could she have forgotten it? It stood straight up, and the head grazed his flesh just above his navel. When he came to her, it barely moved, it was so stiff. She saw a mark on his chest. Gently, she put her fingers on it, but he captured them in his fingers and moved her hand away. "Just a scar. I got it . . . in the

Carpathians." He gazed at her intently. "It's nothing. Octavia, I want us to trust each other."

She nodded. She trusted him in bed. That much was true.

"I want to pleasure you every way I can. I want to teach you about some pleasures I know you've never dreamed of."

"What exactly do you mean?" she whispered.

He didn't answer. He lifted her into his arms, cradling her like a hero with a damsel in distress. But they were naked, so his erection brushed against her bottom.

"I want to show you pleasure that will make you scream."

She wanted to be brought to screams. But at the same time, screaming sounded a bit . . . frightening.

"Don't be frightened," he said, as if he'd read her thoughts. "Be prepared for delight."

He laid her on the small settee near the fire, so her naked bottom was in the air. The silky stitching of embroidery brushed her bare stomach and breasts.

Sutcliffe parted her legs.

From behind, his hand cupped her privates. His thumb swept back and forth, brushing her tingling clit.

"Oooh."

"Shh," he murmured. "We are in the parlor of a public inn."

"But you said you wanted me to be screaming."

"You can scream," Sutcliffe said. "But around this."

Something leathery and smooth slid across her cheek. She parted her lips in surprise, then a round ball slipped into her mouth. Leather straps were attached to it, and he tied them behind her neck. She shook her head and made sounds of protest. He was gagging her so she couldn't make any noise! Was he going to kidnap her?

"It's erotic play." His deep voice brushed over her ear. "Just a game. You have nothing to fear. Did you once dream about tying me to the bed?"

She nodded. How could he know?

"I shared your dreams," he murmured. "I suppose it is part of your powers. When you dreamed we were together, I dreamed it too. It was as if we were really together. Now, I'm going to tie you up, because I intend to do some naughty things, and since you are gently bred, you might feel embarrassed or bad. But it isn't bad. Nothing we do in bed together is wrong."

Now he had her terribly curious. What would she find bad—by which she gathered he meant scandalously naughty? So naughty, he had to tie her hands—which he was doing now—and gag her. He looped soft rope around her wrists, tying them together just over her tailbone.

It was rather erotic to have her arms bound, the backs of her fingers brushing her bottom.

"You look so sensual and beautiful," he said hoarsely. "Seeing the black velvet ties against your ivory skin makes me want to come right now."

She moaned around her gag, aroused by his words. Her tongue ran over the smooth ball in her mouth. It did feel . . . interesting. Her teeth brushed it. She bit lightly into it.

His finger slid between the cheeks of her bottom.

Her teeth sank hard into the ball.

What was he doing? Something touched her anus and stroked that opening. She was frozen with shock, even though the most amazing sensations were rushing through her.

She half turned, trying to ask him what he thought he was doing—

It was not his finger that was stroking in the valley.

It was his rock-hard erection. He was ruthlessly pushing it down to point between her cheeks.

Her cunny tightened and pulsed.

"I'm going to slide my cock up your derriere, my dear."

She shook her head, stunned.

"I can fuck you that way. I promise you will enjoy it. Your ass is so tight and hot, it will be heaven for both of us."

Could they do it? She thought of the courtesan at the duke's orgy. Men had done it to her, and she had truly been screaming her pleasure.

It looked so scandalous, but it felt . . . so very good to have the tip of his cock teasing the entrance of her rear.

"But first, let's ensure you are very aroused," he said softly.

He left her. Turning her face and resting her cheek on the sofa cushion, she could watch him. He opened a velvet bag, and he drew out a long, white wand. It was carved in a phallic shape, and it was almost as big as his cock. Velvet ties dangled from its base. He took something else out, but she couldn't see what.

"First, let's fill your sweet cunny," he said when he'd returned to the sofa.

Gently, he nudged the ivory cock between her nether lips. Slowly, he eased it in and out of her. "Are you sore at all, Octavia?"

She was just a bit, but then her juices were flowing, and it felt good. She ached to be filled.

"Do you want more?"

She nodded yes, vigorously.

Soon he had slid the cock all the way inside her. It filled her completely. It felt so good she was sobbing with delight around the gag. Softness brushed her legs. He tied the ropes around her thighs to secure the play toy inside her.

"Now for your nipples."

Her nipples? What could he do—?

His hands slipped under her. Cool metal brushed her right nipple, making it stand up hard. A gentle pressure clamped onto it. He did the same to her left. It was a velvet-lined clamp, and the tug of them on her nipples made her cunny clench around the toy.

She was rocking on the sofa. She wanted to make love with him, but this felt so good she was beginning to pleasure herself.

Then he mounted her from behind. His cock pressed against her anus, gently opening her. She moaned fiercely around the ball.

As he pushed his cock in just a bit, she cried out at the sudden sensations. Intense. Good. Intense. Amazing. Too intense! The gag muffled her wild sounds.

He thrust farther, opening her, and she felt a soft pop as he pushed fully past her opening, and it widened for him.

Goodness, he was soooo large.

Yet it felt . . . incredible.

And she realized it meant he was fully inside her. His crisp nether curls brushed her bottom. Her rump was stretched, and it felt as slick and aroused as her cunny.

Instinct told her to move on him, to thrust her bottom along the amazing rod buried inside it.

Oooooh.

"Like that, do you?"

More nodding, this time fiercely.

"You move as you want. Pleasure yourself on me." He reached round her, clasped her breasts, and teased her nipples. But he didn't move his hips.

Caught by his questing fingers, she rocked her rump back. It felt amazing to draw back so just the head was inside her, then to surge her rump to his groin and take his cock deep.

She worked harder. Harder. He tugged and pulled at the clamps secured to her nipples. It should have been too harsh, but it wasn't. It was perfect.

She banged her bottom against him, slammed him. Her clit was swollen and throbbing and she touched it, just for a little relief.

But just a brush launched her orgasm. It exploded in her.

Then he began to thrust into her, riding her bouncing ass as she climaxed. Her whimpers around the ball seemed to urge him to pound deep. She rubbed her clit madly.

Again, she climaxed, moaning and gasping around the ball in her mouth. Somehow being gagged made it more erotic.

A third brought sobs to her lips.

By orgasm number four, she was screaming around her restraining gag.

Sutcliffe groaned, thrust his hips forward to collide with her cheeks, then she felt a stream of heat squirt in her bottom.

He collapsed on her back, but caught himself with his taut arms. "Beautiful. You are more spectacular than any dream, love."

Her heart ached to melt, and she was dizzy enough with pleasure to let it.

But she fought for control.

Matthew pressed a glass of sherry into Octavia's hands. He had wrapped his robe around her, and she sat on the bed, the velvet dwarfing her. The hem spilled over her feet; the sleeves covered her hands to her fingertips.

They had thrown on some clothing, then had slipped out of the parlor hand-in-hand and had come to her bedroom. In a soft whisper that had wrenched his heart, Octavia had told him how naughty and adventurous it felt to sneak together up the stairs in their disheveled state. In her room, they'd made love again. A long, slow, luscious bout of pleasure. Now that sex was over, she looked worried, and her hands shook.

Still, her skin glowed, and her cheeks were pink. Before she had looked pale, and she'd had dark circles under her eyes. It had showed how much the search for their child had exhausted her.

He had to thank De Wynter again for giving him the gift of the sex toys.

He sat at her side. "How many families you have gone to in your search?"

"Three," she whispered. "I have two more. I'm terrified that she is with a family who is not on my list. I took the whole ledger, but what if—what if I'm wrong?"

"Sip the sherry, Octavia. It will make you feel better." He cradled her against him as she sipped. "We will find her." At least Octavia had managed to search without being attacked by the beasts like the satyrs and werewolves and vampires. He learned the mysterious Mrs. Darkwell had taught her a spell to disguise her scent, which let her elude the assassins who wanted to hurt her.

He was certain they would find the baby. They had to, because he couldn't accept losing his child forever.

"Will you come with me tomorrow?" she asked. "But when we find our baby, I'm not just going to let you take control of us—"

"I know, Octavia. I am not going to dictate to you. But you are in danger, and you have to be safe." He tipped up her chin. "The threat against you is serious. De Wynter explained it to me. You are being hunted by male assassin groups from the werewolves, and dragons, by vampires, and male witches. You can't fight beings like that alone. You need me—and we both need the help of the Royal Society. Will you trust me?"

She nodded. "I will."

This had to be a good start toward capturing her heart.

But the moment she learned what he was, her love would die.

De Wynter survived without drinking blood from mortals—De Wynter could drink his blood from a glass. But Matthew couldn't. The curse forced him to drink from human prey. He had refused to behave like a vampire and he would deny his hunger as long as he could, then it would take control of him.

He'd attacked men and had drunk until they almost died. De Wynter had stopped him before he killed them. Admittedly, he'd deliberately picked brutes—one had been a London footpad; another one had been beating a prostitute; yet another had been punching his wife. But even they didn't deserve to be killed by a vampire.

Octavia finished the last drops of sherry. "I'm tired," she whispered. "Will you sleep with me?"

He couldn't sleep at night. But he lied and said, "I would be honored. After all, we've only slept for one night together."

A little sound woke her. Octavia opened her eyes, blinking to get used to the dark. She was hot, engulfed in warmth, and all that comforting heat made it hard to wake up and think. She pushed the covers down—the heavy coverlet was over her head. Her nightgown had slipped up in her sleep and something remarkably warm was pressed against her bare bottom.

It was Sutcliffe. He was naked, and his body lay behind hers, so his crotch pressed into her rear. His steely forearm was around her, just below her breasts.

When she moved, he grumbled, muttered something. Then he rolled over onto his other side, leaving his back facing her.

She was accustomed to the dark now. There was no one in the room, no threat. The fire had banked into glowing coals—perhaps it had been a crackle or a hiss of the fire that had woken her.

Octavia looked at Sutcliffe. She heard steady breathing. He must still be asleep.

He was naked beneath the warm sheets. Tentatively she reached out. Her fingers touched his spine. Daringly, she traced down, down to the top of the hot valley between his cheeks.

He didn't stir, but her heart raced. With desire, not fear.

She liked sharing a bed with him.

But she couldn't let lust make her weaken. She was going to

stay with him now, because she had to do it to keep their baby safe.

She snuggled against Sutcliffe. He was deliciously warm; his buttocks were almost hot. His long legs stretched out beneath the sheets. She lay beside him, so close there wasn't an inch of space between them. Amazing to think she could wrap her arms around him. Even stroke him with her toes.

A light tapping filtered into her warm cocoon. She sat up, shivering as the cool night air touched the exposed skin of her upper chest where the bodice of her nightgown scooped. "Who's there?"

Sutcliffe sat up immediately, the covers falling off him. He mustn't have been sleeping, after all. There was no way he could have become so instantly alert. She suspected he had been faking sleep, breathing steadily so she would be fooled.

Why? Had he thought she would run away?

He slipped out of bed and dragged on his robe. Prowling to the door, he turned the key and opened it an inch.

With his body in the way, she couldn't see what was happening. She didn't trust him to share honestly with her. Anyway, if there was danger, he was facing it alone and without a weapon.

She got out of bed, snatched up the fireplace poker, then tiptoed behind Sutcliffe. It was hard to find a place to watch—his back was so broad, it filled most of the doorway.

When she saw who was out in the corridor, she sagged with relief. Not a satyr, or a snarling werewolf, or a vampire ready to plunge fangs.

A young boy stood there. He clutched a cap with his hands, twisting it. "Lady Octavia? I thought this were 'er room. I've a message for 'er. A liddy gave it to me. She says she knows ye're looking for a babby, and she knows where the babby is."

Hope soared and crashed all in the space of one moment. It had to be a trap, one set up by Mrs. Darkwell.

Without hesitation, Sutcliffe opened the door, grasped the boy by his shoulder and pulled him into the room. "All right, lad. The whole story. Who is this woman? If you can't give us her name, tell us what she looked like. Where did she approach you?"

The boy trembled, wringing his poor cap mercilessly. Octavia hurried forward. "You are frightening him, Sutcliffe." She led the boy to a chair by the fire and urged him to sit. The small, thin child perched on the edge.

She was wearing a sensible nightgown, not a scandalous one, but the boy was staring with large eyes, and he looked shocked to be seeing her intimately dressed. She put on a robe, then approached him. "What is your name?" She couldn't let Sutcliffe terrify the boy. Likely they'd learn nothing.

"Samuel."

"Can you tell us who the 'liddy' was, Samuel? We will reward you for your help."

"Didn't give 'er name to me. She was old and had gray hair. All in ringlets it was, under a fancy hat with a long feather."

Not Mrs. Darkwell . . . unless the woman was disguised. But it could have been a woman in the employ of Darkwell. She had to be careful. But she wanted so much to hope. . . .

"Where did this woman approach you, Samuel? In the village?"

"Aye, on the green. She asked for the most clever lad of the group of us, and I said it were me. 'Course the others 'ad to go 'ome at dark anyway. She gave me three shillings, then told me to bring the letter at midnight. For that much blunt, I slipped out of me house to do it."

"Where did this woman say the baby is?"

"The great 'ouse that's 'alfway between 'ere and Kindelwell. Revel House, it's called. She said they stole the babby? Is that true?"

"Not exactly."

"Could you take me there?" Sutcliffe asked the boy.

The lad nodded, and Sutcliffe told the boy to wait for them down at the inn's entrance. He gave the lad a few more coins and sent him out the door. "I might be following the boy into a trap," he said, as he dropped his robe, then pulled on trousers. "But I've got to follow it through."

She tugged her nightdress off. "You aren't going alone."

His brow rose. Icy arrogance seemed to wash over him. "Octavia, I will not let you go after the child. It is too risky for you."

"You are dictating to me! I want to see our child."

"It is late at night, a time when vampires, werewolves, and other assorted monsters are everywhere. It is too dangerous."

"I can disguise my scent—remember, I told you I could. *You* might lead these monsters right to our child."

He stopped, with his shirt halfway on. His chest was bare, his arms in the sleeves, his face hidden by the linen. From the way he froze, it was obvious he hadn't thought of that.

"But if we are both there, armed, we can protect each other," she continued. "It will be much easier to watch out for danger. Together we can protect the baby. If I'm there, I can use my . . . my powers." Even though they were alone in the room, she whispered the word. "Please. I need to find our baby. I cannot stand it anymore. I feel . . . I feel guilty for having made love with you, when I should be hunting for our child. Even though she is safe, I need to hold her again. I need to be with her. I'm going to go, even if I have to follow you secretly through the dark."

He jerked his shirt on. "Damnation, you would get yourself killed. At night, there's going to be assassins out, searching for you. It's dangerous—" He groaned and pulled one of his boots on. "So is leaving you here."

He looked haunted. "I lost my brother by being foolhardy. If I lose you . . . I couldn't live with that."

His words speared her to her heart.

The boy turned out to be telling the truth.

Matthew had no idea who the gray-haired woman was, but her information had been accurate and honest. And for a generous payment, the family—who had been the next ones on Darkwell's ledger list—had returned their baby to them.

Their small, beautiful, helpless, lovely daughter.

But it was now almost three o'clock in the morning, and Matthew was hungry. Dangerously, viciously hungry.

He dragged his hand through his hair. Octavia sat at his side in the simple carriage Matthew had rented from the inn, her hands wrapped tightly around the baby. The baby had slid down in her arms, curling up. Octavia looked stricken as she tried to reposition the little infant. Then she stared at him, confused.

"Sutcliffe, I don't understand. Why haven't you wanted to hold your child?"

He did want to touch their baby. He longed to cradle her. But he could smell his own daughter's blood, and it piqued his hunger. He could control it, but he hated himself for even being aware of his child's blood. Wasn't it proof his daughter didn't belong with him?

He was a vampire, damn it.

And he was afraid. Could he hurt his own child? Could he hurt Octavia?

He could hear the rush of Octavia's blood through her veins, and it was driving him mad.

His hand gripped the edge of the seat. The velvet cushion tore; the wooden frame began to crush under the grip of his hand. He had to keep his face turned to the window, and he had refused to let her light the carriage lamps. It would turn the windows into mirrors. It could reveal his secret.

But his teeth were out, and his jaw was screaming with pain—once his teeth grew, he felt this hot, intense pain until he sank his fangs into a mortal.

His own wife had made his fangs elongate.

He was supposed to be ingratiating himself into Octavia's heart. She couldn't understand his cold, aloof behavior. He could almost see her hardening her heart toward him.

If she needed him to cradle the baby, he would have to do it. He was sure he could do it, without hurting either Octavia or their daughter. He turned to her, thankful that darkness hid him. He held out his hands. "I'll take her," he said gruffly.

She turned away from him. He saw how the baby's swaddled bottom fit in her hand. "I am not going to hand her to you when you make it sound like a chore."

Obviously, he was not about to win her heart this way. "I don't know what to do with a baby," he muttered. "I'd likely hurt her."

Octavia stopped. "You are afraid of her. Is that why you are keeping your distance? She's an infant. How can you be afraid of such a small, innocent thing?"

"I'm not afraid of her," he growled. "I'm afraid of me."

Damn, that was too close to admitting there was reason to fear him.

"Afraid I might drop her or squeeze too tight," he added quickly.

Smiling, Octavia carefully set their infant into his arms. To his surprise, Matthew found he *was* afraid of dropping the little baby. His normally adept fingers suddenly felt large and clumsy.

This was his little girl.

As a vampire, he had excellent vision in the dark. He could see his daughter's fair eyelashes—her eyes were shut, and the spidery lashes lay on her pink cheeks. Her skin was fair, and beneath the lids, he could see the tracing of fine veins. But her cheeks were the pink of fresh roses, her lips were ruby red and pursed as if always ready to start sucking. Soft blond hair curled like silky wisps at the top of her head and on the sides, over her ears.

So small, so delicate, and so innocent.

His brother had been fair haired.

In the baby's pretty features, he could see Octavia, and the baby's coloring obviously came from her mother.

What kind of father could he be to her? Hell, unless Octavia fell in love with him, he would be a dead one.

Their carriage rumbled through the gate of the inn's court-yard.

Octavia shared a look with him. "We're back, and nothing has attacked us. Could it really be this easy? Are we safe?"

Probably from everything but him. "I don't know. You go up to bed. I want to look around first, ensure all is well, then I'll come up." He walked Octavia into the inn. It touched his heart how carefully she cradled the baby, and how she kept giving loving kisses to the tiny head.

Once she had gone up the stairs, he borrowed a pen and paper from the innkeeper. The scent of the man's blood—rich, spicy, strong—was driving him mad. He kept his face turned away to hide his fangs. Damn, it felt as if he could smell every drop of blood in the inn.

It was haunting him.

After dipping quill in ink, he quickly scrawled a note to De Wynter to let him know he and Octavia had found the baby. He handed the message to a servant, along with two shillings to find De Wynter and give him the note. No doubt his friend expected Matthew would want a private night with his wife. The servant's blood smelled sweet, like strawberry jam, or honey, making Matthew think of him as a potential dessert after the stronger blood of the inn keeper. The young man strode off to take his message to De Wynter, and Matthew got out of the inn, shoving out through the door into the dark yard.

He had to get away from people and the smell of their blood.

Outside, he drew in a breath of cool air. The night sounds were magnified. Intense.

Then he smelled skin—the warm, intoxicating smell of human skin.

A maid came out to dump a bucket of kitchen waste. Moonlight made her pale neck glow like a beacon. The tang of blood flooded his senses. He wanted to hunt down the maid. Wanted to sink his fangs into her pretty neck—

No. No, he wouldn't do it. He wasn't going to be a beast, like the one that had attacked his brother.

Pure agony went through his jaw, vibrating through his skull.

He ran in the opposite direction, long strides putting yard after yard between him and temptation. He would not feed from the woman. He wouldn't hurt her or kill her.

He stopped at a stone wall, one surrounding a farm field. Perfect.

Matthew slammed his head against it. Lights burst in front of his eyes, but as a vampire, he could endure a great deal of pain. He pounded his head against stone until his fangs retreated and until the gnawing, agonizing hunger receded.

More pounding was needed, he thought, just to make sure.

And like added torture, he suddenly remembered the afternoon he had hunted his brother Gregory to the dark cave in which he slept. He had gone with a stake, a blade for removing his brother's head, with silver balls for his pistol, with garlic.

Caught in his day sleep, Gregory had been unable to fight him. But his brother could show the agony of death on his face. He'd seen it. He'd also seen Gregory's shock at Matthew's betrayal, then his brother's desperate and panicked fury when he'd realized Matthew was going to destroy him.

He had done that to his brother.

But he was a coward—he should kill himself, but he couldn't do it. He was just as selfish and arrogant as he had been when he had freed Esmeralda.

He staggered away from the wall. His own blood dripped from a cut in his head. He could smell his own blood without feeling the pain of hunger.

He'd conquered it. He'd fought the primal urge of a vampire to take blood. Now he could go to Octavia.

But soon, the hunger was going to come back. He wouldn't be able to stop it.

He couldn't go on like this—he either had to get his freedom from being a vampire, or he had to destroy himself. He couldn't take Gregory's undead life and spare his own.

It was better his daughter never knew him than that she knew him as a monstrous beast.

Then glass shattered upstairs, and he heard a scream. He was halfway up the stairs when he heard an explosion, then smoke began to pour out of Octavia's room.

15

Fangs by the Dozen

His heart jumped into his throat, wedging in there like a cannon-ball. "Octavia!" Matthew hollered her name, racing up the stairs so fast he crashed into a man in a nightshirt and cap at the top of the landing. He pushed the man toward the stair, shouted, "Get out. The place is on fire. Get the hell out!"

The man screamed and stuttered, "W-who's there?"

Suddenly, Matthew realized he had run at a vampire's speed, so quickly the mortal man hadn't seen him.

Other people streamed out of their rooms, shouting and crying and clamoring for answers, and the man in the cap frantically claimed a ghost had shoved him to the stairs.

Matthew leapt over the people in the hallway and reached the open door of Octavia's room. *Don't think. Just get in there; get them. Don't think they might already be gone—*

He kicked in the door and stood on the threshold, his brain flooding with panic.

Something was growling in Octavia's room. The bed was ablaze, as were the drapes on the window. It took him a minute to see—the room was filled with choking smoke, and his eyes were watering. Even vampires were affected by smoke, and Matthew cursed the frailty.

Then he saw them.

Four wolves stood in a semicircle around the corner of the room farthest from the fire. Crouching in the corner, with their baby hugged to her chest, was Octavia. She held her hand over the baby's mouth. Trying to keep the smoke out, Matthew guessed. The baby's fists waved, and she was crying against Octavia's hand.

She was so tiny, so innocent. Octavia was white with fear, trembling.

The beasts had to be werewolves in their animal form. There were four of them, but Matthew had a pistol with a silver ball, stakes, blades.

He was about to find out how strong a vampire was.

"Leave them alone," he said softly.

One of the wolves growled loudly, then barked, and leapt around. The beast was in the air in an instant, with teeth aimed at his throat.

Matthew yanked out the pistol and fired.

The wolf fell to the ground. Its body jerked, then it changed back to human form. Blood flowed out, and the naked man twitched twice.

The other wolves had turned from Octavia and the baby and were inching toward him, hackles raised, growling in their throats. With his pistol spent, he pulled out two knives.

The baby started squalling, but in a weak sort of way, as though the poor thing was already suffering from the smoke. Flaming pieces of the bed canopy dropped to the carpet, which was starting to smolder.

He tried to force his thoughts into Octavia's head. *You and the baby must get out. Start moving toward the door, but behind the wolves.*

She was staring at him, and his heart sank. Apparently, he couldn't speak in her thoughts.

"My lord? Are you in there, my lord? Can we help—?"

It was servants of the inn. "Get out of here!" he roared. "Save yourselves, damn it." They couldn't fight werewolves—they would be torn to bits. And any survivors would probably tear him to bits after this, realizing he was not human. What frightened him more was that they might guess Octavia wasn't a normal countess.

The three wolves launched at him at once. He lashed out with his two knives. Blood sprayed over his shirt, and he'd wounded one in the throat, but not enough—the wolf drove its teeth into his arm. He slashed with one blade and wrenched his arm free, but his forearm was torn open. He could see red flesh, muscle, bone—

Pain lanced him, but he ignored it. He still had a good arm. But he felt a rush of warmth and tingling—the wound was healing.

He punched at the wolves, kicked at them. It was easy to fight them, because he knew they were really human. He couldn't hurt an animal that just needed to eat, but he could kill men who wanted to assassinate an innocent woman and a baby.

He drove his knife into one werewolf's throat. It retreated, and then it turned tail and leapt out the window, through the frame of fire created by the burning drapes.

Then, the other two wolves moved back, barking, preparing to lunge again.

God, Octavia was still there. She was pressed back against the wall, her eyes wide with horror.

Run, he shouted, desperately trying to push his voice into her thoughts. *Take the baby, get to the carriage, and get to safety. You've got to get out of this inn—it's going to burn to the ground. In the carriage, you should be safe.*

"I—How can I hear you?" she cried. "Oh God, I can't leave you to die!"

Thank God it had worked. Or could vampires thank the Lord? *I won't die,* he lied to Octavia, just as one of the wolves leapt at him. Claws swiped, ripping through his coat, his shirt, and leaving four streaks of blood on his chest. He wouldn't die, but he could be destroyed.

"No, I can't let you be hurt. It's my fault—"

Hugging the baby tight to her chest, she held out her hand. A wolf jumped for his throat, but it sailed over his head, skidded across the wood floor, and slammed into the wall. The second wolf suddenly flew out the window.

How had she—?

Damn, it didn't matter. Saving his family did. Matthew ran to her. He gathered their baby out of her arms, then gripped her hand. "We've got to get away. We're going to that damned castle of mine. It may sound like a prison to you, but it will make a damned good fortress."

Matthew found their carriage and dragged it to the entrance to the courtyard of the inn, far from the fire. He ran to the stables. Grooms were bringing out the horses, and it was there he found De Wynter, leading their two mounts outside.

"Where in Hades were you?" Matthew barked. "I was attacked by werewolves."

The golden-haired vampire grinned. "I know. You appeared to be in control of the situation when I saw you from the hallway. I believe Lady Sutcliffe was quite impressed with the way you raced to her rescue like a knight in gleaming armor."

"You left me to fight alone so I could impress my wife." Matthew was sorely tempted to punch De Wynter in the jaw. But he had no time. "Now I have to get her and our child to safety."

De Wynter nodded. "And I will return to London and the Royal Society, to find a way to help you."

* * *

They had been on the road for hours. His chest had healed, but his clothes were soaked with blood. Matthew was afraid for Octavia and the baby. At first, he had been worried that the poor infant had breathed in a dangerous amount of smoke. But now he felt fairly certain his daughter's lungs were all right.

They had made sure the fire was under control at the inn before leaving. Octavia had been wracked with guilt, sure she had caused the fire, so Matthew had given the innkeeper a promissory note to help with the repairs and to purchase the carriage.

"A howling baby makes more noise than barking wolves," he murmured.

"I don't think so," Octavia said thoughtfully. "I think it just bothers us more, because we are parents. It drives us to do something."

She sounded calm, but he saw a tear glitter in her eye. Since they had left the inn, he had held her close. He'd wrapped her and the little baby in one of the fur throws he always kept in the carriage, since she had been forced to flee in her nightdress on a cold November night.

"You're safe now. I promise," he whispered.

"It's not that. I know. You saved our lives, and I am safe—now and always—because I am with you."

Fleetingly he remembered she was supposed to fall in love with him—if she felt safe, it must mean she was opening her heart. For the first time he didn't feel afraid of her love, didn't feel weighted by the responsibility of it. He did, however, feel like a bastard for getting it under false pretenses.

"You saved me, Octavia. The wolves might have overpowered me if you hadn't magically sent them out of the window. Now, if you know you're safe, why are you crying?"

Christ, was it over him? Had she noticed that his wounds had healed with surprising speed? "If you are wondering about my wounds—"

"I did it," she said quickly. "With my magic. I commanded your wounds to heal. It seemed to work."

He breathed a sigh of relief—he'd healed because he was a vampire, but she hadn't suspected. He choked on his sigh when she said, "Our baby must be fed. She's crying with hunger."

He looked at her helplessly, then at her breasts.

She shook her head. "I don't know if I can. When the baby was taken away, my milk stopped coming. I don't know if I can feed my own child," she whispered. "I don't know what we are going to do if I can't."

"You're magical, Octavia. Can you use magic to produce the milk for the baby again?"

Tears dropped off her cheeks. Haggard, despairing, she stared helplessly at him, yet he felt a lot more helpless. He was an earl, he was now immortal, but he had no idea what to do to feed their baby.

"I don't know!" She hiccupped between the words. "My magic never works on me."

"What do you mean?"

"I cannot do things to myself by magic. I can't make myself taller, or change the color of my hair, or make my voice different, or anything like that. I can't make any physical changes to myself. So how could I make the milk come back?"

"Try, love. This magic is for the baby. I believe it will work."

She gave him a wobbly smile. "All right, I'll try."

He watched as she pushed down the blanket, then undid the tie of the neckline of her nightgown. He caught his breath as she exposed her full breast. The baby stopped crying and turned to the nipple. So tiny, yet she knew food was on the offing.

It was the most remarkable and beautiful thing he'd ever seen.

Octavia rubbed the nipple against the baby's mouth. "Women at Mrs. Darkwell's told me how to do this, before she was born."

Speechless with awe, he watched as she tugged their daughter's lower lip down a bit, and the baby latched onto her nipple.

"Beautiful," he whispered.

Octavia looked up with a shy smile. "We must think of a name. I feel so guilty that I haven't given her one. Should we keep the name the family gave her?"

He shook his head. "She is our daughter, and you've moved heaven and earth for her. You should name her, Octavia."

"It should be both of us. A name we both agree on."

"I think we should name her after her remarkable mother."

She blushed. "That's sweet, but I want her to have a name of her very own."

"What name do you like?" he asked.

They debated like that for many minutes, each one telling the other to choose the name, while their daughter drank her fill. Octavia lifted her to her shoulder. "I believe she is now to be burped."

Matthew took their baby and rested her gently against his shoulder. Her little tummy was remarkably round and full.

"You pat the back," Octavia instructed.

He did so, and nothing happened. He tried again, more firmly. Suddenly, a huge belch erupted from the tiny baby, and his back was wet and sticky.

"Oh! A towel. The midwives told me one should use a towel or a blanket."

He grinned ruefully. Still he deserved worse for lying. And their daughter had settled to sleep. "Perhaps we should call her 'Fountain'?"

"We can't! What was your mother's name?"

"No—I won't use my mother's name. My mother ended up so unhappy. I don't want to see my daughter's smiles and remember my mother's broken heart and sorrow and anger. I'd like a pretty name for her . . . hmmm, but not one that encourages rakish men."

She laughed. "Charlotte. I like the name Charlotte."

"I do too. She is the perfect little Lottie."

The carriage stopped so swiftly, Octavia almost fell forward. He caught her and drew her back to the seat. He handed Lottie to her. Then he moved to the carriage door. Rage brought his fangs out. Through the windowpane, in the darkness, he saw two men. Both wore black cloaks; both had white-blond hair that spilled over their shoulders.

One of the men lifted his hand, and suddenly there was a loud thud from the box as if the coachman had fallen, then the horses were free of their traces, running away.

Matthew pushed the carriage door open and jumped down.

He was going to protect Lottie and Octavia. But he couldn't let Octavia know how he was going to do it.

"You cannot go out alone," Octavia cried. "I could use magic. I can help you."

He couldn't let Octavia see how he was going to protect them. "I will be fine. You will stay here and protect our baby."

Werewolves he had been able to fight with brute force . . . and sharp knives.

Male witches were a different breed.

The moment Matthew jumped to the ground, lightning bolts shot through the air toward him. He couldn't let them hit the carriage, so he could not move out of the way.

They slammed into him, but he stood his ground. Amazing—his body withstood the force. He tried to run toward the witches, but they threw everything at him: trees, dirt, waves of wind. He lured their magical strikes away from the carriage.

Searing heat filled his body—no doubt, they were throwing

spells at him to make him burn to dust, but for some reason, their magic didn't work.

He transformed to bat shape and flew through the darkness at an incredible speed. He reached one of the witches unscathed and transformed back instantaneously. He drove his knife into the witch's heart.

Witches were the closest to mortal men. This one fell, clutching the hilt of the knife.

Matthew leapt on the second witch and sank his teeth into the man's muscular neck.

Out of the corner of his eye, he saw the carriage door swing open. Saw a flash of golden hair.

Damnation, Octavia hadn't listened. He tore his teeth free of the witch's neck. *Get back inside,* he roared in her thoughts. *Now!*

His teeth had torn open the man's throat, rendering him helpless.

Octavia drew back at once, and as soon as she couldn't see, Matthew plunged his fangs back into the warlock's throat. Blood rushed out through the wound, filling his mouth. Quickly, he drained his opponent. Sparks of light flew out of the warlock's fingertips. They slammed into Matthew's body, hitting like dozens of hot needles.

But the bolts weren't strong enough to kill him.

He was winning.

Octavia cradled Charlotte to her chest and peeked out of the carriage window. There was no moon, and everything around them was a fathomless black. Through the glass, she couldn't see anything in the dark. Even when she'd opened the door, it had been almost impossible to see.

All she had been able to detect was a male form, which had looked almost ghostly, leaning over a struggling man. Then her husband, who had sounded angry and not wounded, had ordered her to look after Lottie.

She'd hated leaving him out there, but he was right—she had to protect their baby.

And somehow Sutcliffe could see in the dark. He was able to fight. She could tell the three men were battling like madmen by the roars of anger, the flashes of lightning between the trees, the *thud* cracks of punches, the cries of pain.

How had her husband withstood bolts of lightning?

How long could he continue to do it?

She had to try to use a spell and save him—

Then everything went quiet. Plastering her face to the window, she spotted a movement in the dark. The slow steps of a man. He seemed to be prowling carefully toward the carriage.

Her hands shook against Lottie, and she heard a mewling sound of fear escape her baby.

Courage, Octavia.

If only Sutcliffe had let her help him, he wouldn't have been killed. . . .

Now he was *gone*. She'd never known such pain. It gripped her heart and squeezed, stopping a heartbeat, making her dizzy. It slammed onto her shoulders, making her sway. It tightened and dried her throat so quickly, she couldn't draw breath. But it hit her so hard and so fast, she didn't cry.

It was like the horrible moment of waking up and finding her baby gone.

She lifted her right hand, ready to send her power to kill— before she and Lottie were killed. The door swung wide.

Sutcliffe stumbled into the carriage doorway.

He was safe. Dear heaven, he'd survived.

Octavia's knees almost crumpled. She rushed to Sutcliffe, gripped his wrist, and hauled him inside. His clothes were dirty, torn, and half-open. She pushed him onto a seat, then she sat at his side and pressed close to him—as close as she could, for she had to be careful of Lottie.

She lay her head against his chest. "Thank heavens. I thought you were dead. I was so afraid—"

Something dripped on her chest, just above the neckline of her nightdress. A red droplet.

She jerked her gaze up. Blood ran down her husband's lower lip and dripped off his chin.

She stared, horrified. Then she reached up, searching for the wound.

Sutcliffe jerked in surprise, sliding away from her. He swiped away the blood with the back of his hand. "I must have cut my lip. It is superficial, and nothing for you to fret about. I destroyed the two men—male witches."

She nodded. Blood was smeared everywhere on him—in his hair, on his shirt, on his trousers. Closing her eyes, she wished him healed. When she opened her lids, he was gingerly touching his mouth. "The wound is gone. Dawn is close—and we can safely travel in daylight. We are going to head to the castle as quickly as we can."

"How? What of the horses and of the coachman? Was he not killed?"

"No. The witches used a spell to keep him frozen, and he had fallen onto the footrest of the box. The spell was broken as soon as the witches perished. And I was able to round up the horses."

"So quickly—?"

"They had not gone far. Do not worry, you will be safe now." He drew her to him on the seat and adjusted her so she lay on his chest. His strong arm kept her secure, and she cradled Lottie to her.

She closed her eyes.

She was so exhausted, her head felt as if it was stuffed with wool. She was weak with relief, yet ice-cold with fear there might be another attack.

And she was aroused. It was insanity, but she was. Perhaps because she had been afraid she'd lost Sutcliffe, only to get him back.

But she couldn't have sex with him here, now. Not with Charlotte with them. Not when they were hurtling up the Great North Road, seeking his Scottish castle.

She closed her eyes with her cunny aching and her heart pounding.

Next thing Octavia knew, she was in the middle of an orgy, and her husband was stripping off his clothing to join them.

This was the dream his wife wanted to have?

Slumped on the seat of his carriage, with Octavia and his baby sleeping on top of him, Matthew had closed his eyes but he wasn't sleeping—as a vampire he couldn't sleep until dawn came fully. But he was drawn into Octavia's dream.

So he joined her. Just as two young courtesans grasped her by the hands and led her, giggling, to another courtesan and group of three Regency bucks who had just taken off their clothes.

Groups of cavorting peers, rakes, and beautiful light-skirts filled the room. It was an elegant ballroom with a soaring ceiling and six blazing chandeliers. Oval beds had been arranged throughout.

Heat and the smell of sex wrapped around him. Matthew was already naked—Octavia had dreamed his clothes away. Crossing his arms over his bare chest, he decided to watch. His cock felt as if it were watching, the way the head bobbed to and fro.

The three young men bowed over Octavia's hand. She wore a gown of sapphire blue silk, one that made her eyes look as dazzling as a sunny sky. Each quick breath strained her full breasts against the scooped neckline.

He didn't think the lavish kisses the men gave her hand, her fingers, her palm were exaggerated. They were struck by her beauty. And who wouldn't be?

She blushed as they bowed to her. It made their cocks wobble. He wondered if she was noting differences in size and shape of their different equipment, then comparing it to his? He made a good showing, though he would have liked to be the largest. One of the lads was longer, but his cock had a smaller head, thick base, and heavy veins. Not as attractive as his, Matthew thought.

Another young buck had a thicker member, but it stuck out straight forward and looked ungainly. It didn't have the attractive curve and taper of his cock.

The last one was smaller, which gave Matthew a sense of satisfaction, though the lad was good-looking, with blond hair, a thick pelt of it at his crotch, and a body like the statue of David.

Would Octavia want any of them more than him? What if she desired them equally as much as she wanted him? Hell, he had no idea how to cope with this. He just watched her, trying to see if she looked at their naked bodies any differently than she looked at his. . . .

"My name is Desiree," cried one of the courtesans, who had exotic uptilted brown eyes and thick brown hair. "The blond is called Honey, for she is sweet and tempting. The redheaded girl is Flame."

The other two pretty light-skirts, Honey and Flame, curtsied. Octavia curtsied also. In this orgy, only the men were naked. The prostitutes wore elegant gowns. Again, was that his wife's fantasy—where the men were the ones expected to take off clothes?

"Would you like to see what two men can do together?" Flame asked, looking mischievous.

Octavia looked mystified, then smiled. "Ooh, I think I would."

Always the explorer, always curious. It made Matthew smile. He already knew what she would see—what intrigued him was how she would react.

The courtesan pointed at the two youngest men, striplings in their early twenties. Both so young, they had smooth hairless chests formed of lean muscle, tight stomachs that sucked in, prominent hipbones, and the long legs of colts.

Octavia looked entranced as she studied their naked bodies. They stood beside each other, nudging each other, laughing.

Matthew felt an acid spurt of jealousy at her wide-eyed appreciation.

This was a dream; it wasn't real. None of these other people were real. They had been conjured, by her powers, for seduction. He had to remember that, or he'd start punching men right and left for even looking at her.

Matthew waved away a woman who approached him. He just wanted to watch his wife. That was his fantasy at this moment: watching pleasure through Octavia's eyes.

"The gentlemen are Viscount Cayne and Mr. Dashwood. His Lordship has the blond hair, and of course Mr. Dashwood is the dark-haired gentleman," Honey whispered to Octavia. "Lord Cayne is my most favorite gentleman."

Matthew had expected Cayne, who was more slender, more boyish looking, would prove to be the man on the bottom. He was wrong.

Dashwood got on all fours on the bed. Matthew tried to look on the scene and see what Octavia would see. The golden light of the chandeliers accentuated Dashwood's muscular arse and the indents of his haunches. He had well-muscled legs. His hair was black and fell in waves to his shoulders.

All in all, he was a damnably good-looking man.

Octavia was waving a fan before her face. Her cheeks were fetchingly pink as she stared at Dashwood's rump, which was pointing at her. The redhead, Flame, led her around, so she was watching the bed from the side. "A better view," Flame explained.

Cayne mounted from behind, getting on his knees on the bed. It was an ungainly, graceless thing—getting on a bed, holding one's cock down, and aiming it at the orifice on offer. But Octavia looked fascinated. She gasped and squealed as Cayne managed to push his erect prick downward, and got it wedged between Dashwood's tight cheeks.

Matthew let out a low whistle. His wife had a vivid imagination when it came to dreams.

Then he saw her fingers. They had strayed to the bodice of her dress and were gently stroking. She wasn't doing it consciously. Watching the men had inspired her, and she was lightly caressing her breasts.

His cock jumped so smartly it smacked his stomach.

"You will have to wait," he muttered, glancing down at it. "It's too much fun watching her watching them."

Dashwood let out a restrained moan, and Cayne pushed his hips forward. He gripped the hilt of his cock and braced his other hand on the curve of the other man's ass.

Matthew could guess the moment of penetration. Cayne gave a thrust, and Dashwood reacted. His back curved, his hands tightened into fists, and he hissed.

Cayne withdrew, waited, then tried again. The men didn't speak. They knew what to do, and likely conversation felt awkward.

Octavia was panting and fanning herself fiercely. Her hand now cupped her breast.

Then the girls attended to her. Desiree undid Octavia's dress with quick, efficient movements. "Let's get her naked quickly," the dark-haired courtesan giggled.

"Indeed," agreed Flame, who set to work on undoing Octavia's garters, then pulled off her shoes and tugged off her stockings. In minutes, the three girls had her completely nude.

She looked so lush and beautiful after having the baby. Her belly had a slight round, her hips were generous, and she was plumper, which gave her full breasts and sweet thighs.

For several moments, he got to enjoy the sight of three women caressing and kissing his wife. Their clever mouths sucked Octavia's nipples to long, reddened points. She moaned in ecstasy even when they tugged hard. Matthew instinctively gripped his cock when Honey's hand slid into Octavia's nether curls. He could smell his wife's desire.

She was wanton and lovely.

How could he have planned to trap her in his castle, to hide her like a prisoner in a gothic novel?

How could he not do it? Now she was in danger. He had to protect her, and no one knew how to free her from danger. As long as she was the sixth female demon who could take over the world, there would be no real safety for her.

The girls moved away from Octavia, giggling. The third handsome young lord approached. He dropped to one knee, and grasped Octavia's bottom, and pulled her juicy cunny toward his mouth.

Suddenly, Matthew realized what he was watching—another man kissing her sweet cunny.

Hell, no.

He strode to the two of them and pulled Octavia back from the young man's mouth. "I'm cutting in," he growled.

He picked Octavia up, sliding his cock into her with one

thrust. She let her head fall back, moaning loudly. "Oh yes, Sut-cliffe—"

"Matthew."

"Who?"

"Me. I am Matthew." Damnation, he realized he'd never even told her his given name. "Call me that. I was a damned fool to try to close my heart to you, Octavia. I love you."

Guilt speared him, even as he said the words. He was a vampire; he was cursed to die; he needed to make her fall in love with him. Every one of those things made it wrong for him to say those words.

They should mean something. They should be a promise of forever.

But she was wriggling on him, rubbing her cunny along his shaft, and he couldn't think. "You don't need to dream about sex anymore," he said hoarsely. "You can have it whenever you want, with whatever fantasy you want . . . with me."

One thing he'd learned from this dream: He couldn't share her.

Holding her bottom, he thrust into her. Her arms wrapped around his neck, she buried her head against his chest, and they fucked together—

She was coming.

He lost control. Pleasure exploded in him like one of her out-of-control fires. It seared his heart. Holding her, he climaxed in her, and he was so weakened, he had to drop to his knees. At least he didn't drop her.

She moaned and squealed and screamed, but between her lovely, erotic sounds, he caught three distinct words. I. Love. You.

The world was shaking around her. . . .

"Wake up, Octavia."

No, the world wasn't moving—someone was shaking her shoulder, trying to wake her. Her erotic dream was over. Octavia rubbed her eyes. Then she remembered where they were and what had happened before. "Are we in danger?"

She managed to focus on her husband's face. On Matthew's face. She hadn't even known his Christian name, and he'd only been willing to reveal it in a dream.

He gave her a wry smile. "Time to wake up, love. You've slept for almost a whole day, and we've arrived at Castle Grim."

16

In the Depths of the Castle

In the dream, he had said, "I love you." She had said it, too, in the middle of her wild climax. She had opened her heart in those three simple words, and so had he, yet when they had arrived at the castle . . .

As soon as they had entered the soaring entrance hall, her husband had sent his skeleton staff of servants to prepare the nursery for Lottie and to open the master's and mistress's chambers. Then he had sent her to her room to bathe and requested that one of the maids loan her a dress. It was a simple gown, and the maid had been embarrassed to hand it to her, but Matthew had explained they'd lost all their belongings in a fire. Then he had locked himself in his darkened bedroom and had gone to sleep.

He had deserted her, and it was the middle of the afternoon.

That left Octavia surprised, though they were safe and he must be exhausted. She didn't think he had slept at all during the journey back.

She spent her day with Lottie, cuddling her daughter. She had enjoyed her bath, was grateful to wear something other than her scorched and torn nightdress, and had savored the delicious lunch prepared by the castle's kitchen staff.

Charlotte seemed to be healthy, sound, and happy. She waved her fists happily and tried to bite Octavia on her jaw with her toothless mouth, as though hoping there might be milk there.

But as soon as the maids took Lottie to the nursery and she was away from her daughter, fear and doubt took root in her heart. Why had he left her and not let her come to him?

He had said he loved her in her *dream,* not in reality. She had dreamed what she wanted him to say. In reality, he had not opened his heart to her. He had not fallen in love with her. How could he love her when she was a witch? How could he love her when she'd put them in danger? He had risked death for her. Was it possible for a man to ever love a woman who had brought him nothing but trouble?

She didn't know.

Now, with nothing else to do, she set off to explore the castle. He had called it the "Castle Grim," and this was supposed to have been her prison.

Their rooms were in the main part of the house. There were two round towers at each end, with battlements on top. Octavia walked down the immense and seemingly endless hallway. She was alone, but she felt afraid to make any sound.

With stone walls twenty feet thick comprising the outside wall, a drawbridge over a dry moat, then an impregnable house sitting within the courtyard, they should all be safe.

Why, then, was her heart pounding so hard?

She made her way down the grand staircase to the enormous entry. It seemed large enough that a three-mast ship could be dragged in. Plaster had been applied to the stone walls and larger windows had been added, filled with colored, leaded glass. But the floor was made of huge flagstones, and it sent up heavy, echoing thuds when she walked upon it.

A helpful young footman came to her, bowed with a stiff spine, and asked if she required anything.

Safety? Escape? Clothing? Her husband's love?

She was accustomed to running a house, but she gave an awkward "no," and hurried away.

For hours, she wandered through the house. There were hundreds of rooms; some were almost original, with stone walls and tapestries and furnishings that must have been five hundred years old. Others had been modernized and had flocked wallpaper, and dainty furniture, and enormous beds. Even though the castle was rarely used, everything was immaculate.

Then she found a small door, narrow with a pointed top. Pushing through that entry, she found she was in one of the towers.

Octavia made her way gingerly up the winding stair. There was no banister or railing. The steps hugged the wall, spiraling up. If she slipped, she would fall to her death.

When she reached the end of the stair, she faced a door. It proved to be locked. Rather than worry about finding keys, she simply commanded the lock to open, using her powers. Though it took a push of considerable strength to make the heavy, reluctant door open.

Octavia held the door, then peeped around it.

It was a gentleman's room, but decorated in an Arabic style. The bed was a large oval, the cover trimmed with gold and glittering jewels. The sun was setting, and the red-gold light leapt off the facets of the gems.

Curtains that were cinched with ties surrounded the bed. There were no chairs, just voluptuous cushions, all covered in silk.

There was a dresser with a mirror that was encrusted with a decorative mosaic and depicted a sultan amidst his harem.

Whose room had this been?

Had it been her husband's?

Octavia crept to the dresser as if she were committing a crime by walking into the room. Silly. She straightened her shoulders, strode to the beautiful piece, and opened drawers.

In the first she found a journal. Her husband's name was scrawled on the first page, but there were no entries.

Then she found a bundle of letters tied with a scarlet ribbon. They had to be love letters. Did she really want to see who had written love letters to her husband?

Damning herself, she untied the ribbon. The letters spilled onto the marble top of the dresser. She picked up one, and it unfolded as she lifted it.

Startlingly familiar handwriting stared her in the face.

Confused, icy-cold and sweating hot at the same time, she looked down at the signature. It was just one name. *Mellelle.* She recognized it—that had been a pet version of her mother's middle name, Amelia, that she remembered her mother's family using. No one else of the *ton* would know it, so using it would keep her mother's identity a secret.

Her mother had written letters to *Sutcliffe?* To . . . Matthew? She jerked her eyes to the top of the letter.

My dear Frederick, it said. And the date . . . Sutcliffe was six years older than she was. He would have been a boy when this had been written.

A glance at the address revealed the truth. Her mother had written letters to Matthew's father, the previous earl. Octavia quickly read the first one. In it, her mother had begged Matthew's father to forget her, insisting that she would not have an affair with him.

Octavia swallowed hard. Her mother's letters revealed how desperately in love Matthew's father had been. His father had killed himself over a woman he had loved but could not have.

Heavens, had that woman been her mother?

* * *

"What are you doing in the dungeon, darling wife?"

Octavia spun around on her heel, aware she had been staring at one of the walls of this bizarre cell without seeing a thing.

Her husband—Matthew—leaned against the door frame. He wore a shirt, open at his throat, breeches, and polished black boots. The heavy door with iron hinges and grille stood open, throwing light from torches into the room. The torches— and fires—warmed this place, keeping out the wintery cold.

She pointed. "When I saw the lit torches I had to investigate. This place is . . . like the perfect setting for a gothic novel."

"You aren't going to be the imprisoned heroine."

She remembered what he had told her about his father— how he had taken his own life over his unrequited love. Matthew did not know it was over her mother.

What was the point of telling him?

At least she had pushed her mother's letters back into her pocket when she'd come down to the basement of the castle— to the stone corridors and dungeon-like cells. Once she had squinted in the shadows of this creepy place, she'd realized she wouldn't be able to read a word.

She looked at him as placidly and innocently as she could. "Your ancestors kept prisoners here?"

"Perhaps not just my ancestors." He moved to a set of iron shackles on the wall and closed one of the iron cuffs around his wrist. "Do you remember tying me to the bed?"

She goggled at him. "You would make love to women down here?"

He laughed. "Actually, I never have. Dank and cobwebs aren't my particular fantasy."

"Are they anyone's fantasy?" she asked, mystified.

"I'm not a great connoisseur of people's sexual predilections, but I've seen a few curious ones. Some people like to be abused."

She shuddered.

"Mrs. Hastings, the housekeeper, said you had gone up into the tower. To my father's rooms."

"There is a housekeeper? I haven't seen her yet." She spoke to distract him, but then, she hadn't asked, had she? She had wanted to hide away from everyone.

"That used to be my room. When my parents were battling, I wanted to be as far away as possible. So I decided to use the tower room, and decorated it in the most exotic way I could. I was a boy, dreaming of adventure."

"It is a beautiful room. I thought it was yours. I found—"

"You found letters to my father, didn't you? I do not know who the woman 'Mellelle' was. His love for her was the reason he killed himself."

It was over her mother. Oh, she didn't want to talk about this. "I should go upstairs—I should speak with the house-keeper, be introduced to the servants. I've been derelict in my duties as mistress of the house."

She didn't know why she had been skulking around the castle. They had been attacked, but it wasn't as if she were leaping at her own shadow. . . .

She had wanted to be alone, just as she'd been when she ran away. She had been afraid his servants would guess her secret. That she would start a fire by accident, or break a mirror, or send dishes hurtling through the air.

She didn't . . . fit in anymore.

How could she live in a castle amongst normal, human people, when werewolves and warlocks were trying to attack her? What if her powers did something unexpected? What if she did start another fire?

What if she hurt Lottie . . . by accident?

Maybe she shouldn't be a prisoner in a castle—maybe what she should be was alone. Completely alone. Where she couldn't bring danger to anyone, and where her powers couldn't hurt anyone.

What would the servants do if they learned she was a witch? Would they turn on her and kill her to protect themselves?

"What's wrong? You're white as a sheet." Matthew caught her just as her feet and legs suddenly felt weightless beneath her.

"I don't know," Octavia mumbled. "I've been wandering the castle, hiding from people. I'm afraid. I'm a witch—If people knew, they would lock me up in a place like this. They would burn me at the stake."

"Shh." Matthew cradled her to him and kissed the top of her head. "None of those things will happen to you. I will protect you with my life."

As Matthew said the words, he realized he actually had done that. He had given up his life in his hunt for Octavia. He would willingly be clawed apart by werewolves, ripped to pieces by a vampire, blasted by a warlock's spell, if he could guarantee her safety.

After losing Gregory, he'd vowed never to open his heart to pain again. As for love, he had seen how it destroyed a man— he'd had the evidence of his father's suicide.

What he hadn't expected was that love—and this had to be insane, mad love—made a man willing to face destruction. In their shared dream, he'd told her he loved her. It was the truth.

He needed her now. He yearned for her.

This wasn't a hunger for blood—he had quenched that last night with the warlocks.

This was something deeper. The vampire queen had told him he had a soul, but right now, all he felt inside was empty.

He loved his wife; but he had no right to take her love. Not without giving her the truth. She feared that people would destroy her for what she was.

Once she learned he was a vampire, she would hate and fear him. He could not lie, cheat, win her heart under false pretenses. It would not win him his life, his soul, and his freedom because she would find out the truth and hate him.

Matthew lifted Octavia into his arms. As a vampire, he now had incredible strength, and he wanted to use it for loving, not fighting. He undid his trousers with one hand. She tugged up her skirts.

He backed against one of the rough stone walls, so that he could brace himself and lift her lush bottom up and down.

Her skirts were all the way up, and she wrapped her legs around his hips. She wore sensible woolen stockings—a maid's—but her creamy thighs were naked. And no drawers, so the head of his rock-hard cock brushed springy curls, then sticky lips.

He pushed inside her and she rocked on him, taking him deep.

They made love wildly. He moved her around the dungeon, driving his cock up into her, falling back against the walls as his legs weakened with pleasure.

She covered him with kisses. She wrapped her legs tight around his hips, and when she came, she hammered his ass with her heels.

He intended to hold on, but this was so fierce, wild, erotic. A searing heat shot through him as he slammed back against the wall, braced his shoulders against it, then fucked her with long, slow, agonizing strokes.

Her eyes rolled back. "Oh, oh, oh, oh," she cried. Her hands clutched his shoulders, slapped his chest, and her head lolled.

Then she screamed with pleasure and his control snapped.

He came so hard, his legs gave out, and he sank to the floor with Octavia on top.

She took quick breaths. "It appears cobwebs and dust are not so terrible, and your castle is not so grim after all," she gasped.

He laughed.

"This is my fault," she whispered. "You are trapped here now because of me."

"Love, I feel like I've been trapped in the dark, and you've brought me light. I was afraid to love anyone after I lost my father and after I had to kill my brother. But I love you.

"What happened to Gregory was my fault," he continued. "It unleashed a demon—the one who is hunting for you now. Her name is Esmeralda, and she wants to rule the world—"

"Yes, Mrs. Darkwell told me everything."

"I love you, Octavia. It's the truth. But I don't deserve you."

Hours later, she found her husband standing on the top of the tower—she had discovered another set of stairs that led from his old bedchamber to the roof.

It was twilight. The sky was slate-blue, streaked with indigo and purple clouds. Snow lay on the ground in patches, and her breath misted in the air. She wore a fur cloak that had been found and provided for her.

Matthew leaned on one of the crenellations at the edge of the tower, resting on his elbows. His shirt was out of his trousers, flapping in the wind. It was open at his throat. His sable brown hair was tossed by the breeze.

Octavia came up behind him and wrapped her arms around him. She pressed her chest against his back. His skin was cool to her touch. "I'm the one who doesn't deserve you. I'm a witch, and I've brought you into danger. And you should not be out in the cold."

"The cold does not bother me. The danger is my fault," he growled. "If I hadn't freed Esmeralda, who is determined to rule the world, no one would be hunting for you. There's more, Octavia—" He broke off, and pushed her to the side, so she was behind the taller section of stone.

"Stay there. Stay behind the stone."

"What is it?" she whispered. Pressing close to the stone, she peeked through the open space intended for archers to fire.

Light—the faint light left in the sky—reflected off something in the trees. She heard a series of muted growls, as if an entire pack of wolves was in the woods, watching and waiting. "It's werewolves, isn't it?"

"Yes, and they aren't alone. There are a lot of beings out there. A lot of different smells."

Smells? She couldn't smell anything.

Matthew had closed his eyes and frowned, as though he was thinking hard. "The servants," he muttered. "We don't have much weaponry, and there are few men on the estate, but we have no other choice. We have to fight."

The last glow of sunlight disappeared, and the sky turned a dark purple. Then the moon brightened, and she could see as moonlight illuminated the forest.

Beings were moving. She heard growls and grunts. Between the dark tree trunks, flames flickered. The light made shiny scales glow, revealed wings and tails.

"Dragons," he said tersely. "Along with vampires, werewolves, and warlocks. They've grouped to attack."

Like an army of powerful, unimaginable beasts. Octavia closed her eyes, and she held up her hands, and she willed a huge wind to blast at the trees.

She hadn't been able to stop the warlocks from attacking her husband, but her powers could not fail her now.

They didn't. She felt the wind sucking at her as it left her and rushed down the wall. She screamed as she was almost pulled off the edge of the wall.

Matthew grabbed her around the waist.

But she didn't stop the wind from flying over them. She envisioned all the beasts flying through the air, being carried miles away, tumbling through the air.

With a roar, the wind she'd created hit the trees.

Just as she had imagined, hundreds of dark forms flew through the air, silhouetted against the sky.

But some held on to trees and stood their ground.

Howling with fury, the remaining creatures rushed at the stone surrounding the castle bailey.

The wall held most of them off, but then something ripped the drawbridge out of the wall, and ran inside. It was heading toward the bailey—toward their fortified home. Octavia didn't know what it was, but she heard it roaring. She had run along the battlements, and now she must use her magic to fly across the courtyard to their house. Below, servants were flooding out of the house, armed with axes, pistols, swords. They ran toward the wooden drawbridge that had been torn off. But Matthew had few men on the estate, and whatever the beast was that had gotten through, it crashed through his small army of servants, knocking them over like skittles.

Men screamed and fell. Their faces and chests were slashed.

"Octavia, stop!" From behind, Matthew grabbed her.

Octavia tried to wrench free. "Lottie," she screamed. "There are only two nurses watching her. She's in danger. I must get back to our house."

Matthew released her. "Stay up here; you should be safe."

He ignored her protests and left her. He ran as fast as he could along the wall to the stairs that led through the wall to the courtyard. As soon as he reached the ground, he transformed into the shape of a bat. It was dark; Octavia wouldn't be able to see him, and he had to get to Lottie as quickly as he could.

He swooped across the yard and flew up the side of their fortified house. He flew through the window of the nursery. Glass shattered; wood splintered. Charlotte was howling, waving her fists and kicking in the bassinet. A man stood over the baby. Instantly, Matthew took in every detail of the naked man with large muscles, black hair on his head and his body, and the wickedly lethal-looking set of fangs.

Then he returned to the form of a man, launched through the air, and tackled the werewolf to the floor.

The beast sank teeth into his shoulder and tore off some skin. Matthew howled in anger, but the werewolf had incredible strength. The huge man dragged Matthew's arm behind his back. It broke like a snapped twig.

It healed almost as quickly, working perfectly as he threw punch after punch at the beast's jaw, ears, nose. Claws shredded his clothing, leaving gouges that stung with pain. Then he went to punch the werewolf in the stomach but it moved, faster than he could.

Teeth snapped at his chest, the tips plunged, but he threw the werewolf off before his heart was torn out.

The werewolf fell to the floor with a thud that shook the bassinet. Lottie shrieked. He had to get rid of the assassin. And Lottie, fortunately, was too little to understand what he was going to do.

He lunged and bit the beast in the throat.

Strong arms threw him off, but his teeth had opened wounds. Blood flowed down the werewolf's neck.

The rich, heavy, metallic tang of it filled the air of the nursery. The scent overpowered him. It made his body shake and shudder. Shooting pain raced from his fangs through his head.

Hunger . . . all he could think of was sating his damned hunger.

Roaring, he plunged his teeth in again, into the neck of the beast who'd intended to hurt or steal his daughter. A river of blood was released by his teeth, filling his mouth.

He reveled in it. It felt good to suck the life out of this monster.

The werewolf writhed in his arms, his muscles trembling and popping under Matthew's tense grip. Matthew moved his hands off the body as it shifted shape, but he kept his fangs sunk deeply into the neck.

Legs transformed from human to animal; muscular arms became legs with paws. Though the beast writhed to escape his teeth, his vampire strength made it impossible for any prey to break free without ripping its neck open.

This is for coming for an innocent baby, he growled in his thoughts.

A girl child must die, along with the succubus, the werewolf snarled in return. *Destroy me, but it won't end. There'll be more. They will both die—*

Matthew jerked his fangs along the neck, slicing the throat of the assassin who was halfway between man and wolf. In his peripheral vision, he saw Octavia rush in and scoop Lottie out of the bed. She hugged their child to her and backed toward the door.

"Matthew—?" she whispered.

Horror made her tones soft and raspy. He knew—he could hear it. But he couldn't stop. He drank the rest of the creature's blood, then let the drained body flop to the floor. Blood soaked the carpet and floor. Toys and tiny chairs had been scattered in their struggles; things had been broken.

His daughter's bedroom had been desecrated.

Slowly he stood, towering over his fallen victim, and he brushed his hand across his mouth, wiping off blood with a quick sweep.

Tears rushed down Octavia's cheeks. "You saved her. You saved our baby's life. But you—" Her voice died away, and he heard the sound she made—a smothered gasp of shock and pain.

There was no hiding the truth now. She had seen his mouth fastened on the man's neck. Blood was everywhere. It had squirted so fast he hadn't been able to drink it all. Red was smeared on his hands, had soaked his cuffs, dripped from his lips.

"How," her voice came, as a tiny squeak, "did you do that?"

"Now you know the truth about me," he answered grimly. He took a step toward her, and his heart fractured as he saw her clutch Lottie more tightly to her breast. Octavia shuffled back as though she wasn't even aware she wanted to escape him.

Matthew glanced out the window. His servants were fighting off the vampires and shape-shifters. Another great gust came, and it formed into a maelstrom. His servants retreated, and the whirling wind picked up the enemy and carried them away.

The attack was over.

Matthew gave a hollow smile. "I'm a vampire."

17

Hell and Back

He had thought she would run from him, or try to stake him in the heart, or use her magic to throw him out the window, as she'd done with the other monsters.

Matthew watched Octavia as she laid Lottie in the bassinet. He'd commanded it be brought to Octavia's bedroom, while the nursery was cleaned. The cleaning had been done by Octavia's magic. She had made mops and water-filled buckets appear, and had used her powers to make those things clean the bloodstains. Then, with some whispered words and a wave of her hand, she'd sent the fallen body of the werewolf tumbling through the air to land with his companions.

Her magic was growing more powerful.

Even with the nursery clean, neither of them had wanted to stay in it. They hadn't wanted to try to put Charlotte to sleep there.

"Now I understand—so many things are explained," Octavia said softly, as she moved away from the bassinet, toward him. "The blood on your lips when you chased the male witches—it wasn't your blood, from a wound; it was *their* blood. This is why you left me this afternoon when we came here—

you had to sleep. It must have been hurting you to stay awake in the day. . . ."

"Yes, all that is true," he said humbly.

"Why—why didn't you tell me the truth?" she whispered.

"You seduced me without telling me who you were," he pointed out. They had both made mistakes.

But his words made her go pale. "So you mean because of that, we should never have to tell each other the truth, or trust each other?"

"No." He groaned. "I thought you would run from me, if I told you; that you would be terrified. Yet you aren't afraid of me."

"We've been together for days. I expect if you wanted to drink my blood, you would have done so."

But she didn't know how much he had craved her blood. It was only because he'd sated his appetite on warlocks and were-wolves that he had been able to last.

What would he do when he had no assassins to kill and feed from? What if they were here for days, hiding inside for safety? He would have no source of blood.

He wouldn't be able to deny the hunger.

But he now had less than one week before he would be destroyed.

Octavia had said those remarkable words: *I love you.* But it was before she knew he was a vampire. Now that she did know, he had not changed back to a mortal. Was it because he hadn't really captured her heart and her love?

The way she glared at him now, he guessed she wasn't in love with him

Lottie fussed, letting out little squeaks and squawks in her bassinet. Octavia leaned over her at once. Matthew stayed where he was—Octavia's anger and disappointment with him felt like a wall around his daughter's bed. He felt that he had no right to go to her.

He had betrayed Octavia's trust. He could understand why

she hadn't told him her identity: She had needed sex to survive; she'd chosen him to give it to her, and she'd known he wouldn't do it if he'd known he was ravishing a virgin.

Her life had depended on it.

So did his; he could only save his life if he won her love.

Matthew looked over at mother and daughter—his wife and child—and he'd never felt so alone. That was what he'd vowed he would be. Alone, with his heart untouched.

Now, if he got his wish and ended up that way, he would welcome destruction.

He prayed Charlotte was so young, she wouldn't understand or remember the carnage in the nursery.

Suddenly Lottie lifted her legs. She gave a funny smile, with her brows pulled down in a serious frown. Then a loud squirting sound came, along with the ripe smell of a baby's excrement.

Lottie glowed with peaceful delight, then she frowned again, and there came more squirting and more smell.

Octavia looked to him. "We must change her."

Knowing she wanted him to help was like a weight lifting from his heart. He'd never felt happier in his life—or in his undead existence. He'd never dreamed he would feel such joy at the prospect of dealing with his daughter's soiled nappy.

It meant Octavia might still care for him.

Or, he thought ruefully, she just didn't enjoy dealing with an infant's smelly mess. He had to know. "Do you think you could find it in your heart to forgive me? I should have been honest with you."

She gazed at him, and he saw so much wisdom in her eyes, he was stunned. In just months, she seemed to have gone from an impulsive girl to a strong woman.

"I'm a witch," she said. "That would terrify most people, but you have accepted my powers all along. You have never run away from me because of what I am. You even married me after

I told you how sex with you had saved me. You should have thought I was insane, but you listened to me. I'm not going to run away from you because you are a vampire."

Her strength and courage shook him to his core. He was the most fortunate of men to have her forgiveness, to have such a remarkable, beautiful wife.

His father had told him that love was a dangerous thing, that it couldn't be trusted, that it always betrayed a man.

His father . . . Hell, he was beginning to think his father had been wrong.

Octavia wasn't betraying him. He was the one doing it to her. He still wasn't telling her all the truth. He couldn't. How could he tell her he was condemned to die, that he needed her love, that if she did not love him despite being a vampire, he would be destroyed?

All his life, he'd been afraid that love could hurt him.

The curse was proof that love was the only thing that could save a man.

For the first time since she'd had her daughter back, she was able to change Lottie's nappy and her swaddling blanket in only a few minutes, instead of a quarter of an hour.

Octavia saw Matthew watching her as she laid the little bundle that was Lottie on the soft sheets in the bassinet. He was smiling a sweet and adoring smile. She smiled as well—she could not help it.

"Success," she whispered. "All clean and changed."

"I think we just might get the hang of this business after all," he said.

That made her smile all the more, a grin that came from her heart.

Gently, he set the bassinet swinging. "She's gone back to sleep, Octavia," he said softly.

Octavia watched her husband watch their baby. His smile

brought out the dimple in his cheek. His eyes glowed with warmth. It wasn't because they were a vampire's eyes reflecting light—they were brilliantly illuminated from within.

Matthew looked happy, and he had once told her he was incapable of love or happiness.

But then his smile faded. Her heart gave a nervous lurch. He had looked as if he'd forgotten about pain and guilt for a few seconds, then it came rushing back. The haggard look returned to his silvery blue eyes. Lines formed across his brow and around his tense mouth.

"Do you think it is over?" she asked. "Do you think we've driven the assassins away?"

He shook his head. "I'm afraid not. But you need to sleep tonight. Don't worry—I'll be awake to watch over you."

She sank down onto the bed. She wrapped her arms around her knees. "Would you come to bed?"

He cocked his head. How vulnerable he looked. "You want me to?" he asked. "Even though I was an idiot who didn't tell you the truth?"

"I need you. I—I want you." It was the truth. She needed him—she was beginning to feel weak and dizzy. But she wanted him for more than just sex. She wanted him to hold her. She ached to hold him.

She had run away thinking she could survive alone. Perhaps she could; using her powers she could protect herself. But she didn't *want* to be alone any longer.

She glanced up at Matthew. Her breath vanished. It left her so fast she almost fell off the bed.

He was naked. In a heartbeat, he'd stripped off his clothes.

He padded to the bed. When Matthew felt guilty, he always left her, Octavia realized. So if he was returning to bed, this had to be good. He was opening his heart. He was capable of love and happiness. She was going to be patient and keep stoking that warmth growing in his heart.

Assuming they both lived long enough.

She wouldn't think of that. Right now, she couldn't. Right now she needed happiness and . . . and pleasure. She needed it as if it were as potent as a drug.

Using her powers, she had her clothes off in an instant, too. Octavia slid under the covers as her husband lifted them to get underneath. She rolled to him, but he tucked the sheets and counterpane beneath her chin.

"Sleep," he urged. "Lottie will want to be fed soon. When she wakes, I'll bring her to you. It's one of the advantages of being a vampire and a father."

Matthew gave a rueful smile and held out his arm, so she could snuggle in his embrace.

But it wasn't enough. Octavia climbed on top of him, saw his brows shoot up. She was so aroused, and so was he—his cock slid in her tight passage as soon as she straddled him.

"I have to make love," she whispered. "I need it—and right now, I am very glad you stay up all night. For I think I'll need to do this for *hours*."

She had indeed done it for hours, exhausting him to his core, but leaving him almost drunk with pleasure and sensual satisfaction. His cock was limp, his heart was thundering, and he had never felt like this. They were in danger; he felt actually . . . content.

And finally, Octavia was asleep.

Matthew eased away from her. She had snuggled her bottom against him. She needed to sleep, and he had to go.

But she lay on top of his arm.

He wished he had magic powers, to lift her so he could escape without waking her. Matthew used his superior speed to slide his arm out from beneath her.

She woke. She blinked, then frowned. "You're leaving?"

"You aren't to leave these rooms, my dear. It would be too risky. Stay locked in here, with Lottie."

Eyes wide, Octavia sat up, the sheets tumbling off her full breasts. Matthew saw her dusky nipples and swallowed hard. His cock bucked against his belly. He really wanted to rejoin her in bed. He couldn't.

"Where are you going?"

"To ensure you and Lottie are safe. I'm going to end this."

"How?" she gasped.

"That's what I intend to find out. They're going to hunt us forever, unless I can find a way to end this. I'm going to find De Wynter."

"You're going to travel all the way to London?"

"One advantage to being a vampire: I can transform into the shape of a bat and fly there in a few hours. But you must stay inside, stay here and be safe."

The sun was setting.

Holding Lottie tightly to her chest, wrapped in a thick fur throw, Octavia ventured as close to the battlements as she dared. She half crouched behind the tall part of the crenellations and peeped over the stone ledge. A cold wind whipped through the slot intended for archers. It whirled across the tower's roof. She was afraid if she went any closer she would be shot by an arrow, hit by a warlock's spell, or the wind would drag her baby from her arms.

Eyes glinted below in the dark of the forest. It was almost nightfall. An entire day had gone by.

Matthew hadn't returned, but the assassins had.

She had tried to send the fierce wind again to blow the assassins away, but it had hit the trees and then rushed around the men hiding in the forest, leaving them untouched.

She had tried to throw anything she could think of at them.

In desperation, she'd tried to start the woods on fire. Nothing had worked.

She had thought her powers were growing stronger. Now, when she desperately needed them, they had failed her.

Where was Matthew? Was he dead—or whatever it was called when a vampire ceased to exist? Or was he still in London with De Wynter, while she and her daughter were trapped here?

She believed he would have raced back at once to protect her and Lottie.

He must be in trouble. Or he must be destroyed.

The thought made her shake with horror and pain. Blinding, stinging tears leapt to her eyes. They blurred her vision when she needed to see. She felt weak. Her faulty powers had drained her strength.

She felt completely drained by the thought that she would never see Matthew again.

She *couldn't* have lost him now, when she finally knew how much she loved him.

Heavens, she couldn't have lost him when, without him, she and Lottie had no hope.

The monsters were emerging from the woods, massing at the edge of the dry moat that ringed the castle walls.

Without her magic, there was nothing to stop them—

My dear Lady Sutcliffe, if you want to find out how to free yourself, let me speak to you.

Octavia whipped around, crouched behind the battlements. Lottie was pressed to her shoulder, whimpering, smacking Octavia with her small fists. There was no one else up here. Yet she'd heard Mrs. Darkwell's voice, quietly, as if the woman had whispered in her ear.

But who was she to doubt magic?

You can hear my voice in your head, my lady. You caused me quite a bit of bother. When you ran away that night, my house burned to the ground.

"Did I hurt anyone?" she whispered in horror at the thought of what she'd done. "Did the girls escape the fire?"

They did. But your magic started that fire because of your strong emotions. As you are learning, you cannot yet control your magic. Let me help you. We need to set you free from these assassins. We can do that by destroying the woman who wants to use you to enslave the world. Help me to do this, and I'll help you. You need to learn how to live in the world, not hide from it. Lord Sutcliffe is not the right gentleman for you.

"He is my husband, and I love him!" she cried to the dying light. The wind whisked her words away, throwing them over the trees. Below, the army of beasts and warlocks were grouped at the edge of the dry moat, in the shadow of the forest. Some were leaping over the moat. Vampires changed into bats and began to circle. They were staying in the shadow. As soon as the sun dropped and darkness fell, they would attack.

But my husband is gone, she added, in her head. Saying it aloud would make it too real—she might lose control over her emotions.

He left you now, when you are danger, Mrs. Darkwell accused.

"He went to the Royal Society," she whispered. "He hasn't come back."

He won't. He cannot. Even if he were alive, he would never make it in time. He had to know that. He deserted you. Abandoned you.

"He didn't. I don't believe it!"

If he put himself at risk of destruction, if he is dead now, he abandoned you. Even if he had lived, and you were not hunted, do you truly think he would not make you a captive here? He would do it for your own good—that's what he would tell you.

Even if he did not keep you a prisoner, what would you have done when he went away for months or years on his travels and adventures? You would be alone.

"None of that matters if he's dead." Octavia sobbed each word out.

I will take you, and you will fall in love with another.

"I won't! I have to escape, but I have to protect my child and the servants. And Matthew . . . What if he is alive and is coming back? He will need my magic." She didn't care about love. All she wanted was Matthew safe.

Look in your heart. Do you really believe he is coming back? Or does your heart know he is gone?

"I—" That was the worst. When she searched her feelings, all she found was emptiness. She didn't have hope.

Without love, you will die. You must listen to me. Your husband is cursed. I have learned this, and I must tell you what this means. He is cursed to die unless he wins a woman's love. Your love. He doesn't love you; he hasn't changed. He is still arrogant, and he would still keep you as a prisoner. But he will die in days if he does not lie to you and make you believe he loves you.

"That—that can't be true."

The wind suddenly swirled in a maelstrom in the center of the roof. It threw up dust and dirt and small stones. Then the funnel of debris fell, and Mrs. Darkwell stood there.

The last golden light disappeared from the sky.

Mrs. Darkwell held out her hand. It was bare, pale, elegant. "Take my hand. Come. You must come with me. Your magic won't work. The warlocks are combating it."

Without magic, she could do nothing against dozens of vampires, warlocks, shape-shifters. "But what of the people in the castle? They will all be killed."

Mrs. Darkwell grasped her by the wrist. "Close your eyes. It is like falling into a dream."

"No—" Octavia began. But then darkness swallowed her up. She clung to Lottie, and then she was falling through space.

Hours earlier in London

"We have hunted all over England for the vampiress Esmeralda. We have not been able to find her."

Matthew growled in frustration as Lord Eastworth, a member of the Royal Society, explained why they had failed. He was stunned that a society of vampire slayers would welcome vampires, but he'd learned that not only was Sebastien de Wynter a vampire, so was Yannick De Wynter, Sebastien's brother and the Earl of Brookshire.

"All six women are needed." Matthew paced. "That is what Guidon told me."

De Wynter perched on the corner of the large meeting table in the private office. His brother, the Earl of Brookshire, sat at the head of the table, presiding over this reporting of what the Society had accomplished.

Which was nothing.

"How can she be hiding so well from us?" Brookshire leaned back, scrubbed his jaw.

"What about the London house?"

"She abandoned it after you escaped, Sutcliffe. The six demonesses were also gone."

Matthew slammed his foot into the wall. Then he staggered back, realizing he had drilled a round, deep hole through plaster and lath. "I need to find her. If we destroy Esmeralda, then Octavia will be free."

"She won't." De Wynter spoke in grim tones. "Another vampiress will step into Esmeralda's place, because she will then be the strongest female vampire. She will absorb Esmeralda's power and become stronger."

Matthew's heart sank. "If there were some way to set Octavia free from being a succubus, the way I can escape the curse. If she were no longer a succubus, she couldn't use her power to rule the world. She couldn't turn males into slaves, so there would be no reason to kill her."

Silence greeted his words.

Finally Brookshire said, "It is a brilliant idea, but—"

"Go to the devil," De Wynter interrupted.

Matthew jerked to face the vampire, his hands fisted. "What the hell—?"

"I meant it literally, not as an insult," De Wynter said, grinning. "If your wife serves the devil, you need to go to him to have her set free."

It was damned hard to accept that Octavia served Satan, but as a succubus that was what she did. "All right. So how do I get to the devil?"

"What we have to do is find someone who did it before—and survived."

If he could free Octavia from being a succubus, the assassins would leave her alone. She would be free. But it was almost dawn. At nightfall, the beasts would be back, and he had to be there to protect her and Lottie.

"Let's go then," Matthew said. "We have to find a way to Hell and back."

Blackness changed to a purple-colored mist that swirled around her. Octavia felt uneven softness beneath her feet, and smelled grass and the perfume of blossoms. In her arms, Lottie bumped her thumb against her lip, then sucked on it, and she didn't make a sound.

The mists cleared, revealing a beautiful garden. Octavia stood on a grassy path with roses on both sides of her, so tall she couldn't see beyond them.

"After the London house burned down, my patron, the duke, let us use this cottage on one of his estates."

The soft voice belonged to Mrs. Darkwell.

Cradling her baby, Octavia turned. Instead of her normal black gown and pelisse, the woman wore a flowing Grecian gown of white. It was a mystical fabric—almost translucent—and the hem floated in the air, dancing on an imaginary breeze around her bare calves. Her hair was loose, pouring in silky waves down her back.

Mrs. Darkwell smiled. "For one moment, I wanted to be as I used to be. That is all I receive: a few seconds of pleasure, before I have to change back into a staid, corseted Englishwoman."

In the blink of an eye, her white dress was replaced with her ordinary clothes. And the garden and sunshine vanished, replaced by a wintery scene at twilight.

Octavia stared. "How did you bring us here? Are you a witch?"

"Oh no, Lady Sutcliffe, I am not a witch."

"What are you then?"

"Fallen. What I am is ruined and fallen, but in a different way than what you would understand."

"What do you mean?" Octavia demanded. "I am tired of cryptic answers. I am tired of feeling—feeling as if there is something I should know, but that I don't." She stalked to the nearest now bare rose bush, and she broke off the rose hip, the remainder of a dead flower. A thorn tore into her bare hand, raising a line of blood droplets. "How did we travel from a castle in Scotland to here instantaneously? How could I be a witch without knowing I was? How is my husband cursed?"

Mrs. Darkwell smiled. She patted her pinned hair, ensuring it was in place. "Let us have a cup of tea, and we will talk."

"This time, I want my questions answered," Octavia warned.

She followed Mrs. Darkwell on a path that wound through the wintery gardens—with evergreen shrubs, skeletal trees, and dead flowers. Eventually the path gave out onto a small lawn dusted with snow. In the center of the stretch of white, a manor house sat upon a raised knoll. Octavia turned. Several hundred yards away, on higher ground, stood an enormous house. Given its grandeur, it must be the duke's estate house.

Feminine laughter rose—Octavia saw a group of Mrs. Darkwell's young ladies. They were hurrying inside, and were dressed in cloaks and boots, with hands tucked into fur muffs. She recognized Ophelia's pale blond curls, sticking out from her bonnet.

Octavia followed Mrs. Darkwell into the house.

They went into a parlor that looked like an iced cake. The colors were all pastel shades; the chairs were white and gilt, and covered in pink, pale blue, and mint green silk cushions. A large, cheery fire blazed, filling the room with warmth.

Mrs. Darkwell rang a bell, and a young maid appeared at once. "Take the baby up to the nursery."

Octavia shook her head. "I don't want to let her out of my sight."

"She will be safe, and there are two nurses there to care for her. Besides, you might find it easier to speak of matters without the baby."

It was true, even though she was sure Lottie wouldn't understand anything. She handed Charlotte, who was sleeping, to the maid. The young girl smiled and made cooing sounds and carried her baby away.

Mrs. Darkwell sat down, but Octavia couldn't. She paced in front of the window with its view of the dark gardens and the large house.

"There are two very important things about your husband that you must know. Firstly, he is a vampire—"

"I know. I discovered it for myself."

Mrs. Darkwell nodded, with one brow raised in disapproval. "You found out by accident. He wanted to hide the truth. He did not tell you first."

"Yes, but—"

"Are you willing to forgive him for knowingly putting both you and your baby in danger? *You* were honest with him."

"Not quite," Octavia said. Heavens, she sounded mulish and defensive. "I ran away from him. I can understand why he didn't tell me. He feared I would reject him." She turned and stalked toward Mrs. Darkwell, hands on her hips. "These are not the answers I want—"

"This might not be what you wish to hear, but it is what you need to know. Lady Sutcliffe, a woman's soul mate trusts her. Sutcliffe does not—he cannot truly open his heart to anyone, and that will destroy you. I told you that you need love. If he is not destroyed, if he returns to you, can you truly tell me you can survive in a shell of a marriage, without true love or trust?"

Before she could answer, the woman continued. "He carries a curse. As I told you, he is not quite immortal—he will die in days unless he can capture your heart."

"I do not understand this. How can this be? I know vampires can be destroyed, but they are supposed to be immortal."

"Lord Sutcliffe is not. Vampires have the power to make an immortal being, but a goddess wields much more powerful magic. A goddess cursed him. To survive, he must woo you and win your love, or he will be destroyed."

"I don't understand."

"He has to make you fall in love with him." Mrs. Darkwell waved her hand dismissively. "That was why he pursued you and found you, and why he brought you back to his castle. His lovemaking, his smiles—they are all false. He is trying to win your heart, but he is only doing so for selfish reasons. He is not in love; he is just desperate to survive."

"How do you know about this?"

"I know because I am a goddess. I am Aphrodite. I foolishly fell in love with a mortal, and I committed a . . . well, it would be considered a crime in my world. So here I am, banished and captured in the form of an ordinary Englishwoman."

Octavia frowned. "That's madness. I don't believe you—"

"I cursed your husband. He either had to change, to be worthy of your love, or he would lose you forever."

"You did what—?" Octavia wanted to smack this awful woman—this madwoman who thought she was a goddess—but Mrs. Darkwell held up her hand. Octavia found she could not move.

"I did it to protect you. I know what is in your future, if Lord Sutcliffe comes back to you. He will not be able to fight his vampire tendencies—he was created by Esmeralda, who is evil and vicious. He will kill you and the baby, and he will be unable to stop because he is a vampire. Or, when he attacks, you will kill him to protect your child. Do not tell me you would never destroy him, because in that moment of great emotion, you will want to lash out at him, and your powers will do it for you. You won't be able to control them. So either he will kill you, or you will kill him. He had two weeks to win your love. He has only days left. He will fail."

In a flash of purple and lavender-colored smoke, Mrs. Darkwell disappeared.

"The journey to the Underworld is supposed to be hell," Sebastien de Wynter observed. "Your own personal hell. I learned this from a friend who is no longer a vampire—a man by the name of Zayan who had to travel to hell to save the woman he loved."

Cold water dripped on Matthew's head. The air of this tunnel was dank and smelled of the sea. They were in the network of underground caverns and tunnels that led from the Thames and ran under London. These were the remnants of old, underground rivers. Ahead, he heard the pounding of the Thames water. At high tide, this tunnel would fill with water, and they would be submerged. "You're certain this is the entrance?"

"There are other entrances, but many have been sealed up. This is the best one I know of."

He couldn't see how they would go down from this tunnel without drowning. But then, vampirism was thought to be impossible, yet he was one.

De Wynter led them onward, until Matthew, using his ability to see in the dark, pointed out, "This is a dead end." A wall of rock stood before them.

"Not exactly. Walk up to it and give the reason you want to enter Hell."

Matthew stepped up to the wall, feeling idiotic, but if this would get him to the Underworld, he would try it. He had to do this and free Octavia.

Behind him, De Wynter said softly, "On your journey, you will be subjected to tests, Sutcliffe. The things you experience will feel real, but they aren't. They exist only in your mind."

"I suspect that will be bad enough," Matthew muttered. He faced the dark, wet rock, and shouted, "I want to speak to the devil. He holds my wife Octavia in his service, and I want to have her freed."

The rock gave a grinding sound. A crack formed, rushing up the rock, until it became a door. Groaning, the door in the stone swung open.

Matthew stepped into darkness. On this journey, he had to go alone. Anger rose in him—why did the damned devil have to use Octavia? She didn't deserve this.

The door swung shut behind him. He glanced around, and the crack sealed, filling in the rock. The door disappeared.

His own private hell.

De Wynter had warned him he would walk through thousands of bugs, through groups of female demons who wanted to steal his soul. But the hell he found was worse.

It was so dark in this tunnel to Hell, even he could not see, and he had a vampire's ability to see in the dark. But what he saw were visions—of Octavia's life when he was gone. He saw her be seduced by man after man. Young, handsome men who told her how beautiful she was. He saw her glow for other men. He saw her lift her skirts or let her full breasts spill out of her open bodice—

His heart was thundering and hatred flowed through his veins.

He wanted to rip Lucifer apart.

He started to run, determined to get to Hell as fast as he could.

The floor vanished beneath his feet, and he fell.

De Wynter had told him everyone saw Hell differently. Matthew slammed onto a floor and felt soft wool under his hands. He surged to his feet. He stood in a lavish bedchamber, and a seven-foot man with horns lay on a large, oval bed, having his enormous erection sucked by a pretty woman with golden curls.

Lucifer grinned. "Lord Sutcliffe, I believe you came to ask me to free your wife?" The girl stopped her duty, curtsied, then vanished into the dark. The smell of brimstone hung in the air. Out of the shadows, a three-headed dog emerged, straining at its chains. Then another appeared.

Lucifer held up his hand, and the dogs were silent.

"Yes, let her go. She is a gentle and good woman, and she doesn't deserve to be a succubus."

The devil's handsome features contorted into an evil leer. "She is lovely, and she pleases me. She has done a good job of taking your soul."

"But you need a woman who will go to other men's beds.

That's not Octavia. She has a heart; she needs love. She deserves a loving husband, a family. Free her. I demand that you let her go."

"You demand it?" The devil snarled. "I think not. "

"No?" Matthew roared. "What the hell do you mean *no?*"

"Unless you ask me properly, I will not let her go."

Matthew gritted his teeth. But the devil got off the bed. He stood seven feet tall, and his body bulged with muscle. He had claw-like nails that were five inches long. Matthew wanted to fight, but he decided to ask properly. Swallowing pride and anger, he asked again and again, very politely.

Each time, Lucifer sneered and turned him down.

Damnation, he was done with polite. Matthew leapt at the devil, drawing a blade out of his boot. Surprise gave him the advantage, and he swung behind Lucifer. He grappled the devil around the chest, using his vampire's strength, and pressed the blade to Lucifer's throat.

"Let her go, damn it, or I destroy you."

"You will, will you?" mocked Lucifer.

The blade instantly transformed to molten metal. The heat burned Matthew's palm. He had to drop the knife, and it clattered to the stone floor.

The devil clapped his hands. Suddenly, human figures streamed out of the shadows. They looked like black specters. Horrible moans flew from their open mouths. They had no legs, just tattered cloaks, and they swooped around him.

"Protect me, my souls," roared Lucifer.

The ghostly beings flew at Matthew. He tried to fight, but his hands went through them. Their hands clutched at him and tore at his skin. They pulled his flesh off in chunks. Each time, he healed, but there were so many of them, he was losing too much skin.

"All I want is my wife's happiness," he shouted. "Kill me but free her."

"I am Satan," the devil snapped. "I do not grant favors. I

provide eternal damnation and torment. However, I will do one thing for you. I will spare you."

Flames roared up around Lucifer, and stinking sulfur-scented smoke filled the room. The black specters vanished. Then, the devil disappeared. But his voice came into the empty bedchamber. "You have one hour to make your way back from Hell. If you do not get out, you will be entombed here forever."

18

Pleasure in the Theater

That night, she dreamed of Matthew.

Octavia was in a box at the theater, watching a performance, and her husband was down below her, in the pit. There, he was being accosted by voluptuous orange sellers and fondled by bold prostitutes.

She wanted to go down to him, but the crowd was too great. She was with elegant people she did not know. Each time she tried to leave, someone dragged her back, warning her that she must stay where she was safe.

She needed to be with him, so she ignored their entreaties and tried again. This time, a beautiful woman with blond hair pulled Octavia back into her seat and clasped her hand. Wearing a devilish smile, the woman furtively glanced around, and when she saw no one was looking, she winked at Octavia and began to trace circles in the palm of Octavia's hand.

The soft touch made her skin tingle.

Onstage, a famous actress appeared, wearing skintight men's breeches and shirt. Every member of the audience stared at her generous figure.

Although they were in public, they might as well have been alone. The blond smiled and cupped Octavia's breast.

A jolt of surprise went through her, quickly followed by a warm, aroused sensation from her bosom. The woman's hand cradled her gently, then her thumb brushed Octavia's nipple, making it grow hard.

If someone turned . . .

If someone paid attention . . .

Octavia's heart pumped madly.

The blond bent to her ear and whispered, "I am Lady Vane. Do you like this?"

Octavia nodded, and Lady Vane squeezed her breast. Octavia swallowed a gasp, so no one would turn. Onstage, the actress had turned, displaying a rounded bottom in the tight breeches.

She was going to do something shocking and scandalous; something that would astound her husband and that would drive him mad. For, though all the audience stared at the stage, he was watching her.

Lady Vane whispered, "Let us go somewhere private. Somewhere we can have fun." Then she stood and said aloud, "I must excuse myself. Off to the retiring room." She held out her arm. Octavia took the hint, linked arms with Lady Vane, and they quickly left the box.

Octavia had a glimpse over, down into the pit. Matthew left his spot, following them from below, fighting through the crowd.

As soon as they were in the corridor that ran outside the boxes, Lady Vane giggled like a schoolgirl. Then Lady Vane slipped her arm free and scampered off.

"Where are we going?" Octavia breathed as she followed.

"Here." Lady Vane glanced around, then pushed open a door. They were in a box, but it was empty, and the curtain was drawn. "Now we can be alone." The woman's large green eyes flashed wickedly, then she quickly undid the top fastenings of Octavia's dress. "Your breasts are so plump and lovely. I've been watching them all night, wondering what they taste like."

Octavia hadn't expected that. The woman pulled Octavia's bodice down, so the neckline trapped her arms, but slid off her breasts.

Lady Vane stuck out her tongue and licked Octavia's bosom. Octavia giggled nervously, shyly.

"Your skin is so soft and sweet. Now I want to taste your nipples." Lady Vane's plump lips closed over her areola and suckled. Octavia moaned—it was so good. Her lover had a soft mouth, a warm tongue, and sucked just perfectly. Her nipples stiffened, becoming as hard and full as thimbles.

There was a soft click. The door was opening. Octavia had embraced Lady Vane as the woman kissed each of her nipples. Over Lady Vane's gleaming blond curls, she saw Matthew step in. He quietly closed the door behind him.

"Your husband?" Lady Vane asked softly.

"Yes," Octavia whispered. "Do you want to stop?"

"No." Lady Vane's full pink lips curved in a smile. "No, it will be exciting to have him watch."

Octavia heard her husband's soft moan as Lady Vane sucked her nipples again. Pleasure streaked through her, pleasure she wanted to return. She caressed Lady Vane's large, round breasts— they were almost spilling over her bodice.

Lady Vane breathlessly stopped. "Let's open our gowns."

Quickly, they fumbled with fastenings. Tripping over skirts, they both sank to the carpeted floor behind the rows of seats. Lady Vane pushed up Octavia's skirts. She had never dreamed she would like the thought of another woman lifting her gown. But the sight of Lady Vane's silk gloves on her lace-trimmed hems made her juices flow. She was aroused, feeling wet stickiness between her thighs.

"You smell divine," cooed Lady Vane. Then the woman

bent and kissed Octavia's nether curls. She shivered in pleasure as Lady Vane's tongue flicked out and caressed her. The woman tongued her quim more gently than Matthew, but it felt so good.

Especially when she knew her husband was watching. She saw him in the shadows. His jaw had dropped open in shock.

Flirtatiously smiling at him, Octavia reached down and caressed Lady Vane's full breast. It was a lovely, soft globe. She saw Matthew's reaction of astonishment, then he had to adjust his trousers.

It was so erotic to see Lady Vane's skirts spilling out as she leaned over to suckle Octavia's cunny. She was an attentive lover, paying much attention to Octavia's swollen, throbbing clit. Lady Vane gently stroked it with the flat of her tongue.

Octavia had wanted to make this a pretty scene for her husband, but soon she couldn't think about poses or seductive moans. Lady Vane's clever tongue was giving her incredible pleasure. Her hips rocked fiercely; her clit quested more of the lovely licking.

Her moans were desperate and frantic.

Lady Vane giggled against her quim, then suckled her clit. At the same moment, Octavia felt Lady Vane's gloved finger slip up her bottom.

Arching off the floor, she came. The orgasm took her like a fierce wind. She felt buffeted. She was crying out.

Then, as she gasped for breath, she whispered, "I want to do the same to you."

She heard Matthew's hoarse groan.

"We will lick our pussies together," said Lady Vane. Holding up her skirts, the woman moved around on top, until her mouth was over Octavia's quim and her cunny was positioned over Octavia's mouth.

This was daring, to do this to another woman. She almost lost her courage, but she knew Matthew would love to see this.

Closing her eyes, Octavia put her mouth to Lady Vane's wet, slippery nether lips. She tasted different than Octavia, but the same, too. It was a familiar, erotic taste.

Octavia tried to do to Lady Vane what she herself liked.

It appeared to work. Soon Lady Vane was pumping her hips and grinding her quim on Octavia's mouth. Octavia was close to orgasm again.

When Lady Vane suddenly clutched her legs, and her pelvis jerked up, Octavia came, too. With a wail absorbed by Lady Vane's soaking wet quim.

They fell apart, then both of them looked at Matthew.

He was stroking himself. His large hand was clasped around his thick shaft, pumping madly. Heavens, he did it so roughly, giving long, fierce strokes. Every so often, he would take his hand down to the head and squeeze it mercilessly.

Then he clutched his cock and his hips jerked forward. He moaned loudly, threw his head back.

His seed jetted out, spattering on his hand, even on the floor.

Enthralled, she sat up. She wanted to go to him and wrap her arms around him, but before her eyes, his image began to fade.

I have to go, Octavia. I can't stay with you now. At least I know you are safe. I left London and returned to Scotland. I got here and found you and Lottie were gone. Servants were safe but the creatures are attacking again. I have Brookshire and De Wynter with me, with other vampire slayers on the way. We will win.

She tried to send a message to him. *I have been taken by Mrs. Darkwell to another house.*

*Octavia, try to speak in your thoughts to Lady Brookshire. She will be working to hear you. If you can talk to her, I believe you can tell her where—*He vanished before he finished his sentence.

Octavia knew, somehow, that it was true Matthew was at the castle now. He had left London, and he had gone back for her.

Was he in danger? Were the assassins still there? Had people been hurt at the castle?

She had to go there to be with him—

Someone grasped her shoulder from behind and stopped her.

It was a tall woman with flowing black hair. Her fangs flashed in the faint light. "I am Esmeralda," the woman said. "I am the strongest female vampire. I have come for you. You are one of the six."

Octavia jerked free. "Leave me alone. I have no intention of bonding with you, or of taking over the world, or enslaving men."

In the dream she was brave and foolhardy. She was telling a being who could kill her that she would never cooperate.

"You will change your mind," Esmeralda declared.

"I won't."

"You said you wanted answers, yet no one has given you the truth. I can, and I will."

She should resist. Esmeralda was probably lying. But she couldn't resist. "And what do you know?"

"I know you are not a witch," Esmeralda said. "They have all lied to you. But I will not. I will give you honesty. There is a reason you need sex to survive. A reason that you meet your husband in dreams and the lovemaking feels real. You are a succubus."

Octavia knew what such a thing was—from the legends in her father's notes from his travels. Succubi were demonesses. They were sultry, alluring, deadly. They went to men while the men dreamed, and they seduced the men. And when the men climaxed with a succubus, they gave up some of their soul.

It made logical sense. It explained everything that had happened to her.

"D-does Sutcliffe know?"

"Of course he does," Esmeralda said. "As does Mrs. Darkwell. Everyone has lied to you. But with me, you can be powerful and strong. We will rule the world." Esmeralda held out her hand.

"Oh no, we won't." Octavia knew she had to escape the dream. She had to force herself to awaken.

She had to do something—

She scrambled up onto the window ledge. It was a long way down—and a stone terrace was right below the window.

"Damnation," Esmeralda howled. "Stop. Don't go back to them. Come with me. What of your daughter? Your husband wants to imprison you. What will he do to her, because she might be a succubus, too? Come with me and find—"

Octavia jumped.

She fell and fell, much farther than the distance from the window to the flagstones. Everything roared past her so quickly, she saw only a blur. Then she saw nothing at all. . . .

Octavia jerked awake and sat up. Her heart galloped in her chest. Falling had freed her from the dream.

She could not live without having answers. She had to know who or what she was. She had to find out whether she was a witch . . . or something else.

She had to find out what Charlotte was.

She needed to know where she had come from.

Quickly, she would get answers, then she would return to the castle to find Matthew.

To start she had to get to London, to the Royal Society. Matthew had told her she could try to speak in her thoughts to Lady Brookshire.

She must try.

19

Into the Fire

How did she speak in her thoughts to a woman she did not know?

Octavia went to her window. It overlooked the wintry gardens at the rear of the house that stretched toward a forest of skeletal bare trees. Bars covered the window panes; her door was locked from the outside.

L-Lady Brookshire, can you hear me? My husband, Lord Sutcliffe, told me to try to speak to you. I saw you once . . . at Vauxhall in a supper booth. Your husband and brother-in-law are with my husband at his castle in Scotland, fighting vampires and werewolves and witches.

How could she do this—speak through minds—if she was not in a dream? Octavia sagged in frustration, her hands on the window sill.

She would have to rely on herself.

On her magic.

First she would get Lottie, then she would escape.

She strode to her door and glared at the lock. The door handle exploded and flew off the wooden door, bursting out into the hallway. The paneled door swung into her room, a large splintered hole where the doorknob had been.

She hesitated in the doorway, expecting to see Mrs. Darkwell rushing up the corridor, or a servant sent by the woman. But there was only silence.

Octavia rushed to the stairs and sprinted up them to the uppermost floor, to the nursery. The large room was filled with bassinets and all were empty but one.

Panic ate at her stomach as she crossed to her baby's crib—the farthest from the door. It was the fear of being caught now, only a few feet from her child, and being taken prisoner again, unable to protect Lottie. She crept on tiptoe to the crib. Holding the side, she leaned over, her heart in her throat.

Covered by lace-trimmed blankets, Lottie slept peacefully on her back. Heart thudding, Octavia scooped her little girl into her arms.

Lady Sutcliffe.

She heard a female voice in her head, just as clearly as she heard voices in her dreams.

It is Lady Brookshire. We will come and rescue you.

I do not know exactly where I am, Octavia answered in her thoughts. *Mrs. Darkwell brought me to a house in the country, but I don't know where. I can get out of the house, and perhaps reach a village nearby and then I will know where you can come.*

I can follow your thoughts, Lady Sutcliffe, Lady Brookshire answered. *You need only to keep talking to me, and we will come as quickly as we can.*

I am going to get away from the house first though, Octavia answered. *That way, I will feel my daughter will be safer.*

Just take care of yourself and your child. I will be there as quickly as possible, with other vampire slayers. I will bring an army of men to keep you safe. I am a mother, and it worries me greatly to think you and your baby are in danger.

Lady Brookshire sounded indignant, even in her thoughts.

Octavia held her hand to the nursery window. The glass exploded. But it was too high off the ground to escape that way.

"You cannot go out of the window with your child in your arms."

Octavia whirled. Mrs. Darkwell stood at the door

"Vampire slayers are coming for me," Octavia cried. "You cannot stop them from rescuing me. Let me go now."

"I will," the woman answered. "I will not try to stop you. But you will come back to me. I will let you leave now, because I know you will return."

She had spent most of her life surrounded by books.

While her father had traveled the world for much of the time, he had amassed a remarkable library. Octavia used to work in it when she drew the illustrations for his books.

But Guidon's Charing Cross bookshop was stuffed with more books than she had ever seen. He had several rows of shelves, and the books were piled upon these, crammed between the shelves. Every horizontal surface was covered with books, and stacks towered on the floor.

Before she had walked through the doorway, the door itself had opened by magic. That hadn't surprised her. Then she'd seen the cords running along the wall. Curious, she'd tugged one, and the door shut with a swift slam.

A trick, not magic.

She was so used to magic now that a trick seemed more remarkable. She moved forward to let Althea, Lady Brookshire, into the tiny open space at the front of the shop.

"Goodness, it is packed to the ceiling with books," Lady Brookshire remarked.

Once she had escaped from Darkwell's house, Octavia had taken Lottie to the nearest village. It had been the village of Reading, very close to London. Lady Brookshire had arrived within hours.

They safely reached London and the Royal Society. There, Octavia had confirmed that Sebastien De Wynter, the Earl of Brookshire, and Matthew had flown—literally—to the castle in Scotland. She had been torn: Should she go to Scotland at once to help Matthew, or try to learn what she was? Lady Brookshire had insisted Octavia come here, to this tiny bookshop, to meet a vampire named Guidon, who could tell her about her past. Lady Brookshire had given birth a few months before, and her child was at home with nurses. She had insisted on carrying Lottie for Octavia. Fortunately Lottie had fed in the carriage and was now a sleeping bundle.

Octavia suspected Lady Brookshire had insisted they come here because she wanted to keep Octavia away from the castle and danger. She suspected Matthew had asked the lady to do it.

But once she had answers from Guidon, she was going to her husband's side.

"Mr. Guidon?" Octavia called.

Clattering sounded in the back of the shop, then a tiny man with tufts of frizzy yellow-gray hair appeared between two rows of shelving.

"Ah, Lady Brookshire. I am honored." He bowed deeply to Lady Brookshire, and turned to Octavia with a puzzled smile. "Indeed, your face is quite familiar to me." He stroked his chin. "I believe I knew your mother. Yes, I am quite sure of it."

Octavia was about to speak, when Lady Brookshire clasped Guidon's hand and gave it a squeeze. "This is the Countess of Sutcliffe. Her husband, Lord Sutcliffe, has recently become a vampire, turned by a vampiress named Esmeralda. Lady Sutcliffe possesses strong powers of her own."

It seemed madness to hear Lady Brookshire speak so coolly about all these things.

"She believes she is a witch," Lady Brookshire began.

"But she is not," Guidon finished. "She is a succubus."

"So it is really true? How can you know this?" Octavia cried.

A high-pitched whistle came from behind the stacks of books. "I put the tea on when you came in," Guidon said cheerfully.

"Please," she begged. "I want to know how you know what I am. How can I be this thing, when I—I was always quite normal? I must know right now—"

But the bookshop owner shook his head. "You must have tea, then we can deal with questions. All news is easier to digest with a cup of tea."

She didn't believe that, but Lady Brookshire took her arm. "We must humor him," she said softly. "Even my husband cannot escape here without having tea, and he is a most stubborn man. My other husband, Bastien, is even worse, yet he always takes tea with Guidon. I promise you it will be worth it."

She must be hearing things. "I misunderstood. You did not really say your 'other husband,' did you?"

In Lady Brookshire's arms, Lottie began to fret.

But Lady Brookshire smiled, stroked the baby soothingly on her back, then whispered, "After Guidon's tea, I will explain. And you must call me Althea. In your thoughts, I could tell you are calling me Lady Brookshire."

"You can read my thoughts?"

"Only a little. A few words come to me. It is because we are friends that I cannot read more than that—it is the same way with my husbands. I can speak to them in our thoughts, but I can't hear anything private."

Althea propelled her to the back of the shop. They went through a door to a tiny sitting room. Guidon was leaping up and down in front of his almost miniature settee. He took their cloaks, bonnets, and fur-trimmed gloves. Then Althea cradled Lottie to her chest and took a delicate wing chair, while Octavia perched on the small sofa. Guidon sat at her side and poured tea. "I promise this will set your nerves at ease."

Octavia did not believe it, but she took the cup to be polite. Then she realized the vampire would not continue until she actually tried his tea. She took a sip. It was warm, aromatic, and it did seem to ease the tautness of her muscles.

Guidon smiled at Lottie. "A lovely little infant." He made cooing sounds. Then he turned to Octavia, and his smile disappeared, his expression turning grave. "Yes, my lady, you are a succubus. This means you are a type of demoness, but you are not an evil one. What you do is not a deliberate act on your part."

"Do you mean my magic? That is what I do. Esmeralda called me a succubus—I do know what those are, and it cannot be true." She feared it was, but she wanted to deny it.

"No, Lady Sutcliffe, I mean your true mission. Your purpose. A succubus goes to men in their sleep; she seduces them, and she takes a little of their souls. When she has taken a man's complete soul, she brings it to Lucifer. He then claims his victim: He takes the man's life, and he claims the man as a slave for eternity in the underworld."

She shook with horror. "How could I be one of those?" Dear God, how was it possible? She did not serve Lucifer. How could she?

Guidon paused and refilled her cup. He drank his tea in one swift swallow. "You were dying before you . . . uh . . ." He turned pink. "Before you gave your innocence to Lord Sutcliffe. Once you reached womanhood, you were beginning to die slowly, because you did not begin to gather souls. They nourish you and keep you alive. Once you . . . gave your innocence, you acquired your powers. As Mrs. Darkwell told you,

you have very unusual and strong powers. You were destined to be a queen amongst succubi. You were given the strongest powers by Lucifer."

"How can I have been given anything by Lucifer?" she protested desperately. "I had a father and mother, and I lived an ordinary life. How could I be this thing and not know it?"

"Humans may not have many special powers, but they excel at keeping secrets. Until you blossomed into full womanhood, you would have never suspected you were different." His tufts of hair jiggled as Guidon nodded. "Now I must tell you about your past. What you suspected is correct—Lord Sutcliffe's father did indeed fall passionately in love with your mother. She, however, was devoted to your father. But your mother was killing your father. Her powers were slowly destroying him. She loved him too much to leave him, yet she could not bring herself to hurt him."

"How was she destroying him?"

"By making love to him. Little by little, she took his soul. When she realized she either had to leave him and go to other men or die, she chose death."

"Oh dear heaven. But why did Lord Sutcliffe's father die?"

"He could not live without her. So he took his own life."

"That was because my mother was a succubus?"

"It might have been," Guidon answered. "Or it might have been because she was a beautiful woman with a good heart. Those qualities can make a gentleman lose his head."

"How can I make this all stop? I don't want to be a queen of anything. I don't want to be hunted. Is there any way to save my husband and to be free?" She quickly told Guidon about the curse.

"Of course there is," the vampire said. "If you and your husband love each other, the curse will be broken."

"But what happens then? Will he be safe from me?"

"What we must do, Lady Sutcliffe, is save him first."

She nodded, but in her heart, she suspected Guidon was not speaking of what would happen beyond that, because there was no solution.

Would she have to do what her mother did? Chose between leaving her husband forever and taking her own life? And what of Lottie? It had been awful to be without her mother, from when she was young—only nine years of age. How could she do that to Charlotte? If she died now, Charlotte would never know her at all!

"What about Mrs. Darkwell? I think she has . . . rigged the curse somehow. She wants my husband dead—"

"No." Guidon shook his head. "She wants love for you. She has to find love for you—it is the only way she can escape her imprisonment in this world."

Octavia had told Lady Brookshire about this, as quickly as she could, in the carriage. "Is she truly Aphrodite, the goddess of love?" Althea asked. "Who imprisoned her? Guidon, why did you not tell us she had taken Octavia before?"

Guidon gave a sorrowful sigh. "You did not tell me her name was Darkwell."

Althea arched an eyebrow. "Indeed. Well, is this woman really a goddess?"

"She is beautiful," Guidon answered, "but she is not the real Aphrodite. She uses her mother's name—she is the daughter of the goddess Aphrodite. Aphrodite had a love affair with a dangerous vampire and the product of that union is the woman you know as Mrs. Darkwell. The name given to her when she was born was Darkwell, for she had great power and the capacity to bring love to humans, but she has a dark side, inherited from her father."

"If she is bad and evil, should she not—?"

"No!" Guidon cried quickly. "She is good inside. But sometimes, the darkness her father gave her becomes too strong. She is trying to prove she can fight it. Mrs. Darkwell was given the task of finding true love for one hundred preternatural females. Once she completes this task, she will be set free." Guidon's face softened, and his eyes looked dreamy.

Octavia had seen such a look on love-struck young men at balls. The strange little vampire Guidon was obviously in love with Aphrodite's dangerous, beautiful daughter.

Holding Lottie, Althea stood. "We must return to the Royal Society and prepare for our journey. We need to be properly armed to deal with vampires, werewolves, and warlocks."

But in the carriage, Octavia took Lottie from her friend and cuddled her baby close. "All right, Althea. Why did you use the term *husbands?*" Then she thought she understood: Althea could have been a widow, and Lord Brookshire could be her second husband.

The true answer shocked her utterly.

"I have two husbands," Althea said simply. "I was in love with both Yannick and Sebastien De Wynter. Though in the eyes of Society, I am the wife of Lord Brookshire, I am shared between both men. I love them both dearly, and they love me."

"They share you?" She felt her eyes grow big as saucers with surprise. But she remembered the things she had seen at the orgy involving eight men and one courtesan.

"Yes." Althea explained it, blushing delicately. The men were quite content to do it, which startled Octavia. The three of them had two children including the new baby, and both men looked on themselves as fathers. The men didn't care who had actually sired the children.

"We are happy," Althea said. "Though I had to make them understand how strong a love between three could be. Octavia, you could do the same thing. You could have Sutcliffe and another husband—a vampire. Or you could have other lovers, so Sutcliffe would be safe."

Octavia shook her head. The thought made her heart feel empty. "I couldn't. I don't love anyone but him, and I couldn't make love to another man. Matthew is all I want."

"All right. Then we need another solution."

But Althea remained quiet for the rest of the journey to Birdcage Walk. Octavia could see no solution. All she could think of was her mother. How frightened and desperate and unhappy she must have been to take her own life.

Father must have known what her mother was. Yet he had loved her anyway. It was such a tragedy.

Then there was Matthew's father. He had loved her mother hopelessly—

The carriage pulled into the gate. Octavia went down the steps, then took Lottie from Althea. A footman hurried to them, his breath a frosty mist. He held out a note to Octavia. "This was delivered for you, my lady, by a young urchin."

It couldn't be from Matthew. Octavia quickly unfolded it. The words leapt out at her; her gloved hands shook around the note, and she could read, but she couldn't quite think what the words were actually saying—

"What is it?" Althea asked.

"It is from Esmeralda," Octavia answered. "She has taken my father, and she will kill him if I don't go to her."

They thought she was mad for going alone, but she had argued that Esmeralda needed her alive, not dead. Octavia did not think she was in danger of walking into a trap. But she feared if she brought anyone else, the vampiress would sense it, and Father would die.

Octavia hurried through Hyde Park, her fur-lined cloak swishing around her legs as she ran. The note had told her to come to the Serpentine at midnight.

Normally the *ton* flocked here in the spring afternoons—

this was the place to see and be seen. At midnight in winter, it proved to be dark, still, quiet, and eerie.

The perfect place for vampires.

She hurried over frozen grass dusted with snow and reached the end of the small lake. The open water was blue-black, and some of it was frozen, covered with a silvery sheen.

The shadows moved, and five women stepped out of the darkness to stand in the moonlight. Octavia swallowed hard—this was not just about rescuing her father. These women expected to combine their powers tonight. They had brought her here to begin to take over the world.

How in heaven's name did she rescue Father, yet defy these other powerful women?

She walked forward, her head high. The woman who had come into her dream stepped out, meeting her like a general on a battlefield. Esmeralda's hair was loose, and she wore robes of black velvet trimmed with sable. A choker of diamonds glittered around her neck.

"I want my father," Octavia said simply.

"All right." Esmeralda shrugged. She snapped her fingers, and two large men in greatcoats and heavy boots dragged Father forward. He wore a coat over his clothes but no hat. His head hung down, as though he were too weak to lift it.

"Father." She rushed to him, wrapped her arms around him, hugged him, then stepped back when the two male servants growled.

Her father lifted his head. He was eerily white, as though Esmeralda had drained his blood. "Octavia? Dear God, what are you doing here?"

She whirled. "What did you do to him? Have you turned him?"

"No," Esmeralda answered. "I merely kept him weak and under control. I cannot imagine why your mother loved him so much, why she was willing to die to protect him."

"Quiet, you monster," Father roared with surprising strength. "Do not listen, Tavie. It is all lies."

"I know it is true, Father. I know that I am like my mother. You did understand what she was?"

"Aye." Deep lines ringed her father's mouth, and dark shadows lay under his eyes. His cheeks were shrunken and hollow. "I did, and I did not care. I loved her dearly. But what I did not know was that loving her would mean my death. When I found out, I made my decision—I would risk dying to be with her. But instead, she believed she was a monster, and she . . . she killed herself. I am so sorry, Tavie. I couldn't tell you." Pained eyes gazed at her. "I didn't know how to tell you. I thought you were mortal . . . like me."

"I'm not. I am like my mother."

"I should have told you, but I was afraid. You always seemed so happy, and I feared the knowledge would destroy that. Your mother said it was a horrible burden to be different. To have a power and duty that would be condemned by our world. She told me she had prayed you would not be like her."

Tears leaked to her cheeks. How could she blame him for not telling her?

"Even when you became sick, I tried to pretend it did not mean you were like your mother. I should have accepted it. I could have helped you."

"You did the best you could—" She broke off. "But if you had the suspicion I was like Mother, you knew what would save me." She could not say it to her father. But she realized he had known what she had needed but he had been willing to let her die, rather than let her survive as a succubus. If she had not seduced Matthew, she would have died. And Father would have preferred that.

It told her what he thought of her.

It stunned her to her soul.

She had wanted to hide what she was. She had feared Matthew

would not be able to accept it. She had never dreamed her own father would not.

Esmeralda smiled confidently. Her face was a pale oval above her sumptuous cloak. "Now you know, Octavia, why you must join with us. Never will this world accept you. Never will men, who have the power in this world, accept you. We must create a new world, where women who have special powers are not persecuted and killed."

"It is not just women," Octavia protested. "Men who are different are hunted, too."

"Then we can change that. But we must take control to do it. That is why you are here. I am Esmeralda, and I am Number One."

One by one, the women stepped forward. The werewolf female quickly changed into her wolf form and paced ahead on nimble paws, her silver and black fur rippling in the cold wind. Then she changed back. "I am Number Two."

The third was a tiny, slender woman with flame red hair. She bowed her head, and her body writhed in what looked like agony. Wings exploded from her back, and a tail grew from her spine, a long, mobile tail with an arrowhead-shaped scale on the end. Scales covered her skin, multiplying at a stunning rate. She turned into a dragon, then opened her jaws, and a small, precise line of flame shot out. The woman changed back. "I am the last of a rare family of dragon-shifters called the Fiorenze. I am the third."

The fourth laughed gently, then wrapped her arms around herself and bowed her head. Suddenly her arms became huge wings of gray and brown. They unfurled, and the hawk-shifter soared. She flew back to the others, became human again. "I am the fourth."

Mrs. Darkwell had spoken of a witch and a demoness. Octavia had thought she was the witch. Now she wasn't sure.

The fifth woman stepped forward. Octavia gasped—the woman looked like her. She wore a plain gown of green, had long blond hair twisted in a bun at the nape of her neck and large blue eyes. "I am Number Five, the witch."

That meant she—Octavia—was the demoness, because she was a succubus.

"Now," Esmeralda said. "We begin."

"No, I have not agreed," Octavia cried, but her words were drowned out by a deep, cold, masculine voice that barked, "No. Let her go, damn you, Esmeralda. Let Octavia and her father go free."

Matthew—it was his voice, which meant he had survived at the castle. She whirled around. He was striding out from the shadows of a grove of trees.

"I told you to come alone," Esmeralda snapped. She rounded on her two male servants. "Kill her father—"

"Stop," Matthew growled. He held up his hand, and the two servants stopped in their tracks, holding her father between them. "She did come alone. I followed her. I can scent her, and I tracked her here."

Esmeralda seemed to grow taller, like a giant snake rearing up. "Are *you* alone, Sutcliffe?"

"Of course." He shrugged and crossed his arms over his chest. "I thought you might be willing to bargain with me if I were willing to put myself in danger."

Octavia gasped.

"He does not truly love you," Esmeralda said. "You are a succubus, and you have an allure that makes men desire you. He fears his love for you is not real. He wanted to harden his heart to love, to protect his heart, so he would not make the same foolish mistake as his father. So now that he cares for you, he does not know if it is because of Lucifer's power, or if it is real."

"I—I don't believe you."

"Then let us see." Esmeralda turned to Matthew. "You knew your father died because he loved a woman he could not have. That woman was Octavia's mother."

Matthew recoiled. The wind sent his greatcoat snapping around him like enormous wings, as he snarled at the vampiress. "That's a lie."

Esmeralda laughed—soft, evil laughter that seemed to echo all around them. "It is the truth, isn't it, Octavia?"

She couldn't lie. "Yes," she said softly. "It is true."

Matthew looked stunned. "You knew this, yet you didn't tell me?"

"I didn't know until you took me to the castle. I found the letters you had kept, the ones sent to your father. I recognized my mother's handwriting."

"Her mother was a powerful succubus. Perhaps that was what drew your father to her and that was what made him love her so intensely he lost all rational thought. Perhaps he never would have loved her, certainly never would have taken his own life, if she had not been a succubus."

Octavia stared at her husband. "But it might not be . . . He might have just loved her." She hated Esmeralda. The only reason his father would have killed himself, if not because he was caught by a succubus's allure, would be because he was unstable, weak, mad. Would Matthew think that about his own father, or would he rather believe the man had been bewitched—and destroyed—by a succubus?

She feared it would be the latter. Surely he would rather think succubi were dangerous, that they drove men to madness.

It might be true. What if he really did only love her because of her succubus powers?

"There, you see, Octavia. He is filled with doubts now. You

can never trust a man. Men were afraid of me, and they hurt me," Esmeralda said. "They tried to destroy me. If any man is allowed to have power, he becomes a brute with it."

"I don't think that is true," Octavia said.

Esmeralda turned to the dragon-shifter. "You must begin the fire that will meld our powers."

Fire? The woman shifted shape and sent out a blast of flame as Esmeralda spoke an incantation. The fire suddenly grew, but it was burning two feet off the ground.

"How does the fire meld our powers?" Octavia asked.

"Surely you can guess," Esmeralda answered. "We all walk into the fire together, and it melts us, changes us, bonds us together. We will emerge as a new, stronger being."

"I don't want to become a new, stronger being," Octavia said. "If anything I would want to be normal. What of the rest of you? Haven't you ever craved just being normal? Having children to love? Enjoying the beauty of a spring day?"

"It is impossible for us," Esmeralda spat. "We are hunted always because we have power. If you do not join us, your father will die."

"If I join you, he will also die, and so will other innocent people." She had to stop this. The only way to do so would be to kill Esmeralda.

She had come alone, but not completely unarmed. Slipped up her sleeve was a sharpened stake. Shifting her arm as Althea had explained, she felt the point of the stake slide into her palm. "I won't join you."

Esmeralda roared, showing long, curving fangs.

Octavia stepped back, trembling. She couldn't give in to fear. Her husband moved forward, but the witch held up her hand and suddenly Matthew could not move.

"I could kill you," Esmeralda said. "In your place, I would

take your daughter. She has the same powers as you; they are just dormant now."

"She is an infant," Matthew growled.

"As long as she possesses the same strong magic as Octavia," the wolf-shifter said, "if Octavia dies, she will ultimately take her place as one of the special six women. I will keep her with me and have her powers awakened as soon as she is old enough."

Octavia shook her head. "No, I will never let you take my daughter."

Matthew fought to move. She saw the extreme strain in his face. Esmeralda glared at her. "It is time. If you do not come with us, we will kill you and take your daughter. Your husband is a mere man—he does not have the strength to fight us. You have a choice. Help us, or lose your father, Sutcliffe, and your child."

Octavia knew if she attacked now, she couldn't win. She had to drive the stake in Esmeralda when she wasn't expecting it, when she thought she had won and was overconfident.

Esmeralda was driven by hatred. Octavia had to make the vampiress believe she had won.

"I will do it," she declared. "My husband does not love me. He wants to imprison me. No man would ever accept me for what I am."

Matthew grunted and growled, trying to fight the magic. "Octavia, no!"

"I must," she said simply. She turned to Esmeralda. "What do we do?"

"We take hands and walk into the flame."

Damn. Fear shot through her. She would have to slide the stake back up her sleeve, and she would have to break the hand-hold to use it. She would lose the hope of distraction. The flames would kill her.

Or would they? She could start fires with her emotions.

Could she use the control she had developed to control this fire and to protect herself from it?

Octavia adjusted the stake back into her sleeve. She held out her hand to Esmeralda. "For my daughter's sake, I will go with you."

The dragon-shifter took her other hand. They made a ring around the flame, then Esmeralda commanded them to walk forward. She breathed in smoke and coughed. The heat of the fire was terrifying. Around them, the light cover of snow was melting.

She had to do this.

Esmeralda shouted a strange incantation, and the fire exploded in size. Octavia, silently, commanded the flames to lick around her but not touch her.

She heard Father shouting and Matthew's howl of horror. At her side, Esmeralda screamed, "Betrayer. I will kill you."

In that moment, Octavia jerked her hand free. The stake fell into her hand. Then something grabbed her by her arms. Even without looking, she knew it was Matthew. He wanted to save her.

She had only seconds. She lunged, driving the stake into Esmeralda's chest. The vampiress was weakened by the flame. She couldn't escape Octavia's killing blow.

Esmeralda dropped to the ground. The other women ran out of the flames, and Matthew pulled her free.

Would they be attacked by the other women?

But Octavia saw they were no longer alone. A dozen men stood there, holding crossbows, and leading them were Sebastien De Wynter and the Earl of Brookshire. The werewolf, dragon-shifter, and hawk-shifter changed shape. The wolf loped away; the other two flew.

They must never have been alone. Despite her plea to the

Royal Society that she must go unaccompanied, they must have followed her.

Crossbows lifted. "No!" Octavia shouted. "Let them go. Esmeralda is gone, and I don't think they wanted to do this."

"It is true," the witch said. "Esmeralda was the oldest of us all and the most powerful. We were brought here by threats. We do not want to rule the world; we want to exist in it and be happy."

"Yes," said Octavia. "That is what we want. Let them go."

De Wynter nodded. He issued the command, and his group of slayers lowered their weapons.

Strong arms went around her. Octavia turned—and her husband pulled her into his embrace.

"How did you escape the power of the magic?" she asked softly, and she sank against his chest.

"I don't know." His arms tightened, and he kissed the top of her head. "I was not going to let you walk into a fire and lose you, Octavia."

"What happened at the castle? I did not want to leave people there unprotected."

"I arrived just as the attack started. De Wynter, Brookshire, and I were able to drive the assassins back, and we ensured no one in the castle was hurt."

"Thank heaven," she breathed.

"You are all right." His concerned gaze searched her eyes. "And Lottie?"

"We are both fine." She could see De Wynter's men tending to Father.

"It should be over now," Matthew whispered. "With Esmeralda gone, and the other women unwilling to join their powers, the males have nothing to fear. The assassins will no longer bother you."

"There is still the curse. We have to try to save you." She

told him about Mrs. Darkwell. She remembered how the woman had said she would return. It appeared Mrs. Darkwell had been correct.

"We will do that. But I want to see Lottie, and we should get your father home. Then I want to spend the rest of the night making love to you. In peace, joy, and pleasure."

20

Cursed

She loved to watch her husband strip off his trousers and his underclothes.

Octavia had seen it quite a few times now, but it still left her breathless.

Matthew grinned. "You look adorable in the tub, Octavia. Or may I call you Tavie, as your father does?"

She sat up. In the bathing room attached to her bedchamber at Sutcliffe House, she had been lying back in the tub, washing off grimy ash and the smell of smoke from the fire. She had to make room so her husband would join her. Steam rose from the water, and the air was filled with the heady, exotic scent of sandalwood soap.

"Do you truly forgive . . . me for what happened to your father? I know it . . . well, it ruined your life, for it took your father from you and turned your mother into a unhappy woman."

He frowned. "It wasn't your fault."

"But I am what my mother was."

"It wasn't your mother's fault that my father died. Nor was it his fault. It also wasn't mine—"

"Heavens, how could you have felt responsible?"

He looked away, arranging towels on a stool. "I . . . I guess I couldn't understand why I wasn't worth living for. Why Father did not want to stay for Gregory and I."

Octavia moved through the water, making droplets splash over the edge, but she didn't care. She reached out and stroked his hip. "It had nothing to do with you. Your father was in the thrall of a wicked magic—"

She stopped. No wonder he had said he would never fall in love. His father had claimed to be "in love," but he had really just been a slave to an evil magic.

It was the same for Matthew. Could he ever really believe he was in love with her? Or would he always think it was just a succubus's dangerous, deadly magic?

She realized something else. "I never asked you when you were cursed! How long ago was it?"

"I was given a fortnight. I have two days left."

Two days! Panicked, she moved to get out of the tub. "We must go to Mrs. Darkwell and convince her to remove this curse—"

He grasped her arm. "Later. Sex first." Swinging his leg over the side of the tub, he drew her to him as he lowered into the water. He slid both legs in, so he was sitting on his bottom beside her.

She was floating in the water, and he gently pulled her though the water so she floated over him with her bottom gliding over her thighs. Then her cunny floated over his cock. Her nether lips brushed over him as she bobbed in the water. It was barely a touch, but it made her heart pound. Water lapped at her breasts, which also bobbed.

He reached down; his hand stroked her bottom before he took hold of his shaft. She felt the drag against her sensitive lips as he pushed his cock down.

Like a mermaid, a siren, she pushed down through the water, so her quim took his hot, slick cock inside. Her bottom pressed against his hard groin and thighs. Her moans of delight, of agony, of anticipation and encouragement floated out in the perfumed, steamy air.

"Yes," he groaned. "Take me deep. Sit your lovely arse right on top of me."

Water sluiced off his arms as he lifted his hands. Then he slid them back in the water, to squeeze and knead her breasts. Filled with milk, her breasts were enormous . . . and sensitive. She squeaked. He lightened his touch.

"They are so lovely and big," he whispered, then nibbled her neck.

That made her freeze, until she realized he was just using his hot, firm lips. His tongue stroked her wet skin.

Oh, this was so good. She lay back against him, reveling in the pleasure of his tongue and his hands. His hips began to move under her impatiently.

Of course—she had him inside, he wasn't doing anything, and in male fashion, he was rather eager. "I want to celebrate having you with me, having you safe." His voice was rough, throaty.

Pushing off with her hands, she lifted on him, then dropped. His hoarse moan sent shivers down her spine.

One thrust really made him feel so good? She could make him feel so good?

The water made it feel elegant to rise and fall on him. The warmth and slipperiness felt erotic and sinful. All her skin felt as her cunny did—hot and silky and slick.

His hips arched, thrusting his cock hard.

Oh yes, this was perfect. She was exhausted from the confrontation with Esmeralda. Walking into the fire had drained her strength—and had tested her courage to its limits.

This made her feel strong.

Strong enough to fight Mrs. Darkwell, to triumph over the curse.

Matthew leaned back into the tub, so he could thrust his hips with great force. His crotch banged her bottom, his hard cock drove deep, and he lifted her through the water.

"Touch your clit," he rasped. "Pleasure yourself while I fuck you."

She loved the sheer naughtiness of what he'd said. She felt wild and wicked, and she liked it. Splashing water everywhere, she pumped on him. Her hand knifed through the water, and she found her private place and rubbed mercilessly.

She panted. Moaned. Screamed.

Oh God, the pleasure struck like a burst of lightning. She arched forward on him, then fell back. Her body was out of control.

She'd never felt so good . . . or so strong.

She bounced and bounced, then he moaned, "I can't last much longer. Will you take me in your ass?"

Yes. She was tingling there, in her entrance there, surprisingly sensitive after her orgasm.

He lifted her; she held her breath, then she felt the thick, full head nudge against the round opening. Even just that touch felt stunning, wonderful.

She was floating, poised on his cock, and it was magic and naughty.

Then he arched his hips and pushed his thick member in, just a little.

"Oooooh, yes," she gasped. Her head flopped back against his shoulder.

Two more slow and gentle thrusts, and his cock was all the way inside. She couldn't deny the arousal of this. She liked this.

His fingers slid between her nether lips to touch her clit.

He pleasured her three ways—his cock up her bottom, his fingers on her clit, his hand on her breast.

Hazy with pleasure, she moved with him. Her groans and cries grew louder, like music coming to its wild, fervent climax.

"Oh yes!"

Then he growled, like a wild beast, and he thrust his cock deep. Heat filled her, and she felt the spasms of his out-of-control body against her. They gasped together, cried out together, laughed in unison.

"I never dreamed I would find this. A woman I could admire, respect, love, and lust for—all in one. I thought it would be easy to resist love. You make it impossible."

What did he mean—that because she was a succubus he couldn't resist her?

Desperately drawing in breath, she managed to whisper, "All right, we must go now to Mrs. Darkwell."

"Octavia." He let his head fall back and rest on the rim of the tub. "There's no rush, love."

"There are only two days. How could there not be a rush?" Then she understood. "You don't think you can be freed. Do you not believe I love you?"

"Mrs. Darkwell does not want me to be with you. So I don't believe she will free me."

"You think she wants you to die?"

"Apparently she doesn't believe I am good enough for you."

"I hate calling upon females," her husband grumbled, as their carriage drew to a halt in front of Mrs. Darkwell's manor house.

Octavia arched a brow. "This is hardly a social call—we are here to have you freed from a curse. Besides, you are holding a female on your lap, and you seem very happy to be with her."

Her heart lurched as her husband smiled down at Lottie. Beneath her blankets, Lottie wore a pretty baby gown of lace, along with a lacy bonnet trimmed with silk roses. She blew bubbles at Matthew, making a wistful smile come to his lips. Octavia knew he was fighting his need for day sleep.

"Do you really thinking bringing Lottie will work?"

"If Mrs. Darkwell's tasks on earth involve finding true love, I want to make it appear we have found it. Whether it is the truth or not."

"It is the truth," he growled.

But she saw the uncertainty. He just did not know.

Feminine laughter could be heard outside. Octavia looked out, and she saw Mrs. Darkwell's tall, elegant form step out from the house, onto the front step.

She stood. "It is time, Matthew. We are going to win."

Minutes later, she was seated in the front parlor with Matthew and Mrs. Darkwell. Matthew cradled Charlotte and from his arms Lottie gazed at the world around her.

"We have come to break the curse," Octavia said simply. "Matthew had to win my heart within a fortnight, and he has done so."

Mrs. Darkwell held up her hand as a footman entered, bearing a tray of drinks. Matthew had brandy, and two slender glasses of sherry were for the females.

Matthew took a sip. Then he made a face and put it down. "Damnation," he muttered, "I cannot drink anymore."

"Just blood," Mrs. Darkwell pointed out. "It is how Esmeralda sired you." She took her drink and sipped. "The curse can only be broken if you truly love him."

"I do."

"Do you love him even if he doesn't love you in return? Even if he can never believe in his love for you, because he is afraid of it? Once you attempt to break the curse, you will set it in motion. If you cannot break it, Sutcliffe will die."

Panicked, Octavia looked to her husband. She knew she had to try. The curse required him to win her love. It did not say he had to love her in return to survive.

She was willing to love him without certainty he would ever love her. It would lead to heartbreak, but she was willing to do it.

She was willing to take an enormous risk.

All her life, she'd dreamed of traveling like Sutcliffe and her father. She never would have dreamed the greatest and most dangerous adventures lay in love and marriage.

"He lives or dies by your answer," Mrs. Darkwell whispered. The woman stood, lifting her arms toward the heavens. "And your answer must be the truth. You can never lie well enough to outwit a curse. Do you love him, Octavia?"

She hesitated. She wanted to be *sure*. It was only months ago that she had run away from this man. Love could be terrifying: Her mother had died of love for her father; his father had died for love of her mother.

Could she love the Earl of Sutcliffe even if he never loved her? Could she survive a hopeless love?

Matthew was watching her. He'd dipped his head. Obviously he believed he'd failed—he didn't think he'd captured her heart.

Then his gaze slipped away from hers. In that one moment, when she needed him to look at her and she needed to see that he cared for her—

He looked at Lottie. Tenderness leapt into his eyes, and they glistened with tears. His lip quivered. She'd never seen him make such a vulnerable gesture. He was Lord Sutcliffe, the fearless explorer.

Inside though, he was a man who needed love but was afraid to ask for it.

He had moved heaven and earth to save their baby. He had walked into a fire to rescue her.

Watching that sweet delight in his eyes as he looked longingly at their daughter, Octavia knew the truth.

"Yes," she shouted, her voice echoing through the entire house. "I love him."

At that instant Mrs. Darkwell swiftly moved to her husband and scooped Lottie from his arms.

Octavia rose to her feet, fearing she had been tricked, until she saw her husband's face. She gasped in horror.

Blood. The hunger for it roared through him. His jaw twisted, distorted, and shifted back and forth with a loud *crack*. His fangs shot forth, driving into his lower lip and drawing blood.

Delicious, tasty, beautiful blood.

Then his every muscle screamed with pain, and Matthew grabbed the nearest chair for support. He jerked helplessly as his muscles seemed to expand, then contract. His pulse galloped; his heart felt on fire and pain shot from it, down his arms and through his gut to his legs.

The pain was so great, he slammed his head against the wall.

He roared like a beast, staggered to the middle of the room, so he was facing his wife and Mrs. Darkwell, who held Lottie. Like a wild animal, he was slavering over them. He could hear Octavia's heartbeat, and he could literally see the beat of Octavia's pulse beneath the pale, creamy skin of her neck. She grasped their daughter from Darkwell, and backed away from him, hugging Lottie close.

He wanted her blood. The vampire in him was taking control.

No. Hell, he would not hurt her. Blindly, he turned from her and ran to the fireplace.

"Matthew? Matthew, stop!" she cried.

He grabbed a piece of kindling. It wasn't sharp, but he had

enough strength to drive it through his chest. He pressed the end of the stick to his coat, over his heart—

"Stop!" Mrs. Darkwell commanded. "Wait."

She was right. The hunger receded. The pain around his heart stopped, and his muscles no longer felt as if they were burning. Panting, chest heaving, he held the stake. If the hunger came again, he would use it.

"Matthew?" The soft, questioning voice was Octavia's.

"It is over," Mrs. Darkwell said. "You are free. You were willing to destroy yourself rather than hurt her. Not only have you won her heart, you have proved you are worthy of her love."

Matthew fell to his knees. There was a strange pain in his mouth, then it went away. He felt weak; his heartbeat pounded like a mortal's.

What drove him to his knees was not the pain of being freed from a curse. If he was being saved, it meant Octavia truly loved him. He had actually won her heart.

How had he done it? What did she see in him worth loving? He should have told her he didn't doubt his love for an instant—that he believed in true, unconditional love, because that was what she deserved.

That she would love him anyway humbled him.

That he was worthy of her love amazed him. He hadn't been able to save Gregory, or his mother from the despair that had made her drink herself to death, or his father from suicide.

But he had been determined he would do anything to save and protect Octavia.

He loved her deeply, intensely, with his heart and soul. There was nothing like almost dying, after being a vampire, to make a man understand what really mattered in life.

Octavia mattered. And Lottie mattered. Giving them all the love and devotion they deserved mattered.

He opened his eyes and saw Octavia's worried face above him. He grinned. "I think you saved me, my beloved."

Tears sparkled in her eyes. Tears for him. He cupped her face, drew her closer, then kissed her. No fangs to get in the way or hurt her. No temptation to take her blood. All Matthew felt was the fierce need to show her how much he loved her—

She pulled back. Worry had been replaced by wide-eyed fear. She spun toward Mrs. Darkwell, who had stood up from the sofa.

"You made him a mortal again, and you have freed him from being a vampire, but that means I will kill him!" Octavia cried. "I am a succubus, and I will destroy him." Heavens, it meant she was faced with the same choice her mother had made. Leave the man she loved, the only man she wanted—the *only* man she had ever wanted. Or stay with him, selfishly follow her heart, and destroy him.

Mrs. Darkwell waved her hand gracefully. "Perhaps not. If you truly love each other, you will work together to survive—and to have both love and passion. This is why you felt weak again once you saw him: You two are intended to be soul mates. You need his love and passion to keep you strong. I was the one who ensured you found your child. I gave you and Lord Sutcliffe the location of the baby. It did exactly what I wished it would do: It forced you two to recognize and find your love. Now, I must go. It is my duty, Octavia, to ensure you find true love, but that does not mean I can let it come easily to you."

With that, the woman left in a burst of purple-colored smoke.

Damn—why did the woman do that? Why give only part of an answer, a hint of hope, then vanish?

"Should we pursue her?" Matthew asked.

Octavia shook her head. How she wanted to, but she had to accept the truth. "I don't think it will do any good. I think—I think this is some sort of test. What I don't know is how we pass the wretched thing."

In Octavia's experience, it was nursemaids who took babies outdoors. But the next morning was wintery but not too cold, and Matthew oversaw Lottie's preparation for a stroll in her perambulator.

He had dressed her in a frilly white baby dress, then a pretty coat, and wrapped her in many blankets. He selected her hat and tied its ribbons in a large bow beneath Lottie's tiny chin. Charlotte promptly spit up milk that leaked toward the ribbons, but he just grinned and wiped it away.

Octavia stood back and watched him work. She couldn't help smiling. Really, the man was adorable around his daughter. "She looks perfect," she said.

His dark brow lifted. "Perhaps too perfect. I don't want her to start breaking hearts just yet—"

He broke off. For one moment, his expression sobered, then his smile returned. But Octavia knew it was a forced one. She knew what he was thinking. It was the thing they had skirted around for two days and never spoke of directly.

Esmeralda had said that Charlotte had the same powers Octavia did, but had the vampiress lied to coerce Octavia to help her? The wicked and vengeful woman had not been someone Octavia believed would tell the truth. They would have to find out what the truth really was, but she was not sure how.

"Let us go for a walk," Matthew said, his voice gruff but cheerful.

She banished worries. It was a beautiful, crisp day, and she didn't want to let fears darken it.

Cradling Lottie in one arm, he offered the elbow of his other. "You saved my life, my lovely countess, and I want to savor every moment of sunshine with you."

Her lower lip wobbled a bit, so she stayed quiet. Savoring sunshine. That was what they would do, and she refused to worry about the future. Later she would try to understand how to pass this damnable test so they could have a future.

Together, she and Matthew went downstairs, crossed the lane, and entered the gate to Hyde Park. On such a chilly day, there were only nannies out with babies tucked into perambulators. She enjoyed watching Matthew reveal what a devoted father he was.

The afternoon was filled with laughter, then they returned home. Octavia fed Lottie, and the nurse took the baby to bed. Matthew and she had a very hasty supper.

Then her husband clasped her hand, and they ran to their bedroom. Sharing laughter, they tumbled together onto his enormous bed.

"I love this. I love making love to you when you are giggling," he said. He nibbled her neck, which tickled. He kissed under her arm. She hadn't expected it, and it made her laugh so much she could barely breathe.

He kissed down her tummy, and she was almost doubling up with giggles. Then he rolled onto his back and pulled her with him, planting her cunny right on his face. Wickedly, she turned on him, as gracefully as she could, clambering over him. She wanted to pleasure him while he pleasured her.

His cock was thick and hard, twined with veins, with a full, taut, velvety head. She smiled: Seeing his erection was like greeting an old friend. It was only months ago that she had felt so unsure with him, that she had felt apart even when they were intimate. Now they seemed like two halves of one whole.

Especially in this position, when his tongue slicked over her clit, and thrust inside her, and even—heavens—teased the rim of her bottom.

She bent and took his cock in her mouth. How she loved the

taste of him. And she loved making him moan. When she sucked hard, his legs shook.

Then he began to lick her clit wildly, and she could barely suck him, she was so weak with delight.

She was going to make him come when she did. She was determined.

With no idea how, she tried suckling hard, then licking, then just giving much suction on the head. She tongued his ballocks, tugged his nether hair with her teeth. She played with him, happy, confident. Savoring love.

Then his hips began to buck fiercely, driving his erection into her mouth. She concentrated on taking him deep . . . until he grasped her hips, clamped her cunny to his face, and did amazing things with his tongue.

Melting things. Soul-shattering things—

She came with a wild scream. At the same moment, his cock went rock-hard and swelled in her mouth. His hips thrust up abruptly. A stream of hot, rich-tasting semen filled her mouth. She swallowed, the motion tugging on the head, and he moaned intensely into her quim.

Then Octavia let him out of her mouth and fell off him, panting with pleasure.

Matthew was in heaven. His wife did the most amazing things with her mouth. He wanted to get up and cuddle her, but his arms and legs wouldn't obey him.

What was wrong with him? He couldn't move. He managed a gruff laugh, though it hurt his chest to expand. "You've made love to me so intensely, you've just about killed me."

"Oh no," Octavia whispered. "It is because you are mortal again. We cannot do this anymore. I can't make love to you anymore. I'm doing exactly what my mother did, and I have the same choice. I can't hurt you with sex. And to protect you, I can never make love to you again."

* * *

White's. It was a feat to be admitted as a member to its famous rooms. Yet vampires came here to gamble, and none of the snobbish members were aware that shape-shifters and blood-drinkers mingled amongst them.

Matthew found Sebastien De Wynter lounging casually in the famed bow window overlooking St. James Street. With his legs outstretched and crossed, De Wynter looked completely at home, adding his wicked comments to the ribald dissection of the fashion sense of gentlemen passing by.

Matthew took a seat, waited for a few minutes, then leaned toward De Wynter. He knew his friend was watching him. Waiting.

De Wynter had not spoken to him since he had been transformed from vampire back to mortal.

You look worried, Sutcliffe. De Wynter spoke in his thoughts. *I take it you have been celebrating your freedom with your lovely wife? If I were you, it's what I would do. I would still be in bed, in fact.*

He answered the same way, knowing Bastien De Wynter could read his thoughts now that he was mortal again. De Wynter could both project thoughts and hear them. *I would be, except Octavia realized she was killing me and refuses to hurt me anymore with pleasure.* Frustration and anger at fate made his words, even those spoken by thought, sound like a growl. *So we went through hell together with Esmeralda and survived, broke a curse, and I'm going to die if I keep making love to her. Darkwell says we can have a future, but insists we have to find the answer ourselves.*

Let us go somewhere we can speak quietly, De Wynter said. He stood and stretched. "It's time I go in search of deep play." He bowed. "Gentlemen."

Matthew quickly rose. "I'll join you, De Wynter."

Together they left. De Wynter's carriage already waited at the door, and he grinned. "One of the benefits of being able to send messages by thought—and of using a vampire coachman."

Matthew had learned De Wynter and his brother, Brookshire, employed preternatural beings. It gave them work, money, and safety. De Wynter leaned elegantly on the seat.

He joined his friend. "Whom can I go to for answers? We've spoken to Darkwell, to Guidon. Lucifer will not let her go. There has to be a way."

"It is possible that if she were to make love to other men, she would not drain you—"

"Share Octavia? Hell, I can't." He remembered what Mrs. Darkwell had said, about Octavia's needing his love and passion. Even if she didn't, he couldn't let her go to someone else.

De Wynter gave a slow grin. "Let me explain about my unusual marriage."

Matthew frowned. "You aren't married."

"I am. My brother and I both consider ourselves married to Althea. We were both in love with her, and we are both vampires. We were destined to have a threesome for eternity. Of course, nothing naughty happens between Yannick and I— there are some things even I would not embrace, one of those things being my brother. We share Althea."

Matthew's head reeled. "Your brother accepts your sharing a bed with his wife?"

De Wynter nodded. "Althea belongs to us both, and we both love her dearly."

"I—Hades, I don't think I could do that with Octavia." He rubbed his jaw. Without Lucifer's help, what could he do? "Couldn't a witch turn her into something else? If I could be made into a vampire with a soul, one cursed to die, couldn't someone free Octavia from her need to drain a soul through sex?"

"I don't know. For that, we have to speak to Guidon. If a miracle can be had, he would be the one to know."

He had been jammed into the crowded bookshop for hours; he had fetched book after book like a lackey for the gnome-like, gray-haired librarian. If he was offered another cup of tea, Matthew thought he could break every piece of crockery in London.

With each thump of a book shutting, each tug of Guidon's hands in his straggly hair, a little more of Matthew's hope drained away. De Wynter sat, drinking tea—his friend had stayed quiet and had let him do the work of bringing books.

Finally, Guidon pushed aside an enormous leather-bound book, one filled with tattered pages, secured by a tarnished, silver lock. "Nothing." Grimly, the librarian shook his head. "There is nothing. She cannot be changed." He picked up his tea and sipped it. "I wish I had better tidings for you, Lord Sutcliffe."

"I was cursed to die and cheated my damned destiny. I've heard the vampire queens possess great power—can't they help? What of Mrs. Darkwell?"

"She cannot interfere directly in a woman's discovery of love."

"Interfere? She cursed me to die."

"And yet you are alive, and you and your beautiful wife are in love. She merely nudged you two on your way."

He had been cursed to die. That was a *nudge?* He had traveled most of the world, and had been arrogant and confident at every step. He'd never really believed he could die—he was too clever, too rich, and he was a powerful earl.

Now, he felt powerless. Confused. And humble.

"The vampire queens cannot help you," Guidon added. "They cannot help a succubus."

Matthew jumped up from his chair. He had been told many times that things were impossible. He'd been told he would not survive hiking in the Carpathians at night. He had been told he would perish if he climbed mountains in the Himalayas. He'd steered ships through storms that should have torn him apart.

He'd cheated fate dozens of times, even surviving a curse. But the one time he really needed to do it . . . he couldn't. "So there's no happy ending for us—for Octavia and I." He growled the words, hearing the bitterness in them.

"The only way you can make love to her and not lose your soul is if you are changed back into a vampire."

Could he do that? He had hated being a vampire before. And then he remembered. "It won't work. She needs to take a piece of a man's soul. If I kept her faithful to me, and I became a vampire, I could kill her." He shook his head, then faced Guidon. "How long can I expect to survive?"

"Do you really want to know? If I do not tell you, you can"—Guidon blushed—"have your marital relations with your wife until you expire without warning. That might be for the best."

"No. I want to know. I'll wait." As he spoke, Matthew caught De Wynter's gaze and read the most damning of emotions in it. Sympathy. It was almost worse than pity. Hell, how long did he have?

"I will have to find out," Guidon said. "Wait here."

The gnome-like librarian leapt off the settee and raced back to his stove. Soon a strange smell filled the shop. Guidon returned with a gilt-decorated white china cup, filled with a dark fluid. The vampire handed it to him. "Drink. This will tell me how long you have."

Matthew gulped the entire thing down. It was like drinking the sticky sap of a fir tree. "Ugh," he spat after he'd finished it.

Guidon cocked his head and walked around Matthew. "Your body and your soul suffered great strain when you carried your curse, Lord Sutcliffe. Even the magic that freed you from the curse left you weaker. It drained some of your soul. You carried a great deal of guilt while you kept your vampirism a secret from your wife, and that has also taken its measure on your soul."

"That does not sound good," Matthew muttered.

"The next time you are intimate with Lady Sutcliffe . . ." Again Guidon turned pink. "I am afraid it will very likely be your last time."

21

The Last Time

"Do I tell Octavia? Or do I keep it a secret?"

Matthew drained his tumbler of brandy and paced in his study. His baby daughter was up in the nursery, tucked beneath the lacy blankets of her bassinet. Octavia was in bed, either asleep or wondering why in heaven's name he wasn't with her. He stopped stalking back and forth and looked to De Wynter. Why ask the question? Any answer De Wynter gave him would likely be wrong.

He had just needed to put out the question. To air it, so he could think it through himself.

De Wynter rested his arse on the edge of Matthew's desk. "That sounds like a question where any answer is wrong."

"I wasn't really expecting an answer." Matthew groaned.

"I can give you one piece of advice," De Wynter said. "Keeping secrets from wives is more dangerous than facing an entire clan of murderous werewolves or fire-breathing dragon-shifters. There is a solution: If you don't make love to your wife again, you survive."

Matthew gripped the marble mantel and rested his forehead

against it with a thud. "You can't really think I would never make love to Octavia again. I couldn't do it."

His friend nodded. "Well, if you didn't, she would die. However, you have to understand that if you die, she will still need sex to survive. She will have to go to other men anyway—"

"No." He slammed his hands on the edge of the mantel. Facing De Wynter, he growled, "I know you have found happiness. But you also share your wife with only your brother . . . I assume there is no one else?"

De Wynter crossed his arms in front of his chest. "Touché. There's no one else."

"Do I just accept what Guidon says and give up hope? Do I warn my wife that I'll die with my next orgasm with her? If I tell her, I suspect she'll never let me into her bed again . . . until she has no choice. Damn it, this is madness. I won't let her die for me. But why does it have to be this choice? What if Guidon is wrong? He's a librarian—"

"He knows everything there is to know about preternatural beings. He is never wrong."

"I intend to prove he can be."

"Go to your wife," De Wynter said. The vampire came to him and clapped him on the shoulder. "I would suggest honesty. Don't make love to her and die in front of her. Think of her. That would be highly disturbing, and it would both anger and upset her if you hadn't given her the chance to decide."

Matthew pushed open the door of Octavia's bedroom, inhaling delectable scents: the rosy perfume she wore, the lavender water she used, the sweet smell of her skin on her bedcovers. He stopped in the doorway in surprise. Her bed was empty.

She must have gone to his bed, to wait for him there.

How long could she go without making love? Before, when she had lasted for months, they had shared dreams together.

And she had been pregnant. Guidon told him that lessened a succubus's need for sex.

Tonight, he had to give Octavia the truth. He had to tell her what Guidon had predicted.

He had spent most of their time together not being honest with her. He'd tried to hide that he was a vampire, hide from her the truth that she was a succubus. He had only been truly honest when he'd told her he loved her.

De Wynter was correct, and Matthew had learned the truth of it. Honesty was all there should be between Octavia and him.

He went through the connecting parlor to his room. The door stood open. Moonlight poured in through an open curtain. It threw a slant of silver light across the bed. Octavia's golden hair spilled out from beneath the sheets.

He had faced an army of assassins, but he hadn't felt as nervous then as he did now.

Gently, he planted his arse on the edge of the bed. She had the covers pulled right up, so shadow hid her beautiful face. He bent over and kissed her. Smiled as his lips touched moisture on her cheek—she'd drooled onto her pillow.

It was so sweet it made tears prickle in the corners of his eyes. Damn, gentlemen did not cry. He would not. But it was hard to keep his lips steady when he knew he was going to die; he would never see Octavia and Lottie again.

"Mmm." Octavia rolled on her back, and her lids lifted. "You are finally home. You are very late. Are you coming to bed?"

"Tavie, there's something I have to tell you."

Her eyes went wide, and in the next instant she sat upright in the bed. So quickly, she almost bumped her head against his. "What is it? You wouldn't tell me you were a vampire, or that

I'm a succubus. If you are admitting something to me, it must be terrible."

Her words brought forth a spurt of guilt. Once he had not cared about his life because he had felt so damned guilty for not saving his brother. Now he hungered to live, to be with Octavia and Lottie.

He needed to be close to her. He wrapped his arm around her. This embrace would not last long: Once he talked to her, she would probably push him away.

He feared Octavia would focus on saving him.

"When we made love earlier, it left me weak—"

"I know. I'm killing you again. You don't want to go to bed with me, and I don't blame you. I'm so sorry. I don't want to hurt you. I'd rather die than do that."

"No," he thundered. "Don't say that."

Tears glinted in her eyes. One fell to her cheek, wringing his heart like he might wring a wet shirt. "I went to White's to find Bastien De Wynter, and he took me to Guidon's."

He told her everything Guidon had told him. Even the warning that the next time he made love might be his last.

"Heavens, no," she whispered.

She had never looked lovelier. The softness of the moonlight caressed her oval face and made her lips look even more full and luscious than normal. Her eyes sparkled like silvery jewels.

Matthew looked down, and his throat dried. The valley between her full breasts was a deep, shadowy space, one that beckoned him to delve his tongue within. Her curves looked so round and generous his hand ached to cup them.

He knew he wasn't reacting to her with such intense desire because she was a succubus. It was because she was the woman he loved.

"There is no way on earth I can never make love to you again."

"But I refuse to hurt you," she protested.

"You will die without sex. I am not going to let that happen."

"You are the only man I want," she whispered, staring into his eyes. Then she shook her head fiercely. "I cannot believe there is no solution! If you could be changed back from being a vampire, couldn't I somehow stop being a succubus?"

She frowned, obviously thinking deeply. But all he could think of was how her lips pursed so sensually when she thought. How her breasts swayed when she was vehement. How much he wanted her—

Hell, there was no way he would be able to go an hour without making love to her, much less a lifetime. "I went to Lucifer and asked him to free you. He refused."

She goggled at him. "You went to the Underworld?"

"Yes. It was an interesting journey. But Lucifer refused to let you go."

She sank down. "So I truly am a being who serves the devil."

Matthew hated to see such pain in her eyes.

The next time would be the last time. The words had broken Octavia's heart, but she knew she must be strong. "Then we won't make love again," she said firmly.

Matthew was sitting on the bed beside her. He shook his head. "Tavie, I can't do that. You are far too tempting."

"We could live apart," she said swiftly. "So you would not be tempted. I know that men have needs, so you could take mistresses. I would understand. This is my fault—"

His eyes blazed at her. "It is not your fault, and I do not want to take mistresses. I don't want anyone but you."

"Your father died over my mother. My mother died because of what she was. I don't want that to happen to us. I don't want us to both perish over love."

"So we have to walk away from love and happiness?"

It broke her heart, too. "We can still love each other. We just cannot be together," she whispered.

"Tavie, I want to show my love to you. Every night. In fact, I want to show my love to you at night, in the morning, and every afternoon. I cannot walk away. You need sex to survive. I don't want you to go to another man. Making love with you means too much."

"If only I could break this curse of mine," she said sadly. "It is a horrible one. I want someone who could make me just a mortal woman."

"You would never be 'just' anything."

"What did Lucifer say to you, exactly, when you asked him to free me?"

"He said that unless I asked him properly, he could not let you go. So I tried asking him politely, tried it several times, and he refused. Then I held a blade to his throat and threatened to kill him. I quickly discovered you can't threaten the devil with death."

He spoke lightly, and that gave her a jolt of fear. "What happened to you?"

"First my blade turned into molten metal, burning me. Then I was attacked by hundreds of tormented souls, all seeking—in a perverse, warped way—to protect the beast that kept them imprisoned in Hell."

"You were almost killed, weren't you?"

"I survived. You are worth any risk."

"He asked you to ask him properly. . . ." What exactly did that mean?

"I assumed he was mocking me. He refused to tell me what he meant. He laughed at me."

"What if—" Her thoughts raced. She clasped her husband's

strong, elegant hands. "What if he meant there is a specific way you must ask for my freedom? Like an incantation of magic."

The idea came off her lips at the exact same instant he said, "Guidon."

She nodded fiercely. "We must go to him and find out."

Matthew had to smile. They faced a grim future, but her determination made him smile. She was a stubborn and determined woman. And he loved her for it. He'd loved her for those qualities from the beginning, though he'd been too stubborn to admit it.

"It is the middle of the night," he pointed out.

"Guidon will still be awake—he's a vampire. Lottie is upstairs sleeping. She will want to be fed though, so we must be quick—"

"We could bring Guidon to us," Matthew suggested.

His wife smiled. "An excellent idea. Is he actually a vampire? I never knew. I will dress quickly and prepare some food and drink for him."

"Tavie, I don't think you have to—"

"If he can give us a happy ending, I think he deserves to be treated like a king."

Octavia poured tea for Guidon. She looked into his earnest eyes. "There must be a way," she whispered. She was pleading the words to him.

Guidon patted her hand gently before he took the teacup and saucer. Grimly, he shook his head. "To be a demon is to carry a curse that makes one different from mortals. A curse can be broken, that is true. But you cannot beg for freedom. You must *discover* the path to freedom."

Matthew sputtered, but she held up her hand to warn him to stay quiet.

"So you cannot just give me the answer, Mr. Guidon. But there *is* an answer?"

He sipped his tea. "This is the most excellent tea I have ever had, my lady. If there is anyone capable of finding answers, it is a lady who can brew such remarkable tea."

"I will find the answer." She was aware of her husband looking from her to Guidon. She turned to him. "There is a way, but we have to find it. We must use our wits. I suspect that we have to prove we are worthy of happiness."

Matthew was going to speak, but she lifted her hand. "No complaints. Let us prove it." She faced Guidon. "If you could help us, and give us any clue you can, I could arrange a meeting with someone you care for."

The vampire looked startled.

"I was thinking of Aphrodite's daughter," she said softly.

Guidon's cheeks turned scarlet. "I will do what I can, my lady."

"When Lady Sutcliffe takes a bit of a man's soul, where does it go?" Matthew asked.

"To Hades. But do not look to Lucifer for help. He would never release a succubus. Those little pieces of soul are like a drug to him."

"I know," Matthew said drily. "I asked him to free her, and he refused."

"You must outwit Lucifer to win."

Octavia rubbed the heel of her hand against her forehead. She had to think—

"Damn, I can think of nothing," Matthew growled.

The next time they made love, she would take the rest of Matthew's soul, and it would go to Lucifer and he would die—

"Oh!" she cried. She leapt up, knocking the small table and almost upsetting the teapot. Guidon swiftly rescued it. "I think I know how to do this. I think I know how to win."

* * *

Matthew leaned back in a wing chair and watched Octavia strip off her nightgown. Firelight made the delicate silk translucent. She whisked it over her head. She turned as she did so, so the firelight turned her hard nipples into peaks of gold.

Her idea made sense. Pleasure had gotten them into this disaster. It sounded logical that pleasure could get them out of it.

Octavia gazed up at him with innocent, trusting eyes. "I want you to do the most scandalous and erotic things to me. Any naughty thing you can think of. *Please*."

What a request. It made his legs shake as arousal shot through him. It was hard to think, given his cock was so hard, so heavy, and blood pulsed through it with each beat of his heart.

"I want you to be able to watch me making love to you."

He led Octavia to her vanity table. "Hold the edge of it and bend over," he instructed hoarsely.

She did, and it made her lovely bottom stick out. It was such an arousing position, he almost came on the spot.

Gently, he bent and ran his tongue over her generous curves. With his fingers, he stroked her pussy. She was already wet with anticipation.

He dipped his finger in, then thrust it in and out. After wetting his finger with her juices, he pushed his fingertip into her anus. She moaned loudly.

"I want you inside me."

He positioned himself behind her, with his legs slightly spread. He had to push hard on his erect cock to point it down to her cunny.

One arch of his hips and he was in heaven. Her creamy, hot walls gripped him. His brain was instantly flooded with pleasure. He almost came; he had to fight to hang on while he thrust in her.

In the mirror, he could see her breasts sway, her nipples bounce. He could see the sheer sensual agony on her face. He could see her eyes shut with pleasure when she moaned and squealed.

Just as he'd thought, watching her face while he pleasured her was the most erotic and delightful thing he could imagine.

If this was going to be his last time, he was finding out how heavenly sex could be.

Matthew thrust so deep he made her entire vanity table shake. The mirror wobbled precariously, but Octavia didn't care. How could she, when his cock surged in so far and touched magical places? Each stroke make her knees tremble.

She moved her legs wider apart, bracing herself for his assault. "I love this," she whispered. "I love to feel as though I'm being taken by you, and you are so wild and rough with lust."

"And love," he growled. "I'm wild because I love you so much. Now rub your sweet clit and come for me."

She just brushed her fingers against the sensitive nub, and suddenly fireworks were bursting and pleasure shot through her.

"Oh! Oh! Oh, oh, oh!" she cried.

She heard him laugh, then groan, then his hips collided so hard into her bottom, they both sprawled over the vanity. Heat filled her, and she was certain she could feel his semen jetting out of his cock.

Oh yes.

He stroked her clit for her, moving her fingers with his. His touch was gentle, but it made brilliant stars shoot before her eyes. He had never made her come after he'd climaxed. But he did this time, and he moaned so loudly she began to fear he was losing his soul. "Are you all right?" she whispered.

"Perfect."

He rubbed her harder, and she burst once more. He embraced her from behind as she sobbed with pleasure. Then he pulled back, and she felt his cock slide out of her.

He gasped.

Frightened, she turned in his arms. He had gone deathly pale, and had put his hand to his heart.

"I won't take his soul," she cried out. "I won't take it, and I will give mine instead."

She stood by the vanity, trembling, watching Matthew. Matthew groaned and pressed his hand harder to his heart, making her fear that she'd failed. Then he lifted his head, met her gaze. "The pain has stopped."

He clenched his fist and released it. "My strength is coming back." He stared at her. "Octavia, damn, I won't let you give your soul to Lucifer."

She shook her head. She had only taken this terrible risk because she believed Lucifer wouldn't take her soul. . . .

Or had she guessed wrong? Would she notice when her soul left her? Would she feel pain and weakness like Matthew? Would she die? Surely she would if she lost her soul. . . .

But Matthew would be alive. Lottie would have her father—

The most intense, hot, strange scent filled the room. It smelled like a fire, but one filled with spices. Matthew, though naked, moved to her. He threw a robe around her, then he pulled her back against him. She felt his heart pound and his powerful chest move with deep breaths.

"I think Lucifer is coming for his due," he growled. "I'm not going to let him take you."

"Well, I will not let him have you," she answered fiercely.

A whirl of smoke rushed down the chimney. The fire went out with the whoosh of sooty air. Matthew grasped the fireplace poker and held it like a weapon. But she knew, just as with vampires, such a weapon would do them no good with the devil.

She was going to meet the devil. Was she truly a creature made by him? Was she in his service for eternity?

The smoke whirled into the room, just in front of the fireplace. It rose into a column seven feet in the air and began to take on human form.

Soon a naked man stood before them. He possessed muscular legs, lean hips, and a broad and powerful chest. The smoke had formed wide shoulders and, finally, a handsome face. But he had horns, and the most enormous penis—an impossibly large one.

Lucifer folded his arms across his chest. "You truly want to trade your soul for his?"

"No," Matthew roared.

"Yes," she shouted.

Floating above the ground, the devil circled them. "When I create demonesses, I do a very good job."

"But how did you create me? You didn't—I was born of my mother and father. They created me. I may take souls, but I never wanted to hurt anyone. I am *not* a demon."

Matthew pulled her back, stepping in front of her to shield her. "She is an angel."

"I made the succubus from whom she descended. She is not an angel. She is a wanton demon at heart, but with an angelically lovely exterior."

"She has an angel's heart," Matthew said.

The devil lifted a brow. "This is what you fell in love with? Flowery words?"

"My husband is a good and perfect man."

Satan gave a seductive smile. "If you were no longer a succubus, Octavia, you would lose all your special powers."

"I don't mind losing my magic."

"Your magic is a precious gift. You can move objects with

your mind. You can start fires. You can make mortals do what you wish—"

"I don't want that. But I do want to know: If I weren't a succubus would Matthew love me?"

"Of course I would."

The devil gave a wicked smile. "His lust and love for you has nothing to do with your being a succubus. I will release you, Octavia."

"You refused me," Matthew said.

"She is a beautiful woman. I can't refuse her. But I have a price. Sutcliffe, you must share her with me. One night of decadent sexual pleasure between the three of us. Then she will be yours for the rest of your lives. I will give her freedom."

"I—hell, I can't share her. I love her too much."

"So you will let her die?"

"No, you can have my soul, instead of hers, just as you wanted in the first place."

"You would die rather than share her? A pity. I am damned good in bed." A wide grin flashed the devil's gleaming white fangs again. "Most would think I would happily torture you. It would be much more entertaining than a happy ending. But I cannot. I admire love. It's something I have sought for eternity."

"You could find it," Octavia said impetuously. "It is merely your reputation that stands in your way."

The devil's coal black brows shot up. He tipped his head back and roared with laughter.

Finally, he stopped and wiped his eyes. "For that, lovely Octavia, I give you your freedom."

He lifted his hands. Thunder boomed. Lightning forked outside the window, instantly illuminating the room with its flash. Octavia felt warm everywhere, a wonderful tingling sensation. Then it was gone.

"It is done," the devil said. "You are free. When I am back in Hades, I will wonder what I was thinking. Lucifer is not supposed to grant happy endings—it will ruin my reputation."

"Is our daughter to be a succubus? Would you free her, too?"

The devil quirked a brow, and her heart sank. Then he shrugged. "All right, it is done. She is freed as well. So enjoy each other."

An explosion of thunder came, so loud it shook the house. Lucifer's powerful body dissolved into smoke. And the smoke vanished up the chimney.

Matthew had to know Octavia was all right. He grasped her shoulders. She looked fine. A little dazed. She stared at him, obviously confused. "I'm free? Our daughter is free?"

"Yes. That's what Lucifer says."

"Lottie is crying," she said suddenly. She paled. "I can hear her from the nursery."

"I imagine the lightning and thunder frightened her." He slid his palms down along Tavie's arms to her trembling hands. He squeezed them. "The nurses will attend to her, but I'd like to go to her as well. Let's go to her together."

He had to fight tears. Gentlemen did not cry. But it was not every day a gentleman got his perfect, happy ending.

So Octavia wouldn't see those tears, he gathered her close and kissed the top of her head. With his arm around her waist, he led her out of the room, toward their beautiful baby daughter.

"Is it really over?" Octavia whispered. She knew it was a foolish question, and Lucifer had told them they were free, but since he was the devil, could he really be believed?

Matthew cocked his brow at her. They were walking through his greenhouse. A few feet away, Lottie's nurse was plucking flowers, which their daughter kept trying to eat. The young nurse would rescue each flower before chubby fingers could stuff the petals between Cupid's bow lips.

"There is a way to find out for sure." He gave her a rakish smile. "Tonight."

She frowned. "Guidon told us it meant I was free. I am sure I believe him."

"Love, I just suggested a passionate encounter tonight. I can't believe you'd rather believe Guidon than test it out with me."

"I would like to go to our passionate encounter without fear."

"I know you can, Tavie."

She crossed her fingers. "I hope so."

Octavia was too nervous to wait until nighttime. Once they returned to the house, and Lottie was upstairs in the nursery for her nap, she went to Matthew. She found him in his study. Carefully she locked the door behind her.

"I'm ready now," she whispered, "to determine if we really are going to have a happy ending."

He smiled. "That has to be the most unique way you've invited me to have sex."

After three hours of lovemaking in which she ensured Matthew had three orgasms—and she had more than she could count—Octavia gave a happy sigh. She was lying on the carpet, and he lay at her side.

"I am convinced now," she said.

"Good. Another orgasm might have finished me off . . . for entirely different reasons." Matthew levered up on his arm and smiled down at her. "This was very much the perfect happy ending for me."

"It's not quite the end you know."

"More sex?" he asked hopefully.

Octavia smiled. "I meant, we have our whole lives before us to spend together. But yes, more sex would be good, too."

He rolled over on top of her. "Anything you want, my beautiful Octavia."

She wriggled with anticipation underneath him. "I remember long ago, when I was sick and I did not know why, I dreamed of being with you. Even then, I knew you were what I wanted." She sighed happily. "You are my dream come true."

"You are mine."

Then he was inside her, and they were making love. The moment she climaxed, he moaned and shuddered, and he came, too.

And she knew they would always be perfect together—in bed and in every way.

Turn the page for a sizzling preview of the new book in
Kate Douglas's DreamCatchers series:

DREAM UNCHAINED

An Aphrodisia trade paperback on sale now!

1

It wasn't until a tangerine slice of sunlight flashed above the sharp edge of the plateau that Mac Dugan realized he'd spent almost the whole damned night on the deck outside his bedroom.

Sitting in a hard, wooden Adirondack chair, freezing his ass off while the woman he loved and his best friend were curled up together in the big bed in the room behind him.

He imagined the two of them—snuggled warm and cozy in a tangle of twisted bedding—and didn't know whether to laugh or cry at the visual. Dink, all long, well-formed male with a sexy mat of dark blond hair across his chest, washboard abs, and a strong, sharply masculine face darkened with morning stubble.

And Zianne? Fluffy little gray squirrel.

Last time he looked, she'd had her tail curled around the top of Dink's head and one tiny paw resting on his ear.

It wasn't supposed to end like this.

He took a deep breath, pushed back his fear and the sharp burn of frustrated tears, and focused on what they'd shared last night. Mac, Zianne, and Dink, together again as they'd been so long ago. Zianne had held on to her human shape long enough for them to make love—the three of them connecting in a way they'd not been able to do since her abrupt disappearance so many years ago.

Twenty fucking years. Twenty years wondering if she still lived. Worrying whether or not all of his creative energies, every spare penny he'd been able to raise, and the combined technological advances of the entire research and development team at Beyond Global Ventures would be enough to rescue Zianne and the few surviving members of her people from slavery.

Twenty years, sixty million dollars, and a lifetime of focusing on an impossible rescue would all come down to the next thirty-six hours or so. Fewer than two days for Zianne to live or die, for the few remnants of the Nyrian people to survive.

Or not.

They were so damned close to success, even as the entire project balanced on a razor's edge of failure.

Shit. He hadn't allowed himself to consider failure. How could he, and still work toward such an impossible goal? What fool would even attempt the rescue of a small group of alien slaves imprisoned aboard a spaceship—held by another alien race preparing to plunder the earth of all its natural resources?

It sounded ridiculous no matter how he phrased it, so he did what he always tried to do when the fears surfaced. Mac pushed the negative thoughts out of his head. Refused to consider failure. Reminded himself failure was never an option.

Call it denial, call it what you will, but it was the only way he'd survived the past two decades. Focus on the desired outcome. Ignore the rest. Plan for everything that can possibly go wrong, and then put those plans aside and go with one that assured success.

Mac sucked in a deep breath, centered himself, and locked his fear away. He consciously refocused his energy, squinting at the growing brilliance of the sun as it slanted across the huge array of satellite dishes. He studied them with pride, taking comfort in the fact they worked perfectly, that they had allowed his small team of young men and women to make telepathic contact with Zianne's people.

People of pure energy, enslaved eons ago aboard the Gar vessel and forced to power the huge star cruiser now hiding in orbit behind the moon. Unwilling accomplices in the Gar's plans to plunder Earth of all her riches. To take her mineral resources, her air and water—all that kept the planet alive.

The scope of the threat was beyond even Mac's wildest imagination, and his imagination had no limits. The satellite array was proof of that—the fact it had worked so well, that it had allowed his people to contact the Nyrians from the very first day gave him hope that their plan, what there was of it, would succeed. Somehow, they would rescue the captives.

Somehow, he would save Zianne's life.

Mac shifted his attention to the square cinder-block building they'd labeled the dream shack. The small building was the center of operations for the entire project, the place where his telepathic team members would hook themselves up to the massive antennae and, via the satellite array, focus their sexual energy on the Nyrians.

And the Nyrians had already proved they knew how to work with such a powerful and compelling source of power. Mac had learned their secret from Zianne over two decades earlier, that the Nyrians, a people without a physical form of their own, could take on corporeal bodies through the power of sexual fantasy.

Could take those bodies and hold on to them, and, once they were able to retrieve their soulstones, they would be free of the Gar and able to make a new home here, on Earth.

If everything went according to plan. "Damn but that's a big *if*." Sighing, Mac rubbed his hand over his burning eyes. He'd not slept all night and today he would need to be sharp—on top of his game—if he was going to be any help at all. He stared at the dream shack, watching as the sunlight brushed the glass dome on top of the building. That had been an act of whimsy—installing a skylight so that the team members could watch the sky as they projected their thoughts through space. They didn't need to see the stars to know they were there, but from what feedback he'd gotten, all of them appreciated the view skyward.

He glanced at his wristwatch as the top half of the sun wavered above the dark edge of the plateau. It was barely six, which meant Finnegan O'Toole had a couple more hours to his shift.

Now there was a guy who'd proved first impressions weren't always correct. Finn had come across as a class A jerk—brilliant, but still a jerk. Then he'd shown more character than Mac or any of the others had suspected when he'd volunteered to go aboard the Gar star cruiser to help with the rescue.

A brave and foolish offer by a man who was no one's fool.

What kind of man would willingly step into danger like that?

Me?

Yeah, Mac knew he'd do it in a heartbeat, except he was needed here. This was, after all, his quest, for want of a better word. The culmination of his twenty-year mission to find Zianne, to save her people, to destroy the Gar before they destroyed the world.

It sounded like a grade B movie when he spelled it out, except it was real. Terrifying, beyond belief, yet all too real.

Who in the hell, in their right mind, would think he had a prayer of success? Of course, no one had ever accused him of being in his right mind. Even Mac's strongest supporters figured he had more than a few screws loose.

In all fairness to himself, what genius didn't march to a different drummer? It was probably a very good thing that the world didn't know the truth—Mac Dugan didn't follow any drummer.

Hell no. He'd been following the directions of a beautiful alien who drew her physical form from his sexual fantasies. A woman who wouldn't even exist as other than pure energy without the drunken visual of a twenty-six-year-old postgrad student back in the early days of the computer age.

Only a handful of people knew the truth—that his whole career had been based on a four-month relationship with an inhuman creature he'd fallen in lust and then in love with. The same creature now trapped in the body of a little gray squirrel.

Shit. What a fucked-up mess. What chance in hell—

"Mac? I thought you came back to bed. How long have you been outside? Good lord, man, it's freezing out here."

Mac leaned his head against the back of his chair and stared upside down at the man shivering behind him. "G'morning to you, too, Dink. Couldn't sleep. Didn't want to disturb you guys." He straightened up and waved at the chair beside him. "Have a seat. You don't by any chance have coffee, do you?"

"You're kidding, right? Me? Make coffee?"

"One can only hope." He chuckled. He might be a world-famous investigative reporter, but Nils Dinkemann had never been known for his culinary skills. "I was afraid of that, but, yeah, I know. I lost contact with my toes a few hours ago." A thick down comforter settled over him, still warm from Dink's body heat.

"Okay. This works." Mac drew his feet up under the blanket and tucked all that soft warmth around him. "Damn that feels good. I think it's even better than coffee."

A moment later, Dink flopped down in the chair beside Mac's, wrapped head to foot in another blanket. "I heard some rattling and clanking downstairs," he said. "Sounds like your cook's putting some fresh coffee on. I'll get us some in a few minutes."

Mac grunted in assent. He turned and glanced toward the sliding glass door, but Dink had closed it. The glare of the growing sunlight reflected off the glass.

He couldn't see Zianne. "Is . . . ?"

"She's asleep. Still a squirrel. I left her wrapped in your jacket."

"Thanks." He sighed.

"You okay?"

Mac rolled his head to the right and stared at Dink. "You're kidding, right?"

Dink grunted.

Hell no, I'm not all right. "We'll know in approximately two more days, I guess."

Dink grunted again.

Two more days and Mac would know if all his efforts might actually pay off. And if they didn't?

He sucked in a deep breath. Exhaled. "Cameron was planning to meet the last two Nyrians during his shift last night, which means that by now all of them should have access to functioning human bodies. The first group will be coming to Earth tonight—once they have their soulstones—as soon as it turns dark."

"So what happens today?"

Mac glanced at Dink. There was none of the investigative reporter about him this morning. No, he just sounded like a very concerned friend. Right now, Mac figured he needed the friend more than the reporter, though if all went according to plan, he'd need the reporter even more once the Nyrians were all safe. "Today a couple of the stronger Nyrians are going to show Finn and Morgan how to disincorporate and move through space."

"Holy shit." Whispered softly, more a prayer than a curse.

Mac shrugged. "That's the only way to get them on the ship. Breaking down to molecular particles and traveling with a host Nyrian through space. Sounds good in theory."

"I can't believe you actually got volunteers."

"Morgan Black and Finn O'Toole. Both good guys, physically strong, very sharp. The Gar shouldn't be expecting an attack, but they're always well armed. According to Nattoch, the Nyrian elder who's sort of their leader, the Gar carry weapons that can disrupt the Nyrians' energy field. Doesn't kill them, but can effectively immobilize them. It shouldn't affect humans, though. Once Finn and Morgan arrive on board the ship, they'll have to rematerialize and disarm the guards so the Nyrians can retrieve their soulstones."

And, Nyria help them, Zianne's soulstone as well. She was dying. Would die within the next few hours without an infusion of power from one of her fellow Nyrians, but even their generous gifts of power couldn't hold her here forever.

Not without her soulstone.

Mac sighed. So much could go wrong. So damned much.

Dink reached across the narrow gap that separated them, took hold of Mac's hand, and squeezed it tightly. "This is the one thing I hate most about being a reporter. Learning the plans, knowing the danger, and realizing there's not a fucking thing I can do to alter the outcome."

Mac squeezed back. "You're here, Dink. That matters more than you realize." He gazed into his friend's silvery eyes, but there was too much emotion, too much to consider right now.

Mac glanced away as the sun finally broke free of the horizon in a blinding blaze of orange and pink against a cerulean sky. It was easier to blame the tears in his eyes on the brilliant flash of sunlight shimmering off row after row of white satellite dishes, marching west across the array with inexorable certainty.

The sun would continue to rise, the days would pass, the world would go on.

But life? Not such a sure thing. Not anymore. This might be the last day for Zianne, but if things went wrong with their plan for rescuing her people, it could also be the end of more than the few remaining Nyrians.

If they couldn't stop the Gar, if the Nyrians were somehow compelled to continue powering their huge star cruiser, it could very well mark the end of everything, at least as far as Earth was concerned.

Zianne and Mac's love wasn't even a blip on the radar, not compared to the ultimate risks they faced.

It wasn't like humans had been such great stewards of their world, but they hadn't totally fucked things up yet. If the Gar had their way, once they moved on to other worlds, they'd leave nothing but a smoldering chunk of rock where civilizations had once risen and fallen. Where humans had grown and evolved.

Where Mac had met an impossible, improbable woman; where he'd fallen in love and followed a dream.

A dream that had all the signs of transforming into a fucking nightmare.

He didn't want to think about it. No, he had to believe in success. As Dink kept reminding him, it was the only acceptable outcome. He said it again, whispering the words to himself as he sat there on the deck, his hand tightly clasped in Dink's.

Failure is not an option.

Cameron Paisley's hand shook so bad he couldn't get the damned brush into the jar of paint thinner. This had never happened before. Not to this extent, not this total loss of self, of time and place and space while painting.

His fantastical landscapes of imaginary worlds had always come to him through dreams, but he'd generally been wide awake while he painted them. The amount of money they brought in certainly kept his eyes wide open, but this massive canvas was something else altogether.

He vaguely recalled finding the huge canvas in the closet with a bunch of smaller ones that were already stretched. He didn't recall getting it out. Didn't remember setting it up, pulling out his paints. Didn't remember a fucking thing.

It wasn't just big—measuring at least six feet wide and four feet high—but the art itself was haunting. Beautiful. Unbelievable.

Utterly terrifying.

Even more frightening? He couldn't remember painting a single stroke, yet he knew it was his work, done in his style. It was a world he'd never seen, and yet he knew exactly what it was. Where it was. And he knew, without a doubt, that it no longer existed as it once had. As he'd painted it.

He finally managed to drag his gaze away from the mass of dark and fearsome images, focus his attention on the jar of thinner, and jam his brush into the solvent.

As if someone physically forced him, Cam's eyes were drawn back to the painting. His hands were still shaking. Critics had asked over the years if his work was more than his imagination. He'd always said his paintings were the product of dreams.

This was no dream. This hadn't come to him during his shift in the dream shack. No, this had taken him over like a bad drug trip, had caught him up for . . . He glanced at the clock on the wall. Two hours?

Stunned, Cam stared at the canvas. He worked fast, but this painting was huge and filled with such detail that it should have taken him much, much longer.

Days, not hours.

It hurt to look. To realize what he saw in the bold strokes, the splashes of color, the finer details set within an unyielding maelstrom of shapes and images. He'd painted fear and death, abject loss and total destruction.

A world in the agonizing final spasms of existence.

Forcibly turning his back on the art, Cam grabbed a rag and wiped his hands clean. Somehow he had to clear his head; he needed to make sense of this.

Tossing the rag aside, he quickly slipped out of his clothes and left them in a pile on the floor in front of the easel. Naked and shivering in the morning chill, he walked quickly through the bedroom to the bathroom.

He caught a brief glance of himself in the mirror. As always, he averted his eyes and turned on the tap in the shower. So stupid, the way he always reacted to his own image.

Someday he'd probably wish he still looked like an overgrown teenager, but for now, it would be nice to look his age. It was hard enough getting the established art world to take a thirty-year-old man seriously. A guy who looked about seventeen got absolutely no respect.

Did it really matter? Shit, no. If he believed Mac—and there was no reason not to—if Mac's project failed, there wouldn't be a fucking art world to worry about.

Cam grabbed a washcloth off the rack beside the shower, stepped beneath the spray, and concentrated on emptying his mind of everything but the welcome heat of the water, the way tension slowly eased out of tired muscles beneath the pounding spray. A more welcome thought intruded, that he'd finally experienced what the other members of the dream team had known all along—sending sexual fantasies to Nyrians had one hell of a payback.

After two nights of fantasizing about his art and the pending rescue of the aliens, he'd finally gotten on track during last night's shift.

Had he ever. The thought had barely registered when a coil

of arousal shocked him into immediate awareness. His balls drew close to his body; his cock throbbed with new blood.

"Down, boy." At least this part of him looked and acted like a grown-up. Chuckling, he smoothed his hand over his taut shaft, paused a moment to slip his foreskin over the broad head and back again. A shiver raced along his spine. A shiver of pure carnal pleasure. He turned his dick loose and brushed his wet hair out of his eyes. Even without stroking himself, his arousal seemed to be growing, just from remembering his shift last night in the shack.

And to think he was getting paid for this! Being a member of Mac Dugan's dream team definitely had good bennies. Using his imagination to broadcast sexual fantasies to aliens who gained power from his wild thoughts might sound totally impossible, but when those fantasies were combined with Mac's powerful satellite array to boost their energy, the results were beyond amazing.

He thought of the two women who'd come to him during his shift, the last of the twenty-eight surviving Nyrians to make the journey to Earth for the combination of sexual power and visual images necessary to create their own corporeal bodies.

He'd certainly liked the bodies his two visitors had chosen, and he'd definitely loved what they did with them. Once the Nyrians had a solid form, they seemed to delight in the sensual pleasures their new human bodies allowed.

Granted, everything had happened in his head—or at least he thought it had—but it had felt like so much more.

Sort of like the painting. He wondered if Mac was awake, if maybe he ought to show it to him. Shit. He let out a huge breath. He could be wrong, but he was positive the damned thing was . . .

Oh. Fuck. The soft brush of something warm along his inner thigh jerked Cam out of his convoluted thoughts.

Out of his thoughts and right back here, to what could only be a dream. "Mir? Niah? What are you doing here?" He blinked furiously, clearing the water out of his eyes. Both women, his Nyrians from the night before, here? In his shower? He was awake, damn it. He wasn't fantasizing.

"Hello, Cam." Mir gazed up at him, all bright smile and gorgeous, naked body. She and Niah knelt at his feet, almost mirror images of one another except for coloring. Where Mir was all sultry and dark, with long black hair, dark coffee eyes, and skin the color of polished oak, Niah was her opposite. Platinum hair, eyes of molten silver, and skin so fair and fine as to make her look like a carefully constructed porcelain doll.

Yet her lips were red—deep red, slightly parted, and at this moment approaching . . . no. Oh, crap. They were sliding deliciously over the head of his wide-awake, please-play-with-me dick.

Groaning, he braced his hands against the slick walls of the shower and prayed his knees wouldn't buckle. There was no thought of stopping her—last night he'd quickly learned that Mir and Niah did exactly as they pleased.

Except, that had just been fantasy, right? Holy shit. What did it matter when they were here, now, in his shower? Mir stood. Rising gracefully as a sylph, she slipped around behind him, lightly tugged the wet washcloth from his nerveless fingers, and slowly swept it across his shoulders. She stroked his back, his buttocks, and the backs of his thighs while Niah slowly took him deeper and then deeper still, sucking his full length into her mouth, down her throat.

Oh. Fuck. He tightened everything—his buttocks, his thighs, the muscles across his stomach. Tightened and prayed for control, but he could feel it slipping, even as Mir dropped the washcloth and pressed against his back.

She was tall enough that her breasts hit just below his shoulder blades, her nipples beaded up so tight he felt them, twin little bullet points of sensation. Then she was sliding, sliding down, slowly dragging her breasts down his back, running her fingers over his flanks, dropping to her knees behind him.

This was so much more intense than last night when he'd slipped between fantasy and reality, and he'd wondered then if he'd survive their curious explorations. Now, Niah knelt in front, sucking his cock. Mir had gone to her knees behind him, pushing his legs apart, licking the sensitive curve of his butt and then wrapping long fingers around his sac.

He might have whimpered. Knew he was cursing steadily, though if he'd been asked exactly what words he used, Cam doubted he could have given an intelligent answer. Mir forced his legs farther apart, somehow twisting around so that she had her mouth on his balls and her tongue doing something that had to be illegal in most states.

Probably on the planet.

Did it matter? Hell no. Hell. No. No . . . shit.

He tried to stop it. Honestly, he'd never fought so hard for control in his life, but there was no way. Not any way at all to stop what these two women had so quickly set into motion.

Lips and tongues everywhere; fingers on his balls; a hot, tight mouth and throat taking control of his dick. A finger teasing his ass, pressing, entering, sliding deep, pressing . . .

He cried out. Cursed. Shouted.

Climaxed.

Cam struggled to stay upright, but gravity won and he slowly gave in. His knees buckled and his hands slipped along the wet tiles until he was half sitting, half lying on the floor of the shower with the water beating him in the face.

Mir and Niah giggled with utter delight.

He opened his eyes and stared at the women. "What are you doing here? I thought you were going back to finish your shift."

"Nattoch wanted us to gather more energy." Niah licked

her lips. "You weren't fantasizing enough to provide energy. We decided to help you along."

"You were sad," Mir said. She stood and offered him a hand. He wrapped his fingers around hers and she tugged him to his feet. "Your sadness distresses us. Come. Let's dry off and do it again. This time with laughter."

Cam thought of the painting in the other room. Thought of what it might be, what it meant. Then he looked at the women—two absolutely beautiful, wet, naked women—waiting impatiently for him to make up his mind.

He shut off the water, grabbed a towel off the rack, and ran it over Mir first, and then Niah. They preened like glossy, well-loved cats.

Cam dried himself. His legs had stopped trembling. His erection hadn't subsided a bit, and it was still awfully early in the morning. The painting could wait. He'd talk to Mac later. Tossing the wet towel over the shower door, he followed the women into the bedroom.

He glanced out the window as first Mir and then Niah crawled into the middle of his big bed. The sun was barely up. Mac was probably still asleep. Cam turned his attention to the bed.

To the women on his bed.

It was still made up from yesterday. He'd never gone to sleep at all last night. Not that he intended to sleep now.

At least, not for a while. Mir held out her hand. He took it, let her tug him close, but instead of her slim fingers and the look of pure devilment in her eyes, for some reason he thought of the painting in the other room.

The dark, angry red landscape with its familiar pattern of canals and lines, only he realized, now that he'd actually painted them, they weren't canals at all. Astronomers had been totally off base. Those Martian canals had been highways. He'd painted cities and farms, forests and parks and big factories, all in the midst of terrible upheaval. A once-living planet under attack.

Dead and desolate now, and the image of its change had come from someone aboard the Gar vessel. That had to be the source of this vision. He felt a terrible pain in his chest and thought again of waking Mac, of telling him what he'd seen.

Then he caught the scent of vanilla and honey, and the painting slipped from his mind, his thoughts filled now with the women he'd literally conjured out of fantasy. Gently, he pressed Mir back against the pillows and parted her thighs with both hands. Her skin was like silk, her smile filled with so many promises, so much hope. He sent a quick smile to Niah. "You next," he said. Then he winked as Niah settled beside them to watch.

He knelt between Mir's legs with his palms beneath her firm, round buttocks, lifted her for his pleasure, and discovered that, yes, she did taste exactly like vanilla and honey.

Morgan Black lay beside Rodie Bishop and watched the first rays of morning sun cut across the tumbled blankets. The bed seemed almost empty with just the two of them, but Bolt, their Nyrian lover, had returned to the ship at some point during the night. Morgan had slept through his departure.

Still so hard to believe that in the past few days he had not only interacted with aliens, he'd had some pretty mind-blowing sex with them. His thoughts drifted to the five Nyrian women he'd called with his fantasies—women who now had the human forms they'd need when the DEO-MAP team put their rescue into action.

Five Nyrian women, one Nyrian man.

And then there was Rodie.

She'd caught him by surprise, and yet it was as if she'd always been there, always a part of his life. The feelings he had for her, the woman herself . . . Hell, it still felt like a dream.

He'd never had a steady relationship with a woman before, and nothing all that serious with men. How could so much have changed? Now he had Rodie, though what he had with her was a mystery. How much was real and how much fantasy?

He didn't know for sure, but he was willing to find out.

He had Bolt and the other Nyrians, creatures he'd known for such a short time, and yet . . . they mattered. Mattered to him in a way that was almost impossible to describe. As if the forms they'd taken from his mind had left an indelible imprint on his soul.

Essentially, they had become family. His family. And not just the Nyrians—no, the entire dream team was closer than those few he could claim by blood. These were the ones who mattered.

Finn and Cam were the brothers he'd never had. Kiera and Liz were like little sisters. And Mac? How did he describe his feelings for Mac Dugan? Not just a friend, not even a brother. More a mentor, a trusted male, someone Morgan actually admired.

There were very few men he'd ever admired in his life.

And oddly enough, Finn O'Toole was one of them, which was almost laughable when he thought of his first impression of the irascible Irishman. He'd pegged O'Toole as a jokester without a serious thought in his head, a guy more concerned with bagging his next woman and adding another notch to his proverbial bedpost than with anything of substance.

He'd been wrong about Finn O'Toole. At least he hoped so, since he'd be trusting him with his life. Today, he and Finn would learn how to dematerialize, or disassemble, as the Nyrians called it. Essentially, he'd be reducing himself to the molecular level and hitchhiking within the energy mass of an alien creature in order to travel from Earth to the Gar ship that was currently in orbit behind the moon.

Yeah. Sure . . . and it was a good thing he didn't have a clue how this was going to happen or he'd probably be scared to death, but somehow, doing something that was so far beyond belief didn't register well enough to actually terrify him. Yet.

Rodie let out a soft snore and snuggled against his side. He tightened his arm around her shoulders. She was every bit as far beyond belief as dematerializing. Rodie Bishop was someone else he'd underestimated.

He'd thought she was interesting and kind of cute.

He'd had no idea she would totally rock his world.

Of course, when he'd signed on to this project, he really had no idea what he was getting into. Definitely a good thing, being so ignorant, or he'd never have agreed.

And then, just think what he'd be missing.